Scíath

By
J.A. Castelli

To Wendy,
Thank you for all your help and support.
Please Enjoy!
J.A. Castelli

Eternal Press
A division of Damnation Books, LLC.
P.O. Box 3931
Santa Rosa, CA 95402-9998
www.eternalpress.biz

Scíath
by J.A. Castelli

Digital ISBN: 978-1-62929-075-1
Print ISBN: 978-1-62929-076-8

Cover art by: Dawné Dominique
Edited by: Avril Dannenbaum

Copyright 2013 J.A. Castelli

Printed in the United States of America
Worldwide Electronic & Digital Rights
Worldwide English Language Print Rights

All rights reserved. No part of this book may be reproduced, scanned or distributed in any form, including digital and electronic or mechanical, including photocopying, recording, or by any information storage and retrieval system, without the prior written consent of the Publisher, except for brief quotes for use in reviews.

This book is a work of fiction. Characters, names, places and incidents either are the product of the author's imagination or are used fictitiously, and any resemblance to any actual persons, living or dead, events, or locales is entirely coincidental.

To my family for never letting me give up on my dreams.

To Kathryn, for being there every step of the way.

To Tracy, Laura and Ellie, your advice and good cheer kept me on the path. Thank you.

Prologue

The sound of crunching paper filled the still night. There was no reason for her to be summoned back there. To face the stares and smirks, each of them judging her. Kyra closed her eyes, immersed in the rage flooding her. Her foot lashed out, toppling a pile of pallets onto the dusty warehouse floor. The resulting crash made her cringe. Thankfully, her quarry was still an hour away. She kicked aside the pieces of splintered wood, enjoying the clang as they hit the metal walls with the force of her anger.

She leaned against an intact stack and let the familiar scene of a Scíath meeting enter her mind. The meetings were open to everyone, but usually only fifty or so spectators showed up. Then, her father—the Architect—would be seated behind the podium as usual. Guilt filled her as she thought of him. He loved her so and missed her, yet he could not understand what it was like to *be* her, breathing in the animosity that followed her every step. Most hid it well enough, but she knew it was there. Between the race bias and her track record within the various departments, there was a lot of ammunition for animosity.

Thinking of the departments brought the faces of the Treoraí into the forefront of her mind, and her frown deepened. She had no doubt that all of them disliked her, even if they had been kind enough when dumping her.

Glancing at her watch, she realized she still had an hour until the Serpentile was due to pick up his drug shipment from what he thought was a simple supplier. They were a cold-blooded humanoid race, with a forked tongue and a pension for causing trouble.

Sighing softly, she recalled after all the disasters she had almost convinced her father that she could spend the rest of her time hiding in her room when Galerius, the head of security, had walked in. He had taken her out, without even asking her permission, on a hunt for a rogue lupine that was slaughtering sheep and several farmers.

The scent of the damp grass and the cool breeze dancing over her skin. Even now, it caused her heartbeat to quicken. The hunt had been exhilarating, and she knew then this was where she belonged. Her father had never said a word against it. He loved seeing her happy, but she could read in his eyes that he was not thrilled with the danger involved in her path.

Looking at her watch, she saw she had half an hour left. Time to get into position and check the doors again, etc. Perching on the windowsill, she saw the black BMW drive up; however, instead of the single Serpentine she expected, four exited.

After pulling her second gun, she rechecked her watch. She was going to be late.

Chapter One

Initiation

The warm light from the open door spilled into the desolate, marble hall and glinted off the black veins that wormed through the stone. Kyra heard voices from inside the hall, their tones muted and hushed by the distance.

Closing her eyes, she imagined the scene that lay just beyond that thick, oak door. They were all sitting and waiting, probably for her. Her body tensed as the cold of the air around her seeped into her clothing. She drew it in, using the chill to armor herself.

Moments ticked by, she stood as still as the statues around her, her expression just as distant and solid. Knowing she should head in but simply not wanting to face the looks. Pondering not going in at all, she was already late, and the scuffle had taken more out of her than she expected; however, if she didn't show, it would hurt her father.

A boulder settled on her shoulders. She squared her body and jutted out her chin defiantly. She could no longer avoid the inevitable. Drawing in a deep breath, she strode down the hall, indifferent to the shattering sound her boots made against the marble.

The voices muted further as she reached the door. They had heard her coming. They would be watching for her, some of the older members ready with smug looks at her tardiness. Some would smile but still others would meet her with looks of contempt.

Keeping her facial expression as it always was—stony and neutral—she gave no indication of her feelings or thoughts. She paused mere seconds before pulling the door all the way open. Every conversation stopped as the door's mild squeak gave the newcomer's presence away. She stepped into the light.

Her constant outfit—simple fitted jeans, a plain black V-neck shirt, and her beloved worn leather trench—surprised none; however, it was noted with a few smirks the rip in her jeans and the smudges of dirt. Her long, blonde hair, forced into submission by a tight, leather-wrapped braid, reached almost to her waist. Her indigo eyes—a shock against her almost transparent, luminescent skin—took them all in. Her look was unadorned by makeup or decoration. A thick, braided chain ran along her neck, but her shirt hid whatever was at the end of it.

The Architect looked up from his position at the podium, his back resting against the far wall. He was raised slightly above the others, giving him a complete view of the room and the occupants, their chairs scattered randomly through the large ballroom.

His expression seemed amused as he watched the others take her in. Of all their members, Kyra knew she was the most controversial and his most prized. As she stalked into the room, several of the younger members actually pulled away from her, in awe or fear. If he was further amused by this, he hid it by shuffling the papers on the podium.

"Kyra," he said in simple greeting. He didn't seem to expect a reply.

She flipped a chair around in one swift movement. Straddling it, she sat beside the Architect, never uttering a word of apology or explanation for her tardiness. Low conversations began, and she was sure they were all about her. Internalizing the self-doubt those whispers spawned, she met every look she was given with her own intense stare.

The Architect rapped his hand softly on the podium to bring the meeting to order. The whispered conversations fizzled out as everyone raised expectant eyes to him.

"Ladies and gentlemen, I'd like to thank you all for making time to be here. I know many of you are deeply involved in cases, and some of you had to travel quite a distance to be here." He glanced purposefully at the latecomer. His Irish accent so thick that one unaccustomed to it might find him hard to understand, he continued.

"The purpose of this meeting has weighed heavily on my mind for some months, now. Our organization has a long and prestigious past, well as prestigious as one can be for a secret society funded by the Royal family." He smiled at his own joke and garnered a few polite smiles and nods.

"I have been the Architect since the group's inception. It's time for me to start looking for a successor, someone to take over the responsibilities and secrets of Scíath." His announcement caused a murmur to ripple through the room, surprised and plotting expressions already visible.

Kyra listened to the muffled bong of Big Ben. No one seemed to notice. She closed her eyes as she listened to the chimes. The Architect allowed the chatter to go on a few more moments before rapping on the podium. This time, silence was quick to come as they were all eager and perhaps a bit greedy to hear what came next. She noted the disappointment on the many faces when no more was given.

"In a few moments, three new recruits will be brought in, I expect each Treoraí to stand and tell a bit about yourself and each of your departments to help the Foundlings decide where they wish to go." She sighed inwardly, his litany had not changed in years.

He knew very well that everyone wanted more information on the successor issue. Kyra barely stopped herself from rolling her eyes. She could tell he wasn't in the mood to give them more. They stared at him but accepted his words. It had been nearly a year since they had new recruits. It would be good to have new faces about.

After surveying the group another long moment, the Architect signaled to the men standing beside the doors. The guards stood eight feet in height, and wore flawless suits. As the light touched their pale, luminescent green skin, tiny scales glittered. The fluttering of gills peaked over the collars of their shirts in a soundless, breathing rhythm. As they moved to the doors, the seams of their suits strained, giving a hint as to the power of their forms.

She had always found them to be fascinating to watch, and she had heard they were even more impressive in the water.

Kyra tapped her foot. Just being within this group made her skin crawl. No matter how she tried to ignore it, she could feel the vibes rolling off them—the lust for the possibility of power, the intolerance of her existence, and the competiveness for new talent. For a brief moment, she debated just walking out the door when it opened, but she knew it would break her father's heart. Her loyalty was to him, not to the empire he had built. So, she stayed, her reflexes taut, expecting trouble at any moment.

Another squeak and a small gust of wind accompanied the swinging doors. She watched impassively, even though she was curious. Foundlings offered new opportunity for every department to attain new personnel. Plus, it was always interesting to see what races would be represented. Three figures edged into the light. A sharp intake of breath echoed its way around the room, but everyone was too well trained to let their surprise reach their faces. Leading the trio was an Enoch.

She stood no more than five feet tall. Her midnight skin absorbed all the light that touched it. Her golden eyes took in the room with the quickness of the big cats they were supposed to be descended from. No one of record had seen an Enoch in the last century. Rumor said they were only found in the heart of Africa. How the Architect made contact, much less convinced them to send a member out to Scíath, was just another testament to his skills as a leader and a diplomat. Gapes were not well disguised by some of the curious. The Enoch squared her shoulders and met the stares with her own unblinking gaze. Her eyes fell on Kyra, and they nodded to each other in recognition. This only caused the rest of the room more curiosity.

Behind her and to the right stood a man, his hulking frame casting a long shadow. He wasn't a Giant, perhaps six-foot-seven or so; however, his width made him quite intimidating. His skin was a burgundy color, his hair an orange-red, almost reminiscent of lava. His silver eyes reflected the faces of those around him as he took in the room with a silent brooding. The recruit wasn't a pure Dwarf—rather he was from a tribe that had interbred with the Troll population, as Trolls were on the verge of extinction. Kyra heard a chair groan beneath a massive form. She noted Lev sitting up as he recognized one of his own.

With rugged features, a thick, sloping brow, and characteristically large ears, the Foundling was obviously a Dwarf. Not a Stone Dwarf like Lev, though. Kyra would be curious to discover his tribe.

The third figure—an unassuming ,petite lithe female—could easily be mistaken for a child. Her long, pale hair lay in waves of ringlets over her shoulders, and her eyes were crystalline blue. Her appearance was normal—no outward sign on her race or abilities. A member of the audience leaned toward her to get a better look. In an instant, she was gone. A slight shimmer remained where she had stood, but it quickly faded.

The Architect heaved a sigh. Everyone looked around. Some understood, and some were completely bewildered by the disappearing act. She was another semi-rarity—a Witch from the Avalon colony in Ireland. A mix of magic bloods, each exhibiting varied talents. The silence stretched on. The Architect looked like he was just about to call for the Foundling when she shimmered back into existence, exactly where she had been standing. Her pale skin shone with the high color of embarrassment. She tried to stammer out an excuse, but the Architect simply held up his hand. She hung her head in shame. "Ladies and gentlemen, it is my pleasure to introduce our Foundlings, Anaraba." He gestured to the Enoch.

"Maltruis," the Architect continued, and the hulking form nodded in response to his name.

"Ariel." He gave a kindly smile, looking toward the young one who was intently studying the floor, her face still flushed.

"You have all been through the orientation and acceptance to our society. Now, it is time for you to pick a department to join. Treoraí." He gestured to the woman seated to his left.

Taking his cue, she stood.

Kyra's mind echoed with the sounds of crashing bookcases, causing her to look down as Di began to speak.

Crossing her arms, her mind began to wander through her colorful past. Her father let her choose her first department at the age of sixteen, probably because she was stir crazy and getting in his hair often. Out of all of them, Di had been the nicest to her, so she tried Supernatural Species. The first week had been great. Given the department was dedicated to logging all of the races in the world, they had some of the least amount of bias to be found. She had finally been given duties and, as she was new, they started her easy—just logging books and placing them on the shelves. With the amount of material, and this being pre-computer logging, the shelves were enormous, some of them easily five stories high.

In an attempt to prove she was talented, she had scaled the tallest bookcase in the department, forgoing the ladder, to replace a book on the top shelf. Had she stopped to think on it, she would have been able to guess that the force of her landing on the side of the bookcase would be enough to send it toppling backward; however, she simply jumped with book in hand.

She shuddered recalling the resounding booms as the entire store of knowledge was laid asunder, one member getting his arm broken as the bookcase pinned him to the floor.

Kyra made sure her face was a mask as Di spoke.

"Greetings, Foundlings. My name is Dalamni, but you may call me Di. I head the Supernatural Species department. It is our job to catalogue all known supernatural species, their history, powers, and whereabouts. We are the largest and most extensive department in Scíath. It takes great attention to detail and patience to work with us; however, it is very rewarding if you have an interest in the tapestry of our supernatural world. There are desk as well as field positions available." Her South African accent was easily discernible. Her tall, willowy figure and dark skin weren't that different from the Enoch who stood before her. Her head was adorned with short, flaming red hair, shaved into ritualistic designs. She smiled at them fondly and retook her seat.

Across the room, Doctor Leland Barker—a tall, lean man—stood. Medium height with mousy brown hair, he wore thick, wire glasses. One word leapt to Kyra's mind when she looked at him—ordinary. He wore a brown tweed suit, and in his hands, he fiddled with the brim of a bowler hat. Clearing his throat, he spoke, his tone also timid.

Kyra had spent an entire month moping after another fiasco with Di's department. She took every chance to go out into the city, escaping into the countryside—sometimes, without permission and sometimes, causing a fair amount of panic for her father. Subsequently on a third escape, a security agent was assigned to shadow her.

It was after such an adventure that she returned with the prompting of her guard to find Leland, the Treoraí of Medical, sitting in her father's study. He looked uncomfortable as she burst in with her hands full of sweets.

She assumed he was there to discuss her attempt at Medical. He excused himself, leaving her with an angry-looking Architect. She settled in her favorite chair, munching her toffee as she waited for him to be ready to speak. She still recalled the pain in his voice as he informed her that she would not being going to Medical, because Leland was worried that the race bias that followed her would interfere with her seeing patients who might not want her as a caregiver. While she had been angry, she was more than a little relieved. Looking at weird rashes on strange species did not appeal to her in any way.

"Foundlings, my name is Doctor Leland Barker. I head the Medical Department here. We run a hospital, as well as sending emissaries out to tribes or groups in need. Working for us requires intensive training, as you must learn the systems and illnesses of each supernatural species on record. Though, we welcome anyone who feels that this compassionate job is right for them. Thank you," he said, his clipped accent giving away that he was a native to London's upper crust. Sitting quickly, he looked relived to be finished.

After a long pause ,and an audible groan from his chair, a massive form drew himself to his feet. Maltruis immediately took notice. They shared the size and sloping brow of the Dwarven race. Yet, there were obvious differences that made it clear they hailed from separate tribes.

He nodded to the other Dwarf and then began to speak.

"I, Lev Elstin, Building and Transportation department. All supernatural construction comes from us. Help make cities and hide them from Gillys. Supernatural transport for those who not to be seen." His voice was deep and gravely. His heavy Russian accent in addition to Dwarven speech patterns made some of his words harder to understand. He sat back down with another slight groan from his chair. There had been no warmth or invitation in his voice.

Kyra remembered how Lev had offered to take her in, thinking perhaps Building and Transportation would be more exciting and enough to keep her interested.

The sheer amount of information required to plan field outings, clear the way for supernatural species towns, and maintain secrecy of travel quickly overwhelmed her but, she was determined to stick with it. She struggled for a month, fighting the headache and insomnia born of brain overload.

The breaking point came when she planned a route for an anthropology delegation headed into the rain forest to observe a native tribe. She would never forget the look on Lev's face when he was informed that the entire group was lost deep in the Congo after being taken the wrong way and were going to have to be emergency airlifted out of cannibal territory. Hoping to give her a chance to right her mistake, he let her coordinate the rescue, which led naturally to the rescue team needing a rescue. She was quietly returned to her father's study with a request for her to find somewhere else to be.

A movement from the far corner of the room caused everyone to turn. Standing half in shadows, a beautiful woman spoke. Her waist-length black hair shone in the light, reminiscent of a crow's feather. Her Native American features and skin tone revealed her heritage.

"I am Satinka Mawkawee. Please, call me Tinka."

Anthropology had started off rough for Kyra, but Nyles, her friend from childhood, was already apprenticing there, and having him around always made her feel better. Her placement had lasted only slightly longer than the previous one, though. It had been a less disastrous dismissal than being with Di, but after falling asleep face first in books on more than one occasion, it was fairly obvious that studying the customs of sometimes extinct cultures was not something she could do.

Kyra refocused on Tinka's speech.

"I head the Anthropology department here. We work very closely with Supernatural species. We do studies of tribes and covens in their natural environment, documenting their habits and rituals. Our department requires at least eighty percent field work. We have dedicated researchers who record their findings. The ability to fit in with other cultures is a must. The most important part, however, is to have absolutely no race bias of any kind." She looked pointedly at Lev.

Kyra noted that some in the room did not pick up on the tension. The Architect obviously did, and it caused him to frown. Kyra could bet that he would be making a note of it to address later. He despised inner society tension.

"If you have a passion for cultures and protecting them, we would welcome you here." She sat back in her shadowed corner.

The man who had caused the foundling to vanish stood a bit slower this time. He gave a dazzling smile, and his blonde, highlighted hair was gelled perfectly into place. He let everyone take him in before he began speaking.

"Hello, Foundlings. It is a pleasure to have you as a part of our illustrious organization. You have made an excellent choice for your futures by joining us. We can help you as much as you can help us." He smiled, again.

His speech garnered eye rolls from some. The Architect just sighed.

Americans, Kyra thought.

"I am Jason Stevens. I head one of the most challenging, exciting, and glamorous departments of all. Our department is called Gilly Relations or Non-supernatural Relations. We handle all of the exchanges between the supernatural world and the Gillys. We record crossovers, incidents, and work with the Gilly government to make sure our species have places to live. I welcome all new talent to our department. I am looking for dynamic supernaturals with a passion for making our world run smoothly." He flashed his pearly whites.

"I do hope you are all happy here as well." He finished with a flourished bow toward the Foundlings.

As he sat, a man with military bearing stood up. His close-cropped hair was as black as his eyes, the inky orbs slightly larger than a normal pair of eyes, the color offset slightly by his olive skin tone. His disconcerting gaze was disturbed only by his constant shutter-like blinking. He studied each Foundling intently before he spoke.

"*Buena sera*, Foundlings. I am Galerius. I head security for the Scíath. I take care of external as well as internal security issues. Do not join my department unless you have strong will, discipline, and the ability to follow orders." His back was ramrod straight as he sat.

"Well, I guess that leaves me," came a soft voice from the back corner of the room. Everyone turned in the direction of the voice, but the owner was not immediately visible. The dragging of a chair was heard, everyone looked on with interest. Up popped a dainty woman with blazing, red hair pulled back into a tight ponytail. Her milky white skin was splashed with freckles.

"Well met, Foundlings! My name is Moira Kavanah. I am the Queen of inventory." Her statement drew a laugh from the room.

Kyra's stint at Artifacts had been before Moira's tenure as Artifact's Treoraí. Flynn had still been in charge. On his good days he was a sour puss, and his good days were few and far between. He looked down his long hooked nose, the steel of his gaze making her feel very small and afraid. If she had to pick a moment when people's judgments of her really began to incite anger inside her, it was then. He was a Wizard, and he held many deep and ill-informed opinions about non-human creatures. His superiority of humans with magic attitude had made him unpopular with the general members; however, his efficiency and track record could never be questioned, so he was tolerated.

Kyra could not recall that he had ever actually spoken to her, instead referring his second to "find her something to do". She stayed away from the shelves, hiding everyday at her little desk, brushing dirt off things she could not even recall. She'd had to fight herself every morning to get out of bed and head back under his disapproving glare.

She had been cleaning the same piece of pottery for days, unable to pull herself from the *malaise* that had taken hold. The sound of Flynn's voice even in her memory still caused a knot in her stomach. He had been standing a few feet behind her, dressing down his second for allowing the "lazy" creature to take up desk space. Rage had filled her. Only fear of the sorrow in her father's eyes kept her from lashing out and breaking his oversized nose for him. She fled, noting the satisfied smile on his face through her tears.

The rumor, of course, had been that she could not handle the workload, and she was just the spoiled brat of the Architect.

She listened to Moira's welcome.

"I head the Artifacts Department. We are what we sound like. We collect, document, and safely store all the artifacts that come into the possession of the Scíath. We have a complete coding and storage system that we use. We reign over the vaults. Not a whole lot of field time, but we get to see some pretty cool stuff. We welcome any who feel like they belong with us." Her genuine smile, soft Irish accent, and welcoming speech coaxed a timid smile out of Ariel.

The Architect rapped on the podium to return everyone's attention to him.

"Thank you Treoraí for your welcomes and explanations of your departments. We are going to now give the Foundlings time to think about their choices. Kyra, would you be so kind as to escort them to the smaller library where they may think on and discuss their choices."

Kyra's eyes went wide, and her eyebrows nearly touched her hair line. This expression only lingered a moment before her usual, neutral look settled in. She nodded to him. She went to the door with a half wave for the Foundlings to follow her. The Dwarf caught up with her quickly while the other two hurried to keep up. Her direction was easy to ascertain by the sound her boots made on the marble.

She remained silent as they headed down the hall. *Why did he do this to me? Why bring me in from the field, just to sit through a new Foundling ceremony? I already knew about the successor thing, so there was no real reason for him to bring me here.*

Aggravation bubbled up inside her. She was angrier at the thought of him leaving than she was about being brought in for a meeting, but admitting that even to herself was difficult.

She stopped, turning as she swung a set of large, wooden doors very similar to the others they had just stepped through. Walking unabashedly into the dark room, she was lost from the Foundlings' sight. The trio huddled slightly together, unsure if there were to follow her or simply wait. A single, dim lamp pierced the dark, illuminating the table it sat on and the shadowy outlines of the chairs beside it. Then, another and another were lit, until the whole room was bathed in the soft, yellow glow.

Kyra took in the leather spines of the books that adorned the stories-high bookcases, frowning.

The Architect had been the only family she had even known, Scíath the only home she'd ever had, and now, he was planning on leaving. There was no reason for it. Sure, he was older then he had been twenty years ago, but he didn't appear to age at the same rate as most. What race did the Architect hail from? He never spoke of his life before the Scíath. Of his home or others of his kind, she had asked him once, but she was given such a look in answer that she never dared ask, again.

The Foundlings moved into the room, their footsteps barely audible. They whispered among themselves.

Lost in her own pondering, Kyra startled and whirled around with hand on her knife instinctively.

The trio instantly silenced.

"Forgive us, Miss Kyra. It seems some of our tempers got the better of us," Anaraba said, her accent marking each of her words.

Kyra relaxed. "None of this Miss Kyra stuff, please. Kyra will more than suffice." She took an empty seat beside the Enoch.

Surprise showed clearly on the face of Maltruis, as if he expected a much rougher, harder voice. He crossed his arms. "Upset, no?"

"Now what on Earth is there possibly to get upset about? You are here to decide which path to take. There are many to choose from, and each has its merits and flaws, but there is no need to agree or disagree about them." She slung her legs over the arm of a leather, wingback chair.

They all nodded, and no one seemed forthcoming in what the argument has been about. Kyra decided to let it go.

Ariel sat forward slightly and spoke in a quiet tone, "May I ask whom you work for?"

"I work for Galerius in Security. I handle bringing in rogue supernaturals and incarcerating them as well as handling any issues they may cause."

"That sounds very exciting," Ariel said, though it was clear that excitement was not really for her.

"Oh, it *is* exciting, and dangerous, but it's not for the faint of heart," Kyra added, hoping to delude any visions of grandeur that Ariel may be having.

"Me saw another Dwarf," Maltruis said.

Kyra nodded. Dwarves were not the world's best conversationalists she had come to learn.

"That was Lev. He's a Stone Dwarf from a tribe in Russia. He's brilliant with building plans. His crews are second to none. His transportation routes run flawlessly." Perhaps, the Dwarves would be best suited together. That way, no one would expect normal conversation.

"Me, Mirror Dwarf. Me make mirrors for Witches," he said stonily.

Kyra nodded in appreciation. The Architect outdid himself on this group of Foundlings—two rare types in one batch. Though, she was partially responsible for the Enoch. She had stumbled into their village while chasing a bounty. Still, it was the Architect who convinced her to leave her village and come here .No one ever really bothered the Mirror Dwarves, so there must be something special about this one that would send the Architect underground.

"Me go with Lev," the Dwarf said simply and sat back.

"Excellent," Kyra said. She knew better than to think that his lack of grasp on language meant he was stupid. On the contrary, Dwarves were known to be methodical and resourceful.

Kyra turned to Ariel. Field work was not something for the timid, and Ariel had poofed when startled in the meeting. She had noticed that the only time Ariel had smiled was during Moira's presentation. Kyra knew Moira was also a witch, and her department was pretty routine and normal. It might be a good place for Ariel to come out of her shell.

"What did you think about Moira?" Kyra asked Ariel.

Ariel's soft smile returned. "She seemed really nice and very sure of herself. Her department sounded very interesting." After a moment, she added, "I think I would like to go there."

"I think it will be a good fit for you, and Moira is an excellent mentor." Kyra replied with a reassuring smile. She remembered when Moira had first come to Scíath and had been a rather timid one herself. She had really come into her own in Artifacts. Perhaps, the same would happen for Ariel.

Kyra turned to Anaraba. This was going to be the hardest. Enochs were a secretive society. They had a deep connection with the land and the animals who roamed it. The little information that was recorded about them in the archives said that once they reached a certain age, they could shift into any indigenous animal they chose. She knew for a fact that Di and Tinka would love to get their hands on Anaraba and get more information about her tribe and their powers, but she doubted they would get much. Enochs kept their beliefs and culture secret for a reason, and Kyra doubted Anaraba would spill her guts to two outsiders.

"I think I know where I wish to go." Anaraba's gold eyes seemed to sparkle as they reflected the dim light.

"Oh?" Kyra asked, keeping her curiosity from showing.

"I wish to go into Medicine. There was a healer in my village that I greatly admired. I would like to learn to heal as well," she said in a strong voice.

Kyra drummed her nails on the chair arm. She gave little thought to Leland and his department after his polite rejection of her working for him. The only time she ever needed them was when her Gilly side saw it fit for her to catch the chicken pox. He helped her through it. He was a kind man, a bit unassuming, fade-into-the-wallpaper sort. *Hey, if it's what she wanted, so be it.*

"Well, then. It seems you have all made your choices. I will go inform the Architect that you are ready to come back and join your departments. When you return, only the Treoraí will be present. You must stand in the chalk circle that has been drawn and declare your choice. Please make sure you are certain. Departments here are like a path in life. It is difficult to change paths once you have started down them." She added from her extensive, personal experience.

Kyra walked from the room with the same loud, determined stride she had used to lead them there. After pushing open the meeting room doors, she looked around. The Architect was in deep conversation with Tinka while the others milled about—some chatting, some just waiting. They all, however, stopped and looked up as Kyra entered the room.

"The Foundlings are ready to come and start their journeys within Scíath."

Kneeling down, Moira and Tinka readied the chalk circle, creating the intricate and beautiful knot work that made up the choosing place.

The Architect tapped the wooden panel behind him, and the door slid open to reveal the cloaks within. Kyra watched the Architect finger the heaviness of the velvet and smile. This was one of his favorite traditions. It was a token to help the Foundlings feel like they were part of their new department. In essence, a department was a home and its members, family. He handed one to each Treoraí to be given to a Foundling if they chose their department.

Each department had separate sleeping quarters as well as lounging rooms to allow for conversing during free time. Not that there was any segregation between departments. They were all free to intermingle; however, they seemed to spend most of their time around those they worked with, hence making them like a large family.

The Treoraí all took their seats around the choosing circle, careful not to smudge the chalk work on the floor. The capes lay over their laps as they waited, each no doubt hoping for an addition to their department.

Seeing they were ready, Kyra gave a slight bow of her head to the Architect before disappearing back down the hall to retrieve the Foundlings.

Just as Kyra led them in, the lights dimmed. She stopped the Foundlings just before the opening to the circle. She was to lead each of them through and then to their new department. This was something the Architect usually did, but he looked quite comfortable sitting behind his podium.

Inwardly troubled, she went through the motions she had seen a number of times. Ariel was first in line. Kyra took her hand gently and led her to the opening. She felt the poor child trembling and gave Ariel's hand a reassuring squeeze as she let it go.

"Ariel, step into the center of the circle. State your full name, race, and birthplace." Kyra's voice took an official tone. She noted a few of the Treoraí seemed surprised to see her leading the ceremony.

Ariel paused, and her appearance started to shimmer. Kyra groaned silently. If this kid couldn't handle something as simple as the choosing circle, then she had a hard road ahead of her.

Ariel stayed visible, squaring her shoulders and walking to the center of the circle. She fixed her eyes on a point on the far wall as she spoke, her voice quiet but less timid.

"I am Ariel Dormond. I am Avalon Witch, and I was born on the Island of Avalon." Her eyes never left the imaginary spot.

"We welcome you into our home, Ariel Dormond. Please, choose your department." Kyra had never spoken these words and was not prepared in the least, but she had seen it done so many times, it was very easy for her.

"I, Ariel Dormond, choose the Artifacts Department." She said with an instant look of relief when it was out.

Moira stood, smiling brightly as she moved to the opening and welcomed Ariel with a warm hug. She gently placed the emerald green cape over her shoulders, and together, they went to stand beside the Architect.

Kyra turned to Maltruis. She didn't think his choice would overly shock anyone. Lev was already adjusting the cape on this lap.

"Maltruis, please step into the circle. State your full name, race, and birthplace," she repeated.

He lumbered forward, his giant steps showing no hesitation.

"Me, Maltruis, Mirror Dwarf, born under Mauna Loa," he said.

"We welcome you, Maltruis, into our home. Please, choose your department." Kyra's eyes briefly met that of Galerius, her own Treoraí.

"Maltruis choose Building and Transportation." He walked out of the circle.

Lev met him, his own large strides getting him to the opening easily. He draped the ruby red cloak around Maltruis's massive shoulders. Together, they stood beside the Architect. Kyra noted with silent amusement that the cape fell short to cover his massive frame.

All eyes turned to the Enoch. It was easy to see that many of the remaining Treoraí were interested in having her in their department. As Kyra has assumed, both Di and Tinka looked the most eager. Anaraba studied the room before stepping confidently forward. Kyra realized that Anaraba was barefoot. They had all been dressed in the traditional white silk pant and shirt set, but they usually kept their own shoes. Anaraba had been barefoot when Kyra met her, and she wondered if she had traveled the whole way like that. Putting the wonder away, she spoke her line, again.

"Anaraba, please step into the circle. State you full name, race, and birthplace."

Anaraba stood straight within the circle. Her body never seemed to move. Even as she spoke, the rest of her body was still.

"I am Anaraba Willowmane, I am an Enoch, and I was born in the heart of the Congo in Africa."

"We welcome you, Anaraba Willowmane, into our home. Please, choose your department." Kyra stated for the last time.

"I, Anaraba Willowmane, choose to join the Medical Department."

There were several surprised expressions, but none more so than Leland Barker. He stood quickly, catching himself as he tripped over the edge of the chair. He met her at the opening and laid the royal purple cloak over her shoulders. They took their place beside the Architect who looked over the pairs with intense interest.

"Foundlings, I hope that you will enjoy your new positions within the Scíath. I have an open door policy to everyone here. If you have any issues or problems, please feel free to come to me. As you may know, the meaning of the word Scíath is home. This is your home, and we want you to all feel welcome." He stifled a yawn. "With that, it is late, and it has been a big night for all of us." His eyes lingered on Kyra.

"Good night, everyone," he said, dismissing them all though he didn't move. Kyra retained her position as the rest of them filed out, murmuring good night to each other. In less than a minute, the room was empty. Lev closed the doors behind him with a decisive thud.

Neither of the remaining two moved, but their gazes locked.

"I would have told you I wanted you to do the ceremony if you had shown up even remotely on time," he began in a defensive tone.

"Pish, you could have just as easily told me when you called me in for this." Her arms crossed as her lips pursed. She wasn't angry about leading it, but it was easier to lash out than to tell him what really had her upset.

"You would have said no if I had asked you in advance."

"You're damn right I would have. You know I don't go for all this pomp and ceremony."

He stood. "Angry or not, young lady, you will watch your tone and your language around me."

She stepped back and hung her head. He made her feel like a child with a few words.

He sighed deeply. "Kyra, this is silly. You're angry with me for stepping down. I'm angry with myself for no longer being able to continue as the director. We are taking it out on each other, because we both know in the end we will always be family."

She slipped her arms around him in a gentle hug. "Forgive me, father. I'm just not sure what I'm supposed to do without you."

"Just because I'm not running Scíath doesn't mean I'm going to just vanish. I just feel that it's time for someone younger and stronger to hold the responsibility." He stroked her hair. "You're worried about your position here, because you have always been under my protection."

She smirked. "You're supposed to ask before you go stealing thoughts from my head, you know." Her voice had relaxed and was playful.

"Hey, I can't help it. You're practically broadcasting them." He smiled. "I do, however, understand your concern, and I will make sure the matter of your position and securities are handled before I 'retire', as the Gilly's call it."

"You're scared of something yourself?" She frowned.

"Who's using powers, now?" His tone remained jovial, but his expression failed to follow.

"What has you worried?"

He ran his hand through his snow white mane. She looked at his wrinkled face and, for the first time, really saw his age.

"Even handpicked, you cannot ensure that everyone around you is pure of heart. There are those within our organization who crave power. Those who would do just about anything to become my successor, including killing me before I can name another. I felt it from some of the eyes on me, tonight. Heard them wonder how frail I am, how much power I still have. I do not fear death. I fear the power of the Scíath falling into the wrong hands. The collection of information, artifacts, spells, and pure talent that reside here are enough to do irreparable damage if wielded by the wrong hands."

She nodded, her expression thoughtful. "I will stay for a while, just until we get this successor business sorted out. I've been in the field for a long time. Some time at home base to regenerate might not be a bad idea, anyway." *Who am I trying to convince? Him or me?* He stood, and she clasped her hand in his the way a child might hold a parent's on a walk through the park. They headed silently through the darkness, back to their rooms.

Chapter Two

Responsibility

Kyra woke before sunrise and dressed quickly. Silently sliding the key in the lock, she pushed open the Architect's bedroom door to silently gaze upon the sleeping Architect. His breathing was regular and soft. Her eyes swept the room, looking for anything out of place. Convinced that all was as it should be, she left as quietly as she had come, making sure to relock the door.

Moving through the halls of the compound, she encountered no one. Her path wound through many halls and passages until she stood before two oversized, steel doors. Placing her hand on the scanner, she waited while it confirmed her identity. A hissing of air signaled that the lock was released. She entered the room, being sure to close the doors tight behind her. Lights came on around her as she moved through the room. Its stainless steel perfection gave the place a cold, institutional feel. The walls were lined with gun racks, their cabinets locked with handprint scanners and some even with retinal scanners.

Seated behind a mammoth, metallic desk was Galerius. His head bent over a thick stack of papers. He made no movement to acknowledge her presence, but she knew he had heard her before she had even entered the room. She approached the desk but stayed a few feet back, respectful not to intrude on his work. She stood for a long moment before he looked up. His shiny, black eyes took her in. "I am surprised to see that you are still here. I assumed you would be gone as soon as you saw the Architect off to bed." His tone was neutral as always.

"Well, about that. I'd like to come in from the field for a bit. It's been a long time since I spent some time at home base."

Her voice sounded thin to her. She fought to keep the nervous tension from her eyes as she felt the sweat forming at her brow.

Their gaze met, and even through the fluttering of his eyelids, she could tell he did not believe her. She stood still, her mind scrambling for another story when he simply nodded.

"You have been out a while. I have a new possible safe house that's near here that I want to check out. You could take a squad from here with you. It's in an old Imp-controlled forest, but no one has seen one since the end of the war. The house is in a defensible place and would be fit to put visiting diplomats and such in." Pulling the drawer open with a jerk, ignoring its protesting squeak, he placed a thick file on the table.

She was careful not to allow her relief to show. "I can put together and brief a team in twenty-four hours." She glanced at her watch.

He shook his head no.

"I have Lev securing the Gilly permits to the land, so we can fence it off to keep any unwanted outs. That's going to take about two days. So, take your time. I'll brief you tomorrow afternoon. You have indeed been out in the field for a long time. Take some time to rest." He picked up a different file.

Knowing she had been dismissed, she turned on her heel and left. Consciously or unconsciously, he'd allowed her the opportunity she needed. Not only to protect the Architect but to move through the other departments feeling out the people and perhaps letting her see who was a threat. Her footsteps echoed down the halls as she wound her way back to where she had begun. There were more people in the halls now as the rest of Scíath began its day.

She made a brief detour through the dining hall, coming out with a small tray of covered dishes. She carried them quickly down to the Architect's door. Knocking gently, she waited for him to tell her to enter. *Nothing.* Her heartbeat accelerated. She pressed her ear against the door, straining to hear any kind of sound or trace of movement. All she was rewarded with was more silence. She placed the tray on the ground. Grasping her ring of keys from her belt, she fumbled for the right one. She swore under her breath. Time passed too quickly, and her movements were too slow for her own liking.

In frustration, she took two steps back and kicked the door in. At first, it resisted her attempts. A second, more desperate, kick was rewarded with splintering wood. She pushed her way through the door, only to find an empty room. She searched the room. Nothing seemed disturbed, but there was no sign of the Architect. She raced toward the alert switch when a sound from the bathroom caused her to pause. It sounded like running water and some kind of strange warbling. With her gun out, she edged closer. Nosing the door open with her foot, she ducked to avoid the outpouring of steam. Another nudge brought the shower into view. Standing down, Kyra laughed. The dark form behind the curtain was the Architect. The warbling was his version of singing.

She eased the bathroom door closed and hung her head. It was going to be fun explaining to Lev why she needed a new door. Walking to the hall, she closed the door as best she could.

She was arranging breakfast on the table when she heard the door behind her open. She had to make a conscious decision not to allow her hand to move to her weapon. She turned and gave one of her rare smiles at his appearance. He was clad in a fluffy, dark blue robe, and his snow white hair was tousled. Her eyebrows furrowed at how frail he was. When he wasn't dressed in his polished suit, it was much easier to see what age had done to him. Regaining her smile, she gestured to the table.

"I brought you some breakfast." She waited for him to take notice of his splintered door.

"Why thank you, child," he said with a smile. Walking toward the table, he sat down.

"I assume you have already been to see Galerius," he said as he poured his coffee.

She nodded. Sitting beside him gave her a view of the not completely shut door.

"He agreed to let me stay in. Whether he bought my story or not, I can't really tell. He wants me to put together a team to scout out a new possible safe house." She buttered them both blueberry muffins.

"Oh, yes. The one in that Imp forest. It's not far from here, and he seems to think it would be a good place for visitors to Scíath to stay." He accepted a muffin.

"I have a two-day wait time. I'm going to use it as an opportunity to check out the other Treoraí to see if I can get a bead on who could become a problem." She tried to think of a tactful way to tell him about his door.

"Excellent idea. I have my own suspicions, but I do not want them coloring your observations. He glanced behind her. "Bloody hell! What happened to my door?"

"Ah yes, about that." A sheepish grin crossed her lips as she hung her head, her eyes studying remnants of the muffin. "I knocked, and I waited. You didn't answer, and I couldn't hear any sound. I tried to find the right key, but it was taking too long...I was afraid you were in danger, so I just kicked the door in. I'm very sorry. I'll have Lev get it fixed right away," her words tumbled out in a torrent.

He looked from her to the door then back to her before breaking out in laughter.

"My *chailín mo chroí*," he said through his laughter.

He had called her his darling child, so he wasn't angry.

"I'm better protected than I thought." His laughter subsided. "All laughing aside, you did the right thing. This is a delicate situation, not one we have ever had to deal with before, so there is no such thing as too much caution." He patted her hand.

She exhaled, relieved.

"I think I'm going to start with Lev as I have to visit him, anyway. I need to grab someone from his department for my team as well." She pushed her eggs around her plate.

"This is your first team leader position, isn't it?" He dipped his toast point in a fried egg.

She stopped, fork halfway to her mouth. While she'd been on many teams over the years, she had always preferred soloing. He was right, though. This was the first time she would be leading her own team. She almost wished he hadn't pointed it out to her. Before that thought, she had no fears. Now, she had to consider all the issues that could be tied into this position. *Was Galerius testing me? Had the Architect requested me to lead this team? Am I going to be a good team leader?* A majority of her time was spent alone tracking fugitives, so would she be an accurate judge of who was needed on this team? She pressed her palm to her forehead as the questions volleyed off the walls of her brain.

"Yes, it is." She set down her fork.

"You will do an outstanding job." The Architect placed his fork beside his empty plate. "I intend to spend most of my time in my study today, going over dossiers," he finished, leaving the meaning of his project unsaid.

Her brows knit in thought. "I'll check on you throughout the day. Also, I'm going to leave a radio with you. If you need me, just push the red button, and I'll come running," she said, laying a radio on the table.

He picked it up and pushed the red button. A loud buzzer sound emitted from the one on her hip. He smiled with childish glee and pushed it several more times.

She smiled and rolled her eyes. "As you can see, this is a hard-to-miss sound." She said, pushing back from the table.

He grinned and reached for the button again, but her look stopped him. With a tiny smile, he stood as well.

"I'll come by after I speak with Lev." She leaned in to kiss him on the forehead.

She gently opened the splintered door. It crunched as she closed it behind her. Heading down the hall, her head was swirling. *So much to do. So much to organize and coordinate. I need a list, I need to sit down and make a list of what I need, who I need and then go to them.* She walked through the huge compound, knowing her way without even thinking.

This was home. She had a few fuzzy memories of the place she had shared with her parents, but she had left there as a toddler. She paid little mind to the crowded halls around her, since she was on a mission.

Stopping outside a large, stone door, a long sigh escaped her lips, and her shoulders slumped. Apparently, in her absence, they had installed badge scanners on some departmental doors. She had one, and she knew it was an all-access pass; however, the question was where was it? She started with her pants pockets and then moved on to the pouches on her belt. After a futile search, her brows furrowed, and her movements became exaggerated. She'd been here longer than some of the department heads. It was ridiculous that she had to carry some plastic card. Her frustration turned to indignation.

She raised her hand to knock and inform whoever answered to fetch Lev. When she reached, she felt something in the inside zip pocket of her jacket move. She pulled out the plastic card. Feeling slightly foolish, she slipped it into the card reader and waited. The tricolored lights on the top blinked several times before the green light stayed on, and she heard the door locks click open. Pulling out the card, she placed it back into the pocket, making a mental note of its whereabouts. She pushed the large door open just far enough to permit her to slip in. She shut it gently behind her, noting with satisfaction that no one seemed to have noticed her coming in.

It was a large room, fashioned much like a Gilly warehouse. Half of the room was filled with drafting tables, charts, hanging maps, and building models. The other half had desks, bookshelves, and cases filled with document tubes. In the far back corner was a small room—Lev's office.

She stood still watching as the employees moved to and fro. Some sat at drafting tables while others stood conferring. Overall, it looked to be an efficient chaos. She scanned the room for Maltruis, who shouldn't be all that hard to spot. After a thorough examination of the room, though, she couldn't see him. Frowning, she made her way back to Lev's office. A few people looked up, some with recognition and others with curiosity. She kept her stony expression and moved with purpose—not opening herself up for questions or conversation. Reaching the office, she knocked lightly.

"Enter," said the familiar, gruff voice.

She pushed the door open. Maltruis sat in one of the chairs.

Lev smiled at her from across the desk.

"Hello, Kyra. Good to see you." Lev gestured that she sit beside Maltruis.

She took the seat and gave him a brief smile. "I've decided to stay in for a bit and run the new safe house mission for Galerius."

He leaned his chair back. "You good leader for team. I have layout of house and surrounding mapped out. You want member of my department go?" He pulled a file from the drawer.

"Yes, I would like to take someone with me. I would value your input on a member of your team you think would be suitable for the task," she said, pleased with herself for making her need for help sound so professional.

He steepled his fingers. "I can help you, a favor to ask."

His response surprised her. "Of course."

"Maltruis want to be field agent, best way to attend mission. Send him with chosen person?" he asked, glancing at Maltruis.

It wouldn't hurt to have more help, yet she wasn't sure she wanted a rookie on her own trial run. At the same time, making Lev happy might work in her favor. "I would be honored to help him gain field experience." She did her best to follow the diplomatic, professional example the Architect has set for her all her life.

"Good. Take Maria. She is pure Dwarf. Good instincts about buildings." He opened the file. "Here blueprints and survey. You copy, study before briefing." He handed her the pages.

"Thank you, Lev. Once you have all the clearances, I will set a time for team departure." She stood. "Oh, can you send someone to fix the Architect's door?" She looked at her feet.

He chuckled, his rumbling laugh filling the small space. "Yes, I send crew. I saw whole thing on camera, figured I'd wait for you ask." He laughed, again.

She grimaced in response.

"Go on, get you team," he said, his tone still warm.

She slipped out, thankful to escape that slight bit of embarrassment. She did, however, feel more confident about her mission. Lev had a lot of experience and a good head on his shoulders. His endorsement of her leadership helped. She should have asked him about the succession to gauge his reaction, but she simply could not see Lev with those kinds of ambitions.

Looking around as she walked through the department, she noticed a small woman seated at a drafting table. She guessed since Maria was a pure Dwarf, she wouldn't be the size of Lev or Maltruis. Only a few tribes had stayed pure, retaining their diminutive stature. She would introduce herself to Maria when she convened a team meeting after her briefing.

Now to check on the Architect. Kyra's fingers brushed over the radio clipped to her belt, checking once more to make sure it was on. Finding it in perfect working order, she started off on the trek to his office. She walked past the equipment room. She stopped and backtracked, ringing the bell on the half door.

A young Fae came to the door to meet her. The fluorescent lighting of the storeroom caused her indigo skin to take on a luminescent hue. Every time she breathed, her translucent wings slowly flapped, casting prisms of light across the room. She blinked her lavender eyes, the golden slits widening slightly as they took in Kyra.

"Good Morning. I'm Kyra. Class five security agent. I'd like a requisition form, please." She slid her badge across the counter.

The girl bobbed her head and disappeared into the office. Kyra continued to study the blueprints of the two-story mansion as the girl came back and handed her the form. Kyra took the form and noticed that the Fae was unabashedly staring at her. There was a time when the curious stares really upset her. She understood that the mixture between human and Fae was completely forbidden, and that she was the product of such a union. She had encountered hatred from some Fae over the years. Now, she just brushed most of it off. Curiosity wasn't a bad thing, and this girl didn't seem hostile.

Kyra gave her a slight smile, which caused the Fae to smile broadly in return.

Starting off down the hall, she added a mental note to find out the girl's name and clan. She seemed sweet.

Kyra tucked the other paper in with the blueprints. She'd have to get a binder from the Architect. While deep in thought about what department to visit next, a familiar voice from behind caused her to stop and turn.

"Rumor said you were still here, and I'm pleased to see it's true." The Centaur moved up beside her, his hooves clacking on the stone floor.

"Nyles!" Kyra threw her arms around his human top half in a rare display of affection.

He laughed and returned the hug. "It's good to see you, too."

Stepping back, she took him in. He wore a simple red polo shirt, the color complimenting his deep black hair.

"I didn't know you were back from the Centaur census, or I would have come by to see you, already." She hoped no one had seen her burst of exuberance.

"While going home and spending time around my kind is nice, it's a pleasure best had in small doses." He smiled, his dimples flashing.

"Walk with me. I'm on my way to check in on Father."

"Of course. What do you have there?" He gestured to the papers in her hands.

"Well, I've decided to stay in for a bit. Galerius asked me to lead a team to check out and secure a place they are thinking of using for a new safe house." She was aware of the broad smile on her face. Being around him always did that for her. He was also an orphan whom the Architect had brought into Scíath at a young age. They had spent many days playing in the halls here. Even though he was a pure breed, people still had a prejudice against Centaurs. So, ridicule followed them both, only making their bond that much stronger.

"Wow, team leader, huh? Don't suppose you need the Anthropology department for this kind of mission, do ya?" His expression filled with hope.

"As a matter of fact, this was a former Imp stronghold. So, having someone along who could help us understand Imp culture and look for traps and ritual signs would be very helpful."

"Outstanding."

They walked down the hall in an awkward silence. The attraction and affection between them was clear, but Kyra knew that a romance was just not plausible. More extreme race mixes had been seen; however, it was not something one could conceive of. Even though they had never spoken on it, Kyra knew a barrier existed that neither would broach.

When they arrived at the Architect's study, she paused. She couldn't think of a reason why he wouldn't accompany her to meet with him. At the same time, the topic she knew the Architect would want to discuss needed privacy.

Nyles saved her from a fumbling excuse. "I have to get this data to Simon. Can I steal you for dinner?"

"I would absolutely love that, and you have fun with Simon." She thought of the huge mainframe data system that was the brain of Scíath

"Always do." He leaned in to give her another hug.

"I'll meet you in the dining hall at eight." She headed into the study.

"See you then." His hooves click-clacked down the stone halls.

She watched him go, her emotions swirling. He really was an amazing guy, but some things were just not meant to be.

Determined not to break another door that day, she knocked softly and waited. This time, she was rewarded with a swift answer.

"Enter, Kyra." It was not even noon, and already, he sounded tired.

She pushed the door and took a long, deep breath, the smell of his vanilla cherry pipe smoke wafted through the air to greet her. He sat behind a behemoth, ebony wood desk. Bookshelves lined the walls, and knickknacks covered every available space. Several large, overstuffed recliners were scattered around the room. The fireplace sat idle, awaiting its nightly lighting. More prisms and various crystals hung from the ceiling than when she last checked.

His pipe was clenched in his teeth as he replaced the papers he was reading into the folder. "Come in, and take a load off." He gestured to her favorite recliner.

She complied, sinking happily into its soft cushions. He came out from behind the desk and took a chair just to her right. He sat down with a sigh.

"I did not sleep well last night. I kept feeling the hostile and hungry vibes I received last night. I thought I had built this place on loyalty and respect, brought in only those who were good people, and made this a family. The moment the idea of power came up, that chance at power brought out the baser natures of people. You see, all people, be they Gilly or Supernatural, have baser desires—primitive needs in them. It's up to each of use to suppress theses needs, to act in a civilized and kind-hearted manner. I'm afraid I've let wolves in among the sheep, and the worst part is I cannot discern those wolves. Their sheep's clothing is too well tailored." He took a deep puff off his pipe.

"You did an amazing job building Scíath. You took an idea and turned it into a thriving hub. Think of how many lives you've saved. How many cultures that would be nothing but memories that you have recorded in Simon? You've saved both worlds from an Imp invasion. How many dangerous supernaturals are locked up in Mirartene prison? You cannot doubt yourself and the good you've done.

"As for the vibes you felt last night. There is no way you could truly know anyone. All people hide what they don't want others to see, but chances like the one you're laying out will bring those things to the surface. I will make sure you're safe until your decision is made. You should be safe after that. I will also do my best to discover who could be a danger. I can't say I overly checked Lev, but on the whole, he doesn't seem to have an ambitious bone in that huge body of his." She reached out to place her hand on his arm. She hoped to reassure him, even though she knew the threats were very real and that many within the compound possessed the ability to do him great harm.

"If you want, I will turn down this assignment and stay at your side. There are others Galerius can use." She meant every word. Inwardly, though, she was becoming excited about the opportunity and wanted the chance.

"That's not necessary. I can arrange to be with others while you are gone. I want to see how this turns out. As for Lev, I concur with your assertion of his nature. He is quite content to run his department. I have nothing to fear from him."

"Lev suggested I take Maria on the team, and he asked that I take Maltruis along to garner field experience."

"Maria's got an unparalleled mind for structures, and I think that the Foundling would make a good field agent. What did you say?"

"I agreed. I know what it's like to be the tag-along greenhorn. Also, Nyles is coming from Anthro." She stared into the fireplace, waiting for his response.

He chuckled. "I wondered how long it would take you two to run into each other. While taking him along requires a little more planning on transportation, he's a good choice. His extensive knowledge on Imp culture should be able to help you through any traps you find."

"You think there will still be remaining traps?" Her eyes were drawn again to the blueprint.

"Imps are the most insidious, secretive, and cruel supernatural race. They have killed the innocent for simply stepping on land they claim as their own. Whether that step was intentional or accidental matters not to them. They are brutal, remorseless beasts. Lord only knows what's waiting in that place." His tone betrayed his disgust.

She nodded. The Imps were the only culture that was hated across the board. Not that they would ever seek to enter Scíath under friendly terms. They had been banned more than fifty years before, after they raided a Gilly village and killed nearly twenty people. The war that resulted raged for almost five years, risking exposure of the entire world.

The incident had also served to spark the Freedom Movement. A group of supernaturals from various races wanted to try to coexist in public with the Gillys. They made a lot of idle threats of going public, but in the end, the fear of persecution kept them from following through. Most, if not all, of the Imps were believed to have been killed in the war, leaving strongholds dotting the countryside in many lands. It was fortuitous for Scíath, as they could be converted into safe houses and perhaps off compound living spaces. The Architect was right, though. It was impossible to guess what might be left in that place.

"I stopped and picked up an equipment requisition form, and there was a young Fae staffing it. Who is she?" She asked, changing the subject. Thinking about Imps always upset him.

"I'm glad you brought her up. Milyna comes from a tribe very close to your mother's. I wouldn't be surprised if you weren't in some way distantly related."

She let his comment sink in, even though she went out of her way to ignore both sides of her bloodlines. It had caused her so much pain over the years that it was easier to just be without thinking you were a part of something larger.

She simply sat. She knew what he was trying to do. Her first reaction was to cut off contact and make sure she stayed away from the girl, but a nagging desire to belong and remembrance of the girl's sweet smile sneaked into her thoughts. She shook her head slightly.

"Fae colonies can be huge. It's doubtful we're related. She seems very young to be here," she said, hiding her interest.

"As a matter of fact she is. Less than a hundred, that one, but she has an amazing talent for inventory and supplies. Not to mention that her parents contacted me and asked me to take her, as they were both nearing their Sonria with no family to look after her."

Sonria. Kyra was blessed to have mixed genes that did not demand she follow such practices. Fae lived to be centuries old, but after about 250 years, their bodies need a recharge. Sonria was a twenty-five year hibernation.

Most of them planned their children around those, but there were rare occasions when that was simply not possible, and this seemed to be one of them. To most people, nearly 100 years old would seem like more than old enough to take care of themselves, but Fae aged slowly. In human terms, Kyra was merely a teenager and still in need of guidance.

Kyra watched The Architect sitting silently, puffing on his pipe, and leaving her to her thoughts. He could easily have scanned them, but he afforded her privacy. He probably figured he could guess what she was thinking about, anyway. He had deliberately laid that track of thought for her. She sighed. He always managed to get her to think about things she was dead set against. It was a talent he had been using on her for as long as she could remember, and she didn't think it had anything to do with his magical blood. She couldn't help but allow the curious possibility that they were indeed related, somehow, to seep back into her mind. Well, even if they were, she reasoned she was in no position to look after a Fae teenager herself, so it was best left at a perhaps.

"Anyway, could I borrow a binder? I want to put all of my paperwork together, so I can make notes during the briefing. I need to visit Simon to print out the factoid sheet on each member of my team. I want to utilize them to the fullest on this mission." The softness of the chair combined with the atmosphere of the office and the smell of the pipe smoke make it a hard refuge to abandon. She had forgotten how much she liked it here.

"Sounds like you are going to be an excellent mission leader. There is a stack of empty binders on the second shelf in my closet. You're welcome to them." His eyelids drooped low. "So, while you welcome yourself to one, I'm going to welcome myself to a nice nap." He tapped his pipe out.

"I'll lock the door on my way out, then." She selected one of the larger binders and headed for the door.

She moved back to his desk, taking the radio and placing it delicately in his sleeping hand. She then tiptoed out, silently using her key to lock the study door.

She stood outside his door, deciding where to head next. She didn't have to go to Anthropology—that made one less stop on her list. Which, she reminded herself, she had failed to actually make. She closed her eyes, pulling up a mental map of the compound. The nearest office was Medical. Putting on her stone demeanor, she marched herself down the hall, head held high.

* * * *

A short time later at the medical center, she recalled where her badge was and made a much quicker entrance. As soon as she stepped in the door, she was met by two figures in full sterilization garb, complete with air tanks. Her eyebrow rose. She had not heard of any contamination lock-downs.

The figures guided her onto a glowing round, white circle and a cool, ultraviolet light surrounded her. It lasted less than a minute. She felt no different than she had before, and her papers were unaltered. The two suited beings ushered her through a door that hissed with the force of an airlock. She looked around the bare room. All this was new, although it had been at least a year, if not more, since she had set foot in Medical.

A door on the side slid open with another loud hiss. She stepped out and found she had at last reached the medical ward. To the right was a general clinic office for common illnesses, routine vaccinations, and checkups. To the left was a hub of professionals, each in a lab coat and carrying clipboards or sitting at terminals. Medical didn't really have nurses—just first-year doctors. Everything was learned hands on, and lectures were given when something new arose. Otherwise, you picked things up from the more seasoned doctors.

Directly in front of her was another set of swinging doors that led to the inpatient and operating rooms. Making her way to the hub, she waited patiently until a tall doctor with a red stripe on his pocket, indicating this was his fifth year in the department, greeted her. His hair was shaggy, which she thought rather unprofessional until she realized he was trying to camouflage a pair of horns. "Miss Kyra, welcome to Medical. May I help you?"

"I need to speak with Doctor Barker, please." She didn't recall ever meeting him. How did he know her name? *Oh, wait...my badge.* Sliding it into the door to gain entry had probably popped up her name on one of the computer screens.

"He's down in one of the patient rooms. They did a major bypass surgery on a Griffin. I can take you to him if you'd like."

"Yes, please." She needed to get a medical tech for the team, but she also thought it would be cool to see a Griffin up close. She had only ever seen them in flight.

Picking up a clipboard, he motioned for her to follow as he pushed through the double doors. A spider web of hallways branched out in all directions from a round hub in the center. The hub had varied monitoring devices and computer terminals, including a Simon interface on one side, perhaps for entering new case or disease information. It was hard to count all the moving bodies in the hub, but she guessed there were at least thirty people in that circle—all busy.

All serious supernatural injuries were treated here. Outposts had basic medical facilities, but anything major had to come here. She had heard once that a Hibagon, a Himalayan yeti, had been airlifted all the way from Tibet for medical treatment. It had taken multiple departments working together just to facilitate the transfer.

Further, his injury had given him a rather surly disposition. The resulting havoc he unleashed on one mountain village had taken weeks to repair.

I must really get more familiar with each department if I plan on leading teams in the future. She followed her guide through a series of hallways, looking for landmarks. Feeling lost made her antsy. A few more twists and turns, and he stopped outside a slightly open door. Motioning for her to wait, he knocked once.

"Come in," a gentle, male voice responded.

Her guide slipped in the door, leaving her outside with her curiosity raging. She heard a muted conversation and tried to peek inside; however, the curtain had been pulled. After a long moment, Doctor Barker emerged. He wore a plain, white lab coat with his badge clipped to the pocket. He smiled genuinely when he saw her and extended a hand.

"Kyra, it's a pleasure to see you." He gave her a long look, maybe searching for the reason for her visit?

"You as well, Doctor Barker. I'm not ill, if that's what you're wondering," she said, her expression remaining stoic.

"Leland, please. I'm glad you are in good health. So, what is it I can do for you?"

"Well, Leland, I'm leading a team to check out the newest possible safe house. You always hope you're not going to need medical personnel, but I think it wise to take a medic along, just in case." She kept her tone neutral. She had never thought she would have to work with him, after his diplomatic refusal to allow her into his department. It took a fair amount of restraint not to put on the airs of being a team leader, since he had not believed she could succeed.

A thoughtful expression crossed his face. "That is a very wise call. We like to not be needed, trust me." He led her back toward the hub.

As they walked down the hall, a group of doctors headed toward them. At the front of the group was Anaraba. She looked happy and comfortable, reading a chart to those around her. They stopped to greet Doctor Barker.

"Hello all, this is Miss Kyra. She is heading a safe house mission and has come to me to ask for a medic to go along. Would anyone second-year or above like to volunteer?" He searched them for a response

A look of disappointment on Anaraba's face let Kyra know that though nowhere near ready, the newest recruit was willing to volunteer. Several hands in the group went up. A young male from the back of the group held his hand up, standing on his tiptoes to make sure he was seen over those in front of him.

Leland smiled, obviously proud of his students. Kyra nodded slightly toward the tips of the fingers waving wildly over the heads of his peers.

"Nikkos, you are interested in going?" Leland asked. The crowd parted as Nikkos made his way to the front of the group. He was of stocky stature. His skin had a soft olive tone, and his dark, serious eyes were set under a pair of bristly, black eyebrows. Locks of his tousled, thick black hair fell into his eyes.

"I would be honored to go. I'm the top of my year and well versed in both emergency and on-site medical care." His excitement rang in his voice.

Leland held up his hand. Nikkos fell silent, looking chagrined. "Nikkos, I know you will do the department proud. I will give your dossier to Kyra, and you will be informed of the time and place for your briefing meeting. Now, please finish your rounds."

Nikkos, positively glowing, stepped back in with the group. Kyra and Leland continued walking down the hall. Keeping her smile inward, she was pleased at her progress.

"Nikkos is a good choice. Descended from the cult of Apollo, he has the ability to heal and diagnose by simply laying his hands on a person. It can make a difference in a dangerous situation."

While it was not the way she would have approached picking their medical personnel, it seemed she had struck good luck. Now, back at the desk, Leland walked over to Simon. He tapped a few keys, and the printer spat out what she assumed was the aforementioned dossier. He handed it to her.

"I hope your mission is successful and uneventful," he said with another smile.

"Thank you. I hope for exactly the same. I'll send word when I have a time and place for the briefing. So nice to be working out of home base, again," she said, hoping he'd pry and giving her a chance to see if he was invested in the successions.

"Yes, I can't say that I've seen you around a lot, but I'm glad you're here. I worry over the Architect, and I know you will take care of him."

She could sense nothing but sincerity in his words and crossed him off the list of suspects. Much like Lev, he was not high on the list to begin with. "Thank you," she replied.

With a brief goodbye, she headed out, only to be met by the same suited team as she went to exit. She went through the same process that she endured upon entering. She had meant to ask Leland about that but had forgotten. She stood in the hall, trying to decide which way to go next. She had handled, Anthropology, Medical, Building, and, of course, she was Security. That left Artifacts, Supernatural Species...and Gilly Relations.

I wonder if I even need someone from Jason's department. They did not expect to encounter any Gillys, and the area was supposed to be secured by Lev's team to keep any stray people out. *Artifacts, then check on Father, perhaps ask his advice.* She made her way toward Artifacts. It was on the exact opposite end of the building from where she was currently, but it had to be done. She wanted it all finished, so when she went into her briefing, she could show Galerius how ready she was for this assignment.

The stack of papers in her arms was getting larger. She should have brought her satchel. Weaving in and out of the people in the halls, she pondered her dinner date. It was not *really* a date. After all, it was Nyles, and they had been friends for years. Yet, the feelings that arose when she thought of him were far more serious than just a long-standing friendship. She had spent many nights thinking about him, wondering just how impossible a relationship between them might be. She always came to the same conclusion. Love could overcome many things, but race differences of this extreme were not something that was plausible.

Sighing deeply, she made her way through the corridors. She knew so few of the faces anymore. With so much time spent in the field the last couple of years, she had missed quite a few foundling ceremonies. One year, they split a few departments up and added some administrative functions, resulting in several foundling ceremonies in a matter of just a few months. Each department having perhaps ten participants or more doubled the personnel of some departments.

Father had told her stories of how Scíath began. He and five others had taken refuge in the sewer under Big Ben, fearing persecution by the "normal" world. They made it their mission to enable the supernatural world to be organized and protected. Out of that dream, this multi-leveled compound had been born.

The Architect had approached Queen Elizabeth, offering them protection and diplomacy with the things that go bump in the night. She had agreed and funded Scíath. It had been over sixty years in operation and had come so far from a few scared people hiding in a dank sewer. More and more supernaturals sought asylum within its walls. Kyra had great respect for those who had sacrificed and labored to make this haven. Never in Scíath's history had anyone ever been turned away. They had done so much good, going so far as to building a prison to incarcerate those who were a danger to all.

They had put in place an extensive legal system with laws governing relations between the Gilly's and supernaturals. Kyra had attended a trial once, as she had been a witness to a Lupus on trial for a destructive rampage. It was conducted in a similar fashion to the Gilly British courts; however, the Treoraí drew from a hat to see who would act as prosecutor, defense council, and so on. The judge was always the Architect. The jury was comprised of Scíath employees selected randomly by Simon. The Lupus was sentenced to twenty years. Mostly Dwarves, as well as several Centaurs, staffed the prison. She had been there many times to check on prisoners. It was an impressive place.

Lost in her thoughts, she walked right past the vault-like door to Artifacts. She soon came to a dead-end. *Nice job, dingbat.* She turned around and headed back toward the vault.

The artifact department was behind a large, round steel door. A large, stainless steel wheel was the handle, reminiscent of a super-sized bank vault. She slid her badge into the card reader on the vault door, watching the color lights do their electronic dance, until the light turned green. Removing her badge, she heard several loud clunks as heavy, metal locks released. Grabbing the wheel, she gave it a spin to the right, hearing the metal bars slide back.

The door creaked open. Grabbing a hold of the side, she pulled it just far enough to allow her to slip in. Though, she had no doubt that the door's noise had alerted anyone inside to an incoming presence.

The front of the department contained about thirty workstations, the harsh florescent lighting giving everyone a pale, unhealthy glow. From about midway back, the room was packed with shelves. The room went on as far as she could see, and every spare inch was covered in artifacts. Most were placed on plain, metal shelves; however, some were in glass cases. Those that were considered dangerous were in a special sub vault off the main room somewhere.

A dozen people moved about, carrying things, cleaning pieces, or performing other random tasks. Ariel sat beside another worker who was showing her how to enter information into Simon. She looked up as Kyra walked closer and smiled, brightly waving. Kyra waved back, returning a polite smile. Ariel seemed at home here. Kyra was certain this had been a good place for her. A voice from about 200 yards away called to her.

"Kyra, I'm down here," the muffled voice said.

Kyra assumed it was Moira calling to her. She made her way down the path toward where she believed the sound had come from. Fearful of bumping into one of these shelves and creating a domino catastrophe as she was known to do, she walked slowly. She reached the middle of the section. Peering into the sea of shelves, Kyra caught sight of Moira's slight form.

"Moira?" she called quietly.

"I'll be right with you. I just need to finish stacking theses gnome burial pots."

Kyra stepped back, glancing at the shelf beside her. The top shelf was covered by an intricately woven tapestry piece that portrayed a ceremony of some sort. The corner of the tag was half visible. She wanted to nudge the fabric aside and read what was on it, yet was concerned about touching the fabric. If it was truly delicate, it would not be in the general collection, but it would be just her luck if she were to move it and it were to fall apart. Her curiosity would just have to wait. A moment or so later, Moira appeared out of the masses of shelves. She wore a bright smile and a fair amount of dust.

"It's a pleasure to see you. It's been too long." Moira gave her an affectionate hug. Kyra awkwardly returned it as best she could with her stack of papers.

"I was just thinking it's been a while since I've been here. I hardly recognize any of the faces in the halls," Kyra replied.

"There has been a large influx of people in the last five years. My department has received at least fifteen foundlings." Moira dusted herself off.

Kyra's eyebrows rose in surprise. She recalled when the entire department consisted of twelve overworked people. "No kidding eh?"

"Now, I can tell from that stack of papers in your arms that you are not here to hang out. What can I do you for?" Moira asked, leaning casually against the shelves Kyra so feared could topple at any moment.

"I'm leading the safe house expedition, and I wanted to ask for a member of your department for my team, in case we come across anything. This place used to be an Imp hideout, so we have no idea what could be lurking."

Moira's brow furrowed. "I am the foremost expert on Imp artifacts. Unfortunately, Galerius sent out a memo about three months ago asking that department heads not go out on field mission unless it's unavoidable. Some kind of leadership protocol or some such. If you ask me, he worries too much. So, I guess after me the next best person would be Aieta. She has spent a lot of time in the Imp archives and will be a big help. You want her dossier?"

"That would be very helpful, if you don't mind," Kyra replied.

"Sure, follow me."

As they made their way toward the front of the room, Kyra leaned in, keeping her voice low. "How is Ariel doing?"

"Well, she really has a knack for cataloguing, and her recall is extraordinary. She said you helped her make her decision to come here. Good call." Moira pushed a few buttons, and a nearby printer spit out several pages. She handed them to Kyra.

"I wouldn't say that I helped her *per se*. I just noticed that the only presentation she seemed to warm to was yours. I asked her what she thought of your department." Kyra shrugged. "But I am glad she is doing well."

"So, does this mean you're going to be around more?" Moira asked, her voice still low.

"I'll see how this goes. As well as the whole transition of power, we will see," she said, watching Moira's face for a reaction.

"Well, if you do, we should get together for lunch. We have a lot of catching up to do." Moira walked back toward where they had come from.

Kyra stood a moment, puzzled. She and Moira had never been overly close. Was she trying to let her know that she had some information she wanted to pass on that would be best done in private? Kyra would have to make time to talk with her after the mission.

Kyra walked to the vault door and exited. She was disappointed that her comment on succession had garnered zero response, unless that was what she wanted to talk about at their meeting.

The papers she carried were getting unwieldy, so she headed back toward the study.

"Hey there, pretty lady," a male voice said from behind her.

Kyra stopped dead in her tracks, a scowl commanding her expression. Ignoring him would not work, and she was too far from the office to walk in and shut the door. Setting her face to a blank expression, she turned around to meet a grinning Jason Stevens.

"Hello, Jason." She kept her body stiff and her tone as dry and uninterested as she could possibly make it. Her uncomfortable expression made his smile even wider.

His eyes raked over her body with a suggestive smile before he spoke, "I heard you've been making rounds of the departments, collecting team members for your little field trip." He moved closer to her.

She took a step backward. "It is not a field trip. It is a mission to check out a safe house," she said, her tone carrying an edge.

He waved his hand as if dismissing her comment. "Whatever you want to call it. I've noticed you have not come to ask me for help."

He smiled in a used car salesmen fashion.

"Well, that's because I don't need anything from you. Lev's department will have cordoned off the area and handled all the building permits. There should be no Gilly's in the area. I won't need a representative from your department," she said through clenched teeth.

His overinflated smile wavered a moment, before his cool demeanor took over. "Well, I do hope your *assumption* is right. You would hate to risk an *incident* on your first leadership run." His accent on certain words made her clench her fists. His smile turned to a smirk.

"I appreciate your obvious concern for my team. If you would like to volunteer a member?" She wasn't going to ask him for anything.

He paused as if debating if there was a way he could handle this and still come out on top. He sighed ever so slightly. "In the interest of the mission, I will volunteer up Anna. She's one of my top public relations people, and she is also a Wendigo, so she can alter Gilly memories if need be." His expression changed to no longer jovial.

"Why thank you for being so thoughtful, Jason. Please e-mail her dossier over." He was right—she was an excellent addition to the team. Not having to ask him for it made it all the better. "I'm having lunch with the Architect, so if you will excuse me. I will send the time and place for the briefing over just as soon as I have it."

She turned and walked away.

She still needed to see Di, who happened to be on the way to the study. Once she got to the study, she wasn't going to leave for a while. Walking away with her head held high, she wove her way through the compound. Kyra could honestly say she liked few people. The people she would consider friends was an even lower number, but she had always attempted to be polite and diplomatic. Yet, whenever she was around Jason, all she wanted to do was wipe that fake smile off his face. He was definitely one who bore closer examination. His power hungry motives had already been proven, rising through the ranks to become a Treoraí in a remarkably short time. Not to mention the runner-up for the position disappearing conveniently right before the candidates were chosen.

At Di's office, she placed her key card into the reader and was shocked when it started beeping angrily. Removing it, she was about to place it back in when Di stuck her head out the door with a puzzled expression.

"Kyra, please come in. That thing has been on the fritz. It even denied me access to my own department this morning!" Di said with a smile.

Kyra drummed her fingers absently against her leg. She would make sure to send Galerius a memo when she reached the Architect's study. Kyra followed Di into her department. She noted each table was now equipped with a computer.

"I assume storage of information has gotten easier with the new Simon archives," Kyra said as she followed Di to her office.

"Without a doubt. I'm out of book space. I have a team whose sole job it is to enter all the books into Simon." Di offered her a seat as she settled behind her desk. "To what do I owe the pleasure of this visit?"

Gratefully, Kyra placed the papers on her desk. "I am running the safe house mission and was thinking about having a member from your department along. I have Anthropology, but being overstaffed is always better than under."

Kyra loved that Di always got straight down to business. She and the Architect were the only remaining founders of Scíath, making her at least 100 years old. Yet, she could pass for forty at most. She hailed from an African tribe of nymphs. They lived to be at least 500 human years old; however, they reached maturity and their adult form at around fifty years.

"I think it wise. You never know what you will encounter," Di answered, sliding her drawer open. She pondered for a moment before selecting the right file. "I would like you to take Soro. He has, among other things, the ability to sense the supernatural signature. He will be able to detect any other creature within a half a mile radius." She flipped open the folder.

Kyra raised an eyebrow, impressed. "That would be excellent. I appreciate your help."

"Of course." Di handed her a dossier.

Kyra added it to her pile. They walked back to the entrance.

Di opened the door for her and leaned in, her voice soft, "Please, watch yourself. Without you, he is alone." She closed the door, giving Kyra no chance for further conversation.

Kyra frowned and made her way into the bustling halls.

Perplexed by the encounter, Kyra moved quickly. Knocking on the door to the study, she made her expression neutral as she waited to enter.

Sciath

"Come in," he said.

The Architect was sitting behind his desk, a stack of files beside him. Closing the one in front of him, he slipped it to the bottom of the stack. Smiling, he said, "From the look of that stack of paper, you have a team."

"I do, indeed—one from every department." She placed the stack of papers on a side table before settling into the barrel back chair across the desk from him. Her stomach uttered an audible growl. His eyes crinkled as a grin leapt to his lips.

"I hope you don't mind, but I took the liberty of ordering us some lunch. It should be here shortly."

"As always, your precognition is perfect. I'm starved. Not even seeing Jason could change that," she said, sliding her feet into the other chair.

"Oh, how did he take your request for personnel?"

Kyra had told the Architect many times that she couldn't stand him. Her wide smile returned as she told him of the encounter in the hall.

He laughed. "I would have enjoyed seeing his expression. He'll be stewing for a while over that." He then frowned, and his brow set. "But keep your eye on Anna. I've had two complaints about her using her memory powers on people without permission. I have not been able to prove them yet, but just be cautious."

Kyra felt the knot form in the pit of her stomach. *Was that why Jason wanted her to go along? Was this some kind of setup?* The concern brought a deep crease to her brow, and she pursed her lips.

"You're worried Jason is setting you up. I know you do not care for him, and many others do not as well, but I have never seen anything to prove that he does not play by the rules. He's always been forthcoming about his want to move up." He laced his fingers together to place them under his chin.

"Just because he's honest about wanting it, doesn't mean he will be honest about how he goes about getting it."

"Point taken."

A knock at the door caused Kyra to reach for her weapon. She walked quickly to the door and looked through the peephole. "It's lunch." She opened the door, the knots in her back easing.

"I figure assassins don't usually knock."

She stuck her tongue out at him as she took the cart from the white coated Satyr. Lifting the lids on the silver-covered dishes, she was delighted at his selection of comfort food. A steak and kidney pie met her eyes. The meaty aroma wafted up to seduce her. Being out in the field too long, she had forgotten some of the delights of being home—like home cooked meals. She looked up at the Architect and grinned.

"I take it you approve of my selections, then." He moved to join her.

"Absolutely."

They ate in relative silence. She sat back from the table, her eyes drooping in response to a full belly.

"Moira made a strange comment to me." Kyra decided to unload her mind and get his thoughts.

"Oh?" he asked.

"Yes. She said if I was going to be around more that she and I should have lunch and catch up. We've never been close enough to warrant a catch up lunch, in my opinion. I think she is trying to tell me something important."

He pulled out his pipe, packed it, and lit it before he responded. "Moira has always liked you. I could see her wanting to perhaps start a more serious friendship with you, yet I believe your feeling is right. I would suggest taking her up on it. It may be enlightening." He took a long draw on his pipe.

"I'm going to as soon as I get back. I want to make sure this mission goes as smoothly as possible. Galerius is briefing me tomorrow, early afternoon. I'm going to hold my team meeting later in the day, and I want to leave as soon as I get the okay from Lev. That reminds me. I have to get that equipment request in tonight, to give them time to get my gear assembled." She grabbed her stack of papers as she stood.

"You may stay here if you wish. I wouldn't mind hearing about your team. It's been a long time since I've led a mission, and I'm curious." She smiled at his fatherly mix of pride and interest. She felt very comfortable here, and having his opinion might help her belay some of the fears she was having about her ability to run this team. She sat back down, offering him half of her folders. They settled in to go over the dossiers and information Galerius had given her.

* * * *

Across the compound, in a spacious office, Jason's fist pounded the desk in exasperation.

"I simply couldn't wait for her to come to us. I'm glad I didn't. She wasn't even going to come here at all."

"I understand that, however, she is suspicious, and so is that old codger. They're going to wonder why you were so eager to have me on the team." Anna sat on the edge of Jason's huge, mahogany slab of a desk. She pulled her long, jet-black hair over her shoulder.

He scowled at her. "I had no other option. You have to be out there to see what she knows about his succession plans. If he is confiding in anyone, it's her. Don't you think it odd? She hasn't been in the compound for more than a day or two in almost three years, and all of a sudden, she's running missions out of home base?"

"Of course it's odd, and everyone else sees it, too. She suddenly has a reason to meet with every Treoraí, and no really knows what her powers are. She could be checking up on each of you." Anna's intense, green eyes lit up.

Jason's scowl grew deeper. "Well, the Architect's not the only one who can play this game. Just give her absolutely no reason to think that you're up to anything other than helping the team. I will make sure your presence is required." Jason ran his fingers gently over her mocha skin.

"I'm very good at being needed." She leaned across the desk to kiss him with tender passion.

Chapter Three

Twinkle, Twinkle

At half-past seven that evening, Kyra slipped out of the study, sans her papers, and made her way quickly to her room. She debated showing up for dinner in what she currently had on. The holster and gun might be a bit much. Walking to her closet, she contemplated her choices with a frown. Two dozen pairs of jeans, tanks, T-shirts and two spare trench coats—nothing suitable for even a casual dinner. Digging deeper into the recesses of the closet, she found her long, black skirt. She had purchased it to wear to the international summit dinner. She had worn it for all of two or three hours, and that was at least five years ago. Holding it up, it seemed fine. There should be a red silk shell top that went with it somewhere. Digging further, she found it.

She changed quickly. Looking in the mirror, she nodded in approval. She stepped away. With a second thought, she stepped back and slid the leather bracer off, letting her hair down. It fell in waves over her shoulders. She shook it out, running her fingers through the strands as she looked in the mirror. Untamed but okay. After sliding her feet into her black slippers, she headed to the dining hall, ignoring the stares from passersby. She stepped inside the door exactly at eight. Nyles stood just inside. His mouth dropped agape when he saw her.

He approached her, all rugged good looks, dazzlingly eyes, and hooves clacking against the stone floor. He reached out and gently touched her hair. Her general reaction was to pull away when anyone tried to touch her, but never with him. Intoxicated by his nearness, she breathed in the light spice smell of his skin. She wanted to brush gently from his forehead the single shock of his black hair that always found its way into his eyes. Looking up, her eyes met his. She forced herself to step back. Their magnetism would only continue to draw them closer toward an inevitable kiss.

"So, um...ready to get something to eat?" she tried to keep her tone nonchalant.

"I am. We could grab something to go and head to the planetarium. It's not the same as eating under the stars, but it's close."

"That sounds like an absolutely amazing idea." The thought he had put into their impromptu dinner pleasantly surprised her.

They walked into the dining hall as close as they could without touching.

"Gus pulled a bottle of Fae wine from the cellar for me," he said nonchalantly as they stood in front of the deli menu board.

She could not hide her shock. He made it sound like an aside, but she knew for fact that Fae wine was extremely expensive and hard to come by. He had to get permission from the Architect to access that part of the cellar. No doubt that he had easily said yes, but it showed a great amount of planning and consideration on Nyles's part. Good that she'd changed. Her stomach cramped at the smell of the food, and she hoped it did not make an audible growl. She turned her attention to the menu board. The Architect often teased her about her voracious appetite. Given her hybrid blood, as well as her constant state of action, she kept a strong and slender build. No worries about her figure. She glanced at him and was surprised to see he was watching her.

"Having a hard time deciding," she said quickly, shuffling her feet and looking anywhere but at him.

Gus trip-tromped out of the back room, carrying a picnic basket. A Satyr, Gus's lower half was a goat's. Gray speckling in his black fur showed his age.

"I took the liberty of preparing you a basket for your dinner, tonight. I hope you don't mind," he said with a twinkle in his eye. Gus was the head chef at Scíath and managed a staff of several hundred people of varying races. He had been with Scíath for nearly thirty years and watched bothKyra and Nyles grow up. "Gus, as always, you are amazing," Nyles said.

"I wouldn't go that far, but I am at the least creative." Gus winked. "I've included your favorites, as well as an ethnic Fae dessert to go with that wine." Handing the basket to Nyles, he smiled, again. "Now, off with you kids." He headed back into the kitchen.

Kyra's aggravation at being referred to as a child rose, but she quickly dismissed it. Gus meant no harm, not to mention that to him, she really was a child. He had to be pushing 125.

As they exited the dining hall, they took a sharp left into one of the smaller halls. A feeling of awkwardness seemed thick between them. Kyra fiddled with the radio at her hip, making sure to check the reception as they traveled further away from the hub of the compound. Galerius had pioneered all the underground technology, and it almost never failed.

Turning another sharp curve, Kyra ran full on into Anna. Both women fell backward. Kyra felt Nyles's strong arm around her back, righting her before she was even sure what happened. Bending down, he offered a hand up to an aggravated-looking Anna.

"Are you all right, Anna?" Nyles asked, concern evident in his voice.

"Fine," she said flatly. Dusting off her black silk suit, she resumed her quick pace.

Kyra and Nyles gave one another bewildered looks. Neither of them had a lot of experience with the woman, but her appearance in this less-traveled hallway at this time of night was puzzling. With a shrug, Nyles continued toward their destination. Kyra's mind whirled. Nothing was a coincidence. Jason shows up and pushes this woman at her. The Architect lays out a warning about her, and now, she shows up in an offbeat place in a major hurry? *Something was just not right.* Anna was a mysterious woman who worked for her least favorite Treoraí in Scíath. She joined less than two years ago and made no effort to get to know anyone outside her department.

They came to the large, black doors that housed the planetarium. Nyles placed his hand on the scanner and waited for it to turn green. *At least not everything in the building required that blasted key card.* The reader gave out a

Scíath

short beep, and the door lock audibly opened. He pulled the door open, staring into the deep blackness beyond. Kyra, naked without her weapon, reached out with her Fae senses. She searched for any sound or smell of something lurking in the dark. Nyles clapped his hands, causing her to stumble backward.

His clap had brought all the twinkling stars to life. Kyra smiled up at him. Righting herself, she looked up at the stars. Real or not, they were beautiful. "I can't recall the last time I was down here."

He shook his head. "I can't recall the last time you were in Scíath for more than one day."

She opened her mouth to correct him but came to the realization that she could not. "Conceded."

After walking over to the supply closet, Nyles pulled out a stark white blanket and laid it out on the planetarium floor. "I guess the white makes it easier to see what you're eating in the dark," Nyles said, reacting to her confused expression.

Nyles knelt to unpack the basket. Sitting across from him, she opened containers. Gus had an excellent memory. Didn't hurt that he had known them both for years.

Thick, black doors separated them from all the cares and concerns of their duties outside its walls. The meal passed with enjoyment, and the conversation stayed light.

Nyles poured the violet-colored wine as Kyra cut slices of the pear blossom torte.

"This is absolutely amazing," Nyles commented after his first sip of the purple, fizzing beverage.

Kyra took a deep drink, allowing the fizzy feeling to work its way through her entire body. She had drunk Fae wine a number of times in the past, but tonight, it seemed new. Be it the stars, the food, or the company, it all seemed wonderful to her.

She scooted closer and laid her head on his shoulder.

She closed her eyes and listened to his breathing. Its contented rhythm made her even more relaxed.

A loud squawk from the radio on Kyra's hip made her jump to her feet. She was out the door, but she could hear Nyles galloping down the corridor, trying to catch up with her.

Kyra moved down the hall as a blur, cursing herself for not bringing a weapon. Father was in danger, and she was on the other side of the compound, unarmed. She must be losing her mind to have allowed this to occur. Swerving quickly, she avoided a group of students in the hall. From the sound of the cries behind her, she knew Nyles was not quite so nimble. Another squawk from the radio spurred her to move even faster as she rounded the last corner before her destination.

Kyra stood across from a chagrined-looking Architect. Her hair had tangled from the wind, and her face reddened from exertion. Behind her, Galerius lay flat on his back with one of Kyra's slippers resting atop his cheek. Just beyond him lay a brand new door splintered on the polished stone. Nyles appeared in the doorway and helped a rather stunned Galerius to his feet before making his way into the Architect's quarters.

At Nyles's presence, she turned to him. "He sat on it!" she exclaimed, tossing her hands in the air for emphasis

Nyles suppressed a chuckle as the Architect floundered to explain himself.

"I put the radio on the arm of the chair, you see. Then, I went to get my tea, and it must have fallen into the seat. When I sat on it, apparently, it went off." He pointed at his new, broken door. "Child, having you here certainly means a lot of new doors." He chuckled, trying to lighten the mood.

Despite her fear and anger, Kyra broke into a small smile.

"Oh, Galerius!" She hastened out to the now-empty corridor. Her shoe was sitting beside the door.

"I helped him up. He was okay," Nyles explained as she came back in, slipping her foot back into the shoe.

The Architect looked between them, waiting for an explanation.

"Kyra, in her hurry to get to your side, ran him down." Nyles gave a crooked smile.

She cringed, trying to think of a way she could make this up to her boss.

The Architect grinned. "Well, since you are both here, perhaps we can go over the plans for the safe house mission and have some tea?"

Kyra accepted that the earlier night's peace could not be regained. "Fine with me. Nyles?"

"You go ahead. I'm going to go clean up the planetarium stuff. I'll be back shortly...with a new door." He winked.

The Architect surveyed her outfit and loose hair with a sad expression. "I really am very sorry to interrupt your evening and cause you alarm, my dear." He carefully placed the radio on the table before settling into his chair.

Kyra pulled up a chair opposite him and cat-like curled into it.

"It's probably for the best."

"Nyles is a good man." He sipped his tea.

"You mean Nyles is a good Centaur," she corrected him.

"Ah, yes. That is what I meant, of course." His brow furrowed. "I spoke with Lev. He should have all of your permissions together by the time you brief the team, tomorrow. You will have your choice to leave at night or pre-dawn."

"Wonderful." She could do this. She had never failed a mission. Yet, one question sprung to mind. *Am I ready to lead a team?*

"Yes, you are," he said.

She stuck her tongue out at him. "You're not supposed to do that," she said, her tone bordering on aggravated.

"Oh, I didn't have to read your mind, dear. Concern is written all over your face."

"You always were perceptive when it came to me." With practiced knowledge, she moved behind his desk, pulling a plain black, hardbound book from his drawer. Opening another drawer, she withdrew a pen.

"One of these days, I'm going to rearrange the desk just to confuse you."

"Sure you are." She had forgotten how much she loved their banter. "I'm going to start with the departments and who is coming from them."

"Sometimes, I can't believe you've grown from that little girl I found in a flower bed all those years ago," he said quietly.

She sifted through the large stack of files. "Security is obviously me. I'll use this book to document the mission, so everyone should be noted—obvious or not."

"Good point, and excellent idea."

"From Architecture, I'm taking Maria and, as a favor to Lev, Maltruis. From Anthropology, Nyles." She checked his expression, but he simply nodded for her to continue.

"Nikkos from Medical." She recalled the procedure she had been put through upon entering and exiting the department. "Speaking of which, what was that sterile suit, glowing light business I was put through in Medical?" She reached under the side table to retrieve the box of cookies always stashed there.

He laughed as he watched her pick through for her favorite sweet. Then, his face turned serious. "A Nymph from Australia came in with an Imp-engineered toxic illness. It spread from the doctors to other personnel. We lost six people while others lay sick for months. So, Leland engineered a sterilizing system for everyone coming and going from Medical, so it could never happen, again." He accepted the proffered tin and searched for his own favorite treat.

Kyra stared at him. The implications of his statements reached far beyond the few that had died. Almost two decades had passed since any active Imp treachery had surfaced. Did this mean there were active Imps in Australia? If so, why had she not been sent to round them up?

"Before you explode, let me explain the circumstances in which she became ill. The humans were mining for diamonds and drilled into an old Imp hive. Our field agents went to work clearing it out. Sadly, the young Nymph found a trap—a corpse loaded with this vile stuff. In her attempt to humanely remove the corpses and bury them properly, she was infected. The remainder of bodies were burned in a sterile incinerator to make sure they could no longer harm anyone."

She took a deep breath and slowly released it. "Filthy things." She had only ever seen one live Imp.

In human years, Kyra was merely twenty-one. It was hard to tell which race she was going to favor in terms of life span; however, either way, she was too young to remember the active Imp years. The one she had seen was old and gray, and being transferred between prisons. She had been a child then, so she was sure he was long dead, now.

She dismissed the memories. "Let us get back to the matters at hand."

"Right, you were on Medical."

Kyra nodded and picked up her pen. "Gilly Relations is Anna. Supernatural Species is sending Soro. Moria is sending Aieta." She counted them off on her fingers to make sure she had all seven covered.

She knew the Architect had instant and complete recall. His eyes narrowed at Anna's name. "I wonder if I should have allowed Jason to talk me into bringing her here," he murmured, barely above a whisper. Shaking his head as if to clear the thoughts, he looked up at her. "Where and when do you wish to have the briefing? We put in new conference rooms when we moved the gym to the south tunnel."

"I suppose that's the best place, as I'm not sure all of them have clearance to get into Security." She tapped the pen idly on the edge of the notebook.

"I also don't want to worry about trying to match up diets. Let's do it after lunch. That way, I can just have snack food and water. Having it at 4:00 p.m. would give them enough time to pack. That way, we can head out just after midnight, to give us the cover we need with Nyles and Maltruis along." Her fingers picked up a familiar rhythm as she thought. Looking up, she caught her father studying her with a strange look in his eyes—something akin to awe, which made her feel strange. She jumped up and moved over to the computer console. "Who is in charge of room bookings, now? I'll need to send a catering request to Gus as well." She began typing memos.

"Mrs. Christy, over in Administration, takes care of all the room bookings."

She nodded her thanks, chewing her lip slightly as she banged away on the keyboard. She was absorbed in her planning but not enough to miss a shadowy figure in the doorway.

"It's just me," Nyles called in, carrying a new door.

The Architect went to help him.

A short time later, she was finished. Standing, she stretched as the two men finished testing the new door.

"Hey, Kyra. Lev says he's going to start putting these on your tab." Nyles said with a twinkle in his eyes.

Her eyes caught the time on the grandfather clock tucked into the corner of the study. "Goodness, it's after midnight!" *How could I have kept father up so late?*

"Indeed, it is. Guess I don't turn into a pumpkin after all," the Architect said.

"However, you have a very full day tomorrow, both of you. So, perhaps it is time to turn in." He stifled a yawn.

Kyra hugged him and headed out into the hall.

"I'm right next door," she said, catching his yawn.

The Architect simply nodded and picked up his radio. He closed the door, followed by the clunk as the new lock engaged.

Kyra checked the status of her own radio and walked the few feet to her door. "I'm sorry our dinner got messed up."

Nyles laughed, and with a tender touch, he brushed a stray hair from her face.

"Being with you is always an adventure, dear."

"Oh, briefing is tomorrow at four." She moved to open her door. A quick escape was needed.

He nodded and, in one fluid moment, leaned in and kissed her on the forehead. Without waiting for her response, he turned and left.

Kyra stood still, conflicting emotions battling their way to her head from her heart. With a deep sigh, she entered her room, closing the door with a sharp bang. Flipping on the small lamp just inside the door, the dim light gave her just enough to maneuver safely.

She was about a foot from the door when she realized something was wrong. Sliding quickly to her top drawer, she yanked it open. Pulling her gun out with lightening reflexes, she cocked the hammer and kept her back against the nearest wall. Every object in the room threw suspicious shadows. She edged her way into the bathroom and flicked on the light. The harsh florescence blinded her, but she had already ascertained the room was empty.

She waited for her vision to return to normal before she moved back out into the main room. With her eyes closed, she reached out with her Fae senses, searching for what had triggered her panic.

Even with her eyes closed, her other senses created a perfect picture in her mind. Studying the scene, she found it. Inhaling deeply, she identified it. Someone had been in her closet and left a strange scent behind, lingering just beside her armoire.

Moving to the spot, she inhaled deeply, searching her memory for a scent comparison. After a few moments, she backed away. She knew she had smelled it before but could not come up with from where. After slipping into her holster, she tucked her gun into it. She slipped on her trench coat and made her way out into the hall, closing the door quietly behind her. The interloper could still be near.

Kneeling down, she checked the door for signs of forced entry. Seeing none perturbed her more than it would have seeing any. Whoever did this had an access card to all living quarters—hers was on the same security level as the Architects—or they possessed a power that allowed them to move through the door.

Her frowned deepened. Using such powers inside Scíath for this purpose was strictly forbidden and carried a heavy penalty. It was a large risk to take, and for what? She was in home base so infrequently, what would she have in her room that was of interest? She answered her own question. Whoever had broken into her room did so to see if she had any information concerning the succession of power. If they had the nerve and ability to sneak into her room, what would stop them from trying the same thing on the Architect?

She moved down the hall to the next door. It was the door to his study. She tried to open it gently as not to wake Father. It was locked, as it had been when she exited it a few minutes before. Placing her hand on the door, she closed her eyes. Reaching out with her mind, she brought up an image of the room that she knew so well. She rarely used this power, as it was so much easier to be in the room; however, her quota for doors was up. Plus, if anyone was inside, it might cause them to do something rash. This gave her the advantage of not alerting anyone who might be inside with the sound of the key in the lock. Stretching her mind further, she searched for signatures. She found the lingering scent of Nyles, and it made her shiver. Pushing it away, she concentrated on anything out of place. After long moments, she found nothing.

Moving down to the next door—his bedroom—she once again bent down to check the lock. It was unmarred, however, when she stood the odor from her room crept toward her from the south hall.

Her feet barely graced the floor as she sought the scent, moving soundlessly through the empty halls. Pulling out her weapon, she inhaled deeply while tracing the signature. At cross hallways, she without hesitation made her way to the west. She pulled up her mental map of Scíath. She was headed toward the common areas. Her watch said it was almost 1:00 a.m. *That did not guarantee they would be empty.* Plenty of nocturnal species and workaholics were within these walls.

As if to illustrate her thought, she heard the low din of voices coming from the dining area. She pulled in her Fae senses and placed her weapon in the holster. This many signatures would only serve to confuse her.

Her expression set, and her shoulders thrown back, she entered the lit area. There were about fifteen to twenty people milling around between the food counters, the eating area, and the lounge. Her arrival caused a few people to look up. She looked back unblinking, hoping her stern glance would cause the guilty party to look away. A few smiled, and others seemed uninterested.

After a full visual sweep, she was ready to head back to bed. She could check the security tapes in the morning. Out of the corner of her eye, she caught a glimpse of Moira sitting in a back booth, intently studying the papers on the table before her with a pen clenched in her teeth. Now was as good a time as ever to play "catch up". It would be a long time before Kyra would be able to settle in to sleep, anyway.

She ordered a chai latte from a bored-looking Wizard behind the counter and made her way silently toward the back booth. Moira never even looked up. Kyra paused with enough distance as to not intrude if her project was of a personal nature. After another minute of not being noticed, she spoke in a low tone.

"Moira?"

Moira looked up, startled. The pen dropped from her mouth, making an unceremonious clunk as it met the Formica tabletop.

"Kyra!" She shuffled her papers back into the folder.

"I didn't mean to disturb you." Kyra sipped her tea.

"Not at all. I'm not used to many around here being up this late. I am, however, glad to see you. Please, have a seat." Moira gestured to the other side of the booth.

That side of the booth would put Kyra's back to the room.

Moira seemed to notice her hesitation and smiled. "I'll switch ya." She didn't make a big display out of making Kyra more at ease.

Kyra nodded her thank you then slipped into the booth. She scanned the room once more. Finding nothing, she let her body relax.

Moira took in Kyra's dressy clothing and loose hair. Kyra ignored the question in Moira's eyes. "Well, since we are both up, it seems like now might be a good time for our lunch." She hoped her instinct about Moira's request was right and she was not in for a gossip session.

Moira's eyes darted around the room. "I'm glad to see you staying here. The Architect has not been himself the past few months. I can't say specifically what it is that's different, but I'm not the only one who has noticed it. He's been more Spartan with his visits. More and more memos seem to be coming from the high secretary, whereas he used to handle all of those things himself. His announcement was not as big a surprise as he may have thought it to be."

Kyra understood. Inside, she chastised herself for not paying attention, for staying away so long. She was all he had, and she now was the last to know when something had gone wrong.

"Part of the reason I wanted to talk to you is about the succession issue, but I wish to start with the problems I'm witnessing within my own department. As you know, there are at least a million artifacts housed within our walls. Lev dug us a sub-basement for more storage. As we moved things down, I noted that some items were missing from their assigned spots." She held up her hand at Kyra's shocked expression.

"Now, there are several reasons for this to be. They could be out for cleaning, research, study, or digital logging. So, before I reported the loss, I had to make sure they were really missing. So far, I've confirmed that at least six artifacts are missing. I am willing to stake my tenure here that they were not willingly taken by anyone on my staff." Her unblinking gaze met Kyra's eyes.

"Willingly?"

Moira pulled a sheet of paper out of her folder.

"I have accounts from three of my people reporting blackouts, memory loss, and finding themselves in places and not recalling traveling to them." Kyra's hands clenched, and her teeth gritted as she listened to Moira's words. "Before you ask, the only thing they have in common is they all recall seeing Anna before these episodes occurred."

"Has anyone questioned her? She is a Wendigo, with memory powers." She asked, although as soon as the words were out of her mouth, her mind countered. If it was her, she would be smart enough to have all traces of herself covered.

"I haven't spoken to her myself. I turned my report into Galerius two days ago. What I can't figure out is why whoever it is would have taken the pieces that they did. There's no rhyme or reason that I can find." Moira exchanged one list for another.

"They have all been common items, not even anything in the low-level security cases. I am missing one Fae Sonora cloth, one Gnome calendar, two albino Lupus hair samples, one Tritianian scale, and lastly—certainly the weirdest bristles from one of the Grand Witch's retired broomstick."

"Wow, that is totally random." Kyra searched her memory for anything she could think of that would contain those components. She shook her head, coming up blank. "With all of the valuable things in the vault, if you're going to go through the trouble to steal something, at least steal something worth taking."

Kyra's mind floated back to the intruder in her room. *They had also gone through a lot of trouble for nothing.* Snapping back to the conversation at hand, her pragmatic nature took over. "Have you pulled the entry report? Have Anna or Jason been into the vault recently? Did you requisition help outside the department for moving the collection?" She wished she had her notebook.

Moira smiled.

"Yes, no, and yes." She counted them off on her fingers. "I have already checked the log in—nothing different. The helpers I got were from Tinka and Di—mostly long standing members, but I put their names in my report. I will be filing it in Simon for the Architect before I head to bed.

"There was a time when I walked through these halls believing I was in the safest place for our kind. Now, I just don't know. I find myself doubting everyone's intentions, looking for hidden motives. It's disturbed my sleep. That is for certain." The bags under her eyes bore witness to her statement.

"How could things have changed so rapidly? How could people who have worked together for a decade suddenly change? It is truly frightening what the possibility of power does to people." Kyra replied, her voice sad.

"I can't think he is considering me, and for this, I am glad. I could never deal with the responsibility of this place. Thousands of lives are in his hands every day, and that is far too much for me." Moira tipped up her cup to see if any liquid was lingering in her mug.

It was hard for Kyra to see the grand scheme of things. She found it much easier to focus on her mission—her piece in the puzzle that was Scíath.

"What do you know about Anna and Jason's relationship?" Moira asked.

"Nothing. To be honest, I have never actually spoken to the woman or even heard her name. That is until Jason ambushed me in the hall and thrust her upon me for my mission team." Kyra drained her cup.

Moira's brows knit. "I can't help but think it's a bit too convenient. According to the spell pot gossip, she is Jason's lover. He has allied himself with some of the most powerful among us."

"I understand the logic behind having a Gilly in Gilly Relations, however heading it? I'm still not sure I get that one," Kyra interjected.

"I think there may have been more to that than we realize."

"Oh?"

"More gossip, of course, but a Witch from New York says that he is the child of a Witch and a Wizard. They waited many years for him to develop his magic skill, but he never did. He did, however, know all about our world, so they had to do something with him. Now, he has never shown magic here, but he has taken a number of books out of the library on enhancing social magic."

"Social magic?" Kyra asked.

"Yeah, like the art of persuasion and seduction." A hint of disdain emerged in her voice.

"They actually have books on that stuff?" Kyra was way out of her depth. Fae had a glimmer they could use to calm and entrance people, but she'd never even tried to see if she possessed it. "How do you know what he is checking out of the library?" Kyra added.

Moira grinned. "Well, you know Michauv?" she asked.

Kyra closed her eyes, pawing through her overworked memory to discover what that name connected with. "The library clerk. Didn't he come in your foundling group?" Kyra's eyes took longer to open than they normally did.

Moira said with pride, "He's actually the assistant to the Master Librarian, now."

"And you two are involved?" Kyra guessed from her star-struck gaze.

"We are, and he doesn't care for Jason, either. Jason's visits to the library are few and far between. He had to be directed to the correct book section five times. Michauv thought it worth mentioning to me."

Kyra's thoughts whirled. Seemed Jason was up to something, and he was using Anna to assist him. Jason was indeed shifty and someone she went out of her way to avoid. Although, personality aside, he had done an amazing job, and his track record was spotless. *Too much to process.* Kyra drew in a slow, deep breath. She checked her watch. It read nearly two in the morning. Only fourteen hours until her briefing. She still had to put together packets and check over the equipment.

Kyra sighed. She had no idea what was bouncing around in Moria's thoughts, but she knew her own brain needed a rest. "Did you get my memo about the briefing?"

"I did."

"Good. I want to thank you for coming to me with this. Your concerns will be addressed." Kyra fell back on the observed diplomatic skill of the Architect.

"I knew you were the right person." Moira reached out and gave Kyra's hand a squeeze.

"We both have full days tomorrow." Kyra stood to avoid the uncomfortable physicality of the situation. People used touches to convey closeness and affection, but she had never been comfortable with casual affection.

Moira brought out her papers, again. "I just have a bit more to finish up before I hit the sack."

"I'm sure we will be talking in the morning." Kyra headed out of the dining area. Stopping to drop her cup into the recycle bin, she noticed a group of six or so gathered around one magazine.

Out of curiosity more than anything else, she opened up her hearing to see if she could pick up what was being talked about.

"Hey, isn't that Kyra?" one male voice said.

Kyra sighed and started to move away when another voice replied.

"Yeah, she's really powerful. I heard that she cleared out an entire Imp hive by herself!" the voice exclaimed in response.

A crooked smile appeared on her face as she walked away. It was amazing how myths grew.

* * * *

Moira watched her go. She could see the exhaustion and worry on Kyra's face. It was a much more human side of her than most saw. Moira had seen firsthand the prejudice and distrust Kyra had earned simply by being born. She knew Kyra had absolutely no idea the amount of gossip she alone inspired. She also knew it wouldn't help her if she did. Kyra came off hard as stone, all business with a strict, no nonsense nature. It was whispered she had no human side, even though her body and skin color spoke otherwise. Kyra's mother had been part of an almost Amazonian culture. The women were warriors, and men from surrounding tribes were used for breeding. Despite being slight in stature, their plumb skin and white manes lent to their intimidating natures. Her father had been found unconscious in their wood—animal attack or something. No one knows the rest of the story, except perhaps the Architect. In any case, they had run away, and several years later, the Architect arrived with a small child clinging to his legs.

Fae purists called out for the child's death, referring to her as an abomination. The Architect ignored them, raised her as his daughter, and protected her the best he could. She had grown up mostly in human fashion, although she could be mistaken for a teenager still even though she was nearing twenty-two.

Moira liked to think that Kyra would call her a friend, but she didn't think Kyra really had anyone she considered a friend. She was hopeful that after the Architect retired that Kyra would stay on at Scíath, but a lot of that depended on who came into power.

* * * *

On her way back to her to her room, Kyra's pace was slow. As tired as she felt, this type of exhaustion was new to her. She had chased fugitives for days on end with no sleep, gone through grueling, strenuous, physical activity, but she could not recall a time she felt this drained.

It was because of all of the emotional and mental stress she had undergone in such a short period of time. Dragging her feet, she made it back to her room. Grateful no was around to see her, with her weapon drawn, she did a complete search for anything out of place. Finding nothing, she slipped into a simple pair of black pajamas and into bed. She was asleep before she had a chance to adjust her pillow.

Chapter Four

Sanctuary

Kyra's eyes fluttered open. Even before they could focus, she shut them and rolled over to avoid awakening. It would be 6:00 a.m. She always woke up at the same time, regardless of when she had gone to bed. There was simply no way she could run this day and tonight's departure on four hours of sleep. Knowing that it was in the best interest of her team and not just herself, she willed herself back into the depths of sleep.

* * * *

A few rooms away, the Architect lay in the dark. He knew it was time to start the day, but he lacked the will to do so. Stretching out his mind, he could feel every living being under his care. Their energies combined as one, giving Scíath a heartbeat. When he hid in that dank water pipe—dirty, hungry, and scared—he never could have known that their plan would have amounted to this. Thousands of supernaturals filled this compound, to say nothing of the consulates and outposts all over the world.

Four determined minds had brought cohesion to a fractured world. They had chosen him to lead. He had been the eldest then as well as quite full of fire and reform. Could he have gone back in time, he wouldn't have turned down, shrugged the title. He had learned so much, helped so many. Yet his mind always went back to those he couldn't save.

Kyra's parents were a prime example of a pair he had failed. Closing his eyes, he allowed himself to drift back into that memory…

It was cold—the kind of cold that worked its way through your protections and chilled you to the bone. The sun's rays crept across the dense forest, bringing light but little warmth. He waited. It had been a very long time since a distress call had drawn him from the walls of Scíath. If what this woman had written was true, this was going to be a dangerous task. He sensed movement in the dense undergrowth. Before he had a chance to draw his weapon, he stood toe-to-toe with her.

All he could do was take her in. Her violet-colored skin had a luminous, silver sheen. Her eyes—deep as the night and just as black—stared challenging back into his. Her long, snowy hair flowed down her back in cascading waves. She held a simple looking spear in her hand, though he knew it was anything but. It was charged with Fae magic, and the tip likely held poison as well. She regarded him for what felt like an eternity. When she spoke, her voice was low and carried a great deal of malice.

"You are too late, human. They have been dispatched, and their bodies lie in the grove they created."

"Then, why are you still here?" He knew how close to death he stood but remained calm.

"The same reason you are here—the child." Her unblinking eyes unnerved him.

He straightened his shoulders and sealed his mind. She would be searching it for clues. "My business here is no concern of yours; however, as you've just admitted to murdering a human, I suggest you leave before I take you into custody to answer for your crimes." He kept his tone steady.

The Fae's laughter brought several more Fae out of the woods. He was outnumbered four to one. A colossal bluff might be the only thing to get him out of danger. He needed to scare off the Fae so he could search for the child.

Taking a deep breath, he looked the Fae squarely in the eyes. "You leave me no choice, then." He tilted his head out and let out a long, loud Lupus call.

Panic spread on their faces, and they scurried away. There were no Lupines within call range, but the Fae didn't know that. He waited to make sure they had actually left. Once he was sure, he made his way in the direction from which they had come.

Moving quickly through dense woods, he paid little attention to where he was stepping. An animal hole proved to be his undoing. His foot went in, and he fell face first into a medium-sized oak tree. He lay against its bark, waiting for the world to return to steady view.

Pushing himself up, he smirked at the tree with which he was now well-acquainted. Carved into the bark was the gateway to a Fae grove. Using his powers, he laid his hand on the tree, sensing the pattern. He touched the small, carved symbols in sequence, and they began to glow with a dull, violet light. The tree bark turned transparent, granting him entry to a family sanctuary.

Even before his vision adjusted, he could feel the glimmer. As his vision cleared, he stood in awe of what one Fae had done for her family. This homestead was easily an acre large. A simple, stone cottage sat beside a lazy stream. Fruit trees of all sorts sat off to the other side. The soft sunlight filtering through the trees caressed the scene. It would be easy to believe one had stumbled into a waking dream.

The idyllic vision was spoiled by the two battered bodies lying just off the porch. Though no stranger to gore or to brutality, to him those killed in senseless crimes always seemed so much more horrible. Moving past them, he made his way into the house. His search was thorough, checking under beds and in closets.

Discovering that the child was not in the house, he took the blanket from her parents' bed and laid it over their bodies. When he did find the girl, she'd be spared the sight. Moving into the open area, he stretched out his mind to search for a heartbeat. A small, rapid one thumped to the northwest. He moved quickly. No way of knowing how long his trick would keep the Fae at bay. He moved into a formal garden. He didn't even know the child's name, so he couldn't call for her.

A movement caught his eye in the lily-filled garden. He bent down on one knee, pushing aside a clump of the purest purple lilies he had ever seen. He came face-to-face with a young girl of no more than three. Her bright eyes filled with tears, blades of grass caught in her long, blonde hair.

She pulled away from him, obviously unsure if he be friend or foe. He wished he had time to comfort and coax the child, but he did not want her to share her parents' fate. He was unsure of his ability to protect her against three Fae warriors.

"Little one, I need you to come with me, quickly." He held his arms out to her.

"Are you the one mama sent for?" She surprised him with her courage.

"I am."

She walked out of the flowers and into his waiting arms.

"There is another exit in the ash tree, there." She pointed at a tall tree a few hundred yards away.

This child is a wonder. Her parents must have prepared her for this inevitability. The thought nearly broke his heart. First picking one of the long-stemmed lilies from her hiding place, he then scooped her up and headed for the exit.

His mind traveled back to the present, as he heard Scíath start to come to life beyond his door. He rolled over on his side to stare at the crystallized, purple lily that sat under glass on his table. She had been such a resilient child. Her Fae name was more of a song than a title, so to help her fit in, he had given her a human name. She became his daughter. Effortlessly, she loved him, yet she had always remained guarded around others. He just hoped she was up for what lay ahead.

* * * *

Kyra pulled herself out of bed an hour later. She moved through her morning rituals, showering and dressing mostly on auto pilot. She collected herself and placed her weapons in her holster. Once she walked out that door, even to go two doors down, she was a target again, and she would never be caught unaware.

She moved quickly to the study door and knocked twice.

"Enter."

Kyra walked in but stopped short. Seated across the desk from the Architect was Moira. She gave a nod to Kyra.

"I was just stopping by to see if you had eaten. I'm going to check over my equipment." Kyra didn't want to intrude, especially since she knew what the meeting was about.

"Let's plan on lunch, dear," the Architect said.

Kyra grabbed her book and files. She and the Architect would discuss his meeting with Moira at their lunch. Right now, she needed to focus on the mission. *Supplies first—No wait. Better make sure Lev knows Nyles is going.* It would make a difference in the way they traveled.

Squaring her shoulders, she made her way toward Architecture. *A sane person pops off an e-mail. Oh no! Not little Miss Hands-on, Kyra.* She snorted and shook her head. Once again, she caught herself searching for her plastic card as she arrived at the door. Raised voices behind her changed her focus.

Turning on her heel, she located the kerfuffle—a shoving match. Kyra's eyes narrowed, trying to ascertain what the cause was until she saw the young Fae from inventory attempting to retain order.

Kyra rolled her eyes. Male bravado was often more annoying than dangerous, but there was no reason for it to be going on in the halls. The young Fae was beginning to look distressed.

Kyra's voice cut through the fighting. "Excuse me," was all she said. Yet, it froze both combatants in their tracks. Milyna's face flooded with relief.

Kyra turned her attention on the boys. One was a human Wizard from Anthro. She recalled his face from her visit there yesterday. He was a slight boy with straw-colored hair. His face was red with anger, and his wire framed glasses had slid down his nose. His shoving partner was a good two feet taller and wider. Kyra pegged him for someone with a Giant in their heritage.

"So, who wants to tell me why you two took it upon yourselves to create noise and distress this young lady?"

"This oaf doesn't know how to treat a lady," the Wizard spat out the words.

Kyra's eyebrows rose.

"I said he need find new piece of tail. She Fae," the one with Giant's blood answered honestly.

Kyra took in a deep breath. "While I appreciate your chivalry against this rude and boorish statement, there is no need for physicality. As for you," she said, turning her glare onto the bully. "Let me suggest that when you have such a thought, you keep it to yourself."

He shrugged his huge shoulders and lumbered down the hall.

"Thank you so much, Miss Kyra." Adoration showed in Milyna's eyes.

Kyra studied the pair—the protective way he placed her arm around her, her adoring smile. Part of her wanted to warn them. Wizard or no, he was still human, and she was still Fae. Many came here and became so integrated to the mostly nonbiased, cross-species lifestyle that they forgot what it was like on the outside, back within their tribes or cities.

"Milyna, right?" Kyra asked.

The girl's entire face lit up.

"Yes. That's me."

"You may be enjoying each other's company, but realize that the attitude of that 'gentleman' will be more common than not." Kyra cringed at their crestfallen expressions. "Now, I'm not saying don't see each other, because who am I to give that kind of advice? Just know it won't be an easy road."

They hugged, reassured.

"Oh, and I need to pop by and check out the equipment for my mission."

"It's already in the room. I also took the liberty of putting in a few of the new gadgets that have been made since your last stop in here. I'm going back there, and I'll have a full briefing for you when you arrive."

Kyra was impressed. "I look forward to it, and when I get back, perhaps we can catch lunch." She surprised herself with the invitation.

"I'd love that," Milyna replied.

Kyra went to Architecture. Pulling out her card, she was poised to slip it into the scanner when the door opened and Lev exited.

Well, that worked out better than planned.

The little tiff in the hall had saved her from going all the way to the back of the department.

"You want me?" Lev asked, his deep voice booming.

"I do. Nyles will be accompanying me on this mission. That calls for extra measures in the transportation plan."

The Dwarf grunted. "I figured. Already done." He moved past her.

Kyra wondered how to take that. Was her friendship with Nyles that well known? Did people assume he would be on her team? She frowned deeply. She disliked people knowing anything about her personal life. As small as it was, she liked it private. *I'll think about that, later. Now, to the equipment.* She pushed the unpleasant ideas to the back of her mind.

Head down, she moved through the now-teeming hallways. Should she go review the security tapes from her hall before she went to equipment? Anyone who would go to the trouble to sneak in to search her room would not make the simple mistake of being caught on camera. The film heading to the dining area that night would be more interesting. It could wait, though—mission first.

At the equipment door, she saw the Wizard headed away. His expression was angry. Kyra approached the door. Milyna stood just on the other side. Her expression also bore anger but hurt as well. Kyra hesitated to approach her. She was not great with emotional situations. She lacked the desire to become involved in whatever it was that was going on. Milyna must also be a private person, as she put on a bright smile when she saw Kyra, making no mention of whatever it was that just happened.

Milyna opened the bottom half of the door, admitting Kyra into her office. Though more like a closet than a room, she had arranged it to be efficient. Milyna led her through another door that opened into a much larger space. Kyra didn't recall it being this big. Was it another one of Lev's expansions? She took in the room with its stark white walls meeting a cobalt blue tile. She had never seen anything like this flooring in Scíath.

Milyna noticed her fascination with the tile. "It's touch-sensitive flooring. It records every footprint that is left on it, matching it with the bio-signature that was taken of you when you stepped through the door."

Kyra glanced back at the ordinary-looking door. So many new security measures. Galerius had really stepped it up in the last two years.

"It was done to ensure inventory was never invaded." Milyna continued. "I placed your name in the system before you arrived, or it would not have let you through the door."

Kyra looked at her with a new respect. She may be a young Fae, but she was showing a command of a difficult job. "Do you run supplies all on your own?" Kyra said before she realized the implication of what she has asked.

If Milyna caught the possible undertone of that question, she ignored it, much to Kyra's relief.

"I'm not the head. Actually, the admin office handles the funds. I'm in charge of inventory, filling orders, adding new items as they come in, and so on."

As they walked, the rows of shelves reminded Kyra of artifacts. Moving into an open area, she noted three groups of equipment. The largest one bore her name on the sign in front of it.

Slightly overwhelmed by the amount of equipment, Kyra had to recall this was gear for seven people.

"There are seven packs here—each one suited to the member of the team—"

Kyra broke in, "I didn't give you the crew list. Just a request for generic supplies."

"True. The Architect sent me a crew list, yesterday," she explained, not missing a beat.

Why hadn't I thought of that? It hadn't even occurred to her that equipment would be species specific. *The only one I made accommodations for was Nyles. I will add that to my team plans the moment I get back to the study*, she told herself as she turned her attention back to Milyna.

"In terms of distance, this is considered a short mission. The time you are going to be there is unknown, though, as are the conditions of the house. I packed you camping gear and food provisions for a week. If it is to be longer, I will send supplemental packs up through a courier."

Kyra inwardly cringed. All she had asked for was weapons and other utility gear. She forgot that her team would have to sleep and eat. On her own for so long, she was accustomed to gathering her own things only. Had Milyna not been on top of things, her team would have probably starved. Or at least they would have had to travel into a Gilly town to get food.

"I've been a field agent since I was seventeen years old. In that time, I've been on hundreds of missions. I've become so accustomed to being alone that this is an entirely new world for me. I appreciate your willingness to help without being condescending."

Kyra wanted very much to like this girl, but she could never forget that she was full-blood Fae, and that meant she considered her an abomination. Getting too close would be a mistake.

"Here are the new gadgets I mentioned." She picked up an item that resembled a compass.

After flipping it open, she handed it to Kyra. The thin, golden needle spun erratically. Kyra turned in a circle looking for a way to stop it from spinning. Unable to do so, she handed it back to Milyna.

"The reason it's misbehaving is because it's designed to lead you back here. Anywhere in the world you are, this compass will beeline you straight back here. For that reason, you must take great care to never allow it to be lost. It also works underground, just in case."

Kyra understood that implication all too well. A field agent once had stumbled into an Imp hive—hundreds of tunnels stretching over 200 miles. The lost agent was unable to get out or call for help. His body was found several years later by a Scíath team digging out tunnels for the compound. He had died less than one mile from home, because he was unable to get his bearings.

Milyna picked up a pair of goggles and handed them to Kyra. They were lightweight. Putting them on, they seemed not to change her vision at all. She turned to look at Milyna, who glowed a bright red. As she walked back and forth, she left a red trail.

"Heat signature?" Kyra gently slipped them off.

"Yes. Unfortunately, they only work in open territory. They are no help in a building. They do work in dense forest, though."

"Handy." Those were going to become part of her personal gear as well as the compass.

The last thing on the table appeared to be a simple dagger with a metal sheath. Kyra picked it up. It was lightweight, and the grip was good and firm. She looked up at Milyna for an explanation.

"If you slip the cover off carefully, you will see that built into the blade is a hypodermic needle, and the grip has two additional tranquilizer cartridges. You stab with the blade then press the bottom of the handle, and the drug is released. It is a much more accurate method that trying to toss a needle. It helps with species whose skin may be hard to pierce."

Kyra studied it in appreciation. This was defiantly staying with her, as well.

As if reading her mind, Milyna said, "I've requisitioned these three items to add to your personal inventory. They don't need to be returned."

"Thanks," Kyra replied.

The clock on the back wall read quarter to 11:00 a.m.

"Blast, I have to go put the packets together and get them sent to admin to have ready for the briefing." Kyra added as she turned to the door, "Would you like to come speak to my team as the equipment expert, with a list of what's in each pack, just in case anyone has questions?"

"That would be an honor."

"Excellent, the conference room at four." Kyra exited at a quick pace. No way she wasn't going to be completely ready for this briefing. Rushing through the halls, she made it back to the study. Hopefully, Moira had already left. She needed to use Simon's terminal. She also wanted a chance to talk to the Architect alone.

A quick, hard rap to the door was met with an immediate response of, "Enter."

She opened the door. She sighed in relief to see that he sat alone at the desk, reading over what Kyra assumed to be Moira's report.

"Can I steal your Simon terminal?" She set her pile of paperwork on the desk.

"Of course, dear." He stood stiffly and took the file folder with him as he settled into his recliner.

"I need to get the manuals together before I go to Galerius for my own briefing. Show him I can absorb his written reports." She settled in front of Simon.

"Before you start, can you toss in a lunch order? I'd like a roast beef sandwich, swiss cheese, mayo, and no onions."

She listened to his list. She could have built it on her own as soon as he said roast beef. He hadn't changed his sandwich fixings for as long as she could remember. Having fired off the lunch order, she pulled up a blank document and started typing out everything she knew to be given out in mission briefs. Forty-five minutes later, a knock at the door drew Kyra out of deep contemplation. Her mind told her it was lunch; however, habit had her at the door in a flash, hand on her holster. Her quick moment roused the Architect from his nap.

* * * *

He sat up bleary-eyed, watching her open the door with caution. He wondered if perhaps she had become too cautious, if allowing her to become a field agent had been a mistake.

She accepted the cart, shut the door, and locked it. He had never wanted to let her go out. Due to wanting her protected or his own loneliness, he wasn't certain. It became apparent around her sixteenth birthday that keeping her inside Scíath was going to prove to be a challenge. Her Fae side was cramped by the walls. Underground didn't suit her type well.

Galerius was her last chance. He took her in, prepped her, and took her out into the field. At first, she would be gone a month at most and then home for three or four. That was okay; however, her trips out became longer and her times in shorter. It was obvious she was a solo hunter—efficient and traceless. She had captured criminals who had been on the red list for years. She had no idea, but many people thought her a hero—just as many still viewed her as an abomination. One thing both sides could agree on, however, was they never wanted her on their trail.

* * * *

During lunch, she mentally picked over what was left to put in the document before she sent it off for printing. According to the clock she had only half an hour before she was due to meet Galerius for her own briefing. She should have done this last night. Standing, she moved her own plate next to the computer and tapped out the last pages. The Architect did not disturb her. She knew he'd also eaten many meals in front of that terminal. Ten minutes later, she stood and gave him an apologetic smile.

"I hate to eat and run, but I have to make it over to Admin then back to Security by one, and I don't want to be a minute late."

"I understand. Do you mind if I attend your briefing? I don't want you to think I'm checking up on you or being overbearing. I've enjoyed getting back in on the action, so to speak."

"That's fine. I've also invited Milyna to come in and give an equipment rundown," she replied.

"Nice added touch. Very wise." A thoughtful look crossed his face.

After sliding her jacket on, she picked up her files. She kissed him on the forehead and was off in a blur.

The administrative hub was a place she seldom went. It was the place where things were recorded, records kept, manuals bound, financial records and transactions managed. It was necessary to the running of operations.

Mrs. Pylam, a Tryeyed, worked as head secretary. Amazingly efficient, she ran Admin like a ship. Other than the third eye in the center of her forehead and her organizational talents, Mrs. Pylam was quite bland as personalities go. As long as Kyra had her manuals printed and bound by the time she walked through the door, Mrs. Pylam could be as dull as she liked.

Kyra fought the urge to pop into the dining hall to check on her order for the briefing. It would be taken care of. She obsessively checked every clock as she passed, gauging her pace. The doors to the admin office, unique in Scíath, were tall and solid glass, with the words "Administrative Office" written in gold, block letters. Kyra opened the doors and walked up to what looked like a reception desk. Behind it sat a Fury—a race of being who could never fit in the outside world, given that they were a cross between hawks and humans. Her long, brown hair was made up of feathers, her eyes small and sharp. Instead of hands, she had three sharp talons. Unlike the Furies of myth, they were no longer a warring race and chose to live out their lives in peace.

The nameplate on the desk said Tanya. After another obsessive glance at the clock, Kyra walked quickly up to the desk. Tanya looked her over with a non-blinking stare, her head cocked to the side as she took her in.

"May I help you?" Tanya asked.

"Yes, I'm Kyra. I sent some manuals to be done rush. I was hoping to pick them up, now." She tried to keep her eyes off the clock. Ten minutes to get to Security—thankfully, only three corridors away.

Tanya let out a small squawk in understanding, her talons ruffling her feathers. "Your order is ready in one moment." She went into the maze of cubicles and disappeared behind a large, plain wooden door.

Kyra's fingers picked up their familiar rhythm on the countertop. Adjusting the papers in her arms, she stared at the pattern on the carpet and tapped her foot, desperate for this woman to hurry up with her things. After what felt like an eternity, Tanya reappeared with a stack of manuals. Each one was perfectly bound and each had a name on it.

"Perfect, as always. Thank you so much for getting them done so quickly." Kyra ran out the door.

Feet barely touching the floor, she hurried to the Securities office. She placed her hand on the scanner and waited impatiently for it to beep and release the door. She walked in the door with five minutes to spare.

Galerius didn't look up, but his eyebrow rose in acknowledgement of her presence. She laid her own paperwork and manuals out in neat stacks on the empty table, pulled up her chair, and waited for him to begin.

At exactly one o'clock, he stood in front of her table and briefed her as he had many times before. She listened intently and took notes when needed. Once he had finished, she showed him her manual, team list, and equipment. She knew he would remember everything she had done, but judging his emotions was nearly impossible. His expression never changed, nor did the tone in his voice. Having known him a number of years, she could tell he wasn't disappointed or concerned about her ability to lead the team. *Reassuring.*

Galerius handed her a thick file folder containing the aerial pictures of the house and blueprints from the Gilly building department. He had converted some of the images to projector sheets, so she could put them on the overhead for everyone to see. She studied the plans. It was easy to create an outside route; however, Imp strongholds would be riddled with traps, tunnels, and who knew what. Those wouldn't be visible until they arrived, so she didn't focus much on the blueprints.

At ten to four, she gathered all of her paperwork. Thankful that the door had an auto open sensor, she was piled to the chin with her material. Rounding the corner to the conference room, she heard Nyles's voice. It really was nice having him around. Outside the door stood the Architect, Nyles, and Milyna.

The conference table held finger sandwiches, bottled water, cookies, and a small bowl of fruit. Seated around the table was her team. Kyra moved to the front. She looked over the group, memorizing their faces. The lives of these people would be her responsibility in just a few, short hours.

Kyra put down her papers. "Good afternoon, ladies and gentlemen. I appreciate your promptness. Please, enjoy the treats Gus has provided. We are going to start out by introducing ourselves and our departments, to become acquainted." Kyra glanced at the Architect who was leaning up against the back wall with Milyna. "I'm Kyra, a class-five field agent for the Security Department." She was impressed at how calm and in control she sounded when her stomach felt like a butterfly migration.

Maria sat to her right. Her small stature put her chin level with the table's edge, looking like a floating head.

"Hello, I'm Maria." Her voice piped out strong with a high pitch. "Maltruis," she gestured to the hulking shape leaning on the wall behind her, "and I represent transportation and architecture. We're very proud to have been chosen for this assignment."

Kyra looked to the next chair. Nikkos sat in it, his expression filled with excitement. "I'm Nikkos and represent the Medical department. I am also much honored to be chosen, though I hope not to have my medical skills needed."

Kyra assumed that it was Soro in the next seat. She hadn't met him when she did her rounds.

Of average height and build, with soft brown hair, he lacked traits that would mark him as a supernatural until he looked you in the eyes. Instead of the normal ring of color surrounding the black pupil, his eyes had a black outer ring and an almost neon purple interior.

"I am Soro, representing Supernatural Species. I look forward to working with all of you to make this mission a success," his voice came out as a monotone.

Beside him, a petite woman spoke next. Thin, with deep black skin and snow white hair, she wore a short sleeved T-shirt. White ink enveloped her dark flesh in tribal patterns. "I am Aieta, from magical artifacts." Her deep voice surprised Kyra.

Nyles stepped forward, his hooves clacking on the tiles.

"I am Nyles. I represent the Anthropology Department, and I look forward to working with all of you." He finished his statement with a dazzling smile, causing a wobble in Kyra's stomach. She managed to keep a straight face, especially given who was next in line.

Anna took her time pulling her long, silken hair over the shoulder of her perfectly tailored black suit. She regarded everyone with a half-smirk of amusement in her eyes. "My name is Anna. I have the honor of being part of Gilly relations. I'm so happy to be here, and I know this mission will be successful with such an amazing team," her voice dripped honey. Kyra wasn't buying it for a minute.

Kyra passed the manuals around the table. "We're going to do a brief outline. With a nine-hour train ride ahead of us, you'll have plenty of time to study this and ask questions on the journey. After that, Milyna—our equipment specialist—will brief you on what is in your packs and answer questions you may have. I expect us to be finished by 6:00 p.m., giving us six hours before we meet at the transport dock to depart." She looked for confused faces. Seeing nothing but interest, she launched into her briefing.

A little over an hour later, after answering a few generalized questions, she turned the floor over to Milyna. Kyra moved to the back of the room taking a position against the wall. Cracking open a bottle of water, she drank deeply. She rolled her shoulders, letting go some of the tension and celebrating that things were going well. She even gave a reassuring smile to Milyna, who seemed nervous. After a deep breath, though, Milyna began her presentation, and it was obvious she was in her element when it came to equipment.

Kyra shot a look over at Nyles and was surprised to meet his gaze. The intense moment quickly ended, but it was long enough to bring high color to Kyra's cheeks.

Milyna took a few questions specific to new equipment. At 5:59 p.m., Kyra dismissed the group. Everyone filed out. Soro accompanied Milyna back to the equipment department to have a demonstration on a new gadget. Nyles, the Architect, and Kyra made their way back toward the study, chatting about how well things had gone.

"Why don't we have a quiet dinner in the study, before you two head out?" the Architect suggested.

"That sounds very nice. I'd like another good meal before we head back out on the road." How quickly she had become accustomed to Gus's cooking.

As if Nyles read her mind, he said, "It's easy to get used to Gus's food after being away from it for so long."

"I'm not sure I could go back onto road rations. Although, the adventure of going into Gilly villages and tasting some of their 'Fast Food' was fun," the Architect said.

They chatted about the oddness of Gilly food.

As she went inside the study, Kyra swore she felt something brush up against her leg as they entered but saw nothing there.

Once inside, the dinner order was placed, and everyone settled into a comfortable position. Kyra assumed there was a reason for his dinner invitation; however, she didn't want to pressure him.

He didn't make her wait long. Once he had a glass of port in his hand, he took a deep breath. "I spent a long while with Moira this morning, going over a complaint about Anna. I am almost certain she is guilty of the crimes of which she is accused, but because of the nature of what was done, there is no way to prove it. Kyra shares a deep suspicion of Jason, and I see little coincidence that Jason wanted to send Anna on this mission to be his right hand. I want you to remain on alert. Never allow Anna to be your lone sentry, and any finds of a dangerous nature that you uncover, do your best to keep from her," the Architect's tone was somber.

"The deep bond of trust that lies between you two is a valuable thing in this situation. I'm not saying that any other member of the team is corrupt. In fact all of them put off very positive vibrations; however, the only trust you can be certain of is the one you share."

"I wish I could just fire her from the team. It would cause too much suspicion, and I don't want any bad will." Kyra frowned at the diplomatic need weighing on her.

"Indeed, you need to be in an open working relationship with all departments," the Architect agreed.

"Plus, if she is up to something, we don't want to tip our hands just yet," Nyles added.

A knock on the door, announcing the arrival of dinner, halted the conversation. The meal was eaten in a heavy silence.

A little before nine, Nyles and Kyra departed. Both agreed to a short sleep before their departure. The Architect pulled Kyra in for a long, fierce hug. Surprised by his gesture, she returned the hug with the same gusto. It seemed that he was as worried about her as she was about him.

* * * *

Hidden in the shadows of the halls, a pair of eyes watched the warm embrace with contempt and suspicion.

Chapter Five

Departure

As the loud bells above their heads struck the witching hour, a solemn group ascended the freight lift toward the outside world. Kyra felt she should be talking to them, giving them some kind of pep rally speech, but she could come up with nothing that didn't sound hollow to her. The reality of the situation was they were headed out to the field. Some were on their first mission, with a first-time leader, going into the countryside to investigate a former home of the most wretched of all supernatural species. Kyra drew a very deep breath and willed her face to settle into the most neutral expression she had. Her stomach was filled with knots and her head with doubts, but she'd be dammed if anyone else would know it.

The elevator jolted to a stop, and the crew filed out. Milyna stood on the loading dock where a large lorry idled. Thick fumes belched from its tailpipe, causing Kyra to wrinkle her nose. Milyna handed Kyra a clipboard.

"Miss Kyra, if you could just sign for your equipment. Then, your adventure can begin." Her voice was hushed, even though the truck's labored motor covered any conversation they may have. There was something about the stillness of the night that brought on the need to whisper.

Kyra took the clipboard and scrawled her name across the line without even glancing at the things listed. She wanted it to appear to the team that she trusted Milyna when it came to the equipment. Kyra knew that once she was alone, she would be going over every piece. Kind girl or not, Milyna was still a stranger, and a Fae to boot.

Turning to the group, she forced a jovial expression. "Last chance to ditch," she said with a soft chuckle. Her statement evoked nervous laughter as a response.

"No takers? All right, in we go." She pulled back the white, canvas flap of the truck's bed, so they could all file in.

Once they were all in, Kyra pulled the flap closed. The truck's interior grew pitch black, and her hand automatically moved to her weapon. Small, orange glow sticks flicked on, lit by various members of the party. The lorry jostled and bounced everyone. They were cramped on the bench seats, given that the elongated bed was packed full with the massive bodies of Nyles and Maltruis. Kyra longed for her motorcycle. It had been a long time since she was forced to endure mass transportation. One look assured her that no one was enjoying this ride. Thank goodness the rail station was a fifteen-minute ride from Scíath.

The sound of traffic surrounded the lorry. It was tempting to pull the flap back and take in the city lights of the heart of London. It's a shame they couldn't risk anyone seeing inside.

A hard jolt told her the lorry had left the pavement. Its nonexistent shocks did little to soften the blow of driving on gravel. The pieces of rock being thrown up against the truck's metal sides sounded distressingly like gunshots.

In the dim, yellowish light, Kyra saw fear, anxiety, and excitement in the eyes of her team. When she met Nyles's eyes, however, the look in them caused her to shrink back into the dark corner. She dared not reveal her own feelings.

The lorry slowed to a stop, and everyone readied themselves. Nothing as simple as a train station could be taken for granted. Outside the sanctity of Scíath, they were all vulnerable. Kyra pulled back the flap, revealing an empty, desolate-looking train station. It was meant to look abandoned, and it did an excellent job. A muted colored locomotive with two passenger cars and one cargo car idled in the station.

Holding her hand up to signal her team to wait, she stepped cautiously off the back of the truck. She kept her hand on her gun. Her nature was to be cautious about every situation, regardless of the reassurances of those she was supposed to trust.

Soro poked his head out of the truck. After a thorough look around, he spoke softly, "No one is here except for the engineer in the train, and he is a Dwarf."

His voice startled her to take action. This working on a team thing was going to take some getting used to. "Let's head out," she said, keeping her voice low.

Kyra spoke with the driver as everyone crossed the open space to enter into the passenger cars. A few moments later, Kyra joined them. The passenger cars were equipped with wide aisles and plush seats. She laid her hand absently on one of the seat backs, running her fingers over the fibers. The lights were a harsh florescent but thankfully were not plentiful.

For Nyles, there was a row devoid of seats with the floor covered in carpet. "This is most enjoyable," he said, making himself comfortable. Kyra made a mental note to thank Lev for this thoughtfulness.

The train chugged to life, its clunky movements jarring everyone's bones. Kyra took a seat across the aisle from Nyles. Almost everyone was seated in pairs, either involved in light conversation or reading over papers. Anna sat isolated in the center seat, rows away from everyone else.

Kyra decided to make sure she knew the advantages and disadvantages of each of the three cars as a defensible position. She passed silently through the car and slid the door to the second passenger car open. To her surprise, the second car held two cordoned off areas with chains bolted to the floor. It was set up as a brig. It had never occurred to her that she would find anyone she needed to detain; however, it was damn handy. The end of the car had just plain seats. It was easy to maintain her balance while the train swayed along. Opening the last door took effort, and she was rewarded with a loud groan of steel on steel.

She stepped into pitch blackness. Shifting to her Fae sight, she had almost an infrared view of stacks of gear and an ammunition pile in one corner.

Milyna was a smart one. The two sliding doors had been welded closed, ensuring the only way in was the door from the passenger car.

While returning to the front passenger car, midway through the brig car, she heard raised voices. Running, she stood in the middle of the group in a flash, her eyes narrowed and gun drawn.

It was easy to pick out who had been involved in the shouting. Nyles's face was beet red, and his powerful arms were crossed across his chest. Anna's face wore a smug smile. She was standing, though she hadn't left her row of seats.

"Okay, what's going on?" Kyra put her gun away, and her expression changed from alert to annoyed.

To her surprise, it was Aieta who spoke up.

"Anna made a nasty comment about Nyles, and he fired back." She sat back down.

"Really?" Kyra said, her cheeks flushing with anger, her lips becoming a thin, white line. "We are a team, ladies and gentlemen. Personal and race bias is for children. We are all Scíath. If you cannot control your behavior and remain professional, I will ship you right back to the base." Her eyes settled on Anna. "Understood?" she then asked everyone. She sat, controlling the anger that bubbled up inside her. All her life, she has been the subject of discrimination, and it would not go on under her watch.

With a general agreement, people went back to what they had been doing before the tiff had arisen. Kyra settled into her seat. She crossed her arms and didn't bother trying to hide her anger. She wasn't just angry that members of her team were already fighting. Her urge to lash out at Anna because of Nyles would confirm the favoritism that some already suspected.

She observed Nyles. He held an expression of mixed anger and embarrassment. He shot her a pained look, which seemed to say he knew better than to have risen to Anna's bait. Kyra stared out the windows. The quiet countryside rocketed by as the glow from the city faded behind them.

Opening her folder, she looked at page after page. She flipped through it impatiently, unable to focus on any one thing. Her mind was a tangled web of thoughts. Anxiety over the mission intertwined with worry about father. *Should I have left him?* Especially after someone sneaking into her room? She'd had her suspicions confirmed with a check of the tapes from the hall outside her room. Whoever had entered was able to do so without being seen. Galerius said it would take a bit to get the time frames for the hall near the dining hall she had requested. He would have it ready for her when she returned.

When she told him about the break in, Galerius's eyebrows shot up to meet his hair line. *Amazing.* That was the most reaction she had seen out of him since he came to Scíath. She'd heard that he flew into a rage once and actually yelled, but she had a very hard time imagining that one.

Her head tilted as if all the thoughts on her mind were weighing it backward. In an automatic gesture, as her eyes fluttered closed, she pulled her gun from the holster and laid it in her lap.

* * * *

The train reeled along under the stars, the only light to be had. As if on a timer, the car's lights dimmed. Some team members reached up and tapped their lights to keep them up for reading. For the most part, the car was dim—many, it seemed, followed Kyra's lead. Eyes closing, heads drooping, and allowing the rollercoaster of the day to flow away.

Anna remained awake. Her thoughts were also heavy, but she needed little rest. She certainly wasn't going to take it in a situation like this. A smug smile crossed her face as she recalled the run-in with the Centaur. She had to test how close he and Kyra were. He was easy to rile—a powder keg with a very short fuse. Rumors had flown for a long time concerning the relationship between him and their illustrious leader. Her reaction had been all the proof she needed. If nothing else, the feelings between them ran deep. Could be a useful weakness for later exploitation.

The rocking motion of the train and the monotonous chugging of the wheels made it easy for her mind to wander. How was Jason doing without her? Almost as if her thoughts had summoned him, the transmitter in her pocket began to vibrate. She headed toward the car's restroom for privacy. In her hurry, she brushed roughly against Soro, causing him to wake. He sat up, causing Aieta to also awaken.

* * * *

"I'm sorry to have woken you," he said, his voice still thick with sleep.

"Don't worry about it. I'm a light sleeper and used to awakening during the night."

"Apparently, something Anna ate did not agree with her. She's heading to the bathroom in quite a hurry," Soro kept his voice low as not to disturb those around them.

Aieta snorted softly. "I trust nothing that woman does, even if it is only going to the restroom."

Anna was not well-liked, and no one trusted her. He assumed there had been some maneuvering on Jason's part, as he always found a way to stick himself in—especially where he wasn't wanted. "I will admit surprise to her addition to our team," he shared his thoughts.

"I heard the Architect speaking with Nyles. Jason all but forced her onto the team." Aieta suppressed a yawn. "Kyra didn't even want a member of Gilly relations along."

"I can't say I agree with that. It's a useful department, however, I could think of several more highly qualified candidates than her," Soro said.

"Did you hear about the complaint that someone in Artifacts filed against her?" Aieta whispered.

"I heard about the one that came out of the Medical Department but not Artifacts."

* * * *

Kyra listened closely to them with her eyes closed.

She awoke when Anna had jumped up. Her body was trained to respond to

Sciath

sudden movements around her. Sometimes, feigning sleep was useful, so she stayed still.

"I think it has something to do with the succession," Aieta said. "I respect Kyra. She's a hell of an agent, and she deserves our loyalty. Further, I do not want Jason having any kind of upper hand in this. The succession is a very serious matter, and there is no place in it for scum like him." Aieta responded, her voice taut with emotion.

"Who do you think is the top contender for the new head of Scíath?" he asked.

"Di. She is one of the original founders. I am not sure she would take it, though," Aieta said.

"I know she wouldn't," Soro replied. "She is well set where she is and happy. She's also getting advanced in years. In twenty years, we'd have to go through this, again."

"Hmmm...excellent point. We are going to need someone who is still young or young enough to not have to do this again for a long time."

Kyra found they were both very logical, and their points made sense. It was nice to know that they were loyal to her, and that they both wanted what was best for Scíath.

The bathroom door swung open with such force that it rattled the windows around it. Everyone who was awake looked up. Kyra was on her feet, her gun drawn.

A perturbed and pale Anna stepped out and cringed.

"You must all forgive me. The door was stuck, and I pushed hard to open it. I guess I pushed a bit too hard." She offered an apologetic smile.

Kyra settled back in her seat. Anna was lying. The look on her face was one of anger and not just at a stuck door.

Anna didn't meet Kyra's eyes. She did, however, make a bit of a scene about pulling a pillow and blanket from the overhead compartment and drifting off to sleep. Kyra didn't believe she was asleep.

Only two hours into the trip, and there had already been a fight, gossip, and strange behavior. If this was any indication of how the trip was to go, things didn't look good. She stole a sideways glance at Nyles. His head rested against his chest, his breathing soft and rhythmic. His hair fell across his forehead. She resisted the urge to reach over and brush it away as he himself always did.

The conversation in front of her had stopped. Kyra felt sleep creeping over her. She really wanted to stay awake, just in case, but the importance of sleep when on a mission was obvious. She needed her wits about her when they arrived.

If she had been going alone she could have made it to the safe house in just about four hours. The size of the team and the need to carry all the equipment for them resulted in having to skirt around several cities. She would have gone through on foot or on her bike. *Might as well take advantage of the extra couple of hours and get some rest.*

A familiar dream, one she'd had countless times before, overtook her.

She stood in a garden, beautiful flowers surrounded her, the sun was warm, and the air carried the scent of the flowers as it lazily drifted by. The place looked a paradise, but something was wrong. There were raised voices—voices she knew but could not put a name to. Strange voices, angry words. Frightened, she fled deeper into the garden. Someone screamed. Silence filled the void. She scooted further back into the flower beds, felt the petals brush up against her face, and smelled the dampness of the soil. Then, a voice but not an angry voice. She tried to latch onto it, make it make sense, find out where she was, and why she was here. Though, the harder she tried, the further it faded from her.

Awake, again. She debated telling the Architect about the dream many times, but she wanted to try to figure it out on her own. There were people at Scíath who were experienced in dreams and could help her, but the idea of letting someone poke around her brain did not appeal to her. Her watch told her three hours had passed. Out the window, night faded into gray as the sun began to make his assent into the sky.

Kyra pulled her Global Positioning System from her pack to see how close they were. After a few moments, its glowing numbers informed her they were roughly four hours from the depot. Once they arrived, they would have to travel though the woods skirting the town to reach the safe house on the opposite side of town from the depot.

In two hours, she'd assemble a breakfast meeting to answer questions and make sure everyone was clear on the plans. She set her watch to remind her when the two-hour mark arrived. Pulling out her files, she went over her own plans. It wouldn't be easy. The house could be riddled with traps and tricks. Her mind drifted to the story she had been told about them using their bodies as weapons. *Even after death ,they were vile.* Shaking her head, she delved further into her papers.

The soft chime of her watch caused her to look up. The sun was filling the sky. Everyone but Maltruis and Nyles were awake. Standing, she stretched and rolled her neck to work out the kinks.

"Ladies and gentlemen, we are within two hours of our destination. I would like to have a breakfast meeting in one-half hour so that I may answer any questions. We can go over strategies one last time. We'll hit the ground running when the train stops." She noted that both of the sleepers were now awake and heard her message.

"I'm going to get the breakfast food from the other car."

The notes about the train told her that in the cabinet in the back of the second car was five days worth of food rations. No reason to use up their own supplies when they could use ones that were already here. Making her way into the second car, she blinked as the timer had completely shut the lights off in the unoccupied car, and she was greeted with darkness. The lights flickered on, and she made her way to the back. Opening the cabinet, she discovered muffins, jugs of juice, a few protein bars, and a box of donuts. Piling it all up into her arms, she made her way to the front compartment. *What we need is a table.*

She put down the supplies in an empty row. "Damn, I forgot cups and plates," she muttered as she made her way back to the other car.

When she slid the door open, she was surprised to see Anna studying the restraint systems. Kyra narrowed her eyes but kept the suspicion she felt out of her voice.

"Why, Anna. I didn't even notice you had awoken. Sleep well?" She made her way back to the cabinet as she spoke. Never giving Anna her back, she casually allowed her hand to lie beside her gun.

"I did, but I needed to stretch my legs. I'm not used to being sedentary for this long." Anna's tone was as full of as much fake politeness as Kyra's had been.

"I don't know if you heard my announcement, but we're having a breakfast meeting in about twenty minutes. We are less than two hours out from our stop." Kyra took the supplies, keeping one hand free.

"Thank you for telling me. I'll mosey my way back to my seat, then. I do have a few questions I wish to ask."

Kyra couldn't help but notice the calculation in Anna's eyes.

Anna turned to head back to the car, leaving Kyra to follow on her heels.

Everyone had already gathered around the food. Some had already helped themselves to scones.

She moved into the middle and handed out plates and cups.

When everyone was settled, she spoke, "Here is the plan, and please hold your questions to the end. In less than two hours, we will pull into an abandoned rail station on the outskirts of the town of Farringdon. It's small and very rural. No real Gilly police to deal with, as the town boasts two constables total.

"Its remote location and size were likely the reason it was chosen by the Imps to place an above-ground structure in. They took over a large manor house. Currently labeled as condemned, but due to a low town budget, nothing has been done to demolish it. The estate encompasses almost three acres of forest as well as a small stream. I have no doubt that the forest is also booby trapped, so we must proceed with caution.

"Soro, I want you on point with me, so you can scan the area ahead of us. Behind us, I would like Aieta and Nyles, then Maria and Maltruis. Anna and Nikkos, I would like you to bring up the rear. Everyone must stay alert. Not only are we looking for Imp traps, but we also have to be aware of any stray humans, feral lupus, or anything else that may have taken up residence in the area. Nyles is our diplomat if we should run into any other races. The safe house grounds have been fenced off by Lev's men. Once we cross the gate, our main concern becomes Imp traps. Scíath is the only group who will go into former Imp hives." Kyra looked at everyone's face. She didn't want Anna out of her sight, but she also didn't want her on point. Anna felt like a powder keg strapped to her back.

Kyra's shoulders slumped as if the weight were real. Pulling out the blueprints, she handed them to Maltruis to hold up, as he had the largest arm span.

"We will take the path through the woods and enter the house here." She pointed to the outline of a door listed as cellar. "Given their affinity for being underground, I think we will find most of their living space here. Also, they rarely set up traps where they slept, making this the probable safest point of entry. We'll proceed level-by-level, making sure each is clear and safe.

"Then, we'll do the grounds. This may take a fair amount of time, so we will set up camp just inside the gate. We don't want to draw attention to ourselves by having lights on in the house after dark. The forest is dense enough to hide us during the day." Kyra saw some taking notes and others watching her with interest.

"Now, I will take questions."

Met with silence, she was positive that she could not have explained it so well that no one had questions. Then, an unexpected voice came from the left. It was Nikkos.

"Does the house have power and water? In case of medical needs?"

Kyra blinked. This was something she didn't know. Inquisitive eyes stared at her, and she felt panic rising in her.

Take a deep breath. "We will have to determine this once we arrive," she said.

Nikkos nodded and seemed content with this answer.

"Are we permitted to bring back Imp artifacts for study?" Aieta asked.

"If they are deemed to be non-dangerous, absolutely," Kyra answered, completely unsure if they were going to be non-dangerous, but it sounded good.

Aieta seemed pleased with the answer.

"Are there any Scíath outposts near here, in case we need reinforcements?" Anna asked, her tone a touch condescending.

"No. Once we clear the house, it will be turned into an outpost with accommodations for visiting dignitaries." Kyra knew she had covered that during the initial briefing.

Silence once again reigned. Kyra was about to end the briefing when Nyles spoke, "Have any of you ever been in contact with Imp artifacts or rituals?"

"I have seen a number of artifacts," Aieta responded.

He waited to see if anyone else responded. When nothing else came, he spoke again. "Imps are unlike any other creature on this earth, Gilly or Supernatural. They don't think in any pattern that could be considered logical. So, when looking for traps or inspecting a ritual site, take nothing for granted. Anything and everything could be a trap. That may sound paranoid, but after what happened at the last hive, not even corpses are safe."

Anna huffed. "Then how on earth are we supposed to clear a hive and make it safe? If anything and everything could be a trap, why don't we just burn it to the ground and rebuild a safe house," her voice rose to a helium-sucking pitch.

Anna was scared. Likely, they all were. Kyra was a bit concerned herself, and she was used to dangerous field missions.

"While I understand your points, Anna, here is why your suggestion is not feasible. First of all, we cannot burn it to the ground. It is highly possible that explosives or toxic gases have been planted inside the house. Also, a fire that large would require Gilly firefighter involvement. Then, there is the matter of construction that kind. Small and rural or not, the villagers are bound to notice bull dozers and construction equipment making its way through town, and they will become curious."

She met Anna's gaze.

Anna opened her mouth, but Kyra began speaking again before she had a chance.

"As for how we are going to make it safe, we are first going to defuse and remove all traps we find. Maria will then attest to the structural stability of the house. Finally, Lev's crew will remodel it. This team was handpicked.

Everyone is amazing at what they do. We will accomplish this mission." Her face flushed with the anger that was bubbling just under the surface.

Anna must have sensed that she pushed the wrong buttons. She sat back without uttering another word.

"Now, everyone please collect your belongings. We will be arriving soon." Kyra returned to her seat, folding her maps and organizing her papers.

A wide smile spread across Nyles's face. It was mirrored on the face of everyone but Anna.

The train jolted to a stop just as the sun fully made its way over the horizon. Before the last jolt registered, Kyra was on her way out the door. Cobwebs lined the doors, and grime coated the windows of the abandoned depot. Kyra discreetly pulled her weapon and made a full sweep of the exterior of the building. Sliding her weapon into its holster, she motioned for everyone to exit the train.

They filed out. If not for Maltruis and Nyles, the group might have been a normal set of passengers who had ended up at the wrong station. Moving to the baggage car, they took turns unloading packs while Nyles stood watch.

The area around the station was overgrown. Less than 100 yards from the depot, a dense forest provided them easy cover from any prying eyes. All they needed to do is cross an open meadow to get to the forest. With furtive glances all around, they moved out in the earlier discussed formation. Several yards into the hike, Kyra realized a very large, very loud problem. Maltruis sounded like a herd of large elephants. Kyra held her hand up to let everyone know to stop. Turning, she moved to Maltruis.

"You must walk quietly. Try not to disturb anything around you as you move," she held her voice barely above a hiss.

Maltruis looked startled but nodded his head in understanding. Kyra made her way back to the front, cringing at the reverberating sound of her own footsteps which she knew logically made next to no sound. They started forward, again. Lumbering came from behind her, but it was quieter than before.

After checking her mini map, she adjusted her heading just slightly east. They moved with more ease. Kyra saw the yellow caution tape in the distance. With a hand signal, she motioned them to speed up the pace.

* * * *

Approaching the gate, Soro froze in his tracks. Kyra signaled a stop. He stepped ahead, just one or two steps, his keen eyes sweeping the area and searching for the signature he had seen out of the corner of his eye.

He was silent, knowing that until he had a positive signature, he didn't want to say anything. He had been embarrassed on his first mission by halting an entire team of colleagues because a bright red bird had flown past. It was hard for him to explain how he saw signatures. They weren't an aura or a glow. A quick flash of color, as fast as a breath. Life pulsated, and so did its beacon.

He looked again for the blue-green flash he had seen. If it was a signature, then it would be an earth creature. Something that lived underground. Of course, his fear jumped to Imps, but he knew there were tons of species that used the ground as their home. He refused to look like a scared rabbit.

After scanning everything and not seeing another pulse, he shook his head no.

* * * *

Kyra had absolutely no problem with Soro taking a moment. Better safe than sorry, and his talent was damn useful. When they had downtime that evening, she'd talk to him about it.

They moved closer to the gates. Kyra's eyes went wide as she glimpsed the immense, domineering structure through the trees. How the Imps had ever commandeered this place was completely beyond her.

Arriving at the gate, Kyra slipped under the caution tape. Yellow flags on either side of a narrow path led to the house. Lev's crew had already determined this was a safe area to walk through. Off to the left was another large, circular area that was also flagged off. He had even cleared them a camp site. He was damned efficient.

She gestured everyone down the path to the campsite.

"Set up camp so we can ditch what we don't need to carry into the house. We don't want anything slowing us down," she said just loud enough to carry to the whole group.

Everyone went to work, or at least almost everyone. Anna stared at her pack like a deer in headlights. Kyra inwardly groaned. *This woman is totally useless.* She resigned herself to help Anna after she finished her own tent. When Kyra looked up from her finished tent, Nikkos was putting her things together as Anna smiled sweetly at him.

Kyra sighed.

Her mood was restored at viewing the campsite. Perfect and some had even taken the time to get the kitchen set up.

"Are we ready to head out?" she asked in a normal tone. The forest muted their voices well. Everyone nodded, and no one seemed shocked by the volume of her voice.

Kyra picked up her satchel, already loaded with the things she knew she would need inside the house—and a few things she figured might come in handy. Everyone assembled, and they moved up the slight incline toward the house.

The forest ended, and Kyra looked up. The hulking form before them could not be called a house. It was too beautiful for such a title.

Made of pale stone weathered by time and elements, ivy crept up the east side of the building, covering the façade with its shiny, green life. The few broken windows bore witness to the place's neglect. The black-tiled roof seemed to be intact. The chimney, however, was crumbling. Some of its discarded bricks lay off to the side in the weed-choked lawn. The front door bore the notice of condemnation as well as what looked like a large padlock, to discourage anyone who was curious.

Kyra veered to the right, heading for where the blueprints marked the cellar door to be. Careful to stay to the flagged path, she made her way to the doors mounted on a small, cement foundation. They, too, were marked with caution tape; however, instead of a padlock there was a small thumbprint scanner attached to a lock. Tentatively, she placed her thumb on it. Even though it looked just like the ones at Scíath she was still wary. The red light flashed three times, and the lock released with a small clicking sound. She pulled the lock off and placed it in her bag. Lev had assured the security of the house.

After pulling out her flashlight, she grabbed one of the door handles. Soro took the other. The door came open easily and soundlessly. They must have oiled the hinges. *Lev truly was a wonder.*

The stench that roiled out from below was almost unbearable. Kyra smiled discreetly when Anna gagged. The stairs appeared to be wooden. Kyra lay on the ground in order to get her face close to the top stair. She sniffed it, searching for any lingering scent. Her keen eyes hunted for anything that could be a trap. Standing, she brushed herself off hurriedly.

As she put her foot firmly on the first step, everyone around her froze. She lay on the top step inspecting the second and so on until she reached the cellar floor. She shone the light around her. This had undoubtedly been their sleeping quarters. It wasn't just the smell. Little nests of squalor were spread everywhere.

She called up.

"Everyone can come down—except Nyles and Maltruis. I want you both to walk the path around the house and observe all entrances and exits from the building."

Nyles said, "We'll be glad to." The two started off. Unable to walk side-by-side, Nyles led.

Kyra would normally have done that, but those two were too large to fit down there. The five others filed down into the basement. Kyra cautiously looked along the wall for a light switch. When that turned up nothing, she shone the light above, looking for a pull string. She located it just at the bottom of the stairs that led up into the house. *Makes sense.*

Kyra made her way quickly through the debris, careful to not allow her feet to touch the ground for more than a fraction of a second. It was time to answer Nikkos's question about the electricity in the house. Shining her light on the bulb, she looked for any wires or anything out of place that could be dangerous. Imps never cared much for light. The one place they would likely set a trap in their den was in the thing that only outsiders would be using.

It seemed clear. Kyra pulled the cord, and instinctively covered her head. The only thing that came blasting out was light. The center of the basement was bathed in the harsh glow of a high wattage, bare bulb. The deeper, darker corners were still bathed in shadow. Kyra methodically took her flashlight out and shone it through each corner, looking for danger.

The team blinked, some shielding their eyes from the brilliant onslaught of light that assaulted them. Once eyes had adjusted, they looked around.

From first inspection, there were at least thirty or forty nests varying in size. Each nest was composed of garbage of varying sorts. Tin cans, old boxes of cereal, juice cartons, mixed with mud and substances no one really wanted to identify.

Soro pulled out his camera and began snapping photos. "I'm going to say this is the most intact hive we have ever found." His huge grin revealed his excitement.

Aieta pulled out her own camera. "Part of me wants to take a nest back, just to see if they imbue them with any magic, but most of me has no desire to touch it."

Everyone laughed.

"When they come through to clear it, I will ask Lev to make sure one makes it intact back to your department." Kyra loved people who were honest, and so far, Soro and Aieta had proven to be brutally so. "Well, Nikkos. We know there is power. We will have to test for water once we get up the stairs. Speaking of which, I am going to check them out, now. Once I have cleared them, we can head up into the main manor house."

Kyra, having cleared the stairs of danger, led her group up the stairs. They were in a mud room off the kitchen. The smell of mildew was prevalent mixed with something more pungent. Along the side wall were pails of dried mud, most likely for nest building. Kyra, ignoring the worsening of the gut-turning stench, pressed forward into the kitchen. She searched for a light switch.

Finding it quickly, she flicked it on. Several lights flickered to life. Scanning each tile before stepping on it, she made her way toward the kitchen's central island. The floor at one time had been done in beautiful, blue tiles. The brilliant color was nearly lost in the filth that had built up over time. The counters, made of a blue-veined marble, matched the floor tiles; however, the counters and island were also covered in filth. Rotten, moldy meat was everywhere, and the smell was almost unbearable.

"Is there a spell that keeps meat moldy for thirty years?" Kyra pondered aloud. No one responded. Maybe, it was placed there as a warning?

Anna rushed forward with no regard to where she stepped. Before Kyra had a chance to reach her, she was vomiting into the sink. Kyra rolled her eyes. She motioned Nikkos forward, since Anna had already tested the rest of the kitchen tiles for them.

Kyra had not expected to find traps in the common areas—more likely around windows and doors—but she would much rather have tested them in a safe method.

Nikkos moved forward, taking a pill bottle from his bag along with a paper cup.

"Time to test the water," he said with a smile. The faucet screeched in protest as he turned the handle, but after a few sputters, water ran out. Nikkos cleaned out the sink and fed Anna a pill.

Everyone waited—some more patiently than others—for Anna's paleness and dry heaves to conclude. Once she seemed better, she studied the ground, probably not wanting to meet anyone's eyes.

"Well, we can say for certain that the water works, and that the kitchen is not trapped. I'm going to break you up into teams. Once we find an entrance for our other two to come through, everyone will be given a room. The things that I want you to be on guard for are wire, hoses, or even gobs of muddy paper that seem out of place. Imps generally use low charge explosives to stun the intruder, making it easier for them to overwhelm their prey. Though, they will also rig the bombs with one of their toxins. Those are used less commonly inside hives, as they can also be dangerous to the Imps themselves," Kyra explained.

"Are we certain there are no Imps here?" Anna asked, her voice soft and her gaze still not meeting anyone's eyes.

Soro snorted at her suggestion. Kyra shot him a look, and he was silent.

"I understand that in your department, you don't deal with such things, so I shall explain it as we walk," Kyra said, her own stomach turning.

She led them through the door into what once was a formal dining room. A large fireplace encompassed the entire lower half of the far wall. Above the mantle were the remains of a portrait. All that was left of it was a heavy, silver frame and shreds of canvas hanging loose. The room hosted no table, but the little patches of muddy paper meant this was where the Imps had taken their meals. It was amazing with how inhuman they were, they still followed some human customs.

Kyra turned to the group. "The last Imp that I personally know to have been living, I sighted as a child. He was in holding at Scíath between prisons. So, I can say with almost complete certainty that no Imps have been here since the late 1980's." In their eyes, she saw shock and some incomprehension. *Time for a history lesson.*

"All of us studied this in school, but the events happened before most of us were born. So, I'll give a refresher for the sake of getting us all on the same page. About two hundred years ago, the Imps were a thriving culture. They had huge underground hives, some that stretched for miles. For the most part, there was little trouble from them. On occasion one of their tunnels would displace other underground beings, and a tussle would ensue; however, most the time, it was settled without outside involvement." She checked—no glazed eyes, everyone paying attention. *Good.* Kyra decided to continue.

"In 1950, a new Imp came to power. His name was Cobbwick, and he was one of the cruelest, most manipulative creatures of any species in history. He began to organize the Imps, had them take over above ground structures as well as expanding the hives until tunnels connected as many as possible, giving them a spider web network. At first, no one took much notice of them. Expansion was noted. Complaints from dislodged species were taken. Cobbwick counted on them being under the radar of most as he planned his moves." Soro and Nikkos nodded while others frowned. They were remembering. Even Anna was paying attention.

"In July of 1984, an attack was launched from every hive on every continent at the exact same moment. They killed many Gillies before Scíath could launch a counter attack. The war raged nearly a year. Due to the Imps' love of the dark, it was slightly easier to contain from the Gillies, as most of it went on at night, but the fallout was immense." She shook her head at the needless violence. All continued to be riveted on her. Both Aieta and Maria's eyes had filled with tears.

Kyra pushed on. With a deep sigh, she said, "So many lives were lost, but the Imps were driven back underground. Scíath held a worldwide meeting to discuss what could be done to prevent this from ever occurring, again. It was decided that the race should be eradicated. It was a hard call to make, I imagine, being responsible for wiping an entire race from the face of the Earth; however, it had to be done. "

"It's with 'almost complete certainty' that they are gone?" Nikkos asked.

"Well, it's impossible to be absolute certain about anything really, and I always leave myself a margin for error." Kyra checked for more questions. None.

"We are going to move out into the main hall and foyer. I'm going to check the door while the rest of you check the front windows. If you find anything suspicious, do not touch it. Call me over, and I will take a look. I want Nyles in to help as he knows a great deal about Imp traps and has recorded a number of them for the library," she said.

Kyra used her flashlight to push the swinging door with a rough shove. It swung back and forth, stirring up a fair amount of dust, but nothing exploded or popped. Kyra moved into the main hall. It appeared they had come out behind the staircase.

The walls nearest them were in a semi circle, each hosting two more doors. Kyra could not locate a light switch. She assumed the switches were near the front door. She chose the right side path and moved cautiously, making sure not to touch any walls or furniture as she moved through. Years of dust coated the surfaces with a thick layer. Everyone followed exactly where Kyra had gone, taking care to step only in her footprints.

The front door came into view. She saw the panel of light switches just to the right of it. Holding up her hand for the team to halt, she made her way alone to the switches. It would be much easier to move around when they could see where they were. She flipped the switches on one at a time. Out of the five lights she turned on, only three responded, and those were recessed into the ceiling. They provided overhead light but did little to chase the shadows from the corners.

A flash of color outside the window nearest her caused her to draw her weapon. Edging her way to the window to look out, she was relieved to see Maltruis's hulking form. Nyles stood just behind him on the trail. Unsure if it was safe to open the window, she called out to them.

"I'm going to check the door on this side. You check the door on that side. Once it's clear, you can break the lock and come in." Her raised voice echoed through the empty halls.

She guessed she had been loud enough to be heard. Moving deftly to the front door, she knelt. Her nimble fingers went to work on the spider webs. It was impossible to tell if the door was trapped or not through all of the detritus of time. She all but forgot the group behind her as she worked on the door. She moved up and around the frame in a methodic fashion. After a few minutes, she turned around and declared it clear.

Moving back to the window, she told them it was okay to come in. Joining the group, she heard one loud crunching sound followed by the thunk of metal hitting the stone stair. The door swung inward, and ducking, both of them entered.

"Welcome back, gentlemen. Report? Kyra asked.

"Aside from the cellar door, there is a back door, the front door, nine ground floor windows, and seven upper floor windows. Four windows are missing panes, and the rear door is double padlocked," Nyles rattled off.

"Excellent, thank you. We are going to break off into pairs and each take a room. First, we are going to do the two windows here to give the group a practice trial under supervision."

"Now, for the pairs. Let me see," Kyra said, looking around. "Anna, you and Nikkos will take the first door past the kitchen on the right. Aieta and Soro, take the first door on the left. Maria and Maltruis, you take the door down the hall to the right. Nyles and I will take the one on the left.

You will have one hour to finish your task and return here. Keep in mind, this is not the time for exploring. We are searching for traps. There will be time to examine the things here after we are sure it's safe to move about the house. Now, Soro and Aieta, Maria, Maltruis check this window here." She gestured to her left. "The others, here with me," she said, gesturing to the right.

Kyra watched everyone move into position. They took care to search the window frames as they had seen her do with the door.

Soro's head jerked to the far right.

"What is it?" Kyra asked.

"I saw another flash of greenish blue light came from behind a nearby sapling." She watched him stare intently as he waited for it to appear, again. When he saw nothing, he shrugged.

"It must have been some kind of bird or animal." He returned to concentrating on his portion of the window.

The next ten minutes passed in complete silence. Kyra's team breezed through with experience on their side. She was about to call it over when Anna's high-pitched cry caused everyone to jump. Weapons were drawn as the others came rushing to her aid.

At first, Kyra saw no reason for the alarm. About to rip Anna apart for false alarm, she saw blood dripping down Anna's fingers, leaving gory splashes in the thick dust.

Nikkos was already into his bag pulling out bandages and tape. Anna did not speak again, even though the pain was obvious. Nikkos gently turned her palm over. His touch was delicate as he wiped away the blood to make the wound visible. Kyra cringed. Anna had a gash across her palm. It was close to an inch long and from the amount of blood probably deep.

Undaunted by the blood, Nikkos held the gauze against the wound while he searched in his bag. Pulling out a plain jar, he handed it to Kyra. "Open that, please."

Kyra did as she was told. The substance in the jar had a pleasing, peppermint smell. The color was a shade of a deep green, and it had the constancy of jelly. Reaching in with his free hand, Nikkos gathered a generous amount of the goo and slathered it on the wound. The bleeding was staunched. From the expression on her face, the pain had also been relieved.

Skillfully, Nikkos bandaged her hand in less than a minute.

"What cut you?" Kyra asked. With the immediate crisis over, she wanted to make sure it was a rough edge and not a poison-dipped trap.

"On the far side of the frame, where the wooden crossbar meets the frame? I guess the edge was sharp." Her calm demeanor returned.

Kyra examined the spot. It looked like someone had tried to rip the cross piece off, separating it from the edge and leaving a ragged piece of wood jutting out. It looked accidental, but one never took chances with the Imps.

"Nikkos, keep an eye on her. If she gets feverish or faint, let me know. Also, excellent job."

He smiled up at her.

"Well, team. Is everyone ready to push on? Anna, you are welcome to sit on the stairs here if you don't feel up to it." Kyra, for the first time, felt compassion for this woman. Anna had taken her injury like a trooper.

"I'm fine, but I appreciate the option. Thank you, Nikkos. You're amazing," Anna sounded sincere.

Perhaps, she had misjudged this woman. Kyra wasn't willing to change her opinion just yet, but she was now more open to the chance that Anna might be more than a weight around her neck. The all pared up and headed toward their rooms.

Chapter Six

Glimpse

Nikkos took the lead into the room. Opening the door after a complete search of the frame, he was greeted with a black, nebulous dark that reeked of mold and decay. His flashlight illuminated massive amounts of dust floating on the air. He could find no light switch, but he did spot several lamps on a far end table.

"Stay here," he told her.

Anna tilted her head to the side, remaining still.

His movements were cautious. He treaded lightly as he made his way past the huge, dark masses that he assumed were furniture. Reaching the end table unscathed, he tried the first lamp. It had no bulb. The second simply clicked, giving the impression that the bulb had burned out. All of his hopes lay on the third lamp. He really had no desire to search the room with just flashlights.

His hope was dashed when the third lamp also refused to light. He was about to go ask Kyra if he could take a bulb from the kitchen to aid their search, when Anna walked in. Moving adeptly through the dark shapes, giving clue to her night vision, she clicked on a tall floor lamp.

Nikkos was pleased to have light but disappointed with himself for not having seen the lamp. Clicking off his light, he smiled at her, afraid to raise his voice in the haunted silence.

Looking around, it was obvious that this room had traditionally been used as a parlor or drawing room. For the Imps, it had been a strategy room. A large oak table sat in the center of the room. On it, a map depicted from where they stood now all the way to London. Several red circles placed in and around London showed them as places of interest. Perhaps, they had been guesses as to the location of the Sciath base. Part of the reason they had been so successful against the Imps was that the Imps never could figure out where Sciath was. It was a safe place for housing weapons and wounded during the war.

Behind him, Anna studied the map. It looked like she was trying to discern what other marks on it meant. Nikkos walked around to the large, bay window—so clouded by dirt as to be opaque. He started at the base, checking it carefully. It was hard to know what to look for, having never seen an Imp trap, but he figured he knew what a normal window was supposed to look like. So, if he found anything strange, he'd report it.

Every so often, he would glance at Anna as she moved around the room. His peeks had both a clinical and a personal purpose. Even with his gift, poisons were hard to detect until they begin attacking the system. A personal reason was that she was incredibly beautiful. He knew she was miles outside his league, but it didn't stop him from wanting her. She had an icy exterior—one most would find daunting—but he had seen past it when he had helped her. The look in her eyes as he dressed her wound won his heart.

He had just about finished the window when a small, gray wad of paper in the upper right hand corner caught his eye. It was beyond his reach, so he stood on the window sill to examine it further. Anna, noticing his movement, moved over to him.

"What is it?" she asked.

"Well, it's either a trap or a wasp nest. Neither is overly pleasant, so when we return, I will report it to Kyra."

"Good idea. I think the team should see this map as well. It's from a long time ago, but it shows what I believe to be a number of hives around London. We want to make sure they are all clear. Wouldn't want to risk another Australia incident," she said.

Nikkos trembled. He had been just a foundling when the toxin had come in, but he well remembered the stench of the death it caused.

"Agreed." He jumped down off the sill and began to clear the broken furniture and other litter into a pile against the wall.

Anna watched him, her eyes sparkling. "What are you doing?"

He shrugged. "It's hard to see such a beautiful place befouled by garbage." He dragged a broken chair over.

With a thoughtful expression on her face, she said, "It is an amazing house. If did I not love living at home base, I could easily be swayed to come out here for good." Her icy reserve disappeared.

"I've never been into your department, but the bunks in Medical are reminiscent of the dorm rooms in Gilly college magazines. I'm hoping yours are much better?"

Anna nodded emphatically. "I will say it never occurred to me that the accommodations differed from department to department. I have a beautiful suite. You will have to come over and visit after we return."

Nikkos grinned. "Be glad to. Don't be offended if I don't return the invitation, though. I share a room with a Tryeyed."

* * * *

Nice kid. What would it be like to have a friend, with no ulterior motive for making friends? Outside Scíath, the pressure of Jason watching over her lifted. She couldn't open up too much, as she guarded myriads of secrets, but at least Nikkos seemed to genuinely like her. It was easy to be open around him.

She glanced at her watch. "We had best head out. We're at fifty-seven minutes."

"Really? I guess time flies when you have good company." He finished moving the last broken piece with a smile.

Anna grinned as they headed back out into the foyer.

When they arrived in the foyer, they met Maria and Maltruis. Anna had a notion that dwarves where impossible to talk to, so she didn't even bother. She glanced at her hand. Though the bandage remained white, the wound had begun to slightly ache. Whatever he had put on her hand had been amazing.

* * * *

Right at the one hour mark, the other teams emerged. Kyra's clothing had taken a beating. Her jeans were torn, and her jacket dirty. Aieta and Soro appeared the cleanest of all.

"Well it's good to see you all out here. It means no one got blown up," Kyra said, her traditional frown morphing to a half smile. "This foyer, as we have all been traipsing all over it, is also safe. So, pull up a piece of floor to hear reports." She sat leaning up against the door.

Her flawless complexion bore no sign of fatigue, but her voice carried a touch of weariness. "We will start with Aieta and Soro." She tipped her head back to allow it to rest on the door.

The pair glanced at each other and somehow wordlessly decided who would give the report. Soro spoke, "It was once a library. Shelves lined the walls, but there wasn't a whole book to be seen. The windows are clear; however, one of the outbound tunnels could be hidden by the largest shelf. Dried mud coats the bottom of the shelf, as well as a fair number of muddy tracks from it to the door."

Kyra, who had allowed her eyes to close while she listened to him, sat up quickly. "How fresh are they?"

"I'm no expert tracker, but I would say they have been there a very long time," he replied responding to the urgency in her voice.

Kyra returned her head to the door. She would check them herself just to make sure. She did not trust the entire group's safety to a rookie tracker.

"The only other thing of interest was some painted markings in one corner of the room. Aieta and I know them to be Imp. We'll record them and, back at the base, attempt to translate them," Soro finished.

Kyra rolled her head toward Nyles, who had settled beside her.

"Do you think you will know them?" she asked.

Nyles shook his head. "I have committed a few common symbols to memory. Anything outside those, they will have to be taken in for study."

"Excellent job, Aieta and Soro. Next up, Maria and Maltruis." Hopefully, Maria will give the report. Talking to Maltruis was like pulling teeth.

Maria said, "Our room would be what is commonly referred to as a billiard or game room. The interior of the room is covered with wood paneling. It appears to be oak, but I will know for certain after I take another a sample. The sockets are 110, and each is grounded. The plaster is probably three to four inches thick with wooden support beams. The crown molding is early Victorian style with an ivy and magnolia pattern. The large, rectangular window, despite having broken panes, appears structurally sound. The floor is covered in a shag carpet of a teal shade—closer to blue than green. From the feel of it, I would say it had a one and a quarter inch pad. The Imps have done lots of damage to the décor but nothing that would cause the structure to be compromised."

Kyra stared wide-eyed.

Next time, I'll ask Maltruis.

"Thank you for your detailed report. Did you find any traps?" She hoped to remind Maria of the reason for them being in the room in the first place.

"Oh, right. No, I saw no wiring or foreign substances around the windows or doors. It does not appear to me that they used this room very often." She seemed chagrined.

"Fair enough. Nikkos and Anna. Oh, how is your hand?" she asked.

"It is a little sore, but Nikkos did an excellent job patching me up," she said with a smile tossed in his direction.

Nikkos blushed. "I do my best to keep everyone as healthy as I can. Now, for our room. I would say it was a drawing room. We do have a possible trap to report. Though, it could be a wasp nest. Either way, it's dangerous, so we should defuse it. Also we discovered a map." He gestured to Anna to share in their discoveries.

Anna said, "It shows from here to London. There are several hives marked as well as what I believe were guesses as to where Scíath is located. It also shows tunnels in-between hives. I'm not sure of all of these are documented hives, so I thought it might be useful."

"Excellent on the map. I look forward to seeing it. As for the possible trap, Nyles will accompany you to look at it. You're right that it should be destroyed, just to be safe." Kyra looked round. It was her turn.

"Our room was a manor office. It still held a roll top desk and several bookcases, also devoid of books. I'm going to say that due to its smaller size and lack of windows that it was not used very often. We'll do the second floor, tomorrow. We are about four hours from sundown and have that trap to look at. After we diffuse it, we should head back to the camp and tuck into some supper." Kyra brushed the thick dust from her legs as she rose.

"Perhaps, we might seek out a restroom and clear it. Not having to use the camp shower and bathroom I feel is a major bonus," Nikkos suggested.

"Fabulous idea. When we did our walk around, we noted a small building off the kitchen. I believe them to be servants' quarters. If we clear those, we could use its bathroom and have separate defensible, sturdy shelter should a storm arise," Nyles replied.

Yet another sign Kyra was not accustomed to being with a group. She hadn't thought about such a need.

"Half the group can clear the servants' quarters while the other half checks out the possible trap."

They waited for her to split them up, again. She evaluated what their talents and abilities were before assigning them.

"Maltruis, Maria, Soro, and Anna. Take the servants' quarters, check for its structural stability, and make sure that it has no new inhabitants. Anna, you have a bandaged wound. Even if this is not a toxin bomb, I don't want to take any chances with your safety.

"Nyles, Nikkos, Aieta, and I will take the trap. Afterward, we will check the tracks and see if the markings can be documented." Kyra watched as everyone followed her orders without question, and she felt a surge of confidence as a leader.

She followed the group into the drawing room. Nyles and Aieta made their way to the place Nikkos indicated.

After conferring with Aieta, Nyles turned to Kyra and Nikkos. "You were right, Nikkos. It looks like a toxin bomb set to go off when this window is opened. I will seal it, and then a decontamination crew will have to come through. Explosive ones, I can do, but I'm not comfortable with a toxin bomb."

"Are you comfortable to do that while I go check on the tracks?" Kyra asked.

"Of course. By the time you are done, we should be ready to go meet up with the servants' quarters crew."

"Great. Aieta, can you log this map as an artifact? I want it taken in for more study. Thanks," Kyra said as she headed out the door.

"Mind if I tag along?" Nikkos asked.

"Not at all." Kyra headed toward the far room.

She pushed open the door and was struck by the odor of Imp. It was very faint, but there had to have been many of them in this room, coming and going. At the bookcase, she saw the mud Soro had mentioned. Her fingers ran over the shelves, searching for what might trigger the bookcase to move. Disappointed, she pulled on it. *No luck.* Resigning the secret entrance to later inspection, she turned to look at the runes and symbols. Her foot ran over a slightly raised tile on the floor. With a whoosh of stale air and dust, the bookcase swung outward. Kyra jumped back to avoid being hit.

With care, she knelt beside the large hole. It was at least four feet across and no telling how deep. Pulling out her flashlight, she shone it into the hole. The beam penetrated several feet down but still gave no indication as to the tunnel's depth.

Reaching in, she pressed her fingers to the ends of the hole to determine the freshness of the mud. It was hard, and it crumbled under her fingers. No one had come through this in a very long time. She looked up at Nikkos, who watched her movements with anxious eyes.

"Well, it's been a long time since anyone has used this access tunnel; however, I suggest we block it off, just to be sure."

"After they are done, I can help Nyles bring in some of the debris from the other room. Aieta can record the markings," Nikkos suggested.

"Excellent plan. I'll check on the crew in the servants' quarters," Kyra said.

At the other room, Kyra poked her head in and explained the plan to Nyles. With everyone set on task, she trekked through the kitchen, holding her breath. She did not envy anyone who got to clean that out. She moved through the mudroom, past the stairs to the basement, and out the back door. Blinking, she let her eyes adjust to the outside light. One of the flaws of her Fae-sensitive eyes was that sudden, bright lights rendered her blind for a few minutes longer than most.

She moved toward the servants' building. It wasn't attached to the main house as she had thought, but it was less than ten steps from the back door. Anna stood outside it looking as if her stomach had betrayed her yet again.

She smiled weakly at Kyra.

"All the facilities seem to work, however, this was apparently a meat storage house. Maltruis and Soro are cleaning it up. How did it go in the drawing room? Was it a bomb?" Anna asked.

"Yes, it appears to be a toxin bomb. We've sealed it off for the decontamination crew. The tunnel in the office is also being blocked, just in case. How're you feeling?"

"I am cursed with a weak stomach. Other than that, I feel fine." Another apologetic half-smile crossed her face.

"Excellent. I'm going to head in to check this out. The other crew should be joining you shortly."

Stepping into the cool darkness of the building soothed her eyes. The building appeared to be composed of four rooms. A sitting room as you came in. Off to the right, a simple kitchen where Maltruis and Soro stuffed decaying meat into garbage bags. Off to the left, a room with bunks on the wall was probably a bedroom. Moving into the bedroom, she spotted a fairly decent sized full bathroom. The smell of mildew and age greeted her, but with a bit of elbow grease, they could have working bathing facilities. *Beats a portable shower any day.*

Beautiful. The estate, when refurbished and cleaned, was going to be a gem for Scíath. She drifted back into the main room. As she listened to the sounds of cleaning, she glanced casually out the window, and a cry caught in her throat. She had looked directly into another set of eyes. The grime made it hard to see the rest of the face, but the eyes were a startling gold.

Kyra drew her weapon and sprinted out the door. Anna shrieked at the sudden movement. Kyra, ignoring Anna's cries, rushed around the side of the building to find the creature. Reaching the spot, she swore loudly. The only evidence of the sighting was a small patch of grime cleaned off the window to see in.

Her cursing drew Nyles to her at a gallop.

"What's going on?" He placed a hand on her shoulder.

"I was inside, and I looked out the window. Saw a pair of eyes. We're not alone here." She scanned the tree line.

Nyles joined her in her viewing.

Soro also peered around. It's possible that it's just a curious nymph or sprite that lives close and was drawn by the activity. I thought I'd seen a signature, and I'm glad I'm not alone."

The rest of the group joined them outside, brought out either by Kyra's sprint or her colorful language.

A million possibilities ran through Kyra's head. Not to scare anyone, but even a non-Imp could be dangerous. Especially if they had frightened the creature or if it felt that they were invading its space.

Kyra looked over the group. Aieta carried the rolled up map in her hands. Nyles carried his journal and a camera. She assumed that they had finished inside the house. Soro and Maltruis carried half-full bags of things she didn't even want to guess at.

"Right, who here is the best cook?" Kyra asked.

Nikkos raised his hand. "I don't know about best, but whenever we have a Medical Department function, everyone requests I cook." He shrugged.

"Good enough for me," Kyra said.

"Nyles, can you help Maltruis and Soro finish the servants' quarters kitchen? We may be able to use it once all the grime is removed. Everyone else, back to camp, and we'll start up dinner. All need to be back at camp before the sun sets." She kept her weapon drawn as she headed down the path toward the campsite. The others fell in line behind her. Nyles stayed behind for two reasons. One, he had a very strong stomach for the chore they were doing. Two, she trusted him to get the other two back to camp safely.

The wind picked up, running chilly fingers down Kyra's spine. She shivered, and her pace picked up as the wood she had passed through easily before now seemed dark and unfriendly. Every movement, every sound could be something coming closer. Nameless fear rose in her. Her jaw clenched as the fear worked its way into her muscles. It took every ounce of will she had not to break out into a run.

She scolded herself for behaving like a child. She had been in far scarier places and circumstances than this. She would not allow herself this level of weakness. Holding her head high, she marched the rest of the way back to camp, daring anything to try to frighten her.

Once in camp, the large, cheery fire did wonders for her spirits. The flames drew her in. Dancing their primal rhythm, they stirred her soul. Closing her eyes, she felt something calling to her. She couldn't determine what it was or even which one of her senses picked it up. She stood turning toward the ever-darkening forest. The pull was almost tangible, now. Little, electric fingers pulled at her, prompting her to come with them. To embrace whatever secret they led her to.

Her feet moved of their own volition. They took her down the path and then off it. Though unknowing of where she was headed, it was extremely important that she get there. Ignoring those calling her name, she moved faster, urgency filling her. There was nothing more important than getting there.

Branches whipped at her face. Several times, she almost stumbled, but nothing slowed her. Through the distant trees, she saw a glimmer of golden light. She could hear a stream running nearby. A feeling of recognition filled her. She could not place this in her memory, though.

A strong hand on her shoulder caused her to cry out in surprise.

"Hey. Hold up, Lady," Nyles said, his forehead crinkled in concern.

Kyra turned to look at him. A growl of frustration rose in her throat. He was keeping her from getting to...where she had seen the shimmer. It was gone. Tears welled in her eyes. He had wrecked it. The feeling. The memory. It was all gone, leaving an emptiness she hadn't felt since she was a small child.

"Kyra, what's wrong? Speak to me." Concern scribbled over his face.

She sighed and pulled free from his grasp to tramp back to camp.

What on Earth was I doing? Out in the middle of unchecked territory. What was I chasing?

Someone tried to lure me out there by magic, perhaps even glimmer. Shaking her head, she walked back into the camp without a single word of explanation. She squatted by the fire. Its warmth did little to dispel the cold that filled her.

The entire group had reassembled in the camp. Everyone made busy with dinner and perimeter sweeps. They avoided looking at her. She looked like a fool. She tried to not care.

Weariness filled her—her mind and spirit as well as her bones. The wind carried the smell of something yummy. Her stomach rumbled, its tight knot reminding her of her neglect to fill it. As if reading her mind, the dinner bell rang.

She shuffled toward the makeshift kitchen. Conversation went on around her. What was being talked about? No clue. No one engaged her. Perhaps, they could tell she wasn't feeling overly gregarious. She caught sight of Nyles watching her. He looked like he wanted to come to her. She was grateful that he didn't. Not now.

Settling with the others around the roaring fire, she ate silently.

As everyone finished up, she startled everyone by speaking. "We need to set up guard detail. I would prefer to have two people on four-hour shifts." She regarded the faces around her. "I'm asking for volunteers for the first shift, and then the second set. We should need only two shifts per night."

"I require much less sleep on a whole, so I will volunteer for the first shift," Anna said.

Kyra raised an eyebrow but nodded.

"I will also stay up," Nikkos said with a sideways glance at Anna.

Kyra saw his crush on Anna and worked to keep the smirk from her face.

"Right, first watch is set. Soro and Aieta are you opposed to second watch?" Aieta's dossier said she had amazing night vision. Also, Soro might possibly catch the signature of their new friend.

"Not at all," Soro said.

"Fine with me," Aieta said.

Kyra's yawn drowned out what she had intended to say. "Trying that again, we are set for the night. I, for one, am obviously exhausted. I'm going to turn in. If you need anything at all, don't hesitate to get me. I'm a light sleeper." She placed her plate in the garbage and headed into her tent. Anyone who may want to question her about her earlier behavior could wait until morning.

Good nights were murmured as everyone but Anna and Nikkos settled in for some well needed rest.

What on earth is wrong with me? Kyra lay on her cot. It was unlike her to not volunteer for the first watch. *I'm just very tired.* No, fooling herself was impossible. She hadn't wanted to sit up on watch with anyone, because they might question her about what occurred earlier. She wanted a chance to go over it in her own mind before she had to explain it to anyone.

Her head was on the pillow mere seconds before she was asleep.

* * * *

Anna and Nikkos made a perimeter sweep before stopping where the trail joined the camp. He pulled up a large log for them to sit on.

"Now is as good a time as any for me to check on your hand," he spoke just above a whisper.

"The pain is mostly gone. If I forget and try to hold something with it, then it reminds me. That ointment you put on it really helped," her voice matched his volume level.

"It's a secret remedy from my homeland."

Removing the bandages with great care, he was pleased to see that it was indeed quite a gash, but it showed no signs of infection or poison. "Were we at home base, I may have thrown some sutures in it, just to minimize your scarring."

"I'll have a scar?" She gave a frown.

"I'm sorry to say there is a very high chance that you will have a nasty one," Nikkos said, his tone apologetic. Obviously, she was vain. Scars were not something she would be pleased with having.

"Can you try suturing it here?" she asked, her frown deepening.

"I don't have a sterile environment. I can put more ointment on it. The faster it heals, the less visible the scar." What he didn't tell her was there was still a chance that she had some kind of Imp toxin in her body, and if so, a scar would be the least of her problems.

"Fantastic." Her face lit up.

After reapplying the salve, he wrapped it again, taking care to make it as unobtrusive as possible.

"I am really glad you're on this trip," she said.

"While I'm sorry you got hurt, I'm glad to be the one to help you."

An awkward silence followed.

"Is this your first field mission?" he asked.

"This is my first mission so to speak. I'm dispatched in emergencies where Gilly's need new memories. I go in, do my thing, and leave. I've never been on anything like this. You?"

"Oh, yeah. I did some field medic training, but I have never been in a field to test it...until now."

"What do you think so far?"

"Exciting. I can say now that I'm out here that there were more qualified candidates within my department. Still, I'm ever so glad Kyra picked me."

In easy conversation, they walked around the camp.

* * * *

Kyra thrashed in her sleep.

Running, breathe burning in her chest, her legs ready to give. A familiar, female voice yelled "run and hide" over and over. Then silence. Kyra wanted to go back, but something was behind her. Something dangerous. She kept running.

The light became so bright, it blinded her. Lost in a spiral of light so bright, she had to shield her eyes. Opening them, she was again staring into eyes she had seen earlier. Yet, instead of inquisitive, they were furious. Somehow, she knew she was the cause of the fury. She tried to turn away but was blinded by the light. She tried to speak, but her mouth would form no words.

Tears ran down her cheeks. She closed her eyes tight, once more trying to hide. When she opened them, she was staring at the ceiling of her tent. She wiped away the real tears.

For once, she had no desire to go over her dream, to try to understand it. She wanted it to go away. Her watch said she had only been asleep for two hours. Her body reminded her with a huge yawn that she needed more sleep. Her mind rebelled against the possibility of having the dream come back.

Soft voices passed the tent. Anna and Nikkos were doing fine on guard duty. Amazing how well they seemed to be getting on.

Lying back, she closed her eyes and pushed the dream images to the back of her mind. The heaviness of sleep overcame her, again. Giving in to it seemed easier than trying to keep the images at bay.

* * * *

Anna paused as they passed Kyra's tent. A frown creased her face. Nikkos noticed her hesitation and stopped.

"Is everything all right?" he asked.

"I'm not sure…some kind of energy pulse went by me and into Kyra's tent."

Nikkos mirrored her frown.

"Is she in danger?" he asked.

"I can't tell. It was definitely outside energy, but it went by way too fast for me to identify it. We know next to nothing about Kyra's abilities, though. It could be something normal for her."

"So, for all we know, she is just fine?" Nikkos's concerns lingered.

"Yes," Anna said, not looking any less worried.

"I think we should check on her."

"Agreed. I think she would prefer us be over vigilant than under," Anna stated.

Both stood rooted to their spots. Nikkos didn't want to look foolish in front of their leader. Nor did he wish to have something happen to her on their guard. Time ticked by. A shrill bird cry overhead caused them both to jump.

"Oh, for goodness sakes." Anna stepped boldly up to the tent door.

"Kyra?" she called.

* * * *

Kyra was instantly awake, her hands on her weapon before her eyes were even open. She lay still, unsure of what had woken her. She yawned, ready to dismiss it as her overactive instinct, when Anna called, again.

"Kyra?"

"On my way." She unzipped the tent flap.

Looking from Anna to Nikkos, she knew something was up. Due to their quiet approach, it was either something very serious, or they were unsure of a danger.

"What's up?" She kept her tone calm.

Anna explained what she had felt.

"Thank you for being so vigilant and perceptive," Kyra said, her brows relaxing and the scowl melting from her features. She debated on how much to tell them. "It was foreign energy, and it did disturb my sleep. I would appreciate if you would document any time you feel this energy."

"Do you think it could have anything to do with the eyes you saw earlier?" Nikkos asked.

"It is possible that the creature we encountered earlier is trying to communicate with us. It could be afraid of a full-on confrontation," Kyra mused aloud.

"Trying an alternative method of contact to see if we are a danger to it," Anna noted.

Scíath

"When the next shift takes over, inform Soro. He may not be able to sense the energy as you do, but he will be able to see signatures if it comes close to the camp." Kyra's eyes scanned the dark tree line. "I have my radio next to the cot. If anything pulses again, or if you need me for any other reason, press the red button on your radio. It will buzz here but not make noise where you are. Don't hesitate to use it."

"Will do," Nikkos said.

"We want to catch up on our rounds. Hopefully, we will have nothing to tell you until morning." Anna resumed her gait.

It was odd how she was coming to not dislike Anna. Her inner critic went off in her head. *Perhaps, that's part of her plan—be likeable, get close to you. She is Jason's spy.*

Kyra's eyes narrowed in response. She was getting too soft, and how quickly it happened. Taking a deep breath, she felt her imaginary walls slide up. *Too soft, too fast.* Her mind reiterated on her way back to her cot. Checking her radio, she was fairly sure this time that no one would sit on it. She rolled over, letting sleep find her, again.

The next thing to disturb Kyra's sleep was dawn and the smell of bacon. She lay still, listening to the sound of her team collecting for breakfast. She could not help but worry over them. She felt a responsibility for their safety. She could not deny that she enjoyed the respect they showed her. Mostly because she had earned it.

Many of the fugitives she caught showed her similar respect, probably because she had been able to track them. It occurred to her that the only way she really fit into a group dichotomy was as a leader. Though she followed Galerius and the Architect's direction without question, she knew it would be hard for her to follow anyone else.

To Kyra's surprise, Nikkos—in spite of having first watch—was in an apron and cooking. Getting her plate, she settled beside Nyles. She knew he would want an explanation for her odd behavior; however, he wouldn't push her. Good thing, as she had no such answer to give.

Everyone sat around the now-smoldering campfire, enjoying breakfast and quiet conversation. The food was far superior to field rations. She ate with gusto. Kyra waited until everyone was nearly finished before she spoke.

"First off, I would like to thank Nikkos for another wonderful meal." He half bowed from his seat next to Anna.

"Second, I would like our watch teams to give reports on anything they experienced over their shift." She gestured to Anna to begin.

Kyra studied each face in turn as Anna described what she had felt. Several people in camp had the ability to send such an energy pulse, and experience taught her to always look at home first; however, none showed anything but surprise.

Soro and Aieta reported nothing seen or heard during the second part of the watch.

"Thanks to both teams for keeping us safe through the night. Today, we will make the bathing facilities available for everyone. We head back to the house in one hour. The plan for today is the second floor and the servants' quarters. If time allows, we will do the outbuildings and start on the grounds." She stood.

Breakfast broke up fairly quickly. With camp showers, the quicker you got in, the better chance you had at hot water.

Everything seemed to be going along until a ripping sound and a colorful curse filled the morning air. Maltruis stood wrapped in what had previously been the shower curtain. He held it to his still soapy body, his eyes searching for a dignified escape. Maria walked up to him, mumbling about big oafs with no common sense. Everyone suddenly made themselves busy to give him an escape.

Kyra wanted to laugh at the ridiculous figure of a chagrined Dwarf, but she did not wish to embarrass him. She turned away, mildly aggravated at the need for a new shower.

Kyra chose to enter through the front door. It meant avoiding having to split up and another kitchen encounter for Anna.

Once everyone was present in the foyer, she spoke, "We are going to do the upstairs, and it is quite extensive. Please, pull out your radios and turn them to channel three. I'm going to divide everyone up again and assign halls instead of rooms. Do not, under any circumstances, separate from your partner. If you get into any situation, hit the red button and give your location. If you can't, just hold tight to the red button. We will track you down.

"On these floors, you're less likely to find traps; however, you should expect to find spell components...artifacts. Also, you may find pieces of traps or even toxins. Exercise the utmost caution when handling any and all of theses." She removed a medium-sized roll of clear, plastic bags from her pack.

"Each team will take some of these. I'll leave the roll on the landing if anyone needs more.

"If no one has any objections to yesterday's pairs, we can do it the same way, again." She looked for any unspoken sign of issue.

"Anyone? All right, then. Let's get our bags and head up."

When she reached the top landing, she frowned. This place was far more extensive than the blueprints led her to believe. She knew that this was the original structure. Imps by nature were diggers, not stone masons. The blueprints from Lev were incomplete. This was going to take much longer then she had anticipated originally.

"Soro, Aieta, Anna, and Nikkos...follow me. We are going to head up to the third level. I'll divide it up, then. The rest of you, just hang tight, and I'll be back." She had no idea what was on the third floor.

The frame had no door, so the base of the stairs was visible. It reminded Kyra of an attic. She consciously slowed her breathing. It had begun to rush as her heart started to pound. With hope, she flicked the light switch, and somewhere over her head, a bright light flicked on. All it revealed was a long staircase, its top awaiting them in darkness. Kyra pulled her weapon.

Kyra's steps were soft and metered with caution. The others followed her. Soro was so close to Kyra, he almost caused her to trip. When she reached the top step, it wasn't the proximity of the others that caused her to fall back into Soro. It was shock at what she'd seen.

Everyone behind her also took a step backward in a domino effect that left Anna in Nikkos's arms on the bottom. Blushing, Anna righted herself, straightening her clothing as she waited for those above her to move.

Sheathing her gun, Kyra stood up straight. She forced her face to show nothing as she stepped up into the attic area.

The surprise of those following Kyra was audible. To the left of the stairs were elaborate, ritual markings—the swirls and lines drawn in flaky mud that was most likely a mix of chalk and blood. Several jars, pots, and crudely made idols sat in various places around the space. A thick layer of dust did little to mask the brutality of what had occurred in this place.

To the left were stacks upon stacks of bones. There was no overwhelming smell of decay, so it was safe to assume that these bodies had been boiled—the bones were white with no mummified flesh to be seen. Kyra looked from one side to the next.

"Well, ladies and gentlemen. For the task that faces you, I don't think anyone else would be more suited. From the looks of this, you are in your element. Soro and Aieta, please start documenting the ritual things. I will send up more bags. Anna and Nikkos, if you could get a count on how many bodies are here and species, if discernible from the skeleton? We will be sending all of these back to the forensic lab. I'm sure Leland and company could put more than a few unsolved missing person's cases to rest with these." Kyra refused to let her heartbreak at the carnage show.

Soro pulled out his notebook, handing Aieta a pen as they began to scribble, furiously copying the signs. Nikkos respectfully moved the bodies, causing Anna to sneeze from the amount of dust this stirred up.

Kyra stepped down the stairs to the curious glances of those below.

"It's a ritual room, as well as a storage chamber for a large amount of bones," Kyra forced her voice to be neutral. "They are going to need a lot more bags." She ripped off some for the second floor and sent the roll upstairs with Maria.

Once Maria rejoined them, Kyra spoke again, "All right, we will take the west wing. Maria, take the east. There are two sub hallways in each. It's going to mean more work for us, but we will just have to shoulder through it. I will announce lunch break over the radio, and we will all regroup here," she spoke loudly enough for those upstairs to hear her.

With that, everyone headed for the closest door to see what awaited them.

Chapter Seven

Questions within Answers

After checking the first door, Kyra gently pushed it open. Her ears tuned in for any clicks or other noises that might mean a trap lay within. Thirty seconds passed. Nothing .She stepped in. It was obviously a bedroom. The bed frame still stood, even though its mattress and bedding had long ago been stolen or shredded. The thick, cherry headboard and posts were carved with ornate swirls and patterns. Dominating the far wall was a three-paneled window that overlooked what at one time had probably been a flower garden. Making up the other wall was a brick fireplace with a mantle. Everything was coated with a healthy covering of dust. The floor kept track of their steps as they stirred up a fair amount just by stepping.

Nyles went to the mantle to examine the things it held. Kyra made her way to the other door to the right of the bed. Assuming it to be an en suite bathroom, she still gave it the same consideration after opening the door as she had before.

The floor changed from the deep, cherry wood panels to a whitish marble. Placing her back against the wall she slid across it until she could see what was behind the door, pushing it closed with the tip of her toe.

The only things this room held were a clawfoot tub, vanity, and an oversized mirror. From the looks of it, no one had ever really used this room when the house was occupied. Though beautiful to a human, the facilities were of no interest to filth-loving Imps.

"Kyra," Nyles called.

His voice was calm, so she moved at a regular pace, pulling the door closed gently behind her. Nyles was holding a pocket watch of some kind. He held up to her. Though dusty, it appeared to be solid gold. Taking it gently from him, she used her thumb to clean off the face. Beneath each number was a tiny gem. She deduced that the gems corresponded with the months their number represented. Flipping it over, she looked for an inscription or even a maker's stamp. Finding none, she wound its crown with great care. It would be unlikely that an Imp would use something so small for a bomb, but one could never take anything for granted. The clock began to tick away. Though it's time was way off, it was working perfectly.

"I don't think it's magical in any way. It probably belonged to the humans who lived here when the Imps took over," Nyles said.

"It's beautiful. I bet father would love it." Kyra worked to clean the decades of dirt from it.

"I agree," Nyles said.

"Christmas is coming. I could take it to Moira to get her permission and make sure there is nothing weird with it. Clean it up, and give it to him. Thank you, Nyles." She took care to wrap the watch in one of the artifact bags and slipped it into her coat pocket.

"I think this room is clear. It truly is a beautiful house, and after the rebuild crews get done, it's going to be an excellent safe house." Kyra took a moment to admire the carvings on the bed posts.

"I agree. Most of the original furnishings can be saved and cleaned up. I wouldn't mind coming to see it after it's done." Nyles headed toward the door.

They returned to the main hall. Kyra resisted the urge to go check on those upstairs. She had to have faith in her team. No one liked being micro-managed.

Down her hall, she had two more rooms, and then the small hall that led to two smaller rooms on the side. Whoever built this place had tried to cram as many rooms as possible into the space provided. Listening, there was a murmured conversation from the third floor, but nothing from the other hall.

Nyles watched her and smiled. "Kyra, they're fine. You picked a good team. You set up an emergency procedure, and nothing has exploded."

She mirrored his smile. "If I didn't know better, I'd swear you could read minds."

"Minds...no, but you...yes." He smirked as he opened the second door.

He was the only constant person, besides the Architect, in her entire life. It wasn't hard for her to read him, either. It just never occurred to her that it went both ways. She followed him into the new room. It was yet another bedroom. This one featured two single beds. One had been white and the other blue. A children's room. The faded border on the upper wall looked to be of an animal alphabet. A miniature table sat covered deep in dust and cob webs. Toys sat undisturbed in silent wait for their master's return. Kyra's soft sigh stirred up wisps of dust. It was likely that the children to whom these toys belonged were among the bones upstairs.

"I can't say if they ever came in here." Nyles examined a hobby horse.

"I'm sure they originally scouted it, but this is a far larger place than they usually took. It seems very unlike any Imp holding I've ever seen. I'm completely surprised by the collection of bones." Kyra shocked herself with her burst of honesty.

Nyles said, "I've studied their culture for years. In fact, I did a paper on Imps for my Anthropology specialization. The nests were normal. The rotting food in the kitchen was a bit out of character. I think that maybe the creature you glimpsed yesterday is responsible for it, as nothing the Imps would have left would still be decaying," he said.

"The ritual area sounds normal, though I'm very surprised to see it so far above ground. The stairs looked quite steep, or I would try to make it up to see it," Nyles finished.

"I'm sure Aieta and Soro will take a ton of pictures, and the bones will be heading back to Leland and the forensic team." Kyra was eager to leave the room. It depressed her for several reasons past the obvious.

Nyles moved toward the door.

"Why don't we see if we can't knock out those other two rooms? Then, we can help Maria and Maltruis. It would be great to get the upper floors done in one day," he said.

Kyra's estimate of more time being needed had been lessened by the lack of Imps in the upstairs room. Nyles turned toward the smaller hall with Kyra on his heels.

A huge crash came from across the hall, simultaneous with the buzzer sound from the radio going off. Kyra, gun drawn, headed toward the sound. The buzzer was making it harder for her to tell where the crash and subsequent growling was coming from, so Kyra just threw open the first door she came upon. It was empty. The second, however, was not. A globe whizzed at her head.

"Whoa!" She just managed to avoid the object.

"Maltruis, it's Kyra. Stand down," Maria said.

The buzzer stopped. Everyone else congregated at the bottom of the attic steps. Kyra held up her hand for them to stay. It would be much easier heading into the unknown without having to worry about other people.

The room had been a study. Bookcases lined the walls, and amazingly, most of the books were still intact. Several maps hung on walls as well as what looked to be a small, scale model of London. There was less dust in here. This room had definitely seen action during the occupation. Her gun still drawn, she looked around for what had caused the commotion. Maltruis stood with his back leaning against the window. He looked shaken, his eyes wide.

Maria pointed to the window seat. Its cushion lay half on the floor. Freshly broken objects around it indicated this was the crash she had heard. With her foot, she kicked the cushion aside. She drew a sharp breath in as she saw a tunnel that led down into the walls of the house. The mud smeared around the edge of the hole was fresh, but whatever had been there was now gone. Keeping her face to the tunnel, she said, "Right, so what did I miss?" She kept her weapon out but in a relaxed pose.

Maria spoke up, "We were noting that this room had been used, but showed very little sign of Imp. I intended to fill you in at the lunch briefing. Maltruis was assessing the structural stability of the bookcases when the cushion exploded up off the seat. Whatever it was, it was so fast that we only got a glimpse of it. It appeared to be covered in a blue-green fur. It dashed around the room. Maltruis chose to pelt it with things until it retreated back down the tunnel. I'm not sure it was the most diplomatic way to handle it, but it worked."

"Must be the same thing I saw earlier. You did try to protect yourself. I'm glad neither of you were injured." She looked at her watch. "It's about half an hour before I intended on calling for lunch, but since we are all assembled, let's break now." Kyra headed back to the hallway.

"They'll explain what happened once we are back in camp," Kyra said to alleviate the curious looks she was getting.

Everyone made their way downstairs in silence. They were probably shaken up by the first encounter with an unknown creature.

Once outside, the warm sunlight filtering through the trees seemed to lighten the mood. A couple of conversations about local foliage entertained them as they made their way back into camp.

"I'm on lunch," Nikkos said as they entered the campground.

"I'll help," Anna offered, beaming.

"Nyles, let's do a security check on the campsite, just in case," Kyra said. "Maria, if you want to fill the team in while we inspect the area, go ahead."

Kyra and Nyles made their way around the perimeter. Once they were out of earshot, she filled him in on what had happened. "What could we be up against? Of course, at first, I feared it was an Imp, but they aren't furry and are usually just green."

Nyles seemed to give it some thought as they walked at a slower than leisurely pace. Finally, he said, "It seems to me we have two distinct issues here. The first obviously being the creature that seems to inhabit this place, now.

"The second issue is the indication that the Imps were not alone here. If that is true, then the conspiracy theories that flew around back then may have been correct. There are a number of papers in the Anthropology library from people who believed the Imps had help planning the war." His brow furrowed.

"Our first priority is discovering who and what our visitor is and what his intentions are. Pulling on my memory for tunneling, furry creatures with fantastic speed, it might be an off shoot of Troll. Hell, it could even be a Troll-Imp hybrid which is very worrying. I'd honestly have to get a good look at it. Depending on its rarity, I may have to go back to Simon to get identification, if we even have one on record."

"That's part of the trouble with our world. Not even we know every kind of supernatural being that is out there." Kyra's shoulders slumped, and her eyes were downcast.

"I suggest we trap it. If it continues to pop out of things and scare people, it's going to get shot. I see no reason to harm an innocent creature," Nyles offered.

Kyra rubbed at the knot forming in her back. "The problem with trapping it is tracking it. Until the grounds and outbuildings are cleared for Imp traps, I can't chase after it as I would normal prey." The scent of cooking chicken made its way to Kyra. She breathed in the aroma, and the knot disappeared.

"Point, however, it seems very interested in us. We could set a trap in that one room. We could put another trap on the door to the kitchen. Another also around the camp at night." Nyles practically neighed with excitement.

Kyra grinned at him. "Are you sure I'm the field agent, and you're the book worm?"

"Hey, I learned from the best," he said with real affection in his voice.

They stood very close together. Tilting her head up to look into his eyes perfectly positioned her for his kiss, which he began to do.

Someone hollered "lunch" and broke the spell. They walked back to the group in silence. Everyone ate around the fire, the focal point of camp. Conversation was quiet, staying away from the subject of the house and the events of the morning.

As the meal ended, Kyra stood. "Nikkos, you'd best be careful, or Gus will draft you in as a chef. Another amazing meal. I'd be interested in seeing what you could do in a real kitchen."

Nikkos blushed furiously. "Thank you. Once we get back, we'll have to have our debriefing in the dining hall, so I can show you."

"Deal," Kyra replied. Her voice turned serious, "Now, before we head back in, there are a few things I want to cover. It is apparent that we are not alone here. I am going to be setting traps for our friend. Talking to him is preferable to his getting shot because of startling someone.

"It is now noon. I want us to clear out of the house around 6:00 p.m. I will inform everyone of the location of the traps. After dinner, I wish to discuss the things that we have found and get input from everyone. If we can finish clearing the upstairs in the next six hours, fantastic. Nyles and I are almost done. We'll head out to the servants' quarters to see if we can make it livable enough for us to move into. It provides us more shelter and less chance of being surprised.

"This being the case, we will quit around 5:00 p.m. and move camp. I cannot reiterate enough that you must remain together at all times. If you do come across the creature, and you must defend yourself, please attempt to wound not kill. Any questions?"

Aieta raised her hand.

Kyra nodded to her.

"There are going to be a large amount of artifacts, relics, and bones to move back to the train. What are the odds of getting a truck and trailer out here?" Aieta asked.

"I'm not honestly sure, but I'll get a hold of Lev and see what he can do. Thank you for thinking ahead, Aieta."

"Anyone else?" Kyra waited to see if anyone else wanted to speak. "All right, then. Back to the trenches."

She headed to the supply tent to pick up all the cleaning agents she could find. At the house, Kyra laid their extra supplies right inside the doors for when they were ready for the servants' quarters.

In the hall, Kyra watched each group enter their next room or go back to the attic before heading to the side hall she had left to clear.

The tension in the air was tangible. Every creak or shift of light had people jumping. If being in a place that already held danger wasn't enough, now they had a live, unidentified critter running around.

The hallway was dark. Light from the main hall didn't seem able to illuminate the place. Kyra opened the door in her now well-practiced fashion. The room was much smaller than the other two. It held two sets of bunk beds. The beds were coated in dust but still seemed sturdy. Unlike the other rooms, the beds were neatly made. The rest of the room was simple—a single wooden table and four chairs. Other than the obvious signs of age, this room was clean and ready to be used. Very unlike the rooms that held signs of Imps. It strengthened the theory that the Imps had houseguests during war times.

They stepped out of the room. Finding this information and what it meant to the mission and to history kept Kyra lost in thought. She moved silently to the next room. It was an exact replica of the room before it—neat and tidy, and obviously made more for humanoid inhabitants than the Imps. Kyra was closing the door when the radio on her hip crackled to life.

"Kyra, no emergency, but if you're available, can you come to the second room in the west wing, please?" Maria asked.

"On my way."

Kyra fought the urge to run, as she didn't want to frighten anyone. Still, at half-speed, she made it to the room in less than a minute.

Whatever time she had gained was lost as she stood in shock. Her mouth gaped open as she took in what was before her. Nyles's hoof beats behind her barely registered.

Before her was a lab that would rival the one at Scíath. Dozens of beakers and test tubes sat in racks. Burners and bottles were everywhere. It looked like a place to manufacture toxins, but it was so organized.

"This is too extensive and organized to be Imp," Nyles said from behind her, echoing her thoughts.

"Do not touch anything, but take lots of pictures." Kyra backed out of the room, very nervous.

"After that, should we join you in the servants' quarters for the cleaning?" Maria asked.

"Yes," Kyra answered, but her gaze was distant.

She walked down the stairs, picking up the cleaning supplies as she headed out the door. Her mind was a jumble as she tried to place all the pieces she had seen into a coherent picture. Most of the pieces were obtuse and refused to merge with logic. Kyra frowned as she made her way into the servants' quarters.

Picking up a scrub brush, she started work on the kitchen. The cleaning kept her hands busy while her mind worked the clues over and over. Could the creature they had glimpsed been he who was working with the Imps all those years ago? Though, it was a tunnel creature, feral by nature, and not sophisticated enough for that equipment. It had always been believed that the Imps developed their toxins from plants and herbs. Now, there was evidence that they were chemically created in labs. *The question then begged, by whom?*

In her peripheral vision she caught sight of Nyles scrubbing down the stove and checking the vents above it. She had no doubt his mind was as full as hers.

"I'm looking forward to what the others have to say," she said more to herself than to him.

With the counters, sink, and cabinets scrubbed, she picked up her bathroom supplies and headed that way. As she moved into the main room, Maltruis and Maria entered the building.

"Excellent timing," Kyra said. "I just did the kitchen. Would you two mind doing the bathroom? I'll get the bunks together." She held out the cleaning supplies.

"Of course," Maria replied.

Kyra turned to go into the bedroom, when her Fae senses started to tingle. She stood completely still, allowing whatever it was to come to her. A far off sound caused her to cock her head to the side. Everyone around her noticed and paused. She motioned for them to stay and headed soundlessly out the door.

She moved deftly through the woods, her practiced tracking skills in overdrive. Then, another sound—this one of footfalls near the gate to the property. Pulling her gun, she moved down the path in a flash. Rounding the last curve in the path, she came face-to-face with what she had heard.

Two teenage boys stood just inside the gate. Both threw up their hands at the sight of Kyra's drawn weapon.

"Geez! Hey, lady. Put that down," the taller of the two said, his voice high with fear.

Kyra lowered her weapon but did not put it away.

"What are you doing here?" she asked, her eyes scanning the woods for further trouble, in case this was a distraction to an attack.

This time, the shorter one spoke. His gangly arms and cracking voice betrayed his recent spurt into puberty. "Edwin bet us twenty pounds that we wouldn't come out here and bring back something from inside the haunted house." His eyes flicked from Kyra's face to her gun.

She was sure now that they were alone.

"Come with me." She left no room for question.

She moved behind them, nudging them forward. Pulling her radio off her hip, she spoke into it, "Anna, please meet me in the front foyer. We have a Gilly situation."

"A Gilly situation? What's a Gilly?" the taller one asked.

"You are a Gilly, and the situation is you are somewhere you don't belong," Kyra said simply.

"I'm not a Gilly. I'm a Brit," the younger one grumbled, his face flushing.

"Just keep moving," Kyra said.

As they entered the house, Kyra was pleased to see Anna waiting at the bottom of the stairs. Her eyes widened as she saw the two boys that were being unceremoniously escorted to her.

"Anna, Tweedledee and Tweedledum here were bet twenty pounds that they couldn't bring back something from inside the haunted house." Kyra sheathed her weapon. "I would be pleased if they arrived, were unable to get inside, and left."

"Understood." Anna approached the taller boy first. "Look into my eyes," she said softly.

He stared at her as if she was one of the most beautiful women he had ever seen.

Anna placed her hands on his shoulders and murmured softly against his ear.

"Hey, what's she doing to him? Who are you people?" Squeaky voice asked.

"Who we are, what we are doing, and why we are here is of absolutely no concern to you." Kyra shrugged.

Anna finished with the first, who now stood still with a dreamy expression on his face. The second one resisted, wanting to escape his friend's fate. Anna, in one swift movement, caught hold of his chin and forced him to look at her. Once he was locked in, she released his chin and began the same process she had with the other.

Kyra watched with interest. She had heard of memory workers, but it was a rarely viewed art. A few moments later, Anna was finished, and both stood in their dream state.

"You can take them back to where you found them. You have about five minutes before they come back around."

Kyra placed her hands on their shoulders, propelling them toward the door. She faced Anna over her shoulder. "Excellent job. Thank you for your help. I'm glad to have you along." Without waiting for a reply, she moved the two boys out the door and back to whence they came. Once she placed them a good ten to fifteen feet from the gate, she made her way back to the servants' quarters. She was pleased to inhale the smell of orange cleaner as opposed to mildew and mold.

At the sound of her entering the building, everyone came out into the center room to see what had occurred.

"Two boys from the village were looking for a souvenir from the haunted house," Kyra explained. "Anna handled it, and they are now on their way home."

"This has been the day of surprises," Nyles commented as he headed back into the bedroom.

"While that is true, I would prefer to have no more, today." Kyra picked up her scrub brush to clean the common room.

Time passed quickly as they cleaned. There were three sets of bunk beds in the bedroom. The common room held more than enough space for Nyles and Maltruis to set up their sleeping pallets.

The crackle of the radio brought Kyra back to attention as she finished cleaning the windows.

"It's 5:00 p.m. Should we head down to help move camp?" Aieta asked over the radio.

"Yes, we'll meet you at the front door."

"We ready?" Kyra looked around in pride at what they had done to make the place hospitable, again.

"Yes," Nyles said, leaning against the door frame and cleaning the grime from under his nails.

They made their way to the front door to find a very tired-looking quartet coming from the house. With one look at the team, Kyra made an announcement. "Let's move the camp and call it quits for the day. Everyone looks beat, and hot showers and a good meal are needed." Her announcement brought many grateful expressions.

The next hour was absorbed with moving their camp into the servants' quarters. The potbelly stove in the common room roared. Good thing, as the twilight had brought a chill with it. As night fell, everyone was freshly showered and settled into the common room with bowls of beef stew.

"I think that given our new accommodations, if we make sure all windows and doors are locked, we should not need patrols. There is no basement here and no tunnels. It's the safest place on the grounds as far as I can see," Kyra explained.

"First, we'll do our round table reports, so everyone is up to speed on all the information. I'm going to pose some questions to the team, as I value your opinions. Aieta and Soro, you will start. Then, Anna and Nikkos, Maria and Maltruis, and end with myself and Nyles." Kyra took a long sip of her juice.

Casting a look at Aieta, Soro began.

"We studied the ritualistic markings and drawings that were found on the third floor. Some of them, we have seen before in Imp literature. Others are unfamiliar, but as our Imp information was never complete, it's possible they are deity or worship symbols. I did, however, note that there are two distinct writing styles. More than one person drew them. This is uncommon for Imps.

Either their priest was killed or injured and another took over, or this was a dual project."

He turned to Aieta, who reported, "The artifacts are in amazing condition. They are much better than anything we have in artifacts currently. Several are urns and funeral jars; however, I surmise that the large cylinder was used to offer blood as a sacrifice to their deity. I think the dried blood is too old for DNA, but we will gladly send samples to the labs if it would help."

Kyra nodded. "It seems this find is quite lucrative in information. Thank you both for your exceptional job."

Nikkos shared a look with Anna who nodded at him.

"We are about halfway through the bones up there. Thus far, I have identified five male and three female human skeletons. I have also discovered two male Dwarf skeletons as well as what I believe to be a female Fae skeleton." Nikkos waited for the others to digest the information.

Anna jumped in, "From everything I've read about Imps, though, I will admit it's not nearly as much as others here.." She shot an admiring look at Nikkos. "This stacking of skeletons, almost like trophies, seems out of nature for creatures who sleep in nests made of garbage.

"Once we get them back and get them identified, Gilly Relations will work on returning the bodies to the appropriate family members when possible," she finished.

Kyra said, "Anna, it would be greatly appreciated if after we get back, you continue to be our liaison with Nikkos and Medical." Kyra noted the huge smile on Nikkos's face at her words. *Oh, yeah. He has it bad.* She kept the smirk from her face.

"I would love to continue on this project. I feel a responsibility to returning the remains to their people at home." The passion in her voice gave rise to a few surprised looks from those around her.

Maria took a deep breath before she began speaking, "Well, you all know how our first room went, since it inspired our early lunch; however, the last room we entered was perhaps even more shocking than our encounter with the visitor."

While Maria explained the discovery of the lab, Kyra observed the facial expressions and body language of the listeners. She hoped to see if others came to the same conclusion that she had.

After Maria's report, Kyra gave hers. Proverbial light bulbs seemed to go off over people's heads as they all came to the same conclusions she had. She let it all stew for a moment before she put her question to the group. "It's obvious to me at least that there was someone else with the Imps here during war time. This lends much credence to the conspiracy theory that the Imps did not wage the war on their own. The lab is high tech and perhaps the place where another race engineered the deadly toxins the Imps used. Now, with that in mind, does anyone see any clues that would indicate who or what was aligned with the Imps?"

Her question fell like stones on the ears of those around her. The implications of having your race aligned with the only race that was considered enemy to the entire supernatural world were staggering.

"Due to the accommodations and dimensions of the lab, I think we can assume they were a fairly humanoid race," Nyles said.

"Not same creature who came from ground," Maltruis's voice rumbled like an earthquake. Kyra had forgotten how deep his voice was as he spoke so seldom to her.

"Why do you say that?" Soro asked.

"Fur, claws, smell like earth not bed," Maltruis replied.

Everyone took a moment to process this.

He doesn't waste words, but he gets his point across. "I did not see any remnants of fur in the lab or in the bedrooms, so I'm inclined to agree," Kyra replied.

"It would have to be a race of high intelligence," Nikkos said as he scrolled through the pictures on Maria's digital camera. "This equipment is really high tech. It looks a lot like the bio lab at Scíath."

"There are a ton of possibilities with those few criteria," Soro said.

"We need more clues," Kyra agreed. "So, we shall move on to our next topic of discussion—the aforementioned claws and fur.

"I've been running through my mental files, and I'm drawing a serious blank. I can think of a couple of races that fit some of the characteristics, but not one with all. So, either it's a new species, which is not unheard of. I have no doubt there are more than a few reclusive races we have yet to discover. Or it's a hybrid," Soro said.

"Hybrids are rare, but with what we have seen here, it's more than possible that with that equipment, they were doing genetic experiments." Nyles's brow furrowed as he thought of the implications.

"A hybrid Imp race is a terrifying thought," Aieta said.

Kyra waited for someone to toss out a cruel comment about hybrids in general. The chip settled on her shoulder, and she prepared to fight, but nothing was said. Though surprised, the lack of slurs made her feel more comfortable with the people she led. "I'm going out to set the traps for our little friend, whomever or whatever he may be. Anyone want to come along?"

"I would like to," Soro said

"As would I. Plus, I'm good at carrying stuff," Nyles said.

"Right, then. We'll grab our supplies and head out. Lock the door behind us and open it only for us." Kyra affixed her radio to her belt. "We have our radios. If anything happens, we will call for backup. If anything happens here, call for us, and we will come running."

Kyra flicked on her flashlight as she opened to door to greet the night. Without sound, they made their way along the path to the cellar entrance.

"I'm going to set a simple net trap at the bottom of the stairs. I'll ask you to lower down the components. No use in all of us trying to cram into this little spot." Kyra went down the stairs. Each step she made produced a creak or a groan that sounded like a shot in the night silence.

* * * *

Soro turned to Nyles and spoke. His voice was just loud enough to allow his words to reach Nyles but not down into the basement. "I am very concerned by the things we are finding here. I really need access to Simon. I am uncomfortable being out here with an unknown creature stalking us."

Nyles frowned. He had to concede that Soro made good points, but at the same time, he felt that Kyra was more than capable of keeping them safe.

"Perhaps, we should suggest this be a two-part mission. We could clear it for toxins and traps, take back what we can, and come back armed with more knowledge."

"I see the points you are making. I would suggest taking Kyra aside and asking her thoughts." Nyles didn't wanting to place himself in the chain of command.

Soro nodded, looking disappointed. "I had hoped you would perhaps go to Kyra. You know her best, and she might not take offense."

* * * *

A few moments later Kyra emerged from the cellar, wiping the dirt from her hands on her pants. "I will never get used to the filth these creatures chose to live in." Her nose wrinkled.

"I agree. I know plenty of underground or tunnel species that are just as clean as many at Scíath. This was a choice they made," Soro said.

"Right, let's do the two tunnels inside the house and then the entrance to the old campsite. It may think we have left and want to investigate." Kyra moved expertly through the dark.

* * * *

The other two followed close behind. Nyles knew that even with his strength and speed, Kyra was the most skilled in the field. Watching her expertly set the traps, his mind filled with conflicting thoughts. Professionally, in field work there was none better at her job than Kyra. If she could handle coming out of the field, she would easily be next in line for department head.

As a friend, he could think of no one in his life who had accepted him more than Kyra. The Centaurs shunned him due to his want to associate with the "humanoids", and the humans never got over his appearance. He believed part of their bond had come from both being shunned by society, as well as the fact that he was also an orphan. His parents had been killed in the Imp war, and the Architect had taken him in. Their feelings of friendship were acceptable, even if some thought it odd. It was the love he felt for her that was going to end up costing some heartbreak.

How could he not love her? She was amazing. She was beautiful inside and out, and she loved him. He could feel it, see it in her eyes when she looked at him. There is nothing on this earth he wouldn't do for her, but how could they ever be together? Love was blind to many things, but not even love could blind them to their race differences. Given the bias she already faced, he knew even within Scíath, their union would be frowned upon. With the Architect retiring and an unknown taking his place, they could even be in danger of retaliation simply for being together.

She turned around as she finished the trap and caught him looking at her. A flush colored her cheeks, and she quickly looked away.

* * * *

Soro watched the exchange—especially the way Nyles looked at her. Love was obvious. He felt for both of them. In his time in Supernatural Species, he had advised several mixed race couples on possible issues with offspring and such. Scíath made it much easier for races to intermingle than they did in the outside world. Most of the time, the cases were simple; however, he had once broken the heart of a young female Fury who had fallen in love with an empath. He was human, and with her genetic differences, their chance at viable offspring was small. The couple was still dating, but the Fury had really wanted children.

It was not a part of his job that he enjoyed. He knew that any offspring from a relationship between Nyles and Kyra was not possible. In addition, they would be shunned openly and would never be able to have a life outside of Scíath, and even inside, it was not as safe as it should be.

Nyles with her was uncharted territory, as she was the first of her kind that anyone knew about. So, while it might be "possible" it was not probable, and he knew it was not a chasm they chose to cross. He doubted highly they would ever get as far as coming to him, but it was very hard for him to see such a strong love be shot down before it blossomed.

* * * *

After Kyra laid the trap at the old camp site, they headed back toward the servants' quarters. From 100 yards from the building, they could see the light shining through the windows and made out the shadow forms of their companions within.

Kyra stopped. Her action caused Nyles to run into Soro, who cried out in surprise. She held her hand up for silence. Her body motionless, her ears searching out the sound she had just heard. A foot fall, she had no doubt about it. The question was, where was it from, and who made it? Again, a soft step in the underbrush. It came from the right, about 200 yards out.

Kyra's hunter's reflexes kicked in. Dropping her supplies, she crouched down and moved into the wood. She kept her body hidden behind a tree. At the last moment, she remembered those behind her and motioned them to stay still. Her light steps caused no sound as she crept through the lush forest. The cold night air made her skin tingle. The thrill of the hunt filled her veins with power. This was her high. The rush she felt stalking her quarry was impossible to match. The creature she sought had no idea she was headed for it. It kept on its path toward the servants' quarters. A satisfied smile crept to her lips. She was going to take it unaware, and she never missed.

Cutting around behind it, she moved ever closer, keeping 100 yards between them. Nothing she couldn't cover in mere seconds, but she would prefer a clearer path. So, she could let it exit the woods.

It stopped. She flattened her body against the nearest tree. Its rough bark pressed little daggers against her cheek. The sharp tang of the tree sap made its way into her nose, blinding her sense of smell with its pungent aroma.

Much to her aid, it began to move again, allowing her to distance herself from the offending tree. Just as she felt the blood trickling down her cheek, the creature in front of her stopped.

Although, she got a decent look at it as it rose off all fours, the lack of light made judging its exact color impossible. By its outline, she could tell it indeed had fur. She could also tell that it had four appendages. It stood to its full height, which she estimated was at least seven feet. The outline was perfect. It had a long snout and no visible ears. Sniffing the air again, it turned toward Kyra.

Silently, she cursed, wiping the blood from her cheek. *Damn tree.* She moved back toward the path. If this thing charged, she wouldn't mind having backup, so she wouldn't have to kill it.

It dropped back to all fours. In this position, it resembled a very large bear; however, its size was no bane to its movement. It headed toward her at a steady clip.

An expletive escaped her lips as she judged the distance between it and where she wanted to go. Should she forget hiding and try a straight out dash back to the path? The dense underbrush could trip her. While she fell next to never, now was not the time to tempt fate. Or she could try to creep her way back and hope it didn't hone in on the scent of her blood.

As she was choosing her path, she heard a short click followed by an inhuman howl of pain. She took off at a full run, reaching them in mere seconds. Soro stood before her, his face showing his shock. A stun gun in his hand dangled loosely from his grip.

"I saw the signature. It was—you were, I didn't know. I was..." he stumbled over his words.

"Shhh. Calm down. You did fine. Let me see how the creature fares," Kyra said.

Following the tazer cords, she shone the light out in front of her. Fifteen feet out and lying in the brush, she found the two barbs coated in a substance she assumed was blood. No sign of the creature itself. He had been able to remove the metal barbs and move that quickly away after a serious shock. She upped her estimation of its toughness.

After making her way back to them, she found Soro was a bit better. It was obvious that this was his first encounter with a threatening supernatural.

"How is it?" Nyles asked.

"Gone."

"Gone?" Soro asked. "Did I hit it?"

"You did. I found the barbs lying in the underbrush, and they are coated in what I believe to be blood. The stun didn't stop it." Kyra turned her flashlight up to max to search the forest for their creature. *Useless and a stupid thing to do...*"Let's get back inside. If it's not alone, it's likely to come back with friends. Also, I'm sure the people inside are wondering what in the blue hell is going on."

With Kyra's soft, quick steps, and Nyles trying not to sound too much like a herd of elephants, their pace brought them back to the building. Kyra knocked on the door.

"Who is it," Anna called from inside, her shrill voice carrying through the thick door. They had definitely heard the commotion.

"It's Kyra, Nyles, and Soro." Kyra kept her voice calm to let them know that everything was mostly okay. The bolts slid back to permit them entrance. In the main room, they were met with curious and worried expressions.

"Right, let me fill you all in. We laid the traps, and on our way back I saw the creature in the distance headed toward this building. I tried to catch it, but it sensed me. Soro, looking out for my safety and able to trace its signature, shot at the creature with the stun gun. He did hit it; however, the stun didn't stop it.

I saw a decent outline view of it. It's approximately seven feet tall. It has four limbs and seems to prefer to travel on all fours. It has a long snout and a serious sense of smell. It also moves quickly and is quite resilient," Kyra explained to her enraptured audience.

"That size and facial structure is inconsistent with Imps," Nyles commented.

"I collected the barbs to bag and send back to the lab. We could get lucky. If we do not capture it, we may have its DNA on file." Soro's face was still a shade or two paler than normal, but the shock seemed to be wearing off.

Soro's actions may have been enough to scare it off and keep it away from them for the remainder of the visit. Kyra hid her anger with Soro. He was inexperienced and did what he thought was best to protect his team mate, ruining the perfect chance to trap the beast.

Kyra accepted a cup of tea from Nikkos. He really was proving to be multitalented. Conversation milled around her as she became lost in thought. There was no way she could have prepared for the things that they found here. It was, however, proving to be nearly impossible to do without the technology at Scíath. They needed the lab, they needed the archives, they needed Simon, and she needed to consult with Father. Would any of the team object to coming back out here? *Only one way to find out.*

Clearing her throat, she brought the entire room to attention. "Everyone, this was to be a simple sweep and clear mission; however, as we all can attest to, we have discovered far more than some Imp traps or even some toxins.

"It seems to me the best thing to do is amend our plan of action. Finish the sweep, and make sure this place is safe. Secure it, and take the artifacts, the bones and other things back to Scíath. We can then pick up the information we need and come back better prepared. Would anyone object to heading back tomorrow afternoon and then coming back in three to four days to finish the job?"

"I have absolutely no issue and think it's a very smart move," Aieta said.

Everyone murmured agreements.

"Well, if everyone is in favor, I have one more thing to ask. Other than reports to your department heads, let no rumors or information about what we have found here find its way out." She met each person's eyes to drive home her point.

She was reassured by understanding looks.

"Fair enough. I'm going to call Lev and explain things to him. Tomorrow, we will concentrate on clearing out the rest of the sheds. We can pack up what we need to take with us and head out.

"Now, as far as our new friend is concerned, stay alert. The situation will go one of two ways. It will return with friends and relatives, and we will have a fight on our hands, or it will stay away until after we leave. In which case, when we return, we should have a better idea of what it is and how to deal with it."

"I need to know your personal battle skills." Kyra had read the files on each of them, but she wanted to hear from them directly.

"I'll start," Nyles said. "I have extensive hand-to-hand skill, certified in all the weapons I carry, and I am decent with a stun gun."

Kyra turned her gaze to Soro, who sat beside him. Soro said, "I've now proven I can shoot a stun gun. I know basic self-defense; however, I'm not skilled with fire arms."

"Fair enough. For those who lack skills, I may have to switch pairs around. There needs to be at least one fighter in each pair," Kyra explained. "Also, I suggest if you want to continue to do field missions that you take some firearms training from Security. I wouldn't want to lose any of you." She worked hard to not sound condescending.

No one seemed offended, so she gestured to Aieta, who said, "I am a black belt in Karate. I have all my handgun certs, and I'm proficient with a bow and arrow."

Kyra nodded, impressed with Aieta. "Well, Soro. I think you're safe with her. Your team is good," Kyra said.

Maltruis, next in line, shrugged and simply said, "I smash, very strong. No need gun."

"Can't argue with that logic," Kyra said.

"My turn," Maria said. "I have most of my handgun certs; however, my size can make it harder to defend myself."

"I think I'm going to leave you with Maltruis. He makes up the size, and you can tell him what to smash," Kyra said with a smile.

Everyone chuckled. Next was Nikkos. This was the pair Kyra would bet on having to split up.

"I'm a healer and decent in a kitchen, but I've never done anything past the self-defense clinic Galerius ran a few months ago." Nikkos looked at the floor.

"I gotcha, partner," Anna said with a smile. "I've mastered several forms of martial arts. I'm certified in hand guns, fencing, bow and arrow, and stun guns." She looked rightfully proud.

Kyra said, "I am pleased that you are all are prepared or in a position where you are safe. Now, I think we have all had a very full day and exciting evening. I suggest we turn in." She stifled a yawn.

"Can't argue with that," Soro said, mirroring her yawn.

Everyone settled in for the night.

The dawn chorus of birds woke Kyra. She stretched, hearing others moving around her. She lay still a moment. Despite everything outside of the plan that had happened, she was happy with their progress. Slipping out of bed, she made a quick jump into the bathroom for her morning routine.

The smell of frying bacon hit her as she moved toward the front door. Pulling out her cell phone, she discovered she had one-ish bars. Hoping outside would be better, she unbolted the door and stepped outside. It was immediately apparent the phone call would have to wait.

Outside the door were tracks and drops of blood. Their friend had been back. Examining the door and front windows, she saw no signs that it attempted to enter the building. Kyra frowned. Perhaps, it was hurt and was coming to them for help? Opening the door, she shouted inside.

"Nyles, Nikkos. I need to see you, please."

In less than a minute, both of them were at the door and taking in what Kyra was looking at.

"It came back, and it's wounded," Nyles said.

"I'm wondering if it came to us for help," Kyra said

Nikkos winced. "I can grab my kit, and we can try to find it."

"Let's get everyone else started on their tasks. Then, we will set off and see what we can find," Kyra said. "First, I'm going to call Lev. I'll be a sec." Kyra waved them inside. She saw an anxious looking group awaiting them. Finding a sweet spot for signal, she made her call as brief as possible, rushing to rejoin her team.

Nyles was explaining to them what they had found outside.

She waited until he had finished his explanation before she spoke, "Lev will have a truck meet us at the gate at 6:00 p.m. Then, when we return to London, he will have a cargo truck meet us at the station. So, we have roughly eleven hours to get everything ready for transport and finish the outbuildings and grounds.

"With another team, I might be concerned, but I have absolute faith that we can handle this."

Breakfast was quick, and everyone was ready to go in less than an hour.

"Right, I'm taking Nikkos along to see if we can find the creature. Anna, since you are all in the attic work space, I'm going to send you with Soro and Aieta. We need to get those bones ready for transport. We will break for lunch at noon, barring any unforeseen changes that may occur. While we look for the creature, we will also be clearing the grounds. Maria and Maltruis, I would like you to clear the stable, shed, and the smokehouse." Kyra slid her holster on.

"If all goes according to plan, I shall see you all here at noon." Kyra watched as the team disbursed to their tasks.

"The blood drops are not large. That is a good sign," Nikkos said as he bent down to examine the substance beside the tracks.

Kyra nodded. "Let's follow the tracks to see if we can find its den. Keep your eyes out. We need to sweep the grounds at the same time." Kyra began to track the creature.

It seemed as though it had stayed on the path. Following the tracks, they found themselves back at their old campsite. The blood droplets stopped. The wound couldn't have been too serious. Leaving the camp, it had made its way into the brush, making it much harder to track.

Utilizing her tracking skills, she was able to follow it several hundred yards into the brush before losing its trail.

"Well, one thing is for certain. It is alone. I see only one set of tracks. At its size, were there more, we would see indications of them in the woods," Kyra said with a sigh.

"Kyra, this is one of the hardest terrains to track in. We don't even know what it is. Further, we have zero idea what its powers are," Nyles said gently.

Kyra's shoulders slumped. She appreciated his attempt to raise her spirits; however, she disliked the idea of prey escaping. She had never failed to bring in her target, one way or another.

"Plus, we are coming back with more knowledge. You will find him," Nikkos said, his words warm.

Kyra allowed herself a small smile while her back was to them. They may turn out to be a great team.

"Okay, let's start sweeping the grounds. Keep your eyes open for any signs of our 'little' friend," Kyra said, returning her tone to neutral.

* * * *

For the rest of the morning, the team went about their tasks. Nikkos rejoined Anna to wrap the bones for departure. His foot had barely landed on the first step when he heard the quarrelsome tones from above. His pace quickened. He was sure someone had picked a fight with Anna, and his urge to protect her was strong. Cresting the stairs in a few bounds, he was surprised to see Anna quietly moving bones. Soro's lips were pursed in a thin, white line. Aieta was throwing her hands up in the air in frustration as Soro pointed to a deeply carved symbol on the makeshift altar.

"I know it doesn't fit with the others. I would like to remind you that Supernatural Species has the most extensive amount of information on Imp rituals." Soro crossed his arms.

"While that may be true, I'd like to point out that my knowledge comes from actually handling the artifacts and seeing the things firsthand—not just pictures in books." Her body was taut and on the defensive.

"You would not have the opportunity to be hands-on with the artifacts if people from my department and Anthropology did not go out and bring them in to you," Soro's voice rose.

Anna stepped further away from them, pressing herself against the farthest wall in an apparent attempt to disappear.

Taking a deep breath, Nikkos spoke up.

"We seem to have come across a bit of a rough patch here. For the sake of the project, let's just assume that you both have an excessive amount of knowledge about the Imps. I know all about the interdepartmental tensions at work here; however, I'm going to suggest you learn to respect each other and share on an academic level, or I'm going to have to go get Kyra. I have this strange feelings she won't be nearly as nice as I am," he said letting out a whoosh of breath.

Anna's eyes widened, and a soft smile came to her lips.

Aieta regarded Nikkos, her eyes narrowing before a sigh escaped. Giving a curt nod in supplication to his request, she turned her back on Soro and began logging symbols, again.

* * * *

At the stroke of noon, Kyra's team reassembled. With Nyles behind her, they made their way to the servants' quarters. Just as they rounded the corner, she saw it. Kyra studied it in the light. She had been close on the height, although on hind legs, it was closer to eight feet tall. The fur appeared to be luxurious and soft, its multi-hued blue and green tone stunning. She drew the conclusion that the animal most resembled an anteater or giant sloth. It turned, sensing their presence. Two dark, matted patches of fur on his chest were now visible. Dropping down to all fours, it looked at Kyra. Her eyes locked with its feral, yellow ones. She felt drawn in, as if she was moving closer. Yet, she remained still.

A few moments later, a voice in her head spoke, "*I am Ocalli. This land is mine. You will leave.*" The husky, male tone sent a shiver through her body.

Kyra's mouth opened to reply. Before she could respond, he lay against the ground. Before their astonished eyes, he seemed to melt into the underbrush.

It took her a moment to compose herself before turning to Nyles.

"He spoke to me," she murmured.

"Telepathy?"

"Yes, he said his name is Ocalli, and that this land is his, and we should leave," she said.

"Well, that was short and to the point. I'm going to take a moment to sketch him before my memory fades. I can now say for certain that I have never seen anything like him before." Nyles pulled his sketch pad from the satchel.

The other teams were making their way toward the meeting point. None of them had seen Ocalli, but they seemed to know instantly something was wrong by the deep frown on Kyra's face.

She quickly ushered everyone inside, locking the dead bolt securely behind them. Without a word of explanation, she fled to the bathroom, shutting the door behind her. Everyone turned to Nyles for explanation. He shook his head no and continued working on his sketch.

A few moments later, Kyra emerged. Her face was serene and under control. She went to the front of the group.

"I just had an encounter with our creature. His name is Ocalli. He has the power of telepathy. He informed me that this land was his, and we should leave. Then, he lay down and melted into the ground. Nyles drew a sketch of him, which he will now pass around. The closest comparison I can draw is a giant sloth or anteater," she added as everyone viewed the sketch.

Soro took an extra long look. "I cannot say I recognize it off the top of my head; however, I have a feeling that it is a documented species, as something is tugging at the back of my mind. I'll be able to tell you more after we get back to the archives."

"We are leaving, which should make him happy. At least until we get back." Kyra waited until after everyone had finished looking at the sketch before she spoke again, "We should be gone long enough to put him at ease. That might improve our next encounter. Let's get this show on the road. We have a lot of moving and transporting. Then, that wonderfully long train ride back home."

Nikkos pulled Kyra aside while they were assembling sandwiches to explain what had gone on in the attic. Her eyebrows knit. Given how chummy they had been on the train, she was surprised by the tiff; however, Nikkos was right. The frustrations between those two departments could run quite hot.

As they ate, Kyra listened intently to everyone's brief updates. Wiping crumbs off her shirt, she spoke, "We are well ahead of schedule. If everyone can be finished by two, I'd like to divert to the third floor, so that we can start the transfer of the bones and relics. After that is accomplished, we will see what is left to be done to pack up for our return trip."

Everyone finished eating and headed back to their tasks. On the dot of two, most of them met in the foyer and headed to the third floor. Immediately apparent was the absence of Maria and Maltruis. They had been clearing the last of the outbuildings.

Kyra let out an audible sigh. She was anxious to be ready to get the delicate stuff moved, as it was the easiest possible time for something to go wrong. Directing the others to start the setup, she ventured out the front door. A few feet from the door, the blueprints were stretched out, a pair of rocks holding them down. She scanned the dense forest, figuring it should be fairly easy to spot Maltruis. Nothing.

"Nikkos," she called.

Moving quickly, he appeared at her side.

"Hey, take a walk with me. I want to find our missing pair." The corners of her mouth turned down, her hand sliding to her gun.

Holding up one finger, he ducked back in and swiftly returned with his medical pack. Gun drawn, Kyra stalked silently with Nikkos doing his best to step where she had stepped. Tilting her head to the side, she closed her eyes and allowed her hearing to take over. Insects buzzed, birds chirped, and small animals rustled in the dense undergrowth. Focusing, she strained to hear anything that might give away the pair's location. Nothing.

"Damn." Opening her eyes, she took a deep breath to call out. A deep, rumbling curse cut her off.

In an instant, she was moving toward the sound, her feet a blur. Grabbing the handle of the smoke house door, she grunted under her breath as a splinter dug into her skin. Searing pain ignored, she yanked the door open. The warm sunlight at her back gave her a view of the scene before her.

Maria cowered in the deepest corner, only her arm visible around the hulking form of the pitchfork-wielding Maltruis. Kyra's eyes narrowed as they fell on the violet-skinned Fae whose small wings were fluttering rapidly.

The Fae looked at Kyra, and her eyes widened before they narrowed, and she spat on the ground. "Abomination," she said.

Kyra rolled her eyes. This girl was young. In human terms, she would be considered a child, ten or so. Yet, she was already so full of prejudice.

Lowering her gun, Kyra spoke, "Maltruis, put the weapon down. There is no reason for anyone to get hurt here. I'm sure we can all talk this out," her words were choked out. Her anger at the girl's hateful look raged warm through her veins.

His eyebrows rose nearly to his hairline. His mouth fell slightly agape at the suggestion of disarming himself in the presence of one of the most dangerous species in the supernatural world.

Maria moved out of hiding. Placing her hand on his arm, she gave a curt nod of approval. He slowly laid his weapon down, balling up his fists just in case.

"Now that we are all a bit calmer, perhaps we can talk," Kyra said, holstering her gun to show her intent.

The Fae let out a low growl. She looked between Kyra, Nikkos, Maria, and Maltruis. It looked like her hatred of the abomination was overcome by the logistics of being outnumbered. Frustration filled her voice, and she emitted

Sciath

an ear-piercing shriek. Her wings pumped, and with one swift moment, she moved toward the door. She raked her long, silver nails down Kyra's arm as she exited.

The white hot pain blinded Kyra, her eyes instantly swimming with tears. An arm slipped around her waist to stead her. Gentle fingers cooled the wound, and her vision began to clear.

Turning to leave, she was faced with the rest of her team. They probably had responded to the Fae's angry shriek. Kyra saw them clearly in the sunlight. For just a moment, the light became brighter. She attempted to lift her arm to shield her eyes, but a violent shiver overtook her.

* * * *

Nyles made it to her just in time to keep her from hitting the ground.

Cradling her in his arms, Nyles set off for the servants' quarters at a gallop, looking back only to make sure Nikkos was coming. Glancing down at her pale face, he was terrified by the serenity of her expression. Thick, dark blood oozed from the jagged cuts. His fear was not the wound but the magic or poison involved.

After laying her gently on his sleeping pallet in the main room, he knelt as gently as he could beside her.

Nikkos appeared at their side. Crouching down on his heels, he put his hands over the wound. His brow scrunched in concentration. The others crowded outside the door, obviously wanting to help but unwilling to infringe on Nikkos's healing talents.

Sitting back, beads of sweat formed on Nikkos's upper lip. "Her vitals are strong. I believe it to be a poison they use to stun. Its effects should wear off in a few hours, but she will be weak after that."

Nyles took a deep breath, letting it out slowly. "It's up to us to have everything ready and on the train. Nikkos, I want you to stay here with her while we get everything loaded up and ready. Hit me on the radio if anything changes," Nyles said, slipping into the leadership role.

Nyles created an assembly line, and the group worked quickly. The artifacts and bones were moved carefully to a tarp spread out by the gate. It took them over an hour to get everything moved and situated. The next two hours were spent going through the house, securing all windows, and taking pictures of everything they had found. Nyles made several radio check-ins with Nikkos, positioning the team at the gate before going to collect Kyra. Wrapping her gently in his blanket, his heart soared to see some color returning to her face.

Nyles inspected the driver as he stepped out of the truck. It would be rather difficult to explain to a Gilly driver why they were loading bag after bag of bones from the local spook house, not to mention the Centaur and the orange-skinned Dwarf; however, as he got closer, he noticed small differences in his build and features. Someone who wasn't well versed in Elves might have missed them. The driver gave a broad smile and a bob of his head as he moved to the back of the truck. He lowered the gate, and they all loaded the cargo. The bed of the truck was lined with bubble wrap. Lev never missed a trick.

Nyles lay Kyra in the front cabin of the truck and began directing the team.

By seven, they were all loaded and in the transport, on their way to the train depot. The team was silent—most likely lost in the events that had unfolded.

* * * *

Kyra stirred as she felt the truck pull onto pavement. She was vaguely aware of it being a welcome difference from the jouncing and bouncing of the previous couple miles.

Kyra's eyes fluttered open as Nyles set her gingerly in her seat on the train. "Where, what?" she asked

Moving her arm to sit up, a jolt of pain brought the confrontation with the Fae leaping back into her mind. She looked down, noting the thick, white bandage on her arm.

"We are back on the train, everything is loaded, and everyone is aboard," Nyles said as he settled in his spot.

Kyra managed a weak smile to reassure the faces of her team as they bustled by her.

She closed her eyes and listened to the sounds around her. The rocking of the train was a soothing motion. The chant of the wheels churning lulled her into a restful sleep.

* * * *

Nyles watched her fall asleep. He was proud of her, and he knew the Architect would be as well. She had handled far more than had been expected, been injured protecting her team, yet still managed to bring everyone back safe and sound. She was going to make an amazing leader. *She'd make an amazing wife, too.* He looked away, denying himself any further thoughts on the matter.

* * * *

Several seats back, Anna and Nikkos sat side-by-side. With great care, he removed the bandage from her hand. The healing was coming along well. It was still a nasty cut; however, there was no sign of infection, Nikkos noted with satisfaction. Applying more salve, he rewrapped it, his touch more of a caress.

* * * *

Anna smiled at Nikkos, though she was far from happy. She hadn't failed her mission *per se*. She had gotten in close, gotten the team to trust her. Proven to Kyra that she was needed and useful. She had no doubt Jason arranged for those boys to end up on the property. What she had not counted on was caring for the team and enjoying being a part of something where no one expected anything from her but to use her gift if needed.

She had easily forgotten the reason for her being there and that this was all supposed to be a ruse. Her shoulders slumped with the weight of her assignment from her boss. She'd have to bluff Jason. After all, she had the second half of the mission to get the information he needed. Her mind dallied with the idea of turning Jason in. Going to the Architect and telling him how Jason had spies in other departments. That Jason had been trying to teach himself social magic. He also had wanted Anna to slip into Kyra's mind to see what she knew about the succession.

She shook her head slightly. In order to get them to believe her, she would have to confess to some of the other things Jason made her do in the past. Those transgressions were more than enough to get her booted from Scíath. She couldn't expose him without hurting herself. He counted on that, and she knew it.

* * * *

Nikkos saw Anna close her eyes. He watched her as she slipped off into sleep. Laying his own head back, he meditated on the last two days.

It seemed so much longer. More like a week than just two days, but in those two days, so much had happened. Not only on the mission itself, but in his personal life.

He spent all of his time learning medicine. Supernatural medicine was immensely more involved than human medicine. He worked very hard to earn his place in his class, giving him little free time. This mission had proven to be a wonderful break from routine. He had not been outside Scíath in at least a year. Being in nature again had been pleasant, but the most welcome part had been Anna. He had thought her beautiful upon first sight but dismissed her as miles out of his league.

He'd heard Aieta and Soro gossiping about her and decided it was best to stay away. Then, she had needed him, and after administering aid, she had been truly grateful. He knew it was very difficult for her to show weakness. Yet, two injuries in a short period of time had made her vulnerable. He had not exploited it. He just helped her, and he could see in her eyes and her smile that it meant a lot to her. That smile had gotten more genuine since he helped her. *Could she care for me?* He was more than hopeful but not naive. Time would tell the tale...this little break in the trip would show her colors. Would she still be warm toward him back in Scíath, or was this friendship circumstantial?

He stole another longing look at her serene face before closing his eyes and enjoying a bit of rest.

* * * *

Quiet reigned over the passenger car before a passing train whistle wrenched Kyra from her peaceful repose. Her watch showed three hours had passed ,and she uttered an audible groan, rousing those around her. The effects were nearly worn off, and she knew it was time to get back to business. Standing, she stretched stiff muscles that protested her use of them. In the bathroom, she splashed water on her face. She hadn't intended on sleeping that long. It wasn't as if they didn't have plenty of time to do what needed to be done—she just disliked breaking her own schedule. Exiting the restroom, she saw the others waking and a few waiting to make us of the bathroom.

At her seat, Nyles was waiting with a chilled can of soda. Opening it, she smiled gratefully at him as she downed the caffeinated drink. She waited while everyone went about waking up, taking a drink and a snack before she spoke.

"I'm glad everyone is well rested, but now, it's back to work. We are first going to do a mini debriefing. After that, we are going to put together our objectives for our time at home base and what we need to know before we head back to finish the job, by catching the creature, hunting for more clues about who the second race was, and now, I think we should check out the local Fae," she added, her fingers running over the bandage.

"I want to thank Nikkos and Nyles for taking care of me and all of you for keeping to the plan while I was indisposed."

Various members moved to get a notebook and pen.

"Right. Debrief, first. Obviously, you will each have to do a report for the file after we finish the mission. Your department heads will debrief you for that. I will go first. My impression of this mission was that it was a rollercoaster. We went in with a simple directive and came out with answers that only spawned more questions. Once we are completely finished, process all of the possible information, and have more answers, I can then determine if the mission was a success." Kyra punctuated her final statement with a large gulp of soda.

Nyles hesitated and frowned. "My impressions are such. We have walked into a quandary. I will be very interested to collect information on our furry friend. I wish also to determine what race was staying with the Imps. Further, I'll see if we need to change some of the long-standing anthropological beliefs about Imps and the War." He finished confidently and with conviction in his tone.

Maria was next. "I'm going to speak for Maltruis and myself, at his request. I fully expected to come on this mission, only to check some load bearing walls, determine structure stability, and then be finished. I had no idea that we would be involved in the team in such a full way. We are thankful for the ability to be a part of this and thank everyone for their openness and acceptance. I am curious as to why the third floor was not included on the original blueprints of the house. I could have done without our encounter with the Fae; however, I am glad to be able to say I have seen one and lived.

Kyra nodded her appreciation.

Skipping over Maltruis, Aieta was next.

"I will admit the pure, academic joy I experienced logging those artifacts. Having the chance to study them makes me giddy." Her eyes darted to Soro before she continued. Also, being on the forefront of a discovery such as we may have on our hands is an incredible opportunity. I feel that once we wrap this mission, I will be able to give a complete list of what I discovered—its meaning and so forth."

"Fair enough. I look forward to reading about the artifacts," Kyra added.

Soro cleared his throat before he began, "I have felt elation, academic interest, camaraderie, and flat-out fear. I shot a gun for the first time. I have learned many things from our leader and from my teammates. I am hoping to work with Aieta, once this is over, on the artifacts. Perhaps, we can get an idea about the second race that inhabited that house. Plus, I think our departments could benefit from more friendships. We could learn from each other."

"I will take that idea to the Architect," Kyra said.

All eyes turned to the next to speak. It was Anna. She returned their gazes with serene calm.

"This was my first field assignment. Normally, I go in when memories need to be fixed, and then, I leave. This mission has taught me several things about myself. One, that I have a weak stomach. Two, that I enjoy working with a team—especially one so skilled and well-chosen. Three, that much like Nikkos, I always hope my skills won't be needed, but am glad when I can help. I'm very interested in identifying those bodies and also hope for more cross-department projects after this is over. I want to give families closure on the loss of their loved ones—Gilly or one of us. I hope that you will keep me in mind for future missions and know that if you ever need anything from Gilly Relations, you can come straight to me." Her fingers rested over her bandage.

"Thank you for that offer. It makes me feel good to know that you are passionate about taking those bodies home. I know the assignment will be in excellent hands." Kyra found it harder and harder not to feel like Anna was a part of the team.

Nikkos sat up, a pleased expression on his face. "I'm not even sure where to start. The discovery of those remains was shocking. I pledge to take lead of the forensics on the bones to help them get home. I feel the team is meshing well. I've made new friends that I never would have otherwise. I've field tested my skills and gotten to show off my love of cooking."

He slid a sideways smile at Anna. "Like all the rest of us, I'm curious to see what comes of the evidence of another group in with the Imps. It is possible that things we have always been told and taught about the Imp culture may prove to be untrue or have been influenced and assisted by another group."

"Now, we shall cover our objectives and estimate the time period it will take, so we can figure out how much time before we can set back out, again." Kyra pulled out her notebook and pen. It was easy to see they were glossing over the tiffs, the slip ups, and the mishaps. She let it slide, this time.

"First off, we will need to make sure all artifacts, bones, and samples are taken to the appropriate places. I want to keep the chain of custody as small as possible. We are not going to have time to start on the bones before we need to go back out. Nikkos, I would like you to have Leland start those with a select team. Next, we will need to get the samples of the creature's blood analyzed as soon as possible. Nikkos, if you could personally see to that as well, I would be appreciative." Kyra scribbled notes as she went.

Nikkos said, "I can see to all of that. I don't expect Leland will have a problem with your requests, since the remains came from an Imp hive. He will want them sealed off until we are positive they are safe. I assume, barring no complications, I should be able to get all of this done within forty-eight hours."

"Excellent." Kyra looked to Soro. "Next. Soro, would you and Nyles collaborate on our furry friend? Put together a list of possible races that fit the broad criteria we currently have. It will make it easier as we find out other things that might narrow it down."

"Sounds like a good plan to me. We should also be able to meet the forty-eight hour mark," Nyles said as Soro nodded his agreement.

"Maria and Maltruis, you already know what I need from you. Find out why the blueprints were altered, and if so, why." Kyra was glad that Maria brought up the difference.

"Will do. Put us down for forty-eight hours as well," Maria said.

"Well then, with everyone falling into the same time frame, it is now Tuesday, so we should have a meeting Thursday afternoon, say 2:00 p.m. Same place as before. We can assess everyone's progress, share our findings, and decide our departure time. Does anyone else have any other questions or concerns they wish to bring up?" Kyra asked.

Surprisingly, Anna raised her hand.

"Yes?" Kyra replied.

"Can we have our Thursday meeting in the dining hall? We can reserve it, because I'm curious to see what Nikkos can do," she asked with a broad smile.

Kyra laughed, as did everyone else. "If no one has any objections to that, I'm fine with it."

No one objected.

"Then, our meeting is moved." Kyra checked her watch.

"We have roughly five hours left on this trip. I have nothing else for you. So, feel free to enjoy this bit of the trip. We have quite a bit of work ahead of us." Kyra made her way back to her seat.

The group broke up with people moving back to their seats, and murmured conversations began.

Kyra waited until Nyles was settled across from her before she turned to speak to him, "This was a rough first mission. It had just about everything you could want in your first adventure. Unknown creatures, conspiracy, distrusted teammates coming together to get the job done. Surprise Fae visits." Kyra gave a wry smile.

Nyles returned her smile.

"When we get back, after I make sure all the tasks are in motion, I'm going to go run our finds past Father. I'm sure he will have some insight into this." Kyra scanned her notes.

Nyles's brow furrowed. "Kyra, I want to ask you something," he said. His tone was so low, she had to lean in to be able to hear him.

"Sure, what's up?" Assuming he didn't want this conversation to carry, her tone matched his.

"This whole succession thing...how are you dealing with it?" he asked.

Kyra frowned. Considering everything that had been going on with the mission, she had actually not given it any serious thought since they left the train.

Nyles looked apologetic; however, he did not withdraw the question.

"There really isn't anything to deal with. If Father asks me to help him look through the candidates, then I will." She shrugged, her tone making it clear she had no intention of speaking on it further.

She sat back in her seat and closed her eyes, punctuating that she was done talking.

As they pulled into the London station, Kyra could tell that the night was cold. Pulling her trench coat close around her, she exited the train with everyone else. Within an hour, the trucks were loaded, and they were headed home. Given that it was well after midnight when they returned, the halls were nearly empty. The unload was quick and easy. Kyra accompanied the artifacts and bones to their destination. Once everything was settled, it was very close to 5:00 a.m.

As many were getting up to start their day, Kyra's team was just settling in for a few hours of sleep before the hard work began.

Kyra awoke at 8:00 a.m.—her internal alarm unable to sleep in, as her mind knew there was too much work to be done. After showering and dressing, she made her way to the Architect's study. Knocking gently, she then listened for a response.

"Come in," he said.

He sounded tired. "Hello, Father," she said with a smile. "Hello, dear. Your load in didn't finish until nearly five in the morning. I'm surprised to see you up so early." He settled in his big desk chair.

"Even in your sleep, you never miss anything that goes on around here." She sat in the chair across the desk.

"So, this early return with a departure set in forty-eight hours. I bet you have a whopper of a story to tell me," he said, packing his pipe.

"Do I ever. I'm not even sure where to begin."

"Well, start at the beginning, and when you come to the end, stop. See?" he said with his best Mad Hatter grin.

"So helpful you are." She stuck her tongue out.

"Well, the beginning would be the trainride to the site. Not even an hour in, Anna picked a fight with Nyles. Then, Soro and Aieta gossiped about Anna. Anna then got some kind of disturbing news. Not overly interesting; however, everything that follows is." For the next hour and a half, she laid out everything that had happened, everything they had found, and her own suspicions. Ending it with her own injury, she noticed the smoke from his pipe pouring out faster as she spoke of the attack. When she finished, she sat back in the chair, feeling drained.

Picking up his phone, he ordered breakfast. "First, I have to say I'm proud of you. You fared far better in these circumstances than I think anyone else could have. Second, I am deeply concerned by the things you found. Third, I had no idea there were native Fae, or you would not have been going."

She fought a snarky retort. She had tracked things just as dangerous as a Childling Fae on her own. Yet, she kept silent to listen.

"During and after the war, there were many conspiracy theorists who said the Imps had to have help. Imps were not smart enough to organize the entire thing on their own. Many ideas were thrown out, names were named, and slander and political bickering were ripe; however, no proof was ever found that would decide the truth. You have discovered that proof. Now, we just have to decipher it. I'm sure you stressed the need for secrecy to the team."

"I did, and for the most part, I am sure they will keep it." She mulled over the gravity of what had just been said.

"For the most part?"

"Well, I still can't decide about Anna. Her icy demeanor melted some over the trip. She did her job with those kids and worked just as hard as the rest.

Still, she works for Jason, and I simply can't overlook that," Kyra said.

"I understand and respect that. I do hope, however, that she is loyal to the team. A leak on this could create a rather large headache. Now, about this friend of yours. Telepathy is a rare gift, but to be honest, from the description, it's not ringing a bell. Hybrid or genetic experiment is more than possible—it's probable."

Kyra said, "Soro and Nyles are working on that as well as getting a broad list of creatures who best fit the criteria of the beast."

"Given what you have to work with, I think that's an excellent plan. Forgive me, but I'm still shocked. I had my own idea that the Imps were helped, but I never had anything to prove it. After you clear the safe house, I think you and I should head out to the prison to speak with Cobbwick," he said.

Kyra's jaw dropped. "The leader of the Imp nation is still alive?" she asked, clearly disbelieving.

"He is. Imps can live for several hundred years, and Cobbwick was barely fifty when the war began."

Kyra moved past her shock. "Do you think he will talk to us?"

"I think he can be persuaded. Prison is a miserable place, and the offer of a few creature comforts might go over huge with him."

"Bribe him? Well, if it works, it could shed light on a number of things," she conceded.

"Indeed. How long do you think you need to finish out the house?"

"We are going back to try to trap the creature. We'll hunt for all the clues we can and bag up the lab. Also, make sure we didn't miss anything the first time around." She paused. "Several times while we were there, I felt something tugging at my mind, something that seemed to try to be getting me to come to it, to remember it. I can't identify it or explain it, but those woods felt oddly familiar to me."

A knock at the door announced breakfast. Kyra rolled the cart in. On it sat a large bowl of fruit and a pot of coffee. She served them both.

Thoughtfully, he said, "Well, it could be that the place itself is imbued with magic, or perhaps, it's part of your past. Perhaps, it was something the creature did to lure you away from the group, either to attack you or speak to you."

"Those are all viable options." She munched her fruit.

"I'll note if it happens again to see if it's drawing me to the same spot or to the creature." She put down her bowl of fruit. "I'm going to head out to check on the rest of the team and their projects." She mulled over all the information he had given here before standing. "Mind if I stop back in for dinner?"

"Not at all. I look forward to hearing an update on everything."

"Let's say six. Turn your radio back on to the same frequency as before, and please, don't sit on it."

He grinned back as she headed out the door.

Kyra stopped. She needed to decide what to hit first. Every project was of the same priority, so she might as well hit them geographically. Artifacts were the closest. In the halls, everything was bustling. A few people said hello to her. She murmured back. *The problem with the public is all the people.*

At her destination, she slipped in her badge and waited for the light to give her the go pattern. The click sounded, and she made her way into the vault.

Inside seemed empty. Kyra was confused, until she noted Aieta and Moira heading toward her.

"Kyra, I'm glad to see you," Moira said as they approached. She explained to Kyra that she had given everyone the day off as to not compromise the security of the things that had come in. Work tables were cleared, a tarp laid down, and the items laid out. Each table had a clipboard for notes as the artifacts were examined. "Aieta told me what went on during your mission. My goodness! Sounds like quite the adventure. I have to say that I am envious. The mantle of responsibility keeps me from a good time, it seems."

Kyra returned the smile. "It was a rollercoaster. I'll tell you that. I must take this opportunity to say that Aieta was an incredible asset on my team."

Moira nodded. "I had no doubt she was the best to send."

Aieta beamed.

"Now, I want to talk to you about the things here," her tone turned serious. "The Imp artifacts encompass about three-fourths of what we have; however, some of these idols and some of the drawings on the floor are not common Imp artifacts."

Kyra opened her mouth to reply.

Moira put up a hand. "Before you ask me about where the other things belong, I'm going to tell you that I don't know. I've looked through my catalogues. I've search Simon. We are dealing with something truly foreign."

Kyra's brow furrowed deeply. "Why can nothing be easy?" She sighed. "I heard about your creature as well. It seems this whole thing is a mystery."

"I had hoped we would come back here, punch our items into Simon, and be greeted with a printout of answers," Kyra said.

"The best I can do is see if I can get a religious affiliation and the age of the pieces. To see if the markings resemble anything else we have," Aieta said.

"That's a start. We may be pushing off our deadline. It makes little sense to go back with no more answers than we arrived with," Kyra said.

"Check back in tomorrow. We can better evaluate what we have then," Moira said.

"Will do." Kyra made her way out the door.

Damn. Hopefully, Leland and Nikkos had more uplifting news. Making her way toward Medical, she reluctantly became aware that the scowl on her face was frightening others around her.

Her mood did not improve, as she was forced to go through sterilization not once but twice. As soon as she was cleared, she was escorted to the forensic wing. She was surprised to see a member of Security posted at the door to the lab. He simply nodded as she passed. Apparently, she was allowed in.

Entering the autopsy lab, her nose wrinkled at the overwhelming smell of chemicals. All the tables had been wheeled into the same lab. Eight shiny tables stretched the length of the room, each holding a set of bones. A white-coated individual stood over each table, trying to put the bones back into a complete skeleton.

Nikkos and Leland stood in conference at the far end of the room. Kyra made her way to them.

Leland looked up from his clipboard. "Ah, Kyra. A pleasure to see you."

"Thank you, Leland. I must say it seems to me that you've spared nothing in getting this discovery set up and protected."

"I understand the gravity of this find. I wish to get identifications handled as quickly as possible," Leland said.

"Can you tell how they died?" she asked.

"None have any obvious signs of trauma that we have found, yet. We are going to do some bone marrow extractions to search for poisons; however, it's possible that they had their throats slit or died from a wound to the fleshy part of their bodies. I can tell you this. They were boiled clean. None of them were left to decay," he explained.

Kyra's nose wrinkled at the thought of boiling flesh. Nikkos nodded in agreement at her facial expression.

Leland continued on, oblivious to the disgust of those around him. "This could have been done for several purposes. It might have been part of the ritual, to deter identification, or to avoid smell for storage if they were used more than one time."

Nikkos said, "Until we know who was responsible for this, we won't be able to guess why the remains were treated this way; however, the year of death, age, and race should be possible. This means we can try to match the bones up with missing person reports—both Gilly and ours.

"I know we were hoping for some immediate information from the bones, but due to the shear amount of bones and different tests we need to run, we are looking at more like two weeks than two days," Nikkos added.

Kyra scowled, and both men drew back. Noticing their reactions, she sighed. "Forgive me, gentlemen. I just got a similar report from Aieta and Moira. I was hoping for something to lighten that blow."

"I am sorry," Nikkos said.

"I'd prefer it was done right instead of fast. Never apologize for doing the right thing." As she turned to leave, she paused and turned back.

"Leland, would you mind terribly if I appointed Anna liaison on this project? She worked with Nikkos on the scene and will be able to help." Kyra saw Nikkos's face light up.

"Not at all. I appreciate the help." Leland was completely unaware of Nikkos's look.

"I'll let her know. I'm headed there, now." Kyra was out the door and through decontamination.

Damn, damn, damn. It was looking less and less likely that they would be ready to go back in two days. At least, not ready to go back prepared. On her mental list was to pop in and check on Anna's missing persons data from the towns around the house. Talk to Maria, then Soro, and finally, Nyles. *They couldn't all be bad news, could they?*

Stepping into the Gilly Relations office, she stopped. No doubt it had been at least two years since she had set foot in this place. It had been a dull, unremarkable office. Seems Jason had made a number of changes since then. The floors were marble, the walls were a deep burgundy color, and several large ferns dotted the office. A polished woman sat behind a glass top desk. She looked up as Kyra entered.

"May I help you, Miss Kyra?"

"I need to see Anna," she replied, mirroring the woman's icy tone.

"I will send her a message, if you will be kind enough to wait."

She tapped her perfectly manicured nails on the computer's keyboard.

Kyra simply nodded. Wandering over, she admired the landscape pictures hung on the walls. After a few minutes, the door to the right of the reception desk opened. Anna wore a sharp, gray suit with her long hair bound up into a bun. She looked stark and professional; however, when she saw Kyra, she smiled.

"Hello, Kyr—er Miss Kyra." She shot a look at the receptionist who pretended not to be listening but obviously was.

"Anna, so good of you to see me without an appointment." Kyra was going to enjoy giving this receptionist something to gossip about.

"What can I help you with?" Anna asked.

"I am going to be putting in a request to have you lent to the Medical Department so that you may assist with the project you started in the field. If you wish to, of course. Given the high security of our project, I wanted to clear it with you, first. Plus, it will take you away from your department responsibilities for an extended period." Kyra watched the secretary lap up every word. Leaning in, she lowered her voice.

"Since you are such a major part of our startling discoveries."

"I would love to be a part of that," Anna said, her tone sincere.

"Excellent. I will be scheduling a meeting tomorrow at 9:00 a.m. Can you make it?"

"I can," Anna replied.

"I thank you for your time. Expect the transfer request early this afternoon." Kyra gave her a rare smile. This conversation was watercooler fuel for a month.

Kyra had intended on asking her about the data she had compiled, but she didn't want to give away too much. Moving down and around the winding halls toward transportation, Kyra felt as if she was being watched, perhaps followed. She stopped dead, causing a few people behind her to swerve to avoid running into her. Upon hearing several unkind words, she kept moving, but the feeling never wavered.

On high alert, Kyra had to suppress the urge to pull her weapon. She upped her speed. If she could make it to Lev's office, she could see who was following her. She weaved in and out of the pedestrian traffic, glancing behind her impulsively.

Taking a deep breath, she worked to bring her anxiety level down. She was almost there. Just one more turn and a side hall. If whoever had the audacity to tail her followed her that far, a confrontation could be had. Rounding the corner, she felt the eyes drilling into her skull. Someone was definitely tracking her, and their purpose was intense.

She reached the hall entrance. Whirling around, she prepared to come face-to-face with whoever was tailing her. To her surprise, no one had stepped down the short side hall. Sticking her head back out in the main hall, she searched for the perpetrator, but no one stood out, and the feeling was gone.

She leaned back against the cool, stone wall, allowing its solidarity to wash over her calming her panic. She exhaled loudly. *Ridiculous. Afraid in my own home.* Standing straight, she brushed the nonexistent dust from her clothing, squared her shoulders, and entered Transportation like nothing had ever happened.

Several people looked up as she entered. This department was in full swing. She was unable to spot Maria's small form or the hulking form of Maltruis. Making her way all the way to the back of the department, she heard Maria's voice coming from within.

Kyra slowed her pace to hear what was being said.

"I'm telling you, Lev, something is funny here. The third story was obviously an original part of the house. Why was it not on the blueprints? This was a house the Imps took over. We must research the origins of this house, who built it, and who lived in it. Something does not add up," Maria said.

Kyra stuck her head in the door as she gently knocked. Maria stood beside the desk with the blueprint unrolled on the desk. Maltruis hulked against the wall. He raised an eyebrow when he saw Kyra. She assumed it was a form of acknowledgement, as she had seen Lev do it several times.

"Hello, all. Sorry to intrude, but I'm going around the departments to see how each of the team members are doing." She waited to be invited in before entering the room.

"Perfect timing, Kyra." Maria motioned her toward the empty seat.

Kyra settled across the desk and near the familiar blueprints.

"I was just explaining to Lev what we found and the variations from the blueprints. Not only is the third floor not listed on the original blueprints, but there are no blueprints for the outbuildings. Even if they were added after the original structure was built, there should still be blueprints or, at the very least, a buildings permit, but there is absolutely nothing. I'm going to research who had it built and the occupancy records. It's just too odd to be a coincidence," Maria said.

"I agree. I'm having a briefing tomorrow at 9:00 a.m. Our original deadline is looking unrealistic thus far. We are going to catch everyone up and make some decisions," Kyra replied.

"We will be there," Maria said.

"Thank you. Lev, both of your agents were exemplary in the field. I thank you once again for your suggestions," Kyra added.

"Good people, agreed," Lev responded.

"I hate to talk and run, but I am on my way to see Soro and Nyles." Kyra stood up. "I look forward to your report," she added as a goodbye.

Much less progress than she had hoped for; however, it wasn't as bad as some of the others. She paused as she made her way to the end of the short hall. The main hall was less crowded but still busy. Part of her wanted to stay in the quiet, little nook—safe and in control. She knew, however, that she had to plunge into the hall and take the chance that whoever had been watching her before was waiting to do so, again. With a deep breath, she made her way out as if nothing was wrong. She made her way toward Supernatural Species with her head held high.

She was rewarded for her courage when no feeling assaulted her. She still walked a bit faster than she needed to. She had no desire to chance it.

While slipping her badge into the reader, the odd conversation she had with Di the last time she stood here crossed her mind. She tried to keep the succession from her mind. It was his right, but she was afraid that when he stepped down, she would lose the only home she had ever known.

Sciath

The unlocking of the door brought her back to the present, and she made her way in. The department seemed fully staffed, as usual. Looking around, she saw Soro sitting with Di at a back table with stacks of book around them. Kyra stood a respectful distance away until they noted her presence.

Without even lifting her head from the book, Di said, "Hello, Kyra."

Soro looked up with the same startled expression Kyra momentarily wore.

"Hello, Di. Soro. Looks like a research party." Kyra kept her expression neutral.

"You sent Soro back here with quite a project," Di commented.

"Indeed. Any ideas thus far?"

"Several ideas, though I have a massive amount of information to sift through, and—" Soro started.

"And you don't think that you are going to make the deadline," Kyra finished.

Soro replied, "I take it that is not the first time you have heard that, today."

"No, it seems that we all underestimated the time it would take to get back on the site," Kyra said. "I'm having a briefing at 9:00 a.m.—a chance to get everyone up to speed and reevaluate our plans."

"I can have a preliminary report with a few of my basic ideas ready by then," Soro replied.

"Good. I'm sending out a memo reminder with the room and all that. I'll see you, tomorrow," Kyra said. She turned to head out when Di's voice stopped her.

"Please tell the Architect that I would like to meet with him regarding the implications of some of the things discovered on the expedition," she said.

Normally, Kyra would have bristled at being used as a messenger when a Simon terminal could do the same job and probably faster; however, she had the feeling that this meeting was not one Di wanted on the internal system.

She nodded and left. Di masked it well, but Kyra sensed a deep concern in her tone. *I should swing by and give Father her message before heading to see Nyles.* She had no desire to traipse all the way back across Sciath—especially with her earlier experience. Moving just two doors down, she stuck her badge in, again. After the appropriate time, the door clicked open.

She was surprised to find the department completely empty. No sign of Nyles or Tinka—or anyone else, for that matter. Kyra frowned, moving further into the department cautiously. Dread filled her chest, and she stepped backward. Something was wrong here. She fled for the door, allowing it to slam closed. Making her way across the compound as fast as she could without running anyone over, she headed for her father's study.

Bursting through the door like a demon was on her heels, she met the surprised looks of Nyles, Tinka, and her father. Her face must have shown her fear as Nyles was instantly on his feet and moving to her.

"Kyra, darling. Whatever has scared you so?" Nyles asked, slipping his arm around her.

She laid her head on his chest, allowing the public display of affection as she tried to put together her thoughts. His soft sweater cushioned her cheek.

After a few moments, she pulled away and carefully closed the door behind her. Nyles guided her to a chair as her father expertly made her some chai.

She forced a smile. "I must look like a complete fool."

"I would never say fool. I know that if something spooked you that badly, it's definitely serious," her father replied.

She explained the feeling in the hall as well as the feeling in the deserted Anthro office.

"I've had this sensation in the back of my mind since we left the house. Like something is trying to talk to me or show me something. It's right on the edge of my mind." She surprised herself as she finally put the words to it.

Everyone was silent.

"Well, I can at least explain why Anthropology is empty," Tinka said.

"While you were away, one of our members returned from the Troll census with a case of Troll pox—highly contagious and very miserable. So, on Leland's orders, the whole department was closed. Several of our members are in the hospital wing, waiting out the seven-day course of medicine. Fortunately, I had Troll pox after completing a study on them years ago, so I am immune," she explained.

"Makes sense, though I must say that when deserted, Anthro is kinda creepy," Kyra replied.

Nyles laughed. "I've felt that way a few times, being the last to leave more than a few nights."

"That is why we came here to inform you that we couldn't comply with your request until Medical finished decontaminating our room," Tinka noted.

"You should probably run by Medical and get checked, since you entered the room. Though, I doubt you were in there long enough to be exposed," the Architect said.

"First, I need to send out a memo about tomorrow morning's briefing. There is no way we are going to be able to make our original departure plans. No one is going to be ready, and I'm not rushing back in there until we are better armed," Kyra said to Nyles.

The Architect stood. "Here, use my console." He moved to his armchair.

Kyra had her hands poised over the keys when the alarm sounded. The siren wailed through the halls of the compound, announcing a serious problem.

"What in the hell is going on?" The Architect jumped to his feet.

The siren's wail halted long enough for a mechanical voice to announce.

"Biohazard lockdown, full compound code blue," it said before the wail began, again.

"I can never recall the damn security colors. What in hell is a code blue?" Nyles asked.

"It's a full base lockdown. Everyone must stay where they are until the biohazard situation has been cleared," Kyra answered.

"Biohazard? Where would that come from? The only thing that has entered Scíath in the last twenty-four hours was..." The Architect looked from Kyra to Nyles. "Your team."

Kyra punched furiously at the buttons. "The lockdown originated in Medical. I need to get over there and find out if our bodies are the cause of all this." Kyra stood, not wanting to put the information about the bodies on the internal system given the security level.

"You're not supposed to leave," Nyles protested.

Kyra looked to her father before addressing Nyles, "You and Tinka, please stay here. I will be back soon."

Nyles threw a beseeching expression at the Architect as she walked out the door.

"I've never won against her, either," the Architect said. "If you want to protect her, you best hurry up."

Nyles nodded and rushed out the door behind her.

The halls were empty. A blue light flashed, giving everything a surreal look. Hurrying along, Kyra was about halfway to Medical when Nyles caught up with her. She simply nodded when he approached, as if she had expected him to join her.

Reaching the door to Medical, she saw that the situation was dire. The door was cracked open. She stepped cautiously into the decontamination chamber. Inside were bio suits. She slipped into one and helped Nyles affix a helmet and oxygen tank to his torso before heading into Medical itself. All the wards were closed off with steel doors. Kyra had a knot in her gut that said the answer to this emergency lay in forensics with the bodies they had brought in.

She headed straight for the stairs, as she knew the elevators would be shut down. Nyles followed noisily behind. When she came to the bottom, she found the door was tightly locked. No amount of shoving would make it open.

Kyra peered through the small, rectangular window. She saw groups of workers huddled together, but she saw no sign of Leland or Nikkos.

Nyles moved past her to examine the door. It was a simple push bar access, but the lockdown had frozen the bar in place. Without a word, he pushed her gently aside. Rearing up on his hind legs, he brought his front legs crashing down onto the bar. Sparks flew as metal met hoof, but when all was said and done, the door swung inward.

The group had moved away from the door at the sound of the crash, but they looked relieved to see Nyles. Kyra moved to a tallish med student who seemed to be comforting the rest.

"I'm Kyra. Where is Leland?" she asked.

"He's still in the main lab. We were all out here, suiting up to begin our shift with the remains, when the lockdown started. I haven't found a way to break the airlock doors that encompass forensics to check on them."

Whoever set off the alarm feared whatever it was even reaching the hallway. She looked through the lab doors. The blue light made the entire scene ten times creepier than it should have been. She could see the tables but no sign of life. Lifting her gloved fist, she pounded on the glass, hoping to get someone's attention.

Nothing. She turned away to speak to Nyles when the pounding on the other side caused her to jump. On the other side of the glass was the face of a very frightened Anna.

Kyra was shocked for a moment. Then, she recalled that she had asked Anna to help out here.

"Anna, can you hear me?" Kyra said loudly.

"Mostly," her response was muffled by the door and Kyra's bio suit.

"Good. Can you tell me what happened?" she asked.

"I was down here with Doctor Barker and Nikkos. We were logging in the skeletons. It was change of shift time, so it was just the three of us. Nikkos picked up the skull to show Doctor Barker. Some kind of strange crack or something. This green gas shot out, and they both hit the ground. I ran to the other side of the lab and hit the alarm. They appear to still be breathing, but I'm afraid to go over there." Tears ran down Anna's face.

"You did the right thing. Since you have not passed out, I think it's going to be safe to shut down the alarm, so we can get some medical attention to them," Kyra explained calmly.

Anna nodded.

"Walk over to the alarm box, open the box to the touchpad, and enter the numbers eight, two, nine, and five into the pad. It will ask you to confirm. Push the green button." Kyra kept her voice steady to avoid Anna panicking, again.

Anna walked over to the alarm box. It felt like an eternity to Kyra as she watched her punch in the security code and confirm it. All at once, the siren ceased, the lights returned to normal, and all the doors opened.

Kyra turned to the group of medical workers. "Go up and get a decontamination team down here, stat. We are dealing with a possible Imp toxin. Bring me whoever is Leland's second," she called after them.

Stepping cautiously into the lab, she searched for any evidence that the toxin was still airborne. Nyles went to Anna and began to calm her.

Anna had been right. They were still breathing, and their faces and coats were covered with a fine, green residue. Picking up a plastic bag, she careful slid the offending skull into the bag. The suit made it awkward. Her breath was fogging up her faceplate, but she was grateful for its protection.

The medical team soon showed, suited up, and set to the task of loading Nikkos and Leland onto gurneys. With precise skill, they decontaminated and cleaned up the biohazard remnants. Kyra felt a tap on her shoulder. Kyra whirled around and then had to look down to see a woman which, given Kyra's short stature, was uncommon.

"Miss Kyra?" she asked.

"I am," Kyra replied.

"Oh, good," she said with a smile. "You're the fourth bio suit I tried. Handy things, but they make finding people more difficult. I am Sabrina Monten, Leland's second-in-command."

"Good to meet you, although I wish it was under different circumstances. This could very well be an Imp toxin," Kyra said.

Sabrina's brow furrowed. "Let us head to my office. The team will take care of Anna."

Kyra motioned to Nyles. He turned a still shaken Anna over to the team and followed Kyra up the stairs. Once up on the main floor, Sabrina removed her helmet. She was of Indian decent. The bindi upon her forehead said that much. What supernatural race she was a part of was not apparent. She was no more than five feet tall. Her long hair was bound into intricate braids.

Kyra also removed her suit. She gulped fresh air as she was freed. Nyles slipped off his mask, also happy to be unencumbered.

"We can get rid of the rest of the gear in this bio room." Sabrina moved further down the hall. Kyra and Sabrina freed themselves from the tangle of fabric.

"My office is just down this way." She leaned over to speak to a young woman who sat behind it. "No one leaves Medical without my clearance. Lock the outer door, priority code one," she said in a hushed tone.

Kyra looked to Nyles, who raised an eyebrow.

A few moments later, they settled in a cozy office, its bookshelves crammed with medical books and a few pictures on the wall. Sabrina sat behind the desk, Kyra in a chair on the other side, while Nyles stood.

"I know Leland was working on a forensics project. It was secret. I had no idea it had anything to do with Imps. Those were not Imp skeletons on the tables."

"No. They were skeletons we found on an expedition to clear out a former Imp house to set it up as a safe house. They were found in the ritual area and believed to be part of a sacrifice. They were examined in the field, put aboard a lorry and a train, and then another lorry before they were unloaded here. I am surprised that whatever it was didn't go off before now," Kyra said.

Sabrina took a deep breath. "Because they are still breathing, it was not a killer toxin. That Anna was not affected tells me it was some kind of localized neurotoxin. It was probably planted to keep anyone from messing around with the sacrificial bones. We will know more once the lab tests come in; however, the rest of the bodies will have to be treated as a possible biohazard. They will all have to be irradiated and then examined in full bio gear," Sabrina explained.

Kyra sighed silently. It would add at least a week to the already two to three weeks she was looking at. "I'm not as concerned about the bone results as much as I care that Doc Barker and Nikkos are going to be all right."

"Fair enough. I'm going to call Galerius and let him know he can stand down. If you two will see the team on the way out, they will decontaminate you. I will get word to you as soon as I can about their conditions." Sabrina picked up her phone in an obvious dismissal.

Kyra and Nyles made their way out of the office.

"Why do I get the feeling she is less than pleased about the bones being here and her not knowing the details of them?" Kyra asked.

"I got that, too. She seemed more concerned about deadlines than the health of her boss and colleague," Nyles replied.

They ceased their conversation during the next fifteen minutes while being exposed to different colored lights. After swallowing two rather large tablets, they were released into the main hallway.

"I think we should go fill in your father and Tinka on what's going on," Nyles said.

Kyra nodded, and they made their way back to the study. Pausing to knock this time, she waited for his reply to enter before opening the door.

She was more surprised this time than she had been when she last burst in. Galerius sat beside Tinka at the desk. She had only seen him in this study once in her entire time at Scíath.

"Ahhh, Kyra, Nyles. I trust you will have some explanations for us," the Architect said.

"We do," Kyra said.

While sitting in the recliner, she explained the entire situation and what procedures were in place to deal with it.

Everyone sat in silence after her explanation, taking in the gravity of what could have been a colossal disaster.

The Architect broke the silence. "You handled that well. I am anxious to know the condition of our people. Please, keep me informed."

"Since we are all cleared to head back to our respective places, I'm going to go order some dinner." Tinka stood and stretched.

Kyra checked the clock. Time had flown—it was nearly five-thirty.

Galerius stood. "Kyra, please submit a report to me concerning what happened, today." He walked out without any further good-byes.

"Kyra, Nyles, will you join me for dinner?" the Architect asked.

They both nodded, knowing there were a number of things that needed to be discussed.

After Tinka left, Kyra lay back in her chair with an enormous sigh.

The Architect smiled. "I had a feeling that was coming."

"You should have seen her. Cool as a cucumber during the entire thing," Nyles said proudly.

"Without you and that logical thinking, we never would have gotten into the lab."

He grinned. "Sometimes, theses hooves come in handy."

The Architect grunted in agreement. "We all have our talents, even some we don't know we possess until we need them. Now, let us order up some dinner. We can put some thoughts down and do a bit of brainstorming. I have a feeling this safe house mission is turning into far more than any of us expected."

After dinner was ordered, everyone found a comfortable spot. The Architect packed his pipe while Kyra pulled out her binder and favorite red pen.

"I suggest we start at the beginning. This is going to require a fair amount of recall from you both, so be prepared," he said.

Kyra knew he was looking for specific facts, but he would never say them beforehand, as to not taint anything that might be remembered.

"When you first arrived on-site, remember how it felt. Was anything out of the ordinary?" he asked.

Kyra went back in her mind. Closing her eyes, she saw the scene in her mind. Nothing had felt odd, but wait...

"When we headed toward the gate, Soro stopped us. Then, he said it was nothing." Her eyes remained closed.

"He said later it was the same bluish green color he saw from our furry friend," Nyles added.

"Then, what did you do?"

"We set up camp and headed for the house," she replied.

"I will say that I found odd the lack of feelings or even remnants of energy forces from the size of the house and the number of Imp nests. It should have had at least some lingering energy," Nyles said.

"Yet, it felt sterile—almost as if someone had wiped everything from it," Kyra picked up his lead.

"Inside the house, what were your indications of another presence?" the Architect asked.

They had gone over this when Kyra had returned. Perhaps, he wanted to see if together something new would come out. "The lack of traps in the study and the bedrooms."

"The lab, the map, the organization. It was almost militant." Nyles again finished her thought.

Sciath

"So, it seems to me that we have a humanoid race with advanced thinking and a militant bearing and organization." The Architect summed up. "Search your minds. You both have extensive knowledge of the supernatural world. What comes to your mind when you put those things together?"

Kyra's first thought flashed before her eyes, but she dismissed it and kept searching.

"I've been wondering, would they have to have been supernatural? Could they not have been a group of humans?" Nyles asked. "Perhaps a group of the government's soldiers? We know Gilly relations haven't always been excellent. All it would take is an extremist faction to join up with the Imps in an attempt to exterminate us."

"But would the Imps trust them?" Kyra asked.

"I can see Cobbwick aligning with the humans. Although, I would imagine that if they had won, they would have turned on the humans," the Architect said, considering this new avenue.

"I think we should go ask him. He has no reason to hide anything, now," Kyra added.

"Cobbwick is alive?" Nyles asked, his voice incredulous.

"Yes. I was shocked to find that out as well," Kyra said.

The knock on the door caused all of them to jump.

Kyra sighed. "I'm going to have to start eating in the café. Room service is giving me too many heart attacks."

Her comment drew smiles from both the others.

Dinner held lighter conversation. As they finished up, the phone rang.

The Architect looked puzzled. "No one ever calls me, anymore. I'm not even sure where the damn thing is." Everyone hunted for the ringing sound.

The ringing continued until Kyra found it under a stack of papers. "Hello?" she answered. She nodded, listening to what the voice on the line had to tell her. Her brow furrowing, the other two watched her pace as she listened. The conversation continued on, one-sided, for several minutes.

"Thank you for the update, Sabrina. We will swing by in the morning to check on them," Kyra said politely as she hung up.

"The more contact I have with that woman, the less I like her. Anyway, it appears what they were exposed to was a sleeping mist. They are still out, but the vitals are good, their brainwaves are good, and the scans look clear. Also they should have the DNA on our furry friend ready by tomorrow morning," she told them.

"I'm relieved to know that Leland and Nikkos are safe and that it was nothing more serious. You said the bones were found in a ritualistic area. My guess is that they rigged a few of the skulls with the sleeping mist so that if anyone disturbed them, they would fall asleep and likely end up in the pile themselves," the Architect mused as he headed back to his desk chair.

"That makes sense," Kyra replied.

"Now, I would like to explore your theory about humans and Imps. I think you're right. Cobbwick has been incarcerated a very long time. He might just tell us what we want to know," the Architect pondered aloud while sitting back in his chair.

"I have a meeting tomorrow morning with my team to discuss progress and what not. Then, I have to poke my head in and update Galerius. Other than that, I can leave immediately," she said.

"I know it means more work in travel, but I would love to accompany you," Nyles said.

"Of course, you may come along, my boy. You're never an inconvenience to me," the Architect said with a reassuring smile.

Kyra loved how open the relationship between her father and Nyles was. *If only our relationship was so simple.* She sighed softly.

"What kind of gear do we need? I bet I can slip down to Milyna and get us a stat order put in." Kyra wanted to escape the room and her own thoughts.

"I'll arrange the plane with Lev. I'd say all we need are some light provisions. We'll be landing at the prison and then getting back on the plane. All weapons must be surrendered at the door, but if you wish to get a survival pack to stow onboard, you're welcome to." The Architect seemed to understand her urgency to leave.

"Excellent plan. Nyles can you pop on Simon and send out a memo for tomorrow morning's meeting, same room as before, at 9:00 a.m.?" she asked.

"I surely can."

"Great, then I'll catch you in the morning." She quickly made her way out the door. She arrived at Equipment just as Milyna was locking up.

"I'm so glad I caught you," Kyra said.

Milyna looked surprised. "I was unaware you were back, already. What can I do for you?"

"We had to come back early due to some unforeseen discoveries. Tomorrow, the Architect, Nyles, and I are taking a plane trip to the prison. I would be thrilled if you could pull together a basic survivalist pack that I could toss into the plane." Kyra's words tumbled out.

"Sure. I have several of those all ready to go. I'll toss in some personal appropriate things, and I can have it ready by 9:00 a.m.," Milyna replied. "I'm heading down to the lounge for a tea. Care to join me?"

Kyra was thrilled to have the opportunity to assure herself that she would not meet Nyles again, tonight. "I would love to. Thank you so much for the offer."

They walked down the hall together. The pace was calm and casual.

"I'm sure you will know what on earth all that code blue business was earlier?" Milyna asked.

Kyra debated how much to tell her. She couldn't risk Milyna telling anyone, though Kyra did trust her.

"Seems something down in Medical went off. They called the biohazard as a precaution." Kyra hadn't lied, so she felt better.

"First time I have ever been in a lockdown before. Since I work alone most days, I'll admit it was more than a little unnerving," Milyna said.

"I have only been through two, and it still frazzled me," Kyra admitted.

They entered the lounge. Both women ordered their tea, found an unoccupied booth, and settled in. The lounge was remarkably empty. Only three other tables were occupied. It seemed everyone had been shaken by today's episode.

"If I may ask, what was the other lockdown?" Milyna asked.

"I was nine. Nyles and I were playing tag in the hallways. I hid down in one of the small service ways to ambush him when he came running past. Suddenly, the world was bathed in red, the sirens were blaring. I recall fearing it had been something I had done to set off the alarms. I curled up in a dark corner and hid, which of course caused Father even more panic than the actual break. Red is a security breach, meaning that an unauthorized party has made their way into Scíath. It turned out to be a lost group of University students who fumbled their way into a loading dock. That was cleared in a matter of hours. Due to my falling asleep in my dark corner, that led to another two hours of panicked searching."

Kyra's look betrayed her sheepishness at the memory.

"So, there has never been an actual emergency?" Milyna asked.

"Nope, and I'm hoping it stays that way."

"Me, too," Milyna agreed.

"I suppose I can't ask why you are headed to the prison tomorrow, can I?"

"Actually, you can. I'm heading out to question a prisoner."

It was clear Milyna was hoping for more details. As good as she was at her job, it couldn't be all that exciting. Milyna looked down into her tea, again. Kyra was about to explain that she couldn't divulge the mission details when the girl blurted out, "I'm in love with a non-Fae!" Her words came out so quickly, Kyra had to take a moment to mentally translate them.

Kyra nodded. "The young gentleman I saw escorting you earlier, I assume." Kyra kept her tone kind. This was a tough place for the girl to be. She rejected the annoyed expression that wanted to show when emotions became involved, and she leaned in slightly.

"Yes, his name is Seth. He's a Wizard from Scotland." She looked relieved that Kyra was willing to talk.

"How long have you two been seeing each other?" Kyra asked.

"Almost eight months. At first, it was a fun, flirty kinda thing. I never expected it to become serious."

"You already know the troubles that will face you; however, if you do decide to pursue this relationship, Scíath is the safest place for you to do so."

"Seth has already been promoted to senior researcher. I'm safe in my position. There is no reason for us to leave."

"You have no desire to go back to the Fae?" Kyra asked.

Milyna, after a long moment, pulled out her pocket knife and slit her hand.

At first, Kyra was shocked by her action. Then, the reason became clear. The blood that filled the wound was not blue but white.

"You're a weak blood," Kyra whispered.

"I am. I have few Fae powers. My parents were far too old to have me, and their own blood so thin, that mine became this." Milyna gestured to her palm before placing a napkin on it to quench the bleeding. "You know how I will be treated back there."

Weak bloods were a step above an abomination to the Fae. Perhaps, there had been other reasons Father had brought her here.

"Do you really love him?" Kyra asked after a long moment of thought.

"I do."

"You deserve to be happy, regardless of race or other people's opinions. So, do what feels right," Kyra told her with a smile.

The young girl's face lit up. "Thank you so much for listening."

"I'm the only person who knows what you are going to go through. Remember this. Those who truly are your friends will stick by your side. Those who don't, weren't worth your time."

"I have a close circle of friends, and they support us. I know my superiors or his would never discriminate against either of us," Milyna explained.

Kyra drained her tea. "When you get done with all this mission stuff, I'd love for you to meet him," Milyna said.

"I'm sure something can be arranged," Kyra replied. "Now, my dear, while I have enjoyed the time with you, I need to leave. I have an early morning briefing with my team, and then a long plane ride to the wilds of Siberia. I'm going to head back to my room and get some rest." Kyra stood.

"I will have your packs for you first thing." Milyna stood as well.

Kyra made her way back to her room. Her brain was completely crammed full and in overdrive. So much had happened in the last few days, it was hard to put her thoughts in order.

She paused outside her door. She had forgotten to tell the Architect that Di wanted a meeting with him. She knocked at his study door. She assumed he was asleep, and she would have to tell him tomorrow; however, he called out, "Come in."

He was seated in the armchair. A lone lamp lit a very small circle in the room. It threw dark shadows onto his face. Kyra could see his age, the dark circles beneath his eyes, his hollowing cheek bones, and his shallow breaths.

She rushed into the room and pulled him into her arms in a tight hug. He made several surprised noises before returning her strong hug.

"Well, that's certainly a nice way to wake up," he said, pulling away from her.

"Sometimes, a hug fixes many things," she replied, settling into the recliner beside him.

"With all the chaos today, I forgot to tell you that Di wants to meet with you to discuss the ramifications of our discoveries." She took in a deep breath, letting the smell of his pipe smoke and the peace of the room help her to ease her mind.

"I will call on her in the morning, then."

For several minutes, they both just sat there, enjoying the atmosphere and the comfort of the room.

"Did you know she was a weak blood?" Kyra asked, her voice quiet.

"I did. Her mother came to me, as she knew about you. She wanted safety for her child. After they went to sleep, it would be discovered. She feared the child would not be alive when she awoke, so she asked me to bring her here to shield her."

"She's in love with a human and came to me tonight about it." Kyra leaned her head back against the chair, her eyes closing.

"I can't say I'm surprised she's gravitating toward you. What sage advice did you give her?"

"I told her to do what made her happy. That if they were going to be together, Scíath was the safest place for it."

"That's excellent advice. I admire your ability to take care of your friends," he said.

Several replies came to her mind, but she just let the silence go on.

The room was warm. Kyra felt herself start to drift off. A soft, sweet song played in her mind. She let its melody carry her away. The song ended. Warm sunlight on her face. Opening her eyes, she recognized the meadow, but this time, it felt different. Something was missing—no voices this time. She wasn't afraid and felt no need to run. She soaked in the warm sunlight and inhaling deeply. She smelled the mix of flowers as its aroma floated past her face.

She was enjoying the relative peace, and then, she felt it. The feeling of being watched and the same eyes on her. Spinning around, she searched for them, stalking from one side of the meadow to the next. Hunting for the eyes that wanted her, but she could find nothing. A sound, a branch creaking in a nearby tree. She rushed to the tree. Looking up into the topmost branches, she met the same yellow eyes she had stared down at the house.

"Welcome home," echoed in her mind, forcing her to wake with a start.

She sat up quickly, looking over to find her father watching her.

Cold and vulnerable, her first instinct was to reach out to him to be comforted. Then, she knew she would have to explain her dream, and she simply had no desire to.

Standing, she kissed his forehead.

"I'll come by as soon as I finish my meeting. Good night." She left, not waiting for a reply but making sure to lock the door on her way out.

In her room, she did a thorough search before undressing, slipping into her pajamas, and climbing into bed. As a second thought, she got back up and slipped her gun under the pillow. In the field, she would have slept with it in her hand, and with the way things were going around here, it couldn't hurt to have it close.

Thankfully, the rest of the night was restful. No more images haunted her, and she was granted her sleep.

* * * *

The Architect laid awake most of the night, working to shield Kyra's mind from itself.

He pondered all the things that were going on in his world. Wondering if he would have to postpone the succession, wondering what this meeting with Cobbwick would reveal. Too many variables at a time when he wanted simplicity. As dawn approached, he forced himself to sleep. He would need his rest.

* * * *

Kyra awoke feeling rested. Blinking at the clock, she was surprised to see it read 8:00 a.m. It had been a long time since her internal clock had allowed her to sleep that late.

After dressing quickly, she headed to the dining hall. She headed out with her tea and muffin. Rounding the corner, she came face-to-face with Nyles.

"Let me grab some breakfast. We can head down to see Nikkos, Doctor Barker, and Anna." He stepped past her without waiting for a reply.

Part of her was annoyed that he assumed she would wait, but the rest of her knew she would. Within moments, they were headed toward Medical.

"I won't lie. I'm excited to meet this Cobbwick," Nyles admitted as they waited for their admittance to Medical.

"It will be fascinating to meet a live Imp, I agree. I just hope he is in a gregarious mood when we arrive."

For the next fifteen minutes, they were processed by the bio team. Their breakfasts were confiscated and disposed of. They were dressed in sterile scrubs with face masks. Nyles looked slightly ridiculous as he had several pairs of pants cut and taped together to cover his lower half. After the entire ordeal was over, they were shown to a locked down ward.

The first room held Anna, dressed in a hospital gown and looking exasperated. Kyra entered while Nyles remained in the hallway. Kyra waited until all of the medical personnel had left the room before lowering her mask. Anna looked immediately relieved.

"Kyra, you don't know how happy I am to see you. I do hope that you have come here to inform theses angels of mercy that I am perfectly fine and have a 9:00 a.m. meeting to attend."

"I'll get you out of here in time to make the meeting. I need you there to explain what happened in here," Kyra reassured her.

"Thank you. You have no idea how much it means to me. You're the only person who came to see me," she said, leaving her meaning dangling in the air.

"You're part of my team, and you're in here because of something I asked you to do. I got your six," Kyra said.

"And I yours," Anna replied thoughtfully.

"Now, I'm going to go get your release papers started and check on Nikkos and Leland."

"They won't let me out to check on Nikkos. Tell him I said...I hope he feels better soon."

Kyra nodded and left. It was ridiculous the amount of love that was popping up all around. *Must remember not to drink the water.* She then bullied the resident doctor into releasing Anna. After that fight was won, she went to Nikkos and Leland.

She heard Nyles stifling a laugh behind her. She whirled around. "What exactly has you so amused, sir?" she asked.

"There is nothing like watching a five-foot-two woman take on a Cyclops without a single thought and win," he replied with a chuckle.

"The bigger they come, or so they say," she replied with a wink and walked into the room. This time, Nyles followed her in.

Nikkos and Leland were sitting on the edges of their beds with reports and figures spread out across the bedside table.

"I don't think this is what they call resting, Doctors," Kyra said.

"You know doctors are always the worst patients," Leland said, looking up.

"Very true. How are you two feeling?" Nyles asked.

"Better if we could get out of here; however, my own twenty-four hour protocol keeps me trapped," Leland admitted.

"Well, don't get mad at me, but I sprung Anna for the 9:00 a.m. meeting. She wasn't affected, anyway."

"You saw Anna, and she's all right?" Nikkos asked with anxiety on his face.

"A bit annoyed at being kept but otherwise fine. She asked me to tell you to feel better soon."

Nikkos's face relaxed.

"So, Sabrina tells me it was just a sleeping mist?" Kyra asked.

"Yes, a very odd Imp tactic, to be sure. I think it was used as more of a protection measure for their ritual site than an offensive one," Leland explained.

"They were sneaky about it. They hid it along the line of a skull fracture, knowing that someone would look at it, since all the other skulls lacked marks," Nikkos added.

"Imps are known to be sneaky. I understand that this will slow down the processing of the bodies. I do not want you to be under any pressure. Maintain your safety first," Kyra instructed them.

"The departure has been pushed off. I'll make sure you receive notes from the meeting, Nikkos, so you know where everyone else stands."

"Thank you. I will have the report in your hands the minute it is completed. I think it fair to let you know that we have identified at least two Fae bodies," Nikkos told her.

Kyra's lips pursed. She exited, leaving Nyles to make the good-byes.

He had told her about the Fae for several reasons. First, it was very difficult to take down an adult Fae, lending credence to the fact that the Imps had help. Second, well, she was half-Fae, and perhaps, he expected her to know how the bodies should be disposed of or something. He would have more luck getting that info out of Nyles. She had made a point of delving into neither human nor Fae traditions, as none fit her fully.

Nyles joined her in the hall. They made their way out with Kyra impatiently glancing at the clock. It was the same decontamination measures they had met on their way in.

"I'm going to run to the room and make sure it's set up. Can you swing by the café and see if Gus can throw together a breakfast plate for the team? We have twenty minutes."

"Sure. He's come through for me with less time. I'll meet you back at the conference room," Nyles said.

Kyra half-sprinted to the room, only to find everyone already milling about.

"Well, no one can say my team isn't punctual." She entered the room. "Nyles will be back with a tray of breakfast food by nine." She settled in a chair.

"Oh, good. All I could get in Medical was liquids. Trying to kill me, I think," Anna replied.

"Anna, since Nyles already has the scoop on what happened in Medical, why don't you go ahead and fill everyone else in?" Kyra reached into the podium and was grateful to find a yellow legal pad.

Anna nodded and waited for everyone to get settled. "As you can all see, Nikkos is not here. Even if you missed that, I have little doubt that you missed the code blue lockdown that occurred yesterday afternoon. I was the cause of that lockdown. At least, I was the one who pushed the alarm button. If any of you were seriously inconvenienced by it, I do apologize, but it was necessary.

"I had entered Medical about twenty minutes before the alarm. I went down to forensics, where they were examining the bodies. I was speaking with Nikkos and Doctor Barker. We were about to start tagging the skeletons, assigning a race and age guess to the master list, so I could start looking for matching reports. Nikkos asked me to go wash my hands and don gloves. As I was doing that, I heard Nikkos say something about a remarkable fracture. This loud hissing sound came from the skull he was holding, and a dark green mist covered them. Unsure of what to do, I grabbed a mask and hit the alarm button," Anna said, finishing her tale.

As she was speaking, Nyles crept in as quietly as a Centaur can and placed a large tray of breakfast pastries and fruit on the table. He also laid out a tray of bottled water. Kyra smiled appreciatively at him.

"What I have managed to discover from Medical is that it was a sleeping mist, most likely designed to trap anyone who meddled with the ceremonial remains," Kyra explained.

With thoughtful expressions about what had been said, the members descended on the breakfast tray.

"Nikkos and Leland will be released later this afternoon. What happened will put a delay on their findings, as they now have to treat every single remain as if it is booby-trapped. I can tell you from experience that working in those bio suits is not an easy thing to do. Our timeline on that project is blown. That slows down everything else; however, we are not giving up this project.

"Until that house is cleared of all the clues pertaining to the second race, and all the mysteries solved, you are a team. You are relieved from other duties within your departments, and we are now effectively a task force. After this meeting, Nyles, the Architect, and I are heading out to the prison to meet with Cobbwick," Kyra added.

The surprised if not shocked expressions on the faces around her let her know she was not the only one who didn't know the Imp was still alive. *Good to know I'm not alone.*

"I'm hoping to get some answers from him. He's been in prison a very long time, so let's hope he's interested in improving his living conditions in exchange for information," Kyra said.

"Now, let's get the rest of the reports." She sat back in her chair.

Maria spoke, "I have requested all the documents I can find on the house and the people who lived there. I should have it all within the next couple of days. I'm hoping it will shed some light on the discrepancies in the blueprints."

Soro went next. "I'm knee-deep in research. I'm hoping some of the things Aieta discovers about the artifacts will help me narrow down my search, because at this point, I'm numbering possibilities in the high double digits."

"We have a number of species to go through, but we are hoping that anything we can discern will help the others narrow the searches. I can tell you this. Most of these artifacts are way too complex to belong to the Imps," Aieta said.

"I have not had access to my department, due to medical quarantine, so I've been working here and there. I'm in the same boat as the rest. We just need more data," Nyles said.

Kyra took a long drink of water before speaking, "I'll be back by tomorrow. Hopefully, I'll have more data to give to you. I'll set up another meeting at that time, so we can see where we are and what we want to do next."

It was disappointing that they had no more real answers than when they had returned from the trip, but expeditions like this weren't like bounties. They required research and time. She accepted it, even though she didn't like it much.

"All right, I've got a plane to catch. I look forward to sharing with you what I know when I return." Kyra stood.

Chairs scraped back and papers shuffled as everyone made their way out of the room. Nyles waited by the door. They started toward the Architect's office.

A deep frown set on Kyra's face. "I sense you are not overly pleased about something," Nyles said.

"This is just a different realm that I am used to operating in. In the field, I get the bounty, I track the fugitive, capture him, repair anything I need to, and then leave. This is completely different." *Meeting, meetings, meetings.*

"Well, I can say this. Not many people would be asked to take on something this complex for their first team assignment. Galerius and the Architect have great faith in you. As do I," he added quietly.

She felt a blush rising to her face, but her uncertainty made it fleeting.

"I appreciate the sentiment. I'm just concerned that I'm headed for failure. Not to mention, I'm at home base until all the implications from this trip have been sorted through."

"Is that such a bad thing?" Nyles asked.

Her frown grew deeper. "I enjoy spending time with Father and you, but we all recall the last two years before I was put out into the field."

Kyra's attempts at departments in Scíath were well-known. She had been through all of them, each with their own disaster, before it became obvious that her Fae nature yearned for freedom. She remembered walking through the halls for hours, touching the stones and imagining the earth that lay beyond her stone cage.

They walked on in silence. Nyles changed the subject. "Do you think Cobbwick will be cooperative?"

"I hope so. He could solve a fair number of mysteries, not only for us but for the supernatural world at large." She stopped outside the Architect's door.

Knocking softly, she used her sensitive hearing to determine if he was alone. Hearing absolutely nothing, panic descended upon her, again; however, this time, she forced herself to calmly put her key in the lock. Opening the door with her weapon drawn, she stepped into the room. Only the dim light on the desk was lit. Everything seemed to be in place. Reaching out with her Fae senses, she searched the room for anything out of the ordinary. She found a strong resonation of the Architect. Not surprising, given how much time he spent in this room.

She heard Nyles's steps behind her. Holding up her hand, she indicated for him to wait. She didn't want his energy throwing off her findings, but she found her own love of this room and her own ingrained energy throwing off any findings. Moving to the light switch, she flipped it on, flooding the room with warm light.

"There you are," the Architect said from behind her.

Kyra whirled around, gun still grasped firmly and now pointed at the figure in the doorway.

For a moment, they stared at each other. The Architect showed absolutely no fear, even with a weapon pointed at his face. She felt his calming influence washing over her in waves. It was a familiar feeling and welcomed. Lowering the weapon, she smiled at him.

"I have to say that being home to relax has made me jumpier than I ever was in the field," she said with a dry grin.

"I went down to the meeting room. It was empty, so I figured you were on your way here. Are we ready?"

"I need to stop by equipment and sign out the packs I had Milyna put together." Kyra shut the door behind her, careful to relock it.

"Packs?" the Architect asked.

"Just three basic survival packs." She walked toward the equipment office, well aware of how paranoid the precautions appeared to be. The two following behind her didn't comment either way.

After Kyra knocked twice, Milyna opened the top half of the door. Her face was swollen and splotchy. She had been crying, quite a bit.

Out of a need to protect the girl, Kyra laid a reassuring hand over hers. The young girl smiled up at her before getting to business.

Milyna said, "The packs are aboard the plane. Each one is equipped with a Global Positioning System homing beacon, wired into Security as well as Lev's office. If anything happens, just hit the button, and the cavalry will be deployed."

Kyra scribbled her name across the required forms. They headed toward the exit tubes to the air strip.

* * * *

Nyles watched her. Every time he thought he had her figured out, a whole new series of enigmas presented itself. They arrived at the exit tubes, and he cringed. He knew that the tube would accommodate him. Lev had made sure that all of the larger creatures could use the tubes, as not only did they serve to get to the air strip and the helipad, but they could also be routed to the emergency shelter should the compound ever be compromised. Despite that, there was something disconcerting about laying down in something that could easily double as a coffin and hurtle someone underground at nearly 100 miles per hour with no control over it.

Inhaling deeply, he gave her a smile. Any weakness in front of Kyra would simply not do.

* * * *

They arrived at the tube station. Placing his thumb on the scanner, the Architect waited patiently as the wall slid back to reveal five tracks, which always reminded him of bowling ball machines. Individual tubes of varying sizes waited patiently for passengers. Kyra had used them many times to head out for assignments. It had been on her suggestion that Lev placed ten such stations throughout the Scíath compound. Each track supported three separate tubes, allowing many more people to be evacuated.

The three of them each went into their own tubes and, with a push of the button for their destination, they were off.

* * * *

Kyra stood blinking in the bright sunlight as the other two emerged from the tube station. The midmorning sun shone down upon them, reminding Kyra how much she loved feeling its warming rays.

A small fleet of aircraft sat about the air strip. Everything from a full passenger plane to twin-engine prop planes. They walked to the one and only hanger on the base. It housed the private jet. Its white exterior boasted a single red stripe—no identification or decoration. The stairs were lowered, and the pilot waited beside it.

Kyra studied him. His hawk-like nose and feathered, downy hair led her to believe him to be a fury; however, he had perfectly normal hands and wide eyes. She filed away the thought to ask Nyles about them later. He would know or, if he didn't, he would be in a position to get the answer fairly easily.

They boarded the plane. Kyra noted with satisfaction the three largish packs stowed in the first three seats. This jet was not set up like a normal plane. It had a row of normal plane seats, though only two to a row. The left side was outfitted with a table and chairs as well as a laptop with Simon access. It was a fully functioning office. Two single beds lined the back of the cabin. Kyra knew the plane was normally stocked with a full medical kit, rations, and office supplies. Lev missed not a single detail in making this plane as efficient as any office in Scíath.

* * * *

They settled in, buckling up as the streamline engines started with a near silent purr as they taxied out of the hanger. Nyles would never let it on in present company, but he despised flying. His stomach lurched as the plane climbed into the clouds. He knew that air was the most expedient form of travel, and the only way to reach where they were going, but he would have much preferred a ground method.

The Architect turned and looked at him, giving him a reassuring smile. Nyles had no doubt he was broadcasting his feelings in his aura and vibes, and that both Kyra and the Architect picked those up; however, they would never get him to admit his fear out loud. They floated through the clouds.

* * * *

The voyage was quiet, but the excitement in the cabin was palpable as they descended on the prison. Kyra had her thumb on the seat belt release as the plane made its rather choppy landing on the island.

As they exited the plane, the reason for the turbulence was immediately revealed. A wicked wind ripped at their clothing, making it hard for them to move toward the entrance.

The prison had been built into the base of a dormant volcano. The rough, brown stone walls were resistant to the raging winds that surrounded the island. The winds were one of the main reasons why this island was chosen. They were daunting to Gilly's and most supernaturals. Kyra knew the Architect had been sad when it became necessary to build such a structure. He liked to believe that all creatures could be good if they chose to. The need for a prison showed him that some really did prefer to be destructive.

Fighting the raging wind, they made their way to the guard shack. Kyra recognized the guard immediately. She had brought a fair number of the current residents here. The race chosen to run the prison was Technizoid—the same race Galerius hailed from. They had computer-like brains and were security whizzes. The guard's name was Atorius, and he was Galerius's brother. Kyra always seemed to come in on his shift, so they became friends during her usual wait for her prize to be processed.

He waved to her at her approach. She waved back. Once inside the shack, they were spared from the wind's fingers. Yet, they could feel it battering the windows, like some terrible beast barely kept at bay. Nyles kept glancing at the windows.

After being searched, they passed through the decontamination, again. Kyra was pretty sure she was about as sterile as any one person could be after all the times she has been flashed. They waited just outside the last door, separating them from the interior of the prison. The light was a harsh florescent, giving everyone a sickened look. Kyra felt alarmingly naked without her weapon; however, she understood it being taken. A riot in this place would be disastrous.

A muscular man opened the other door. Well over six feet tall, his well-defined physique was easy to discern in his simple, white golf shirt and black pants. He extended his hand to the Architect.

"It's good to see you again, Sir," he said.

"You as well, Anthony. It has been a number of years." The Architect returned the handshake.

Anthony offered his hand to Nyles, introducing himself.

"I'm Anthony, the warden here."

"I'm Nyles. I represent Anthropology." He also returned the handshake.

"Kyra, I was starting to wonder if you were on vacation. Two red listers went up three days ago." He pushed the gate open.

Kyra flinched. She had the highest count of red listed bounties in history. It bugged her that she was falling behind. Red listers were the most dangerous, and they were her favorite to hunt.

"No. No vacation. Working on a special project; however, I will get back out in the field soon." She followed him into the prison.

The inside was as drab and rocky as the exterior. The cells were all carved straight from the rock. The first cell block was for offenders who had limited sentences. They mirrored Gilly cells with basic commodities. Kyra recognized several of the faces inside these cells. They made their way toward the cell block reserved for offenders who would spend the rest of their lives behind these walls. This, in some cases, was hundreds of years.

Several groups within the supernatural world were calling for a death penalty for the most severe offenders. Kyra agreed with them. There were some creatures that did not deserve to live after their crimes. The Architect had refused to even entertain the idea. She knew better than to try to get the Architect to see her point. He believed all life was sacred, even if the creature in question was rotten to the core.

As they walked, Anthony updated her on things that had been added recently. Kyra's mind, however, wandered to the time when she personally played judge, jury, and executioner.

It had been cold—the kind of bitter cold that crept into your bones and took hours to rid yourself of. It was winter in Russia. Kyra was situated in a tree, watching over the home of a Mantrix. They were medium in size and, upon close inspection, they resembled a pig. Although, their skin was brown instead of pink. This particular Mantrix had taken to stealing children from a nearby village. Kyra was fairly sure he was eating them. At last count, twenty children had been taken. He had to be stopped.

Kyra shifted slightly, which did nothing to alleviate her pain from a branch that had chosen to press into her shoulder. She had been sitting here for several hours. The cramps in her muscles affirmed that thought for her. She was just was about to climb down and attempt it again tomorrow night, when her ears picked up the sound of shuffling feet heading her way. Making herself flush with the tree, she listened as another sound joined that of the shuffling. Rage surged within her as she realized the sound was that of a young child crying for its mother.

Kyra had to strain to keep herself from just jumping from the tree onto this monster. She knew, though, that she would have to make sure the child would not be harmed. Moonlight lit up the scene. The disgusting creature paused at the top of the hole and set down the child, who was no more than two and now wailing on the ground. The Mantrix seemed to be tying up his pockets and weapons before he made the journey underground. Kyra had no intention of letting him get that far.

As luck would have it, he turned his back to her position. Not daring to wait a moment longer, she leapt. Her foot connected directly with the creature's back. Lifting him off his feet with a squeal, he flew forward. Her movements were lightening quick as she scooped up the whimpering child and placed her at the base of the tree. She turned to face the angry Mantrix. He seized her gun, fumbling with the unknown weapon. A swift kick to his jaw sent him skittering through the snow. Still, he clambered toward her in a half crawl. She kicked the gun out of the foul creature's grasp and ran for her weapon. Grabbing it, she turned just in time. She pinned the Mantrix with the barrel of her gun pressed against its snout.

"You are under arrest. I will be transporting you to your trial and incarceration. You are being brought up on the charges of kidnapping twenty-one Gilly children." Kyra had given this speech a number of times.

The Mantrix roared with a horrible, guttural laughter. "Didn't kidnap. Was more like grocery shopping. There have been more like one hundred over the years." He chuckled at his own wit.

Kyra's rage rose up in her. All those innocent lives and families destroyed—all because this beast preferred the taste of child flesh. For him to be laughing about it was simply more than she could take. With the image of the child's tear-stained face in her mind, the child that was to be his next meal, she squeezed the trigger. His head exploded in a mass of gore and blood. She stood and took the time to clean herself off before kneeling before the child.

"Don't worry, little one. I will get you back to your mother," she said gently, hoping her Russian words were the correct ones. It was not a language she used often.

Removing her coat, she placed it around the shivering child clad only in her bedclothes. The child curled up and fell asleep inside the warmth. Kyra smiled. The resilience of children was always amazing to her. She bound the Mantrix body and hid it for later retrieval. Following the Mantrix's footprints in the frost, she made her way back to a tiny village. It was easy to tell from which house the child was missing. One small cottage on the far edge of the building was lit up like a beacon while the rest of the houses were dark.

Kyra took a deep breath. As she carried the child back to her home, she could hear the mother's voice inside. "This creature ripped the shutters from the hinges, showering me in glass and wood. It snatched Anya as she said her prayers." Kyra elbowed her way through the crowd and laid the child in her mother's lap.

The mother looked up, tears streaming down her cheeks.

"Thank you. You are an angel," she said.

"You need fear the creature no more," Kyra said quietly to the room at large. Being around this many Gillys made her nervous.

"Who are you?" the man asked while leaning down to embrace the mother and child. Kyra assumed it was the child's father.

"I'm a friend. Cherish your daughter always." Kyra made her way quickly out into the dark, wanting to answer no more questions.

Though she was pleased to see the girl home, seeing the parents holding her tight and their joy at her return made Kyra long for her own parents. She knew nothing of them, and moments like this made that even more painful.

Kyra was startled from her revelry as she heard the code for the maximum security wing being entered. Even though there was not much difference in the structure in this wing, aside from the size of the cells, the air felt heavier. It was as if those condemned to an eternity in theses walls were able to fill the atmosphere with their despair.

The wing was brown stone and cold, steel bars. The cells were triple the size of those in the other wings. They contained not only sleeping quarters, but a sitting area and workout area. Theses prisoners were never allowed to leave the cells. Fifty of these maximum security cages were in the wing. Yet, even after the war, no more than half were full at any given time. Many creatures preferred suicide over a lifetime of captivity.

"Cobbwick has been informed of your visit, and he seems amicable toward seeing you...well, as amicable as he seems about anything." Anthony explained as they made their way down the winding corridor. "I will be sending two of my men in with you." Anthony, apparently noticing Kyra's raised brow, continued, "I have no doubt you can handle yourself; however, I spare no precautions when it comes to him. He killed four guards when he was transferred here."

"I appreciate your precautions. I recall that incident all too well," the Architect replied as they stopped in front of the iron bars.

Sciath

This cell was made to the Imp's size. They had scrambled to make the accommodations, given that he was the largest Imp anyone could ever recall seeing. Which, theoretically, had helped him rise to the rank of leader. The mammoth, eight-foot doorway made Kyra feel small and a bit intimidated. Anthony entered the code, and the door slid open. Kyra could hardly keep the excitement from her expression. An Imp—a live Imp—and not just any Imp. Cobbwick, the creature who was responsible for the only war to ever have been waged within the supernatural community. Living history.

The guards heralded their entry. Kyra attempted to see around the two guards, the Architect, and Nyles, but it was fruitless. Somehow, in the shuffle, she had ended up in the back of the group, and it was not making her happy.

Her disappointment erased as the massive form of Cobbwick stood. He towered over them. Immediately apparent was his age. His coarse, gray skin was wrinkled, its surface dotted with brown age spots. Only a few tufts of stark white hair remained on his head; however, the most telling sign were his eyes. The large, black orbs were dim. His body was lean, the joints in some places almost painfully visible. He was dressed in the classic black jumpsuit of the prison. His enormous feet were bare.

He regarded them with no change of expression. He sniffed the air as an animal would. He leaned against the wall and closed his eyes. Kyra guessed this allowed his senses to obtain the information he sought. After a long sniff, he laughed, or that was she supposed the sound was meant to be. It was more of a wheezing, wet sound.

"You lock me up. Yet, the abomination roams free," he said in a thick, low voice. His words sounded more like a growl.

Kyra bristled.

The Architect held up his hand. "I am not here to debate with you the race of your visitors," he said, his voice solid and his expression stone. "I am here to ask you some questions about an old hive house of yours we have discovered near the Scottish border."

The old Imp smiled. His gums were as gray as his skin, and not a single tooth had survived. "You can't figure out what all the clues inside mean, and you want me to help you?" His expression was smug.

"I do have a few questions for you. I am willing to bargain with you for the answers," the Architect replied.

"Bargain with me? What do you think you could offer me that I would want? We both know you're not going to pardon me, so what?" he asked, crossing his arms.

Tension came off the guards and Nyles in waves. Though Kyra was also afraid, she would be damned if she allowed this monster to know. Jutting her chin forward, she moved to stand beside the Architect.

"For starters, I can make the outside recreation pad available to you for an hour a day. When was the last time you felt the air on your face? Saw the sky? Felt the ground under your feet?" the Architect asked.

Cobbwick's smug expression disappeared. He was hooked. Kyra masked her satisfaction with the Architect's results.

"I will give you two honest answers for that privilege," Cobbwick replied with a sincerity Kyra was shocked to know he possessed.

"I must tell you that if you attempt to escape or harm any of the prison personnel, the right is immediately withdrawn," the Architect clarified.

The old Imp simply nodded. "Ask."

"Were you performing genetic experiments there?"

"Personally, no. I have no head for science." He held up his hand as Kyra opened her mouth to speak. "However, yes. Genetic engineering to create a beast of war was carried out during our time there."

The Architect nodded. Kyra and Nyles looked at each other. Was that creature they met in the woods a by-product of such experimentation?

"Second question. It was also evident from the quarters that there was a race besides Imp living in that house. What was it?" the Architect asked.

Nothing could have prepared them for what came next. The old Imp appeared to be straining. He opened his mouth to speak, but nothing but guttural, choking sounds emerged. His body trembled, and a long string of slimy saliva rolled down his chin. The guards backed away, forcing everyone else backward.

A rhythmic convulsing took hold of his mammoth form. It continued for half a minute before ceasing. He slid to the floor, where he lay in a crumpled heap. Showing utter disregard for his own personal safety, the Architect rushed forward to check for signs of life. "He's alive. Get the med team," the Architect shouted.

Moments later, the room was filled with guards and doctors. The three of them made themselves as small as possible to stay out of the way. Eight men lifted the giant creature to his bed, and they worked to stabilize him. One of the doctors broke out of the huddle and went over the Architect.

"He suffered some kind of seizure. He has never had one before in all the time he has been here. What was going on when it came on?" He gave an accusatory look in Kyra's direction.

Kyra's anger rose. She had been insulted several times since they had arrived here. Her good graces only lasted so long.

"I was questioning him," the Architect said. "It is my belief that the question I asked triggered that response in him. Someone did not want him sharing that piece of information."

The doctor returned to his charge.

The three of them slipped out of the room, meeting up with Anthony in the hall. It was obvious that he was angry from the livid look in his eyes; however, his face was stony, and his tone of voice level as he spoke, "I hope with all of this that you at least got some information out of him." He took them back toward the entrance.

Time to go. Kyra gritted her teeth in frustration. It was obvious Anthony wanted them to leave.

"Some," replied the Architect. "However, he had a block placed on his memory that prevented him from revealing information. This strengthens our original suspicions." The Architect followed Anthony along the way they had come.

At the door they originally entered through, Anthony hesitated. That he wanted them off of his island, pronto, was clear.

"I will be in touch with you after I arrive back at Scíath. If Cobbwick has not come around, I will have Leland send out a neurology team." The Architect accepted Anthony's hint but made it clear he was not abandoning the care of the Imp king.

Before Anthony had a chance to protest, the three of them were out the door.

Kyra grimaced against the onslaught of wind that thrashed around her. It had grown even fiercer than when they landed. More than once, she lost steps she had gained. Lowering her head, she pushed forward. In her mind's eye, tiny hands tore at her body.

Pushing forward, struggling for every inch of gain, Kyra was unaware of her progress until she crashed headlong into the side of the jet. Entering the plane, she plunked into a seat and released her hair from its braid, so she could recapture the strands the wind had torn free.

The Architect was wiping the unshed tears from his irritated eyes. Fortunately, Nyles had protected him from the worse of the wind's onslaught.

"This is why the prison is on this island. It's nearly impossible to escape that wind. If we hadn't had the jet to come to, we would have been pushed back to the gates or into the rocky water below," the Architect explained.

"I get that. I really do. I will be much happier once this place is behind us," Nyles replied.

The jet lifted into the air. The wind caused it to rock and sway as its powerful engines fought the turbulent winds. The forceful wind howled against the jet. It was the embodiment of the screams of the tortured souls captured beneath.

A few minutes later, it was smooth sailing as they cleared the vicinity of the forlorn island. Kyra broke the silence, "I have to say that was not at all what I expected. First off, he gave in so easily to your offer. Second, I was surprised that given his length of captivity and docile behavior that the guards were so frightened of him. Then, obviously, there is the whole seizure/unconsciousness bit, but I think that was a given." She retrieved a ginger ale from the fridge.

The Architect nodded and said, "I must admit that I used some telepathy on him. I looked into his mind to see what it was that he longed for. I had 'insider information' of what to offer him. I understand and respect their fear. Docile or not, he is an incredibly strong creature. Were he to go into a rampage, he could easily kill many before they took him down. I would not be surprised to learn that he was sedated for safety."

He frowned deeply, placing the tips of his fingertips together. His brow creased with the weight of his next statement. "As for his collapse, I've seen mental blocks before. It requires a great amount of skill and concentration to create even simple ones. One like this that causes the subject to lapse into unconsciousness at the mere attempt of retrieval of the information had to have been done by a memory master.

"A great deal of time and effort went into making sure he never remembered who his allies had been. What strikes me as truly odd about that was the block would have taken weeks to complete. He was captured in the final battle of the war. In fact, it was his capture that caused their offense to fall apart and allowed us to triumph. So, logically, the block would have to have been placed after his capture."

The Architect's words hung in the air.

"How many people had access to him after his capture?" Kyra asked.

"Quite a few. It was a time of war. He was placed in the custody of a number of people on his way to the prison," the Architect answered.

"Whoever it was would have needed extensive time with him," Nyles replied.

"I'd wager it was after he was imprisoned," Kyra said.

"That narrows it down to about three hundred prison staff as well as a couple hundred prisoners. When the prison was first built, everyone was kept together. They didn't add the life timers' wing until about fifteen years ago," the Architect replied, his eyes drooping.

Nyles winced. "Every time we uncover a piece of information, it's accompanied by ten more questions." He clenched his hands. .

"We need an objective list," Kyra said more to herself than anyone else. Pulling out her yellow legal pad and red ballpoint pen from her carry-on bag, she began to write.

"Number one, discover who the ally of the Imps was, which will require more searching of the house and collecting the articles that pertain to them. Number two, discover who placed the mental block on Cobbwick. Number three, figure out what the beast that we saw was and if it poses a danger or help. Number four, get the safe house mysteries solved. Find out why the extra rooms did not show up, scout the area for warrior Fae, and a final sweep for Imp traps, just to be safe. Number five, locate and match the bones with the missing person reports."

"I think those are all excellent points," the Architect said. "However, you might want to add finding out the composition of the sleep toxin that was in the corpses, so it can be added to the archives."

Kyra nodded and scrawled that down as number six. "I think after we meet with the team, I'm going to assign a pair to each number. We have a better chance of getting this solved if we all work together and utilize the strengths and talents available to us." Kyra looked at the floor. "I know that I'm not going to make my original completion date on this assignment."

"I think given the amount of obstacles and new tasks to complete, missing the original deadline is fully understandable." The Architect's words soothed her anxiety. "I've learned over the years that nothing in our world is routine. The simplest tasks can be deceiving, and you must be able to roll with the punches."

"I'm going to have to fill out an open-ended personnel requisition for my team." Kyra scribbled down a note to herself.

"I'm going to suggest that we take this time to relax. Once we set down, I have no doubt things are going to be nonstop." The Architect covered his yawn with a hand.

That was his way of saying that he needed a rest. Kyra laid her head back, intending to think further on the issues.

Sleep crept in and took over. She dreamed. The clearing. Her body tensed for the replay of the familiar nightmare; however, she saw subtle differences in the scene. The trees were unnatural—their twisted, tortured branches bare as they reached for the glaring sun overhead. The air carried a heavy feeling, its touch laden with moisture. She was grown, now—no longer a child stumbling through the dreamscape.

From behind her came distinctive footfalls. Their vibration caused the tree to shiver. She backed away from the oncoming creature, placing her back against the tree. Its cold, rough bark grated through her shirt. That was the least of her worries as the thundering footsteps raged toward her.

She stared into the dense forest. Trying to get a glimpse of what was coming, she was thwarted by too thick trees and a too bright sun. Crouching down in a defensive position, she waited. A moment later, two trees before her split apart as the mammoth creature pushed its way into the clearing.

Kyra's heart pounded in her chest. Fear gripped her like never before. It froze her to the spot. She could to do nothing but stare at the horrific visage regarding her from no more than fifty yards away.

It had to be at least twelve feet tall. Humanoid but covered in blue-greenish fur and with razor sharp claws on its hands and feet. The most puzzling part about it was the face. It was Cobbwick. The same large eyes, sloped brow, and dour expression.

The beast paused and sniffed the air, just as Cobbwick had done when they entered his cell. Its gaze honed in on her. A savage smile lit up its face as it took long strides toward her. Kyra braced for the attack and picked up a decently sized stick to mount her defense with. To her surprise, it came within half a step and stopped. Looking down at her, it began to speak. The voice was deep and husky, and its tone filled with foreboding.

"Tread carefully upon the bones of the past. The secrets they hold may destroy your future." It turned and walked away. The trees shivered as it disappeared back into the forest.

Kyra stood frozen in place, adrenaline racing through her veins. She had been expecting to fight for her life. She moved slowly, still unsure of what to expect. The sky went dark, and she blinked several times. The sudden loss of the sun's overbearing glare left her blind.

The trees whipped as a ferocious wind ripped at them. Some of the smaller saplings bent nearly in half under its fury. She shielded her face from the debris, seeking refuge behind the sheltering trunk of a grand, old oak. The clearing transformed, and she was standing a mere thirty feet from the manor house.

As abruptly as it had begun, the wind stopped. She laid her face against the oak's bark. It was cool and smooth. The other trees lost their tortured, twisted, and bare forms. They now grew straight and tall, their limbs bedecked in gowns of leaves.

She headed for the house, moving with caution. She had been brought here for a reason, and she wasn't going to lose the chance to gain information. Reaching out her hand toward the door, it swung inward, as if expecting her arrival. She stepped inside, preparing for the dark interior by narrowing her eyes.

Once again, she was surprised. The entire staircase was covered top to bottom with white, pillar candles. The smell of vanilla rose up to great her. Due to the sheer amount of candles, the smell was almost overwhelming. Kyra raised her hand to her mouth to somehow stop the nauseous feeling rising within her.

Moving to the window, she looked around. There were no signs of decay. Time and neglect had not touched theses walls. She guessed this was what the place had looked like before the Imps took over.

She turned toward the closed door closest to her, deciding to investigate. Before she could take a step, a sound stopped her dead. She paused—unsure she had heard anything, the sound had been so soft. Convincing herself it had been nothing, she returned to her original course. No, there is was, again. This time, she was certain of it—the soft but unmistakable sound of someone crying. Moving quickly and silently, she followed the sound. She stopped several times to get a bead on where it originated.

Her quest led her to the kitchen, now spotless. The sound stopped, but not before Kyra had tracked it. Getting down on her knees, she opened the cabinet under the sink.

Staring back at her were the eyes of a terrified, little girl. Kyra guessed her to be seven or so. She was dressed in a long, white cotton gown, and her hair done in braids. She stared warily at Kyra with her immensely large, clear green eyes.

"Hello," Kyra said simply and quietly.

The child's pale cheeks were flushed, and her nose red from all the crying she had done. Her tear-filled eyes were wide with fear. "Are you one of them?" she asked, her voice hardly more than a whisper.

"Who are them?"

"The men who came with the ugly creatures. They want our house, but Papa won't give it to them. They were fighting in the hall, and Mama told us to run and hide." Her words ended with a sob.

"No, I'm not with them." Kyra reached out very gently and pulled the child into her lap.

"I'm scared, and I want my mama," she said as she laid her weary head on Kyra's shoulder.

"Well, I will certainly help you try to find her." The rest of this child's family were most likely being used in the attic ritual that had been the cause of all the candles. She didn't like lying to the child, yet she couldn't bring herself to tell her she was an orphan.

Kyra cradled the girl close to her chest. Rocking her, Kyra softly sang the lullaby the Architect still sang from time to time. The little girl went limp against her chest as the soft, rhythmic breathing of sleep took over her choked sobs.

Kyra had an overwhelming urge to protect this child and to strike down those who had brought her anguish. Anger boiled within her. What right did "they" have to destroy her family and leave her alone in the world? Closing her eyes, she knew what she must do. Laying the child gently back in her hiding place, she stood, ready to take her vengeance.

At that moment, the room began to shake. She felt a hand on her shoulder. Someone was calling her name. Struggling, she pulled herself back to consciousness. She stared into the concerned face of Nyles. They were still on the jet. Her cheeks were wet with tear drops. Nyles looked like he wanted to ask a question but didn't want to pry.

Kyra took a deep breath and adjusted herself in the seat.

His words tumbled out, "I'm sorry I woke you. You were crying and jerking around, and I thought..." Nyles blushed.

Kyra smiled sadly at him. "You did the right thing." Kyra wanted to soothe his anxiety.

Taking a long drink of her ginger ale, she told the dream to Nyles. She was unsurprised to see tears roll down his cheeks as she told him about the poor, scared child under the sink.

"Do you think she got away?" he asked after a long moment of contemplation over what Kyra had revealed to him.

She shook her head sadly. "Nikkos mentioned several human child skeletons. I have little doubt that they belong to that child and her brother," Kyra hated the words as they came out of her mouth.

"Do you think perhaps it is her restless spirit that pulled you back into the house?" Nyles asked.

"It's possible. People who die in such a traumatic way are known to leave their specters behind," Kyra replied.

"Tinka is a nut for ghost lore. She's investigated hundreds of hauntings. You should tell her about your dream when we get back. If there is a way to communicate with this child, she could be a valuable source of information. If nothing else, we might be able to put her soul to rest," Nyles added.

Kyra nodded solemnly.

Layers upon layers, mysteries that lead to more mysteries. This assignment had kept her so busy that she had been unable to do much snooping about the succession matter. Her failure bothered her deeply. She never wanted to disappoint her father on anything, and this was a supremely important matter.

"Try not to worry about that, dear. I won't be stepping down until all this is settled and the repercussions seen," the Architect said from across the aisle. His seat was still tipped back, and if he hadn't spoken, one would never have known that he was even awake. Kyra's face flushed, and she inhaled deeply, prepared to set forth with a tirade.

"Before you get all huffy and accuse me of reading your thoughts, you were broadcasting, again. I am fairly certain that a psychic monkey could have picked up on that," he continued with a wry grin.

Kyra instantly deflated. He knew her far too well. "Well, since you are over there playing possum, care to weigh in on my dream?"

"I have to agree with Nyles. Tinka will be an excellent reference. If that little girl's spirit is still around, she could crack this case for us. She saw the men who came with the Imps. She could give us a description; however, I must caution that it could also be a trap. Whoever set up Cobbwick's memory block was extremely powerful and could use such trickery to pull you in and perhaps do the same, if not worse, to you." His expression was somber.

Kyra's frown deepened. A very private person, the idea of someone delving into her mind caused rage to rise within her. She had spent years working on veiling her thoughts and blocking people out. Whatever this thing was, it had to be close to, if not as powerful, as the Architect.

"I'm going to put a top security clearance requirement on all of the material pertaining to this investigation. I need you to issue several security badges to most of my team." Kyra navigated away from her own disturbing thoughts.

"I will issue them; however, they will only pertain to this case file."

Kyra nodded. As much as she would like to believe that her team was trustworthy, she knew that giving *carte blanche* clearance to the team was unwise.

The conversation stalled, and Kyra lapsed into her own thoughts. The smooth voice of the captain coming across the intercom startled her. He announced that they would be landing in ten minutes and to please make sure their belts were fastened.

The ride from the airstrip to the base was just as quiet. Kyra stewed. She had lost an entire day in the investigation process, and all she had been able to come up with was more questions.

Exiting the tubes, she looked at her companions.

"I'm going to head to a Simon terminal and toss out a meeting for tomorrow at 10:00 a.m." Her watch said it was just after 8:00 p.m. "If you want to go to the study, I'll meet you there about quarter to nine. Order up dinner, will you? I'm starving." Kyra used that as her goodbye. She swept down the hall, leaving the other two staring after her.

* * * *

"She is something else," Nyles mumbled softly.

"That, she is; however, we'd best do as she suggests. Her hungry is a rather frightening thing," the Architect replied.

The two fell into step as they headed toward the study.

Shaking his head, he fought back a sigh. As much as he loved her, being the hanger on was getting a bit old. She expected trust and loyalty not only from him, but from the team. She had not openly questioned them, yet. He had seen her leaving the camp, following up on reports. Every piece of information that they had given her, she had checked if possible. He knew better than to expect trust to come immediately; however, he needed to sit her down and talk to her about how taking others for granted would alienate those who wanted to help.

* * * *

The Architect smiled to himself as he pulled out his keys. Kyra never even paused to ponder if he and Nyles would do as she said. While the destination and need for food were perfectly logical conclusions, she never took into account that perhaps they would wish to eat alone. She had eased quickly into her role. He was pleased with her development; however, he would have to find a kind way of showing her that loyalty had to be earned not just commanded. Given the strides she'd made already, though, he would have to be cautious not to deflate her.

* * * *

As the clock on the mantle slipped to quarter to nine, a knock on the door brought Kyra on the heels of the dinner cart. Her expression gave away nothing as she snatched a roll from the cart, tearing off a bite with her teeth.

"Kyra, my dear, your timing is impeccable," the Architect said with an amused smile.

She glanced at her watch, comparing it with the clock on the wall. She shrugged as she peered under the silver dish covers. Picking out which one she wanted, she settled into her favorite recliner and began to eat voraciously. "If I say nothing else about staying at home base, having hot food is amazing. I seriously think that we need to rethink road rations, 'cause honestly, mystery meat in gravy gets old fast," she said between bites.

The Architect laughed. "I'll speak to Gus about it."

"Did you get everything you needed done?" Nyles asked.

"I did. I moved the meeting to noon and requested to have a luncheon sandwich tray set up."

The rest of the meal was eaten in silence. Kyra noted an uncovered dish on the tray. Placing her empty dish on the cart, she lifted up the cover on the mystery dish. A sigh of happiness escaped her. Arranged artfully on a plate, and drizzled with chocolate, lay six *cannoli*.

She picked one up. Then, recalling her manners, carried the plate to the others. Soon, she was seated back in her chair, devouring the two delicate dessert pastries in absolute bliss.

She smiled up at the Architect. "Father, you're trying to seduce me into staying here more with decadent pastries."

He grinned. "Well, is it working?" he asked with a wink.

"It doesn't hurt the negotiations." She returned his wink.

* * * *

Nyles loved seeing the free and open way they teased each other. Unfortunately, it made him realize that no matter how close he thought he was to her, there was another level he could never reach. He felt a twinge of envy as he watched their smiles.

"Lady and gent, I wish to thank you for the field trip, the amazing dinner and dessert, and as always, stellar company. I must now rest my bones before tomorrow's work begins," he said with a smile, wincing slightly as his hooves clacked loudly against the stone floor.

* * * *

Kyra yawned. "That is a wonderful idea. Father, do you need anything before I turn in?" She rolled the cart to the door.

"I'm fine. Shall I see you for breakfast or just catch up with you at the meeting?"

"I'll be over in the morning. I have to set up team assignments." She affirmed his permission to stay involved.

"All right, then. Good night to both of you, and sleep well," the Architect said, though the last part was jumbled by a yawn.

"Good night," they replied in unison and headed out the door.

"I'm going to see if I can hunt Tinka down first thing in the a.m. She might have time in the afternoon to speak with you about your dream, if you would like," Nyles said.

"That would be great. Make it around four, if you can. I have no idea how long the meeting is going to last. I don't want to make her wait around for me."

He stood in an awkward silence as the pull between them intensified. Kyra couldn't help but notice how soft and sweet his lips appeared. *How easy it would be to tiptoe up and kiss them softly.* Her body took her musings as actions. His strong arms circled around her waist. Paused precariously close, she closed her eyes, wanting nothing more in that moment than to kiss him.

The moment was crushed. Footsteps coming down the hall caused them to move apart so quickly that Kyra backed into the wall, hitting her head with a thud.

Her vision swam. It took her a second before she could see to whom the footsteps belonged. To her surprise, it was Anaraba.

Anaraba took in the scene with a knowing glance but made no reference to it. "Kyra, I'm glad to catch you. I did not want to use the radio system, as he says it's higher clearance. I'm sorry it's so late, but Doctor Barker asked me to find you and see if you were available to come to the lab."

Kyra sighed. *What was I thinking?* "I know it must be important, or else, he would wait until morning. Catch you at the meeting tomorrow," she said to Nyles as she hurried away.

The pair of women made their way through the silent hallways. Kyra was pleased that Anaraba chose not to ask or even mention what had just happened.

"How do you like Medical?" Kyra asked.

"I love it there. Everywhere I turn is knowledge and people willing to teach what they know for the good of all. The experience I am gaining is invaluable. You were the first non-Enoch I had ever met. In the time I have been here, I've been exposed to thirty-three different races, and those are just my coworkers! Next week, I start seeing patients. It is exhilarating," her low voice hummed with excitement.

Kyra was pleased that she had taken so well to her new home. Kyra had been concerned when Anaraba had made her choice. Medical seemed a sterile environment for one so used to being in the wilds; however, it appeared to be going fine.

They arrived at Medical and went through the procedure which had seemed so strange to her at first and was now common place. Given that it was nearly eleven o'clock, the halls were empty and the lights dimmed. Kyra gave furtive glances into the shadow-laden corners, only to find that they held nothing more than the things they should.

Anaraba looked completely relaxed. Kyra did her best to emulate her—she did have a reputation to maintain after all. They moved quickly through corridors and hallways. Kyra checked around every time they went through a doorway or turned, looking for any discernible landmarks, but the rooms and halls all looked the same. She was completely lost. She had no idea Medical was this big. Finally, ahead of them in bold, black letters against a glaring, yellow background was the word "Lab". They stood outside the doors. The windows were frosted, so she could not see what lay on the other side of that slightly forbidding sign.

Anaraba took out her badge and slid it into the machine. The light went green, and the doors whooshed outward, greeting the newcomers with a blast of frigid air. Kyra hesitated slightly as the scene that greeted her was an alien one.

The walls were lined with stainless steel shelves. Bottles, tubes, dishes, and jars of all kinds were set meticulously on them. Everything was locked securely behind sheets of glass. The harsh, florescent lights only served to make the scene more outlandish.

Workstations were set up in neat rows of three. She assumed all of the equipment that lined these tables was for the work done here. She had never been big into science. Microscopes and Bunsen burners were the limit of her knowledge. The rest was beyond her. It could just as easily be an alien lab on some distant planet as it was the lab inside her home.

She watched the people working diligently at their stations. They were dressed in green hospital scrubs, with matching caps and a mask. They were sets of eyes that followed her steps inside.

Anaraba nodded to two of the figures whom Kyra could not even tell apart, much less recognize who they were. They nodded back, not bothering to hide their curiosity.

Kyra held her stoic expression, not giving anyone or anything her attention for more than a moment. She followed Anaraba, hoping that where they were going was far away from this place.

Anaraba led her to the back of the room where they passed through yet another airlock and light decontamination. Kyra was pretty sure she would never carry another germ. The room they entered was much like the one they left, except smaller. An oversized table stood at its center. Leaning over a microscope was Doctor Barker. He wore the same sterile, green scrubs as the others, but without the hat and mask. He also sported a lab coat inscribed with his name. Underneath, it simply said "Department Head".

He looked up as they entered. Kyra studied his face, searching for any lasting signs of the chemical he had been exposed to. He smiled. For all appearances, he was completely normal.

"Kyra, please forgive me. I know it's late, and you just got in, but I wanted you to have this information right away." Leland's face was flushed with excitement, his tone animated. In all the time she had known him, she had never really noticed him. Even when he was tending to her, he had been a timid, introverted man. Something certainly had him riled up.

"I have been work on the blood from the creature you encountered in the forest." He motioned her to come over behind the workstation.

On his laptop was a picture of two strands of DNA. One was blue and one was white.

"I was able to find out that it was a genetic hybrid that the Imps had created," Kyra said.

He nodded vigorously. "Oh yes, and after a great amount of work, I have been able to reconstruct the two individual patterns that were merged to make the creature. The blue strand comes from the Imp. Thankfully, we had that on file. Knowing what belonged in that strain made it possible to pull out what didn't belong and arrange it in a sequence."

"So, the white strand is the unknown creature's DNA?" Kyra asked.

"Oh, no. Not unknown. It was also on file. I was able to match it once I had it complete." His hands clasped together like a child celebrating a victory.

Both Kyra and Anaraba stared at him. Kyra was sure he wanted her to ask, but she didn't really go for conversation games. He could just come out with it. It wouldn't be long. He was already fairly bursting to tell her.

As she predicted, less than ten seconds passed before he spoke, "It's an Emus."

Composure and reputation forgotten, Kyra's mouth dropped open. Leland nodded in satisfaction, obviously pleased that his revelation had the reaction he had expected. "Where did a group of filthy Imps get a Fae guard pet?" Kyra asked, her expression still one of shock.

"I have little to no idea," Leland replied. "However, I am absolutely positive that is what it is."

"If you don't mind, Kyra, could you please tell me what an Emus is?" Anaraba asked softly.

Kyra started slightly. That woman was so quiet, it was easy to forget she was even present.

"Of course. An Emus is the Fae version of a watchdog. Usually, the biggest it gets would be the size of a small bear—around two hundred to two hundred-fifty pounds tops. They are covered in shaggy fur of various colors, and they have long snouts." The beast she saw in the forest very much resembled an Emus, and she was annoyed at herself for not noticing it herself.

"How many of these things have you ever seen? With the genetic mutations, the circumstances in which you came across it, no one could fault you," Anarabe said in a determined way.

Kyra simply nodded, then turned to the doctor. "Can you tell the traits it has from each side? Its strengths? Possible weaknesses?"

Leland shook his head no. "I can tell you what it's made of, but I can't tell you what it can do. If I were you, I would assume it bears all of the strengths and by the same token all the weaknesses."

The wheels inside Kyra's head started to turn. She would add that to the list of things that needed to be looked into. The ugly question popped into her mind. *Was it possible that the race aiding the Imps were Fae?* Despite their warrior status, they had entered into the war very late in the conflict—near the end, in fact, when it was certain the Imps were going to lose. The gears sped faster, her brain whirling with the possibility that part of her could belong to the race that almost brought an end to world order as they knew it.

She took a deep breath. Keeping the tumultuous feelings from spilling over into her voice, she said, "Doctor Barker, Anaraba. I want to thank you very much for bringing this to my attention in an expedient manner.

"As I'm sure you can imagine, everything connected with this case has been moved to top security clearance. Nikkos will be receiving a temp clearance and codes, tomorrow. He can continue the work you have done so far. Now, if you will be so kind as to excuse me and lead me back out of here, I have a fair amount of things to assemble before tomorrow morning," she spoke to them with a polite smile.

They both nodded, understand the gravity of the situation at once. Anaraba led her out silently. At the airlock that led from Medical, Anaraba gave Kyra's hand a squeeze.

Before Kyra had a chance to ask her the meaning of this gesture, the girl left. Kyra shook her head. *Too many things to deal with right now than to worry about a simple gesture.*

Walking slowly back toward her room, Kyra placed her hand against her forehead. The millions of things raging inside her skull could burst out at any given moment.

I should stay up and set up all the teams and their tasks, our overall mission goals, and try to figure out what a conceivable time line is for this. I certainly don't want this going on, forever.

Of course, as soon as this is over, I will have to deal with the succession issue. Her body felt heavy, and her steps dragged. *I should just go back out to the field where I belong.* Let someone else deal with all this. Back where your Fae side belongs.

Kyra growled at herself. Pausing outside her door, she felt for any foreign presences. Receiving nothing, she went inside. She saw the shower through the bathroom door. The idea of a hot shower and sleep was incredibly seductive to her. Just let it all go for tonight. You can pick up again in the morning.

She stripped down and stepped into the delicious spray of warm water from the shower. As the water cascaded down her skin, she allowed the stress to go with it. Washing away all of the questions and concerns along with the confusion with Nyles.

As the last drops fell to the porcelain tub floor, she felt warm and sleepy. Not wanting to lose the feeling, she quickly dried off, slipped into a cotton gown, and crawled between the covers. *Sometimes, ignorance is bliss.*

Chapter Eight

Plans within Plans

Nyles awoke with the sun. Even in the underground place, he knew the exact moment the first golden rays crept over the horizon. He got up quickly. He knew he had far too much on his mind to even try to go back to sleep. Washing quickly, he headed out for the cafeteria. This day was going to require a lot of coffee. A few people were out. Some of them were the nocturnal crew, and a few like him were early risers. Making his way to the coffee car, he was surprised to see Anaraba adding cream to her coffee.

She looked up as he approached. She smiled at him. "The fates have indeed been kind to me."

He inhaled the deep, rejuvenating liquid as it poured into his cup. "Oh?" he asked, unsure if she was talking to him.

"I know that you are very busy with your current assignment, but I would like to sit down and talk with you when you have a free moment," she replied.

Thoroughly confused, he just nodded. He didn't want to appear rude. "Sure. As soon as this whole safe house thing is settled, we can do lunch or something." He was completely taken aback by her offer.

"This is good. Send me a memo in Medical the day before, if you please." She snapped the lid on her coffee, and she walked away without another word.

Nyles stirred his coffee pensively. Was it over what she had seen last night between him and Kyra? Perhaps, yet another to lay down a warning against any relationship they may have? Was it about the mission? Was it something completely unrelated? Nyles sighed deeply. It would just have to wait until this other matter was settled. Snapping on his own lid, he made his way toward Anthro, praying that the place was cleared. He had far too many things to do to be displaced, again.

* * * *

Kyra sat up and yawned. The clock read five after six. She had slept surprisingly well. Now, it was time to work. She dressed quickly—a pair of jeans, black T-shirt, and hair braided in less than a minute. After picking up her notebook, she was out her door.

She walked to the next door, pausing and waiting to hear if he was already up. She heard nothing, so she slipped in, bearing in mind to tread softly. Father had looked very tired the night before. She wanted him to get the rest he needed. She sat down at the Simon terminal, sending off a breakfast request. He would be up by the time it arrived. Never in her life had she known him to sleep past 7:00 a.m. Tiptoeing to the door, she opened it just enough to peek in and see his sleeping form beneath the covers. She watched as his chest rose and fell with each steady breath.

Back in the study, she turned the dial on the gas fireplace. After settling into her chair, she pulled out her notebook. She was instantly absorbed in her work. Remotely, she was aware that twenty minutes later, the Architect's shower turned on. Breakfast would soon be there.

A knock on the door pulled Kyra out of her work. She had filled the table beside her, as well as the arm of the sofa, with pages and pages of notes. She stretched as she made her way toward the delicious smell wafting under the door. As she opened the door, the Architect opened the door from his bedroom.

She smiled at him. "Now who's following the food tray?" she asked as she wheeled the cart in.

"I learn from the best." He took his seat as she brought him his plate and coffee.

"Before we start on today's fun, let me tell you what happened last night."

In-between bites of her omelet, she explained the visit to the alien world and what Leland had to tell her. She was pleased to see that he also sported the dumbfounded look she had on her face the night before.

"I simply can't see the warrior Fae joining up with the Imps. They only joined us when the fight was far from their wood. They wanted no harm to come to the families within the groves," he said.

"As much as I would like to say it just can't be, I have to look at all the possibilities and be objective in my observations. Even without extensive contact with the Fae, I do know firsthand how they feel about things from their world interacting with outsiders. So, in order for the Imps to have an Emus, they would have to kill its Fae owners or have it given to them," Kyra said.

The Architect simply nodded. "I guess we have another goal; however, I would prefer if you allowed me to talk to the Fae of the area. While an outsider, I am recognized by most as nonthreatening. Plus, we have already seen how they respond to you."

He was not telling her he was doing it. He was leaving it up to her discretion. Her pride swelled a notch. "I would be thrilled if you would come aboard on this. You are by far the most accepted diplomat in our organization."

"Thank you, and yes. I accept the assignment."

It was obvious to her that he was really enjoying this. "I would also like it if you would go over my objectives for each team, look at my pairings, and give me your thoughts."

It hit her with force. She was no longer a child asking her father for help. She was a grown woman, a highly regarded and distinguished agent of security, asking her peer for advice. Her smile reflected her epiphany.

Kyra laid out her notes in logical order. For the next several hours, they went over the notes, revised, changed, and finalized them. When the badges and codes were delivered by Tanya, they stopped. The alarm on Kyra's watch rung at eleven-thirty, telling her it was time to get her things together and go. At quarter until noon they headed out the door, hands full of responsibility and adventure.

Kyra heard the voices of her team before she even rounded the corner. It made her feel good to know that they were getting along, as they would be together for the foreseeable future. The Architect went in before her, taking a seat with the group. The conversation stalled just a bit, but to her delight it, picked right back up—this time involving him.

Kyra stepped through the doorway, prepared to get the ball rolling. Around her, she saw all the now-familiar faces.

As her foot touched the ground inside the room, a surge passed through her body. It was not painful. It did cause her heart to pound inside her. Its primal beat thudded against her chest. Her vision swam. She reached out for the nearest chair to support herself. She heard a voice, low and husky, unfamiliar, and quite unsettling, *"Look at them, all looking to you for guidance. They want you to stay here, inside the concrete prison, making plans and filling out papers,"* the voice dripped venom.

Kyra closed her eyes, squeezing her entire face as hard as she could, determined to remove that horrible voice from her head. She opened her eyes to see everyone staring at her. She felt an outpouring of concern from them.

She forced a smile she did not feel and said, "I swear going in and out of those lights is having an effect on me." She marched her way up to the podium, allowing her body not the slightest sign of weakness, again.

They all stared at her. She had no desire to discuss it, and ignored their looks. "My team, I want to thank you all for your dedication to this project. I have news to be shared with you. First, I must let you know that this could take several weeks, if not a month or two, to completely wrap up. Given the immense amount of time and work this is going to require, I'm asking if anyone would like to opt out of continuing with this mission. There will be no hard feelings." Kyra serenely surveyed the faces before her.

She allowed an entire minute to pass. No one spoke up.

"Very well. In that case, please pass these around, will you?" she asked Nyles, who had taken his customary position against the wall.

"These are your top clearance badges and codes. They will give you access to all the information, as this file has been moved to a highly classified status. They will, however, only access this case file. The call numbers for the file are on the back of your badges, along with your pass codes.

"Now, I'm going to inform you of what I know. After, I would like updates on what you have discovered in my absence. Then, I will be breaking you up into teams. Each team will be given a set of goals. We'll meet every Thursday to discuss progress. Then, when all the goals have been completed, we will sit down and have a wrap-up." She paused to take in the expressions around her. It wasn't until this moment that she noticed that Anna was not present.

Her frown deepened to almost a scowl. "Where is Anna?"

"I stopped by Gilly Relations to walk with her, and I got the super brush-off. I assumed she didn't want to see me or something and came straight here," Nikkos said.

"I saw nothing from her this morning, either," Kyra said.

A knock on the door announced the lunch trays had arrived.

"Go on and eat, everyone. I'm going to go check on her." She threw a look at Nyles who nodded.

The two of them made their way to Gilly Relations. Their pace was so quick that many people who saw or heard them coming simply stepped aside. Kyra could not shake the feeling that something was wrong. Did the sleeping mist have an ill effect on her? Some latent germ from the house? She pulled the door to Gilly Relations open so hard, the glass in the door rattled.

The same, polished secretary sat behind the desk. As she spied Kyra, her eyes narrowed, and her look took on a decidedly hostile tone.

Kyra smiled. She was in the mood for a battle.

"I'm here for Anna." She crossed her arms over her chest.

"As I informed the young gentlemen from Medical, Anna is unavailable, according to the memo from Mister Stevens," she said it as if that should be enough for them.

"Then, I need to speak with Mister Stevens," Kyra replied through gritted teeth, restraining her anger.

"Oh, I'm sorry, but that's not possible. He is booked into meetings all day." It was clear she wasn't at all sorry, her smile plastic.

"One of two things is going to remove me from this office. Either you give me Anna, or you give me Jason," Kyra said with a scowl.

The woman rolled her eyes and picked up the phone. Turning her back on Kyra, she spoke quietly and tersely.

Something was going on here, and Kyra felt a responsibility to see for herself that Anna was all right. Given how much Kyra had originally not wanted her on the team she had proven herself to be not only useful, but not be that bad at all.

The woman turned back. Her lips were nearly white, and she was restraining quite a bit of her own rage.

"Mister Stevens is on his way," was all she said. She went back to typing up the letter she had been working on when they made their boisterous entrance. Nyles glanced at Kyra, his eyebrow raised.

She shook her head. She closed her eyes, trying to reach out with her mind to find Jason or Anna and see if she could determine distress. A door banged and startled her eyes open. Jason wore his characteristic black suit and greasy smile. Kyra's senses picked up easily on his anger and, more interestingly, on his fear.

"Kyra, Nyles."

"Jason, where is Anna?" Kyra asked.

"She's on her way, actually. Completely my mistake. I double-booked her. I saw your personnel request, and I wanted to get the things I needed from her before I sent her to you."

His fake cheerfulness nauseated Kyra. He was lying. She didn't even need to bother looking into his thoughts, which was something she tried to refrain from doing in general, as it was an invasion of privacy. His aura exuded deception. She just had no way to prove it.

The door opened, and Anna stepped through it. She was dressed in a mocha-colored pants suit, and her long hair was bound into a tight bun. Her expression was blank. For all intents and purposes, she looked healthy, yet Kyra could not shake the impression that she was empty. Her expression and aura were just like a chalkboard that was wiped clean. She nodded to both of them.

"Please forgive my tardiness, Miss Kyra. I'm ready to come along with you, now." Even her voice was monotone.

Jason frowned slightly but then plastered on his fake smile. "Well, I have to get back to my meeting. Please, keep me updated as to how long she will be unavailable. I may have someone fill her position." With a small wave, he disappeared behind the door.

Kyra once again glanced at Nyles. *Something is definitely rotten in the state of Denmark.* This, however, was not the place to discern it.

The trio headed out silently. On their way back to the meeting room, Anna made no attempt at conversation. When they entered the meeting room, the Architect stared directly at Anna's vacant expression and frowned deeply. She settled into the empty chair, refusing any offers of food or drink.

Kyra made her way back up to the podium. She was deeply troubled by what was occurring with Anna; however, it would have to wait until the meeting was over. "Now, where were we…oh, yes. I'm going to tell you what I discovered from Cobbwick and then assign you your partners and objectives." She struggled to focus on her agenda. Between the mystery voice and Anna's rescue, her mind was in a jumble.

"After my explanations and pairings, if anyone has any updates to give, they can share them at that time.

"The Architect, Nyles, and I traveled to the prison to meet with Cobbwick to see if we could get some of our questions answered. He is still a very imposing creature; however, he seemed amicable to talking to us. He confirmed that the creature we encountered at the manor is the product of genetic engineering. When we asked him to name the race that had accompanied them in that house, as soon as he started to think, he had a seizure and went into a coma.

"It is my belief that a memory block was placed in his mind that prevented him from ever recalling that piece of information. Now, a block that well-constructed would take weeks, if not months, to put into place. Which means it has to have been done after his capture.

"Also, on our way back, I experienced a dream of a little girl hiding under the sink at the house. I believe her to be the ghost of the little girl who lived there at the time the house had been taken over. If it is possible to communicate with her, she could give us a description of the people with the Imps, helping us identify them." She took a deep breath and looked up at her enthralled audience.

"Last night, after we returned, I was summoned to the Medical lab. Doctor Barker had been able to separate the DNA of the creature we fought in the woods. The first set of DNA was Imp, and the second belonged to an Emus." Every face in the room save Anna's took on an expression of shock and surprise. Anna was still simply impassive, like a lifeless doll dressed up and seated at the table. Kyra had the urge to stop the meeting instantly and take Anna back to the study to discover what on earth was going on here. She knew, though, that there would be time for that after the tasks had been handed out, and she really did need everyone to get started.

"So, as you can see, we once again went seeking answers and came back with more questions. I'm going to do your pairings and give you your folders, so that we can try to get this mystery under control. First pair is Aieta and Soro," she said while handing them a folder.

Sciath

"I'm going to go over each team's goals with the group, just in case you come across anything in your individual research that could help your teammates."

* * * *

The Architect watched and listened to Kyra. He was truly amazed by her; however, his pride was tempered by his concern for the Wendigo, Anna. He reached out with his mind to touch hers to see how she was. He was met with a disturbing emptiness. There was simply nothing in the forefront of her mind. It was if she was standing in an endless hallway filled with doors, and all of her thoughts, memories, and feelings were locked behind the doors.

He felt Kyra's concern as well and assumed she meant to deal with it after she sent the rest of the team to work. It was wise not to create a circus out of it in front of everyone.

* * * *

"Soro and Aieta, I've tasked you with searching through the ritual artifacts brought back. In addition, check the other clues we have discovered. See if you can come up with any indication of what race we are dealing with. Also, I'd like you to compile a list of strengths and weaknesses of both the Imps and the Emus. See if you can find any sightings among the supernaturals of that area of the creature," she read off her sheet.

They both nodded, seemingly happy with their partnership and list of tasks.

"Next, I have Maria and Maltruis," she said and handed them a folder. "I have set you to discover the house's history, the anomalies in the blueprints, and find out if the ground under or around the house holds any magical significance.

"Nyles and I will be tracing Cobbwick from his capture to imprisonment, to see if we can find any one person or race that had long-term contact with him. We will also be searching through the archives to identify which races can do such powerful things to one's mind. Also, both of us will be available to any pairs that have questions or need of help."

She saw Nyles puff his chest out proudly. She had just named him the second-in-command of the mission, and his pride was hard to contain.

"The Architect will be speaking with the Fae in the vicinity to discover if any Emus had gone missing or if it was gained though another channel," she explained, her fingers lingering a moment over the bandage on her arm.

"Nikkos and Anna, you will be handling the identification of the remains. See from how far away they went missing, discerning races, as well as finding out how far away the people went missing from. It will give us an idea of how mobile they were." She watched as Anna automatically took the folder and laid it in front of her.

Nikkos nodded absently at Kyra's words. His eyes were glued to Anna. Kyra had no doubt he would accompany them to the study.

"All right, ladies and gents. If we have no further questions, I suggest we adjourn. We will meet for updates in one week." Kyra was blowing off listening to their updates, but she needed to figure out what was going on with Anna.

It seemed that everyone understood her reasons and took their leave. Anna stood up to go with them. Kyra placed her hand gently on her shoulder.

"Nikkos, would you mind accompanying her back to the study with us? I'd appreciate it if you would go get your medical bag first, though." Kyra kept a gentle but firm grip on Anna's shoulder, although she made no attempt to do anything but stand.

"I'll be there in ten minutes, tops," he replied, his expression filled with concern.

The strange quartet made their way silently through the busy corridors. A few passing people stopped to look at the glassy-eyed woman being escorted through the halls by their leader.

The Architect unlocked the door. Kyra guided Anna to her favorite chair and sat her down. Kyra looked into Anna's eyes and, for the first time, noticed a slight spark of attention.

Kyra pulled the ottoman over, so she could sit in front of her. "Anna, it's Kyra. Tell me, are you okay?" she asked with her voice low.

"I'm fine, Miss Kyra," she replied. Her responses sounded programmed; however, this time, she met Kyra's eyes when she spoke.

Kyra looked up at the Architect who motioned her to come closer to him. She stood, moving behind Anna's chair. A concerned Nikkos rushed in without even knocking. His face was flushed and his breathing rapid. Kyra guessed he had run all the way here.

"Please, give her a physical. See if you can find any reason for her current state," the Architect said.

"Nyles, please get on Simon and pull up all the info on Wendigos that we have. We can see if this is normal or a common affliction." Kyra took control of the situation. They both moved to follow her instructions.

She looked to the Architect who touched his forehead. She nodded in understanding. Closing her eyes, she opened her mind. The Architect's voice was gentle, *"I looked into Anna's mind, not prying, just looking for her surface thoughts. I could find absolutely nothing. I could feel her presence, but her mind was simply blank, like all the doors had been closed."*

Kyra's jaw set. *"It was Jason. I'm sure he did something to her."*

"It is possible, but would he risk being this obvious?" the Architect asked, sending soothing mental vibes to her.

"Nikkos," Anna said from behind them, bringing everyone to her side. She was staring at him, as if this was the first time she had seen him.

"How are you feeling?" Nikkos asked, his hand resting gently on her arm.

"I have a colossal hangover, and I don't recall drinking." She smiled wanly.

Nikkos continued his base exam.

Nyles stood up from kneeling in front the computer, his back legs knocking over a stack of the Architect's books. "I'm sorry," he muttered.

The Architect smiled. "This place is a mess and a hazard for anyone moving around," he said.

"I think I may have a reason for Anna's headache and vacant appearance," Nyles replied, still looking uncomfortable with the awkwardness of his horse half.

"Oh?" Kyra asked.

"I scanned her race file, and it said that Wendigo's are vulnerable to trance-like states after an overuse of their powers," he replied.

Everyone turned to look at Anna. Kyra fought to keep her sympathy from turning to suspicion. She deserved a chance to explain herself.

Anna glanced around at everyone present. "I know you have no reason to believe me, but if I *did* use my powers, I don't know for what," she said softly.

Kyra studied her. Her overall aura and actions spoke to the honesty of her statement. Kyra was simply not that trusting.

"Can you tell me what you remember last?" the Architect asked, moving around to take a seat in front of her.

Kyra watched him intently. He was so kind with people. He believed all people, Gilly or non, were good by nature, and it simply baffled her.

"I was compiling missing persons reports from the area. Jason summoned me to his office. There was a woman there that I had never seen before. She was Asian. Her beautiful long, dark hair extended halfway down the back of the chair. I sat down, and Jason said something about the mission and my report. Then, she touched me and—" Anna's face screwed up into a look that reminded Kyra of Cobbwick's expression before his collapse.

Nikkos placed his hand on her head. Kyra assumed he was using his power to keep her from imploding.

"Then, I saw you in the lobby with Nyles." She directed her words to Kyra. "I remember everything from the meeting, but it was like I was watching an old movie, not like I was really there."

Her voice gained more strength, but her color had yet to return.

The Architect said, "We'll find out who she is. I've approved no new visitor logs in the last several months. She has to be someone who is already here. Keep in mind how large Scíath is. I imagine there are many people under this 'roof' that Anna wouldn't know."

Kyra knew the Architect was scouring Anna's mind to get an image of the mystery woman. He could be oh-so-subtle about those things, and given Anna's weakened status, Kyra was fairly sure she hadn't even noticed.

"I'm sorry to have caused such a fuss. I hate to be an inconvenience, but..." Anna's eyes implored them. "Since I am part of this team, can I possibly get quarters outside the Gilly Relations Department?" she asked. It seemed she was as disturbed by her lack of memory as everyone else. It was evident she thought Jason was a threat to her.

"I can get you one of the visiting relative apartments inside Medical, if you'd like," Nikkos volunteered.

"That would be so very kind of you. I do hate to be so much trouble. Especially with all the work we have to do," her tone exhibited her relief.

"I will inform Jason that we are studying the after-effects of the toxin on those exposed, and you are needed to stay in Medical until the tests are concluded," the Architect replied.

Kyra was stunned. Not only was he lying, but he has done it with such poise and ease, you would have never thought it wasn't the truth. He went to his computer to send out the message.

Nikkos reassured her that she would be safe. Even Nyles seemed to be trying to help her. *It's all too pat.* A major discovery is made in Medical, and now, Jason's number one agent was being moved there. Part of Kyra wanted to believe and take Anna under her wing. That was her human half, she decided, but the Fae side was suspicious and unsure of the entire situation. Deciding that the entire thing needed more observation, she was content to let the others coddle her and get her tucked in. Not being that close to it would help her remain objective.

She settled in a far chair and watched as the pale woman was ushered out to her new accommodations with a promise from Nikkos to collect her things. As the trio left, she felt her father's eyes on her.

"This has to be hard for you." He leaned back in his desk chair.

"Why do you say that?" She retook her place in her favorite chair.

"You have to decide between your dislike for Jason and your sympathy for Anna's predicament," he said, packing his pipe.

She couldn't help but smile. He knew her far too well.

"Bounce both scenarios off me." He took a deep pull off his pipe.

She nodded. This was an activity they had been doing for a long time. As long as she could remember, they had used each other as sounding boards. Even as a child, she knew he valued her opinion.

"If Jason is the villain here, he may have had this mystery woman in his office to either use her powers on Anna or vice versa. I can see Jason using someone to delve into Anna's mind to pick up the particulars of the mission that may not have been in her official report to him. He was quite avid about having her along; however, I feel that she changed while within the group."

"How so?" he asked.

"When we first started out, she was standoffish. Not that anyone made an effort to get to know her. Then, she demonstrated her vulnerability by vomiting in the sink in reaction to a pile of decaying food. Then, she cut her hand as I was teaching them how to check windows for traps. It progressed from there. Once she was paired up with Nikkos, I think his personality put her at ease. She became more open, and by the end of the trip, she seemed like one of the team. I wonder if Jason didn't count on her becoming friendly with us. If perhaps he sent her as a spy, and she defected."

"Plausible." He blew smoke rings as he waited for the other half.

"Now, the other side also sees Anna in the wrong. It shows her thrusting herself among us, getting friendly, and making us believe she was useful so that she could more easily garner information for Jason. The move to Medical could be part of it. It's easy to deduce with Nikkos's crush on her that if she asked for some place to stay, he would offer, thereby putting her even closer to the test results on the toxin, as well as the blood evidence. Perhaps, Jason is connected to those who were involved with the Imps. He could be doing damage control," she finished.

They sat a moment in silent contemplation.

"While I'm inclined to believe that Jason is unethical, power hungry, and generally not a nice guy, I can't see him being in league with the Imps. If you recall his race is Gilly. I find it highly unlikely that everyday Gillies would join with a race hell-bent on their eradication," he said. "I'm thinking his interests lie more toward succession than treason."

"I see your point," she said as an audible grumble escaped from her stomach. "You missed lunch."

"Yes, I did. I'll order something in a few minutes."

"I'll do it. The tray was devoured by the time I got to it as well." He tapped a few keys on his keyboard.

"Did you manage to get a look at the mystery woman?" Kyra asked.

He frowned. "I get nothing by you, do I? I did, and I didn't say it at the time as not to alarm anyone, but I don't recall her face."

Her eyebrows rose. "You always recall faces, past and present."

"Indeed. I'm going to call Galerius and make sure no one authorized any outside visitors. It is possible that her entry was approved for this date a while back, and I'm simply not recalling it." He tapped his pipe out in his hand.

"I think before we can determine which scenario fits Anna, we need to know who she is," Kyra said. "I guess I can just go to Jason and ask as well."

"I'm not sure we want to do that until we know who this woman is and what she can do. I want no one else hurt," the Architect said.

Kyra thought about protesting. She could take care of herself, but she had zero interest in spending time alone with Jason. A soft knock sounded on the door. Stretching out her senses, she felt Nyles's strong, alluring presence on the other side of the door. "Come in," she called.

He entered, and his face was red. The vein in his temple was pulsing, and his hands were still clenched into fists.

"Good grief. What's wrong?" the Architect, asked obviously picking up on the same clues as Kyra.

"I ended up going to Anna's room to pick up her things. Nikkos wanted to scan her brain to see if he could find any residual energies. Jason is a despicable—"He stopped with a glance at Kyra. "He's a something I won't say in the presence of a lady. He interrogated me, demanded I return 'his' employee, and he was going to have me written up for stealing things from inside his department."

"That's outrageous," the Architect said, color rising on his cheeks. "Treoraí or not, he cannot treat other members of Scíath in such a manner."

The Architect went and began banging away on the keyboard, what was no doubt a scathing memo to Jason. A knock came at the door. Kyra had no need to stretch out her senses. The smell of food was making her mouth water.

Nyles opened the door. Kyra saw three dishes on the cart and instantly marveled at her father's ability to make sure everyone was taken care of. Kyra and Nyles sat down and ate quietly as the Architect continued to stab at the letters on his keyboard. A short time later, he pushed back from the table.

Kyra again saw how frail he really was as he steadied himself, going down the two steps from his desk. He lifted up the remaining lid and sat to eat. No one spoke, no doubt intent on their food and on their recent developments.

Kyra then discovered a small dish with three slices of cheesecake on it.

"I swear you're bribing to keep me here forever," she said playfully.

"I do what I can," the Architect's voice and posture revealed his exhaustion, the rage having left him. "I'm going to send out a message to the Fae chief and request a meeting in a couple of days." The Architect stifled a yawn. "For now, I'm going to take a nap."

He kissed Kyra gently on the forehead before heading for his bedroom.

"Well, I guess we should get started on our list." She finished off her last bite of dessert.

"Where would you like to start?" Nyles asked.

"I'm thinking we should e-mail a request to the warden for all personnel who were present when Cobbwick was admitted, as well as any prisoners. Since he was a prisoner, he was transported by Security, which means his chain of custody would be documented in the records there."

"I can go and e-mail the warden while you go talk to Galerius. He is, after all, more fond of you than me," Nyles said.

"I'm not sure he is ever really fond of anyone; however, I agree with you. It's easier for me to get in than for you to."

Nyles looked at clock on the mantle and did a double-take. He clapped his hands loudly. "Given the mess we just went through, I completely and totally forgot I set that appointment up for you with Tinka at four."

She smiled broadly. "Well, look at it this way. You remembered at three instead of at four, so I'm not late."

"Point. You're supposed to meet her in the mirror library." He gathered his notes.

Kyra was not a fan of the mirror library. There was something disconcerting about dozens of your own reflection staring back at you, but if that's where she had to go, that was where she would go.

"We should meet up and go over what we have later this evening," Nyles said. "I'd ask you for another dinner meeting, but given our recent luck…I think it's best we just meet back here and order food."

"Agreed. This is definitely our home base. If I were to stay in more, I'd have to get an office or something. Though, I can't imagine anywhere being better than this." She surveyed the room that filled so many of her fond memories.

Shaking herself out of the reminiscence, she stood up. "I have an hour. Gives me time to stop in Security to request that chain of command. Let's meet up around seven?"

"Sounds good to me," Nyles replied.

Kyra made her way toward her department. Even though she was one of Securities' top agents, she spent very little time in the department. Debriefs, assignments, and weapon allotment—which was about all she cared to do. She appreciated the stark utility and functional setup of the department; however, it did not welcome its agents to stay long.

She put her hand on the scanner, taking a moment to rearrange the papers in her arms while she waited for the light to turn green. The door hissed open, and she made her way in. The moment her foot crossed the door frame, something was different. Half of the lights were off, giving the entire space an eerie glow. Her steps were cautious. Reaching out with her mind, she felt for the presence of her boss—or anyone, for that matter. She received nothing back. The entire department was empty. This was the second time this had happened to her. Moving slowly toward Galerius's desk, she spied a piece of paper lying there. Her first instinct was to look away and log into the evidence terminal, but her curiosity nagged at her that it may give a clue as to where everyone was. Glancing at the door, she went to the desk. It was a piece of paper torn out of a notebook. Written in Galerius's unmistakable block handwriting, it said, "3:00 p.m. dining hall."

She turned it over looking for more information, but it yielded none. She shrugged and made her way to the evidence terminal. She wanted to get in and out as quickly as possible. Not only did she have a meeting to make, but this place was just downright unfriendly in the half dark. Logically, she knew she could turn the lights on. She had every right to be here, but she couldn't help feeling like she was trespassing, as if turning on the lights would alert someone to her presence.

She typed out her documentation request, glancing over her shoulder constantly. The terminal informed her it would take two hours to retrieve her documents from the archives. Satisfied with that time frame, she picked up her papers and headed quickly for the door. As she stepped out the door, she felt much better. The hall was full of people and well-lit. It quickly dispelled the odd feelings Security had given her. Moving toward the dining hall, she decided to swing through and get tea before meeting Tinka. Plus, she could swing through the dining hall and perhaps see who Galerius was meeting with.

She frowned. She really shouldn't be checking up on her Treoraí, but her gut wouldn't let it drop. Once in the dining hall, she looked around, trying to keep her gaze and movements as natural as she could while making her way up to the counter to order her tea. The clock said 3:30 p.m. Unless it was a very short meeting, he should still be here. With her tea, she went to the bar, adding her nutmeg and cinnamon as she glanced around, again.

She was about to give up when she saw him, nestled in the same back booth she and Moira sat in when they wanted to speak in private. Due to her angle, she couldn't see whom he was speaking to. Moving to throw her stir stick in the garbage and hoping for a better view, she was thwarted, again. Sighing, she gave up and headed out. The only way she was going to see who he was talking to would be to take the obvious approach and walk up to his booth. That was a step she was not prepared to take.

The mirror library was situated below Anthropology. It housed contemporary as well as classic novels. It was a place to find pleasure reading instead of the histories and other non-fiction materials complied in the other library. It had been a very long time since Kyra had time to do any reading for pleasure.

Perhaps, when this was all over, she would take a week of her vacation time and just relax or go to the shore. She had several weeks accumulated but just never had time to take it. After this succession thing, it would be good to go somewhere with Father. The frailty she had noted in him recently concerned her. She felt bad for not spending more time with him.

Kyra was lost in her thought as she made her way through the maze of halls. She looked forward to speaking with Tinka and spending time with Nyles this evening. Checking the wall map as she passed it, she found she was about half way there. She upped her pace. She had no desire to be late. Rounding the bend, she heard the disturbance before she actually saw anything.

"I told you if you ever spoke to her like that again, I would teach you a lesson," a young man's voice shouted.

Kyra's shoulders slumped. *Here we go, again.*

The same young Wizard and the same Giant stood across from each other as a crying Milyna stood off to the side. Kyra shoved her way through the onlookers who had gathered. She took a deep breath and assessed the situation. The Giant's hands were both balled into fists. The Wizard held his wand with a white-knuckled grip. This looked far more explosive than the last confrontation. There was no way to get between them, so she raised her voice.

"It seems to me that both of you should have better things to do than fight in the hallways," she kept her tone hard, eyeing them both with displeased looks.

"He's gone too far this time," the Wizard answered, not taking his eyes off his foe.

The Giant cracked a half-smile. He was obviously enjoying tormenting this couple. Kyra's rage rose. They would have enough trouble without some bigot Giant. "What was said?" Kyra hid her ire. She was the diplomat in this situation. She would not allow her personal bias to be involved.

"He said that we were the beginning of another abomination, and someone should sterilize me," Milyna answered through her tears.

Kyra saw red. Her rage filled her, as she turned on him. Before she was even aware of it, a bolt of energy flew from her, striking the Giant squarely in the chest. The bolt knocked him back into the wall, causing the stones to fracture. The onlookers gasped. Kyra returned to her senses and stared at the carnage she had caused. The Giant was most definitely unconscious. Kyra moved closer to him. Her nose wrinkled as the acrid smell of burnt flesh rushed toward her. His chest presented with a burn several inches wide and long. The scorched skin still smoked in places. Kyra picked up her radio and quickly switched it to the emergency frequency, calling for medics and giving her location. She turned toward Milyna who threw her arms around her.

Kyra froze. She had just attacked someone, inside Scíath. She would be taken into custody. She had hurt an innocent. The Wizard saw her forlorn expression and peeled Milyna off, holding her as she sobbed. Kyra stood dumbfounded as she waited for Medical to arrive.

Within minutes, it seemed everyone was there. She saw Tinka, Leland, Galerius, and Moira. She turned around in a circle. Hundreds of eyes glared at her, judging her. She could hear their thoughts. They feared her, condemned her for simply existing. Her eyes rested on the face of a beautiful, Asian woman. Kyra stared, thinking that this should mean something to her, but her mind was simply too scattered to bring together the thought.

She gaped at the creature she had harmed. Suddenly, her father and Nyles were beside her. The Architect placed his arm around her waist and guided her away from the whispering hordes who stared at her.

Before she knew it, she was seated in her chair with a cup of steaming tea in her hands. The smell of chamomile drifted gently up, clearing her senses.

She looked from Nyles to the Architect. Neither wore judgmental expressions.

"I'm sorry," she said, her voice trembling.

"Of that, I have no doubt. Could you please explain to me what happened?" the Architect said in a gentle voice.

"I was on my way to meet with Tinka to discuss my dream. I came around the corner to see the young Wizard and Giant preparing to fight. This is not the first time I had encountered this situation. I assumed I could diffuse it again, but I had no idea that the Giant had been so cruel. He told them they were the start to another abomination, and that someone should get Milyna sterilized." She fought to suppress the anger again rearing its head.

Nyles's mouth fell open while the Architect's set in a hard line.

"What in the hell is going on around here? Mystery visitors, Treoraí acting like idiots, bigoted morons insulting fellow members?" the Architect demanded of no one in particular.

"I was angry, but I never intend to harm him. Is he going to be all right?" Kyra asked.

"He will be fine. The burns were superficial and the bump to the head negligible, though it may give him a headache," Nyles responded.

The Architect took a long sip of his tea and packed his pipe. When he spoke again, his voice was calm, "This is a new manifestation of your Fae powers, it seems."

"It is. I must gain control over it. I harmed an innocent."

"While I never advocate violence as a method for solving issues, he brought that on himself with such ridiculous behavior," the Architect replied.

"What will happen to me?" Kyra asked anxiously.

"Well, Tinka will be here shortly to have your meeting. Then, I think we should all have a nice dinner. I'm going to call the masseuse we hired and see about getting you into the day spa tomorrow morning," the Architect said.

Kyra's eyes widened. *Why aren't I being charged?* Was he using his power to keep her from justice?

"If you think you are not being charged, because you are my daughter, you are wrong. You did not intend harm. There are plenty of accidents that come about as people mature and learn their powers. Plus, I think everyone there would agree that he had a few lumps coming to him," the Architect replied.

Kyra let out a deep breath that she didn't realize she had been holding. "I really am sorry. Are Milyna and her young friend all right?"

"Indeed, she and Seth were headed back to the garden when I saw them last," the Architect replied.

"They really do seem to love each other," Kyra noted.

"Indeed. I venture to say the large brute would have received far worse than he got had you not intervened," Nyles observed.

Kyra nodded. "Someone must talk with him. He can have whatever opinions he wants; however, he simply cannot go around expressing them like that."

"I will ask Di to sit down with him and explain our policy on racial equality," the Architect said as he searched for his tin of cookies. After removing the lid, he passed the box around.

Kyra took her favorites before passing it on to Nyles. She felt numb inside, as if the rage had ebbed away after burning everything else inside her out. She looked into the eyes of those who loved her. She knew she was truly blessed to have them in her life.

A soft knock on the door made everyone jump.

"Come in," the Architect called.

Tinka stuck her head in the door and looked around.

"Is it all right for me, now?" she asked.

"Indeed, come in. Have some tea and cookies," the Architect said.

She placed her hand on Kyra's shoulder and gave it a brief squeeze before she settled into a chair.

"Please, don't think me meddling, but I took a moment to print off these descriptions of Fae powers. Keep in mind yours may have variations due to your human genes, but this might help you a bit," Tinka said, handing Kyra a small stack of papers.

"Thank you. The worst part about it was I did not even know what had happened."

"I can only imagine. Hook up with Di in the next couple of days. She should be able to help you as well. Now, on to the ghosts. You do know I'm a raving fan of spirits." Tinka changed the subject easily.

Kyra smiled appreciatively at her and launched into the tale.

* * * *

Jason sat at his desk, his hands steepled before him. Across from him sat the visitor. Her hands were folded in her lap. She wore an exquisite red gown, embroidered with gold dragons. She finished her story and sat silently, awaiting his response.

"She attacked him, in plain view of many witnesses. Yet, she was escorted out like a victim instead of a criminal. If that doesn't smack of favoritism, I don't know what does," Jason said with a smile. "We need to make sure it is well-circulated that she was not charged or even taken into custody for this."

"To what end?" she asked.

"I want her out of Scíath. She could foul up many of the plans I have in the works, as well as digging up things that just don't need to be found. If I can stir up enough of an outcry against her, not even the Architect will be able to protect her."

"Won't that ruin any favor you have with the old man?" she asked.

"I'm not as worried about that. There are ways around him to get what I want." She raised an eyebrow, but he had no intention of elaborating on his statement. "I need you to do what you do and keep an eye on her. I want to know everything she is doing, who she is meeting with, and so on," he said.

"What about Anna's inside recon?" she asked

Jason scowled. "You saw the same things I did. She's a loose cannon. I would have had her eliminated. She knew it, which is why she had them protect her."

"I think they protected her, because you sent her out in a near-idiot state."

"What choice did I have? That Kyra is a nightmare. She would have raised the roof had I not given her access to Anna. I made the wrong choice. I should have sent you." His lips pursed in anger. "Speaking of which, you'd best get back into the face on your badge before people start asking questions about who you are." He watched keenly, as he loved the transformation.

The woman took in a deep breath. Before his eyes, her face began to change. The skin tone lightened, the eyes rounding, her beautiful jet hair fading to a tawny brown. She stood, and he watched as her shapely figure flattened out into a tomboy physique.

"That never fails to amaze me," he said.

She clipped on a badge that identified her as Martha Wilkins, a file clerk in Gilly Relations.

"If that will be all, sir?" she asked, her silky voice replaced by a slightly high-pitched one.

"Yes, I expect a daily report," he said, picking up the paper on his desk.

She left, silently fiddling with the thick, metal bracelet that adorned her wrist.

* * * *

Tinka sat back. "I must say, I miss field work. This sounds like an absolutely fascinating adventure! I have a feeling that you are dealing with sinister forces, both corporal and non. We can try to contact the girl's spirit from here, but I think it is bound to the house in which she died. I'm certain that were we to be sitting in the kitchen, we would be able to contact her. I would warn against opening a gate in the ritual room, though. Too many spirits have passed through there, and we might end up with a supernatural melee."

"Tinka, if we arranged a flight, would you be willing to take a two-day leave and help them with this?" the Architect asked.

"I thought you would never ask," she replied with a grin. "I can have everything ready to go by 8:00 a.m."

Kyra wasn't sure she was ready to go back to the house, given all that had happened. Time was of the essence, though. They were four months out from the summit, and they would need a safe house. She sighed inwardly and put on a strong face. "Let me phone Lev and see what can be done." Kyra went to the phone.

* * * *

The Architect saw Kyra had turned her back on them as she spoke into the receiver. He turned to Tinka and Nyles, lowering his voice as he spoke, "Please, try to keep a lid on gossip about the events, today. I know it won't be completely possible; however, given who she is, this event could do her a great deal of harm."

"I know her attack was accidental, but to be honest, I'd have given that idiot a stiff uppercut on purpose had I walked into it," Nyles said, crossing his arms over his chest.

"I know we all feel the same about his remarks, but Scíath preaches nonviolence and diplomaic problem-solving," the Architect replied.

They sat up as she placed the receiver down and came back to retake her chair.

* * * *

"Lev said he can't get the proper permissions and flight plans laid in for forty-eight hours. We can leave first thing on Saturday morning." She was relieved that she wasn't going to have to dash back out.

Tinka pouted slightly. "Ah, well. I will be ready! Now, if you will excuse me, it's getting close to dinner, and I need to shoo out my workaholics and close the department."

"Thank you for everything," Kyra said.

Tinka nodded. "Nyles, I'm going to transfer all your other projects to Brad. It's obvious that you are needed here for the time being. Before you protest, like him or not, he's motivated and has a good track record." She stood.

Nyles nodded, though his expression was sour.

They made their good-byes.

Tinka left, and the trio remained silent until the door clicked softly behind her.

"Brad?" Kyra and the Architect asked in unison

"He's the rising star of the department. He's a Nochi, and his memory and energy levels are high, even in the supernatural world," he explained.

Kyra mind-searched her memory for a description of a Nochi, but she came up blank.

"They are an Asian race, from the mountains of Tibet. They are descended from a trio of priests who received enlightenment and were granted powers of mind and energy," the Architect explained.

"Asian!" Kyra exclaimed loudly, causing both of them to stare at her. "I saw her, in the hall, when the fight occurred—a beautiful, Asian woman," Kyra said.

"May I see if she matches the one from Anna's mind?" the Architect asked.

"Please do." She faced him, and she and closed her eyes. She let her mind go blank as to allow him easier access to the information he sought.

"It's the same woman. I've gone over every approved visitor log and employee badge issued for the last three months. I've found no trace of her," he replied.

"So, we have a breach in security," Kyra exclaimed.

"It would appear so. I've looked back over incident reports to see if anything has been broken into or gone missing, and I have nothing other than the random artifacts that I'm still hoping were misplaced. If she is here to cause trouble, she hasn't done it, yet. I have a meeting with Jason tomorrow at noon to discuss his behavior, Anna's condition, and this woman," he said.

"I will not allow you to meet with him alone," Kyra said.

He raised an eyebrow. "I understand your concern, and whenever I have to do a disciplinary meeting, I have a witness. Di will be present," he explained.

Kyra visibly relaxed.

"I'm going to set up a morning spa appointment for you. You need to relax." His tone left no room for disagreement.

"You two can start work again after she is finished," he said to Nyles, who was nodding.

"I think you will benefit from it," Nyles agreed.

Kyra thought about protesting. She never had time for such things before and had always considered them frivolous; however, after today's outburst, it would do her good to get her emotions back in line.

"Oh, I totally forgot. I need to pick up the chain of custody log for Cobbwick. I ordered it when I was on my way to meet Tinka." Kyra's limbs grew heavy at the idea of having to go to Security, again. This chair was so comfortable. The company was good, and she felt safe here.

"We can pick it up, tomorrow. We aren't going to do anything with it, tonight," Nyles said.

"I concur. I'll order dinner, and we can watch a movie. I happen to have one of your favorites on those little disks," the Architect suggested.

"Which movie is it?" she asked.

"*The Wizard of Oz.* Apparently, we went to all plasma screens. I allowed one to be put in as long as it could be hidden away." He gestured to the space above the fireplace. "I have a remote somewhere that turns it on and a disk player, too. Galerius insisted I have one for reviewing security footage, if need be."

"I think it sounds like a delightful idea. I'm not honestly sure I could concentrate on work tonight, anyway," Kyra had a note of tiredness in her voice.

"Shall I order? Any requests?" the Architect asked as he watched her.

"I trust your judgment," Kyra said.

"I'm going to slip next door and put on some pajamas." She stood.

Nyles stood with her.

Moving over to his computer, the Architect ordered up dinner.

"I'll be fine. I'm going one door down," she said, leaving. When Kyra came quietly back in, she was dressed in a simple set of red satin pajamas, her hair still braided.

"You look more comfortable," Nyles said.

"I'm getting spoiled by being in base. Good food, comfy clothes, and a bed night after night," she replied.

"Careful...you might decide you want to be a squint instead of a field agent," Nyles said in a teasing tone.

She laughed.

The Architect rejoined them. "Dinner will be here shortly. I want to thank both of you for spending so much of your precious time with me. It gets lonely in here at times."

Kyra felt a stab of guilt. She had run off, perusing her own life, and had cut him out of it completely. Unconscionable, given how much of his life he had devoted to her. "I can't think of anywhere else I'd rather be," she replied.

"I have to agree. I'm going to miss hanging out in here once this is all over," Nyles said.

"My door is always open to you," the Architect said to Nyles.

"Thank you," Nyles replied.

The rest of the evening was spent enjoying a wonderful meal and a movie. Shortly before midnight, the Trio parted ways.

Kyra had a restless night. She was thrown back into the fight scene. Though, this time, she was watching from above as a great, red pulse left her body and struck the Giant. In this version, the onlookers were hostile. They began to chant "abomination" as they pelted her with stones. She woke as the sun rose. Her cheeks were damp with her own tears.

She emerged from the shower as someone knocked on the door.

"One moment," she said as she slipped into her jeans and a T-shirt.

Opening the door, she came face-to-face with a man she had never seen before. He was dressed in what looked to be white silk pajamas. He was tall but rather average looking. His appearance gave no indication as to his race.

"Miss Kyra?" he asked.

"I am," she replied.

"I've been sent to escort you to your spa appointment," he said, his voice deep and raspy.

"Oh, yes. Let me slip into my shoes, and I'll be right with you." She had gone back and forth in her mind as to whether or not she would go through with this. In the end, she decided that if Father had gone to the trouble to make the arrangements for her, she should go. She slipped into her shoes and glanced over at her weapon and holster. *I shouldn't need it.* Plus, she had far more dangerous weapons at her disposal, it seemed.

She stepped out into the hall. The amount of traffic was minimal, but as soon as she shut the door behind her, the pace slowed. Everyone looked at her. Kyra saw their expressions, saw the fear, and sensed the disapproval. Kyra turned her gaze downward. She couldn't bear the looks. *As soon as this mission is over, I'm going back into the field. No one to judge me there.* She stayed close to her escort.

They headed past the administration wing. Kyra hadn't been down here since they added the new wing. It was referred to as the amenity wing, and it contained the gym, spa, a clothing store, and the Garden of Peace—a fully working farm with a decorative flower garden attached. The Architect had gone out of his way to make sure that members of Scíath had everything they could want or need—compensation for being kept underground by a world that wouldn't accept them.

It reminded her very much of the Gilly mall she was in once. Her silent guide led her toward a set of sleek, glass doors. She felt no vibes of dislike off him. In fact, she felt really no vibes at all, which was odd. He pulled open the door and gestured for her to walk in.

The wood paneled lobby had in the corner a rock fountain bubbling a serene sound. Inhaling, she tried to place the scent but couldn't. Whatever it was, she decided it was nice.

"Please, have a seat. Jampo will be here to get you in just a few moments." He bowed his head as he disappeared through a frosted glass door to her left. Kyra sat breathing in the scent and listening to the bubbling water. A peace came over her. This had been a good idea.

Kyra closed her eyes. The visual of a peaceful meadow descended upon her. A smile crept to her face as she looked around at the lush meadow, with its clumps of wild flowers swaying gently in the lazy breeze. The trees with their sun-dappled leaves sighed softly as the wind rustled them. She raised her face toward the sunlight, enjoying its feel on her skin. It felt good here, familiar. She tried to place it. She could almost recall it.

A hand touched her shoulder gently, causing her to jump. Her grasp on the memory was lost, and she opened her eyes. A petite, older woman stood before her. She wore a simple robe of orange, and her graying hair was pulled into a bun. She had kind eyes and many smile lines adorning her face. She sized Kyra up another moment before she spoke.

"I think you need our services more than anyone else who has ever walked through those doors." She followed her statement with a sage nod. "If you will follow me, please. We will begin your program." She walked toward the frosted door, not even glancing to see if Kyra had followed her.

Kyra stood. She wasn't sure how to take that statement. It didn't seem that the woman was interested in her thoughts, so she just followed behind her. The door opened into a long hall. The same paneling adorned the walls, but the floor was carpet here as opposed to the stones of the lobby. Kyra inhaled deeply. The scent had changed. It was softer but still pleasant. It invoked no thoughts. The woman stopped abruptly, causing Kyra to jump back to avoid running into her. Turning to the right, she pushed the door open.

Kyra looked around, curious to see what her treatment held. The room held a massage table, an incense burner, and a CD player. She frowned. Somehow, she was expecting something extraordinary.

"Change into your robe. I will be back in a moment with the oils." She walked away.

Kyra shrugged. Doing as she was told, she slipped into the frail, silk robe. Pulling it tight around her, she hoped its cover would make her feel less vulnerable. As she perched on the edge of the table, her thoughts roamed to all of the work she needed to get done. She should also visit Medical, though, and check on the Giant's condition. She doubted she would be welcome in his room. A discreet call to Leland to get an update would probably serve better than risking another confrontation.

The woman's voice caused Kyra once again to jump.

"I must ask that you banish all work thoughts from your mind," she said as she went about lighting the incense and dimming the lights.

Kyra wondered if the old woman had read her mind or if she was broadcasting, again. The soft, sweet smell of lavender rose to meet her, and she smiled.

"I will be taking you through meditation steps as I perform the massage. Please listen, and follow my instructions the best you can." She gestured for Kyra to lie on the table.

Kyra removed her robe and lay on the table, feeling very exposed and uncomfortable. She twitched when the warm oil touched her back. The woman started the massage. At first, Kyra couldn't get her body to relax. Slowly, the woman forced Kyra's muscles into submission, and she felt the tension flee.

"I want you to imagine yourself in the forest—a peaceful, quiet place, lush and green. Feel the breeze as it slips through the leaves to caress your face," she began.

Kyra closed her eyes. She returned to the forest surrounding the manor house. She could see its hulking shape through the dense trees, but it was just a distant landmark.

"Feel the air on your skin. Embrace the solidarity of the trees. The softness of the moss, the warmth from the dappled sun, and the cushioning grass under your bare feet...you are one with the earth, and with nature around you." Her voice melodious, she intoned each spoken word into the actual feeling.

Kyra felt the forest breathing around her. It was easy to feel like she belonged with the sentient beings around her. The forest was alive. She heard the old woman speaking, but it was far and distant. It was impossible to make out the words. It became a soft melody.

Wandering through the forest, she occasionally paused to place a hand on a tree or watch a bird flit through the branches. She inhaled deeply. The sharp scent of pine filled her lungs. She was moving into the evergreens, and the house was much closer than it had been. She turned away. She did not want that place intruding on the peace she was feeling.

Out of the corner of her eye, something flitted, and she turned her head sharply. Again, just on the outside of her vision, another flash of light. She used her powers to reach out to see what it was. She got nothing back. Part of her mind tried to tell her this was just a vision induced by meditation. She was too keen on finding out what it was to listen. She moved faster, catching glimpses of whatever it was as it passed between trees. She broke into a run, catching up to it at the edge of the lawn of the house. It was the little girl. *The ghost.*

The girl still looked so sad that Kyra's heart broke. She looked up at Kyra and cried softly, "I thought you were going to help me."

"Oh, I am." Kyra got down on one knee.

"But you haven't come back." Silent tears slid down her face.

" I will, and I'm bringing people who can help me talk to you. To help you find peace."

"Who?"

"Experts from where I come from," Kyra said soothingly.

"Who are they?" she asked again, with almost an annoyed expression.

Kyra was caught off guard, but she answered, anyway.

"Myself, the Architect, Tinka, and Nyles," she replied.

The little girl nodded and vanished. The scene melted around her, until she was in the dark of her mind. Her eyes fluttered open to see Jampo blowing out the candles.

"You did very well. Your body was very tense, but I managed to work out the major knots. I will show you to the facial area, and then, you will have a manicure and pedicure. I hope you enjoyed yourself and find your way back here, again." She stepped out so Kyra could get back into her clothes.

Kyra dressed quickly. Her mind was much less relaxed than her body at this point. Why had the child been so demanding on who was coming? How had she found her way into Kyra's vision, again? Kyra sighed. She would really rather be discussing this with her father instead of getting more pampering, but she knew he wanted this for her. She stepped out and followed Jampo silently down the hall.

The rest of the morning dragged on. It was hard for Kyra to enjoy any of it. She was anxious to go, now. The sadness in the child's eyes haunted her. Regardless of how weird the encounter had been, the child was waiting while Kyra was getting her nails painted. It felt wrong to her.

At a little past noon, Kyra emerged from the spa. She could not deny that physically, she felt better than she had in a long time. Her mind, though, was a bubbling mass of concern and doubt. Going toward the work part of Scíath, she ticked off the things she had to do.

She would stop by her father's office, thank him for his gift, and check on how the meeting with Jason went. Then, she needed to swing by Security and pick up that paperwork on Cobbwick. She had to go check on Milyna and order equipment for the mission. Call Leland and check on the Giant. She took out a pen and notebook she kept and scribbled down all her to do's. Lists were a savior when the mind was frazzled. Her body set on autopilot, she made her way to her father's office.

She heard the pacing hoof beats before she turned the last corner. Her steps sped up. She came face-to-face with a very angry-looking Nyles. He paced back and forth in front of her father's door. His tail swished in time with his steps, his powerful arms crossed over his chest. He stopped and looked at Kyra.

"What's going on?" she asked. Her instinct longed for her weapon. It was just one door down the hall, so she took a deep breath and quelled her fight instincts.

"The Architect and Di have been in there with that—that, person. For almost an hour, I have heard raised voices. Even thuds, but I can't open the door," he replied through clenched teeth.

Kyra pushed past him, trying the door. It was locked. In a panic, she tossed her shoulder into it, only to be met with the same resistance. She stepped back to kick the door in as she had already proven she could do. It swung open, and she was faced with a very stern Di.

"This meeting is still in progress. We would appreciate it if you would come back in an hour." She closed the door in Kyra's face.

Kyra stood stunned by the reprimand she had received. When the door was open, she had seen her father sitting behind his desk, and he looked just fine. She could only see Jason's back, but his shoulders were slumped and his head hung, so she assumed he was getting what was coming to him.

She stepped back. Though Nyles's expression was pacified, she could feel the anger rolling off him. "Want to accompany me to lunch, and then we can check back here?" She placed a hand gently on his arm.

He looked down at her, and his expression softened. "We can do that," he said, walking toward the dining hall.

"Plus, I have a list of things I need to do before we depart tomorrow morning. Help and company is always welcome." She wanted to keep him from twisting Jason into a pretzel, but she really did want his company.

After they placed their order, they sat down at a table that would accommodate Nyles.

"I like the nail color," he commented as he poked at his salad.

She smiled. "They tried to put this shiny pink color on me. I informed them if my nails were to be painted, then it would have to be some kind of red." She held her crimson nails out for review.

"How was the whole spa trip? I work in the garden occasionally, and I've walked past it, but it's not really my kind of place."

Kyra took the question as an opportunity to get some of the swirling issues off her mind. Nyles listened intently, nodding but never interrupting her.

After her summary, Nyles said, "I'm very surprised that the girl came to you again like that. It was a dream last time. I think, perhaps, we should drop by Tinka's office and give her a rundown." He finished his milkshake.

"I'll add her to the list." Kyra pulled out her notebook. She scribbled it on to the bottom of the page.

"It does look like you have a ton to do. I'll be happy to accompany you and do what I can," Nyles said.

Both their spirits were calmer as they made their way back to the Architect's office.

Kyra was unsure of what they would find, and she did not fancy the idea of being sent away, again. It felt wrong to her that a room had been open to her for her entire life would be closed.

However, to the relief of both of them, they discovered the door was standing ajar and the clacking of keys could be heard. Kyra raised her hand to knock.

"Come in," her father's voice said, preempting her action.

Kyra smiled and shook her head.

The Architect looked up and smiled at both of them. Kyra studied his face, but she knew if he didn't want her to see anything, she wouldn't.

"I would like to thank you both for your patience earlier." He shoved some printed papers into a folder.

"Kyra you look more relaxed, and red suits you. I hope your visit was enjoyable," he added and folded his hands on top of the folder.

"It seems like your meeting was a success." She hoped he would reveal the details.

"Yes. Nyles, you will be receiving a written apology from Jason," he said to which Nyles snorted.

"You're not going to share the rest, are you?" Kyra settled into her chair.

He shook his head. "There really is nothing to tell. Nothing to do with your mission, anyway. He professes complete ignorance as to Anna's condition. Says she came to his office in the same state that he turned her over to you in. As for the mystery woman, he also claims ignorance and offered to comply fully with an investigation of his department."

Kyra pursed her lips. "I don't buy any of it." How could he have accepted such a reply from Jason?

"I figured as much, but I'm not at liberty to use my powers to ascertain the truthfulness of his words. I will say, however, that his aura has changed. The vibes from him are different than they used to be."

"How so?" Nyles asked.

"I can't put my finger on it." He shook his head.

"Well, perhaps, when we get back, we can do a little further snooping into him," Nyles said.

"Perhaps," the Architect replied noncommittally. "So, where are we on our preparations?" he asked, changing the subject.

Kyra pulled out the list from her back pocket, causing the Architect to break into a big grin. "I have to go to Security, call Leland, go see Milyna, and then, I am going to talk to Tinka," she read off.

"I get all of those but Tinka," the Architect replied.

Kyra took a deep breath, held it a moment, and then launched into her vision. Her father's eyebrows shot up.

"I am extremely surprised," he said, denoting the obvious.

"As am I, which is why I'm going to see Tinka. Perhaps, she can shed some light on how this spirit is still speaking to me."

The Architect gave a nod. "Excellent use of Scíath's resources. I have a fair number of things to do myself to prepare for our trip. I have to place all the second-in-command protocols on Simon. Don't want the place to go into lockdown when I leave."

"Who is the second?" Kyra asked, feeling as if she should know this, and she didn't.

"Di," he responded simply.

Both Nyles and Kyra nodded, as this was the obvious choice.

"So, I suggest we all get to our 'to do's' and meet back here around six for dinner?" the Architect suggested.

Kyra glanced at the clock on the wall. It was quarter to two. Four hours should be more than enough time to get her list accomplished. "Sounds like an excellent plan to me." She stood. "Oh, and yes. I enjoyed my trip to the spa this morning. Thank you very much." She mentally crossed that off her list.

He nodded in response.

"We will be back here with bells on and empty stomachs at six." She kissed her father on the cheek. He smiled warmly at her but was obvious slightly surprised by her spontaneous show of affection. She headed out the door with Nyles on her heels, closing the door behind them.

"Where first, *mon capitan*?" Nyles asked with an amused grin

She smiled back at him. It was nice to have him around. His presence comforted her. Hard to admit it, but she liked not being alone all the time. Something deeper stirred within her. Before it could frighten her further, she pushed it away and focused on what needed to be done.

"Let's start with picking up the report. Swing by Medical, order our equipment, and check on the welfare of Milyna. I expect her to still be shaken up. After all that ,we will pop over and see if we can get a few moments of Tinka's time."

"I thought we were just going to call Leland to check on the Giant?" Nyles fell in step with her as they made their way to Security.

"We were, but then, I decided I'd also like to see Anna."

"Any particular reason?" Nyles asked.

Kyra's brow furrowed, her expression clouded. "I don't know what to believe. She's a part of my team, and she was harmed, so I should check on her. Or she's a spy for an unethical, power-hungry slimeball, and is a danger to my team."

Nyles laughed, causing her to turn and give him a look. Before she could respond, he held up his hand. "I'm only laughing, because I love your bluntness and ability to express your opinion about people."

She smiled back at him.

"I just hope you don't talk about me when I'm not around like that," he added.

"You know I don't!" She gave him a light punch to the shoulder to make her point.

He simply smiled back.

They walked on in silence. Kyra did not fail to notice some of the looks she was getting from people as they passed. People in the building were talking about yesterday's incident. Those who opposed her existence were enjoying the scandal.

They reached Security. Kyra laid her hand on the scanner, waiting for the light to turn green. She turned to Nyles. "Do you want me to duck in and just grab the papers?" she asked.

He nodded in affirmation.

She slipped through the door, noting that once again, her department was unattended. This was happening far more often than it should. Making her way quickly to the printer, she noted it was empty. Checking around the printer and even on her desk, she found nothing. Perhaps, Galerius had filed them when she had not returned.

Heading to the file cabinet, her eyes were caught by a weapons cabinet. Not only was it unlocked, but it was hanging slightly open. She was immediately on guard. Pulling her weapon, she scanned the room with both her eyes and her Fae powers for anyone lurking in a dark corner. Once she was certain the room was deserted, she nudged the door all the way open with the tip of her gun. The interior at first looked intact. Guns lined the cabinet, and none appeared to be missing.

Kyra was ready to dismiss it as a lock not catching when a drawer just slightly pulled out caught her eye. Using her gun barrel again, to preserve any fingerprint evidence, she opened the drawer. It was empty. The inventory list on the inside of the door showed that, the empty drawer had held tranquilizer darts. Galerius had spent a long time refining a tranquilizer that was effective on ninety percent of the known supernatural species.

A film of sweat covered her brow. This was more dangerous than a firearm going missing.

Leaving the cabinet, she walked quickly to the phone and dialed her father's extension. She explained to him what she had found, and she listened to his response. Her shoulders slumped. She had no desire to go through another lockdown and search; however, this could not be ignored. After placing the phone back in the cradle, she picked up her radio.

"Galerius, please return to base immediately. Over." She waited white-knuckled for a response.

A long silence met her request. She moved slowly to the alarm button. She would much rather have him here or, even better, have him hit the lockdown.

Her radio crackled to life.

"Galerius. On my way to base, over," his monotone voice answered.

Kyra exhaled the breath she didn't know she was holding. Nyles was still standing outside the door, expecting her to come out any minute with a stack of papers in hand. Moving quickly to the door, she opened it. "Nyles, I need you to go back to my father's study. We are potentially going into lockdown, again. I want you to be safe, and I want someone I trust with him."

Nyles looked confused but nodded. He quickly went back the way they had come. Kyra searched the halls for Galerius's imposing form. Seeing nothing, she pulled the door shut, again. She shivered involuntarily. The room felt more foreign to her than it ever had.

She sat behind her desk and waited. Depending on where Galerius had been, it could take him some time to get here. She hoped there was some kind of logical explanation for this, something that would make her feel silly for panicking.

She heard the door hiss open, and she was thrilled to be faced with the solemn figure of her boss.

"What has happened?" he asked.

Scíath

"I came in for some papers I requested last night. I couldn't find them around the printer, so I thought perhaps they had been filed. When I was standing at the cabinet, I noticed this door ajar. At first, it seemed that nothing had been disturbed, but then, I noted that the tranquilizer drawer was open, and it was empty." She moved to the cabinet to show him what she meant.

He studied the evidence in his characteristic manner. His eyes rapidly blinked as he took everything in. He knelt to examine all sides of the doors and the drawers. Then, he stood, taking a long moment before turning to her. "You did the right thing in calling me here. Anything missing from our department, especially something of this nature, is going to be cause for a lockdown." His words caused her stomach to knot.

"There have been more lockdowns since I've been back than in the history of Scíath," Kyra said with a sad tone.

Galerius nodded in agreement. He walked over and hit the button on the wall. Within seconds, the red lights flashed, and the siren announced a code.

"Code Red. Remain in your current locations," it said.

Kyra's heart sank. Code red, security violation—this day could not possibly get any worse.

"I wish you to report to the Architect as his protection detail, but first, I will have to search you for the missing tranquilizers," Galerius said.

Kyra's eyes went wide. Then, she realized it was not that he did not trust her. He was following protocol. She nodded and stood as still as possible, fighting her inner urges to hit him every time he touched her. After a few moments, which felt to her like hours, she stepped back.

"You are clear. Head back to the Architect. If you see anyone in the halls, detain them and radio me," he said with a dismissive nod.

Kyra picked up the things she had entered with and left quickly. She was glad she had sent Nyles back to her father before the lockdown. She made her way quickly through the halls, keeping her eyes open for anyone out of place. Relieved to have found no one about, she reached her destination. The flashing, red lights made everything seems outlandish. The siren was more than annoying.

A concerned looking Nyles opened the door to her knock.

The Architect sat in his chair, smoking his pipe. Though the sound was muffled, it was still obvious something was going on in the compound. She sat down beside him.

"I'm sorry. I feel like all of this chaos has to do with me being here." Her tone was apologetic.

The Architect took a deep puff off his pipe and then looked at her with saddened eyes. "This hoopla has nothing to do with you being here, my dear. The biohazard would have occurred no matter who was the leader of that team. As for this, I believe it has more to do with the succession than anything else."

Kyra's fingers started to drum against her leg—the familiar rhythm of her annoyance.

"I am not sure what happens, now. Is it even possible to search all of Scíath?" Nyles asked, settling himself beside the fire.

"In theory, yes. In practice, no. There are simply too many places and people. This lockdown is more to keep anyone from getting the weapons outside of Scíath than anything else," the Architect replied.

"Does this stop our mission?" Kyra asked. Even with all the chaos, she could hear the voice of the child begging for her help.

"We will be allowed to leave after, we, our gear, and the plane are searched. I expect shortly that the sirens will cease, and it will be announced that all travel is restricted," the Architect explained.

Kyra pulled out her list and sighed as she looked over the things that were likely not to get accomplished.

"Another lockdown was not on the list, huh?" Nyles asked with a smirk.

"Indeed not. The only thing that absolutely must be done before we leave is to get the equipment settled and to check on the Giant's condition. I suppose the rest can wait until we return on Monday," she replied.

"I took the liberty of checking in on the Giant and Anna for you," the Architect said. "They are both doing well. Anna seems completely back to herself, and the Giant is healing. Though, I dare say his pride is more wounded than his body."

"Thank you for being so thoughtful." Kyra put her hand over his. She could not get over how delicate and frail his skin felt.

"Galerius may share the same suspicions as you do about the reasons for this breach. He has ordered me to stay with you as your protection detail." Kyra checked the clock. Time had flown by since she last left this sanctuary. It was a quarter after four.

"He is a smart man and very good at what he does," the Architect said. "That being said, once the hullabaloo has quieted, I think the three of us should get our equipment together. That way, we are all safe."

As if his words had caused it, the sirens ceased. The metallic voice announced, "This facility is still in full lockdown. You are permitted to work and socialize as before; however, travel outside is restricted. If you have any further questions, see your Treoraí."

Kyra nodded to Nyles who stood.

The Architect knocked the ash from his pipe. "Well, then. Let us be off. I'm going to suggest that Tinka join us for dinner. Perhaps, you can get your chat in with her after all." The Architect opened the door to the hall.

Kyra was in front of him before he could even turn the knob. "I will be going out first, to make sure the way is clear." She cracked open the door and slipped through into the hallway, thankful that it had returned to normal lighting.

Her senses stretched out to feel for anyone in the corridors. She felt nothing, so she allowed her father and Nyles to exit.

"I'm surprised everything is so empty." Nyles winced as his hooves clacked loudly in the silence.

"I imagine everyone is afraid. No one wants to be in the wrong place at the wrong time. All they know is that there was a security breach. They have no idea of what nature," the Architect said.

"An excellent point. I hope whoever committed this crime is just as frightened as the rest," Kyra said.

"As do I. I do not like this place feeling so hostile," the Architect added.

The trio made their way through the long and winding halls until they reached the familiar door of Milyna's office. Kyra knocked softly. She watched as the shadow hesitantly moved to the door. After a long moment in which

Kyra was sure the young Fae was debating the safety of opening the door, it opened. She looked relieved to see who was standing on the other side.

"Kyra, I'm so glad to see you. Life has been such a rollercoaster recently." She opened the door fully to let them enter. "I suppose you can't tell me what is going on?"

"No, we can't. I wanted to see how you were and also to pick up our gear for the mission, so it can be checked before we leave." Kyra wished she had given as much thought to the girl's wellbeing as she had her equipment.

"You are still leaving?" she asked, her tone incredulous. "I just got a memo saying to cancel all equipment packs. No one is leaving until the breach has been handled."

"And for all other people going out, this is true," the Architect said. "However, our mission is time-sensitive, and we will go through the extra steps necessary to clear us before we leave."

"Of course. I mean, who could suspect you," she replied to him.

"I had already pulled all your gear and, as always, the plane is stocked." She gestured them to follow her into the equipment area.

They made their way in when a loud crash stopped them in their tracks. Everyone turned around to see a very sheepish looking Nyles trying to pick up the things his tail had knocked off. Kyra moved to help him, trying to ignore the high blush that colored his face. After the things were replaced, he made his way carefully into the larger room.

Milyna gestured to the four duffle bag packs sitting inside a taped off square on the concrete floor. "They are basic survival packs—not that much different from the ones I sent with your team the first time. Though, since you will be going without a medic this time, I have placed medical packets in each. The plane has a more comprehensive kit. The plane also has more food than the basic rations in each pack. Although it's a two-day mission, I've got each pack set up for seven days—just in case." She seemed to swell with pride at Kyra's admiring look.

"I'm very impressed. When I return, I will be putting you up for the equipment management position. You have shown yourself to be more than qualified," the Architect said.

The young Fae's jaw dropped. Kyra smiled. She had mixed emotions now when it came to the girl. Part of her saw a young woman who would face many of the issues her own mother had battled with. There was a bond between them, as they both defied Fae tradition. Then, there was the rush of guilt that came with the Giant incident. After all this was over, she would have to reconcile her feelings, because she knew the girl would need Kyra in her life.

They all thanked her and left. Exiting into the corridor, there were one or two passing people, but the halls were nowhere near as crowded as they should have been this time of day. They were returning to the study when the Architect stopped short and turned around. Kyra spun around as well. At first, she saw nothing down the long, empty hall. She was about to ask him what was wrong when Tinka and Di came into view. The trio waited for them to approach.

Di smiled at the group.

"We were just coming to see you," Tinka said.

"I know, hence why I waited," the Architect replied with a wry grin. Di simply laughed. The Architect continued, "I would be pleased if both of you ladies would join us for dinner. He peeked at his watch.

Di and Tinka looked at each other and nodded. "I think that would be beneficial to all of us," Tinka responded.

"We just came from the equipment department. Everything is still a go for our trip tomorrow, Tinka, if you're still interested in going," Kyra said as they walked toward the study.

"Interested? I don't think you could keep me away. It's a field assignment. I don't think I have been above ground in five years. Not to forget, this is my absolutely favorite topic. The ramifications of what this could entail for our entire society as a whole…I feel it is my responsibility as a Treoraí to be present," Tinka explained. She looked at Di and then the Architect. "Do you think Kyra and Nyles could be so kind as to head down to the cafeteria and grab something yummy for the five of us?"

Kyra was being given the brush off. She knew also that the three of them would be safe together, and obviously, they had something they needed to talk about that she could not be privy to. Nodding to Nyles, the two of them headed toward the cafeteria as the others walked toward the study.

Even though she knew she shouldn't, she stretched out her hearing and listened to the muted conversation that was going on behind her.

Di said, "I have asked Lev and Leland to meet us at midnight. I would have asked Moira, but I can't risk Jason finding out. Plus, if we invite everyone but him to the meeting, he will smell conspiracy. You only need four out of the seven, and we all know Galerius is too busy with the breach. We can certify your choice."

"Thank you for handling it for me. I want to have it in place so that once we settle this issue, we can proceed with that," the Architect said.

They moved out of range of her powers, and Kyra sighed softly. He really was retiring. Nyles turned to her.

"What did they say?" he asked.

Kyra tried to feign hurt at the implication that she was listening in. She smiled. Nyles knew her far too well. "They are getting together at midnight to certify father's choice for his successor." She was unable to keep the sadness from her voice.

"Look at it this way. Once he retires, you can spend more quality time together." Nyles gently placed a comforting hand on her shoulder.

He was right. She should be happy. She just couldn't shake the feeling that her role at Scíath would be at risk under another leader. This was the only life she had ever known, and she really had no other place to go. She chided herself for her selfish thoughts. She should be thinking about taking care of him, not about herself.

With a weak smile, she picked up a menu. She had absolutely no idea what to order. She handed it to Nyles who gave it the same, confused look.

"I'm not used to ordering dinner for a group of people," he replied.

" I know who will know," Kyra said. She lightly dinged the silver bell.

After a moment or two, Gus stuck his head out of the kitchen door. Seeing who summoned him, he smiled and came out with a towel in his hands.

"How are my two favorite people this afternoon?" he asked with a twinkle in his eyes.

Gus's good humor was infectious. Kyra felt lighter than she had all day. "We are good, but we have been tasked to order dinner for ourselves, the Architect, Di, and Tinka. We are completely lost."

Gus became semi-serious. "That is an interesting crew. Two restrictive diets, and one food allergy, so one must choose carefully," he said more to himself than to them.

"You must have a memory like an elephant to be able to remember all this," Nyles said.

Gus laughed. "I would have preferred the legs of one as well. Then, I would be taller!" Kyra and Nyles joined his laughter. "If you two will trust me, I think I can throw together a good dinner that will work for everyone in your party."

"That would be fantastic. We'll be eating in the study," Kyra said.

"Give me about an hour." He disappeared back into the kitchen.

"Well, we should go back. Let's walk slowly to give them more time to discuss what we can't be present for," Nyles suggested.

"We could always swing by Medical and check on Anna. I know the Architect called, but it can't hurt," Kyra replied.

Nyles nodded. They started off down the hall, and Kyra's mind swirled.

Her thoughts lingered on the successor issue but for a moment. She knew that if she started worrying about it, it would be very hard to stop. Instead, she let her thoughts float to the mission ahead of them. It should be very productive.

Her primary goal should be uncovering the conspiracy surrounding the manor. To accomplish that, she might have to work with the Fae in the area to deal with the hybrid creatures. That in and of itself would prove to be tricky. Perhaps, make contact with the creature or creatures themselves and working out a treaty of sorts.

She could not shake the image of that little girl's sad eyes and her heartbreaking pleas to go back to her family. Kyra, at one point in her life, was that little girl—lost and alone. She had the Architect there to save her. This girl lost her life, and now, her spirit was anchored to that horrible place. No matter if they cleaned it up, and made it a beautiful place, Kyra would never feel comfortable there. She could never shake the vibes of sadness attached to it.

They approached Medical, and Kyra's steps faltered. Even though they were not here to see the Giant, and she knew he was okay, it was still hard for her to enter. The guilt flooded her, but she was not about to let anyone else see her weakness—no matter how close she was to them. Lifting her head high, she squared her shoulders, her stride took on its familiar air, and she waited impatiently to be admitted to the department.

Once through the decontamination, she went to the first desk she saw and asked for directions to the relatives' apartments. They made their way through the labyrinth. Nyles made a face as his hooves clacked against the sterile tile.

After walking for what seemed like ages, they entered a carpeted hall that was cheerfully decorated. Flowers graced the entryway, giving the whole hall a wonderful smell. Kyra felt some of her anxiety lifting, which was no doubt what this corridor was designed for and possibly bewitched to do. Those who came here often had loved ones in dire straits. Anna's apartment was down around the L-shaped bend in the hall. As they neared the bend, the tranquil atmosphere was shattered by two voices—neither was raised, but both held anger.

Kyra motioned for Nyles to stop just out of sight of the pair. Placing a finger to her lips, they commenced eavesdropping.

"I don't care what fake medical diagnosis you are trying to use to keep her from me. I am her Treoraí, and I have every right to see her at my discretion, not yours." The first voice belonged to Jason.

"In your department, your attitude and intimidation may get you want you want, but this is Medical. I am her doctor, and she is in no mental condition to deal with another session with you," Nikkos replied.

Nyles's hands were clenching and unclenching. He was ready for a fight. She sighed. This whole testosterone-filled confrontation thing was becoming tiresome. With a deep breath, she charged forward into the hall with a faked, polite smile plastered on her face.

"Nikkos, just who I was looking for!" she exclaimed, giving an acknowledgement nod to Jason. "I received your report on Anna's state. I do agree that until the effects of the toxin can be fully investigated, she should be kept on quarantine. It would be just horrible if it was still able to spread. Very responsible choice." The huge, sweet smile stretched her lips.

Nikkos's smile spread as Jason's frown deepened.

"Jason, it's so nice to see how dedicated you are to checking on a member of your department. I'm sure you agree that it's best to reduce the chance of any latent spreading of the toxin," Kyra said.

High color rose to Jason's cheeks.

Kyra knew Jason was on thin ice with the Architect. If he pushed this issue, he would risk another disciplinary action.

His face deeply reddened, Jason said, "Indeed so. Nikkos here was just telling me about the extent of her issues. She will be much missed in our office. I trust you will keep me updated and let me know when she can accept visitors."

"Absolutely," Nikkos replied with a broad grin.

Jason nodded to Kyra and brushed past Nyles as if he didn't exist. They waited until his footsteps no longer echoed down the hall before all of them burst into laughter.

"I can't say I've ever seen him so angry," Nikkos said.

"So true, and so worth it," Nyles added.

"Glad we decided to stop by. Can you give me an update on her condition," Kyra asked, gesturing to the door.

Nikkos's expression turned serious. "I have her sedated right now. She is having horrible nightmares. We hooked her up to our machines, and her brain activity during the Rapid Eye Movement sleep cycle is off the charts. She doesn't recall much after she wakes up, other than rivers of blood and grisly corpses. I do not believe it has to do with the toxin but more with the house. She mentioned several times immediately upon waking that she had a very strong urge to return."

Kyra's mouth fell open. She had no idea about this, and she should have.

As if sensing her thoughts, Nikkos added. "We did not tell anyone, because we wanted all the tests back. We wanted an answer to go with the frightening symptoms. I believe that what is happening to her is not medical but supernatural. I think something from the house is trying to bring her back, although, I'm not sure for what purpose."

Kyra debated telling him about her visions of the girl, but she didn't wish to sway his findings. "Do you think I could send Tinka down later this evening to see her? She has been dealing with the house reaching out. Even if Anna can't remember, I think it would be beneficial."

Nikkos said," I trust your judgment, and I should let you know that Maria and Aieta have both come in for treatment of severe headaches. I was compiling a report for you, but today has gone pear-shaped. Lockdown tends to send our clinic into overload."

"Can I see her?" Kyra gestured to the closed door.

"She's not even in there," Nikkos replied.

"I have her in our long-term neuro unit. She is constantly monitored, even when I have to work. I can't allow anything to happen to her," he said with a passion that triggered a smirk from Nyles.

"Nikkos, you have been simply amazing. Once I get back from the house, I'm going to put a commendation request into Leland." The growth of her team still amazed her.

He blushed, but then, his face grew tight. "I'm concerned about you going back to the house."

"I will be very well protected, but I do appreciate the concern," Kyra said.

"You have no medic on your team," he said as he started walking back the way they had come.

"No, but we have advanced medical kits in our packs, and the plane is outfitted," she tried to reassure him.

"Humor me and allow me to put together an anti-toxin kit, as well as a suture kit," he said. "I'm never against being over-prepared."

"Just send it over to Milyna. It has to be checked over before we leave. I thank you very much for taking good care of us." Kyra placed a hand on his shoulder.

He smiled. "What can I say? Nothing is too good for my team captain."

As they exited the hallway, Kyra saw the clock on the chamber door. They had about twenty minutes until the food was delivered. Her stomach reminded her that it was indeed empty.

"I think we can head back, now," Nyles said.

"As do I. I'm hungry," Kyra said with a grin.

Nyles returned the grin.

Their walk back was uneventful and filled with small talk. Kyra dreaded the turn in every hallway. She never knew if another issue lay on the other side. They heard muted voices and a touch of laughter as they stood outside the Architect's door.

"Come in," he called before her knuckles made contact with the door.

Nyles chuckled behind her. She opened the door, and they entered to find Di, Tinka, and the Architect sitting around a cheery fire, all sipping tea.

"We thought you got lost!" Tinka exclaimed.

"We talked to Gus and then decided to go check on Anna," Nyles said.

All three sets of eyebrows raised as Kyra set to filling them in on what had occurred.

"I would have loved to have seen his face," Tinka said with a giggle.

Kyra smirked. "It was well worth it."

"All fun aside, I am very concerned about the effect this house is having on my team." Kyra pulled up her chair, and she filled Tinka and Di in about her own visions as well as the headaches of the other members.

Tinka worried her bottom lip. "I've never seen a structure with so much power. Whatever went on there must have been incredibly significant if it has this kind of resonance. If you would be agreeable, I would like to enter your mind to walk you through the visions. Perhaps, I can glean something from them. Then, I will certainly go and visit Anna. See if I can find any common themes or similarities. I should be able to explore her nightmares, even if she can't recall them."

A knock at the door brought a rumble from Kyra's stomach.

"Right after dinner, that is. It seems we are all hungry," Tinka added.

Kyra inhaled the aroma. She was not able to identify what was under the silver dishes, but it smelled divine.

The waiter set up the table, laying out each dish as well as pouring the drinks. Each lid was lifted eagerly by the diners. Kyra was immediately impressed. Each plate held roast chicken, but the side dishes varied to their eater, and some of the things on others' plates, she could not identify. Gus was amazing. Everyone dug in, and conversation was sparse, as the starving filled their stomachs.

After the dishes had been cleared away, Kyra and Tinka sat across from each other on the floor in front of the fire. Tinka rubbed her hands together and spoke in a low, soothing tone, "Kyra, I want you to relax. Let all the tension leave your body. Feel it flowing out of you. Close your eyes, and empty your mind."

Kyra liked the sound of Tinka's voice. It made her feel at ease and safe. She knew it was part of Tinka's powers and probably assisted her in her work. It was soothing nonetheless. Kyra was adrift in a black sea, and the only thing she heard were the melodious words.

"Think back to the first vision you had. Remember each detail. Play it in your mind like a movie for me," Tinka instructed.

Kyra let it flow back. She watched it along with Tinka, like two friends sitting together, watching a documentary. As it ended, Kyra opened her eyes to see Tinka's tears. The little girl had touched her as much as it had Kyra.

"Let's move on to the second." They repeated the process; however, this time when Kyra opened her eyes, Tinka was not crying but frowning. "I seriously doubt the authenticity of the second vision. The feel was different. It was too crisp, too artificial. I do not think the little girl is behind the second one. I think another force from the house may have used your vulnerability to the child to draw you back in. The one thing I can say without a doubt is that house wants us back, and with certainty, its intentions are not good."

"Should we not go?" Nyles asked.

"We must," Kyra and her father said almost in unison.

"I need to have this issue resolved. If we can stop the house's ill behavior, we may be able to free Anna and the others from its spell," the Architect added.

"We must go about this in a very cautious manner. I'm going to go see Anna, and then Moira to get some magical cleansing items." Tinka stood to go.

"We are wheels up at 9:00 a.m.," Kyra said.

"I will be there with bells on," Tinka said with a smile.

Di stifled a yawn. "This has been a very long day, and the night proves to be just as long. I'm going to catch a nap before the meeting," she said, gently embracing the Architect.

Kyra glanced at the clock and was completely shocked to see it was ten to nine. Time had flown since she got back to the study.

"I'm going to head to bed, myself. I want to be fresh in the morning," Nyles said.

"I'm going to sleep on the settee in Father's room, as we still have missing tranquilizer darts. Nyles, if you want to take my room, as it's right next door, you are welcome to it," Kyra offered.

"That is a good idea. I'll take a radio with me, and that way, if something does happen, I'm here in seconds," Nyles replied.

After the exchanging of radios, keys, and good-byes, Kyra and her father found themselves alone in a silent study.

"I know you were listening. The topic makes you uncomfortable, but I would like to share my choice for successor with you after the council ratifies it," he said.

"If you want to...I know this is difficult for you as well."

"We will have plenty of time to discuss it when we return. I am shocked at all the things that have come from what really was a routine mission." He poured himself a drink. Kyra momentarily became lost in the arcs of rainbow light that arched from the cut crystal inlays of the decanter.

Shaking herself free from the vision, she replied, "No kidding." She sat back in her chair, thinking she wasn't quite ready for bed.

He settled into the chair across from her. "I have decided that I'm going to set my retirement for after the Christmas holiday. That way, there is plenty of time for the replacement to learn the ropes." He sipped his drink.

It was still a week and a half until Halloween—plenty of time for her to get her things in order if she had to leave.

"Speaking of holidays, since you are liable to be in Scíath for an extended period due to this assignment, have you thought about attending the Halloween ball?" he asked.

Kyra's mouth dropped open. Scíath held formal parties throughout the year, but it had never occurred to her that she would be expected to go to one.

"From your facial expression, I can guess you hadn't even given it a thought."

"I must admit that the social side of Scíath is something I've given little thought to. I think the foundling ceremony is the closest I've come to attending a social event in a long time," she said.

"I know that I have a hard enough time getting you to come in to give you your Christmas and birthday gifts," he said.

Kyra cringed. It was becoming more and more evident to her that the years she had spent in the field had left her father alone on important family occasions. "I'm sorry. I've been incredibly neglectful of you."

He laughed softly. "You're part Fae. Stone walls are very difficult for you to stay within."

"Even so, I have a responsibility to you. In truth, the field leaves a lot to be desired, sometimes." Perhaps, her workaholic nature was to make up for her shortcomings.

As they sat in silence, Kyra started to nod off, jerking herself awake. "I think it time we turn in. We have an early liftoff, and if we are not on time, I think Tinka may lynch us." She punctuated her statement with a yawn.

He set his glass on the table. "I find the older I get, the more fatigued I feel, but the less I sleep."

In his bedroom, he pulled out a thick comforter, and after testing all his pillows, he gave her the softest one he had. "This is a switch." He chuckled softly. "I remember spending many a night on the loveseat in your bedroom." He headed into the bathroom with his pajamas, the door closing behind him.

Kyra also recalled those nights. For a six-month period, when she was seven-years-old, she had gone through night after night of horrible nightmares, always awaking screaming. Nothing anyone could do would stop them. Her father took up sleeping in her room so he could comfort her. Then, one night, they just stopped. To this day, she never knew what they were about, and not even her father had been able to pull the images from her mind.

Coming out of the bedroom, he came over and kissed her forehead before climbing into bed.

"I love you, Father," she said softly in a surprising show of emotion.

"I love you too, my daughter," he replied, his tone grateful for her expression.

It had been an exhausting day, and there was no doubt that more like it were on the horizon. Sleep overcame her quickly. She flinched slightly when the Architect pulled up her blankets as he went into the study to attend the meeting.

Chapter Nine

Fateful Return

When Kyra's eyes opened, the room was dark. A sliver of light came from under the door to the hall. She lay completely still. Something had woken her, but it was not immediately evident what. She stretched out her senses. She heard nothing out of the ordinary and felt no foreign presence. She was about to roll over and dismiss it as nothing when she felt it. It was like a gentle, subliminal tap. Someone was trying to invade her mind, again. It was so subtle that had she been awake fully, it would have probably gone unnoticed.

She sat up in the darkness, careful not to make any sound as she did not want to disturb her father. She felt it, again—like someone rapping softly at the door to her mind, seeking entry. She frowned. She had a hard time letting people she knew into her mind much less some random intruder who knocks in the wee hours of the morning. On the other hand, it could be the ghost girl, again.

Her eyes strayed to her father's bed. It was tempting to wake him and ask his advice. From the sound of his breathing, he had finally achieved a deep, restful sleep. She was reluctant to wake him.

She considered opening her mind to this presence, but her paranoia would simply not allow it. Closing her eyes, she forcibly ejected the presence and walled her mind off. She waited several moments to see if it reattempted admission to her brain.

Nothing. She lay back down waiting—again, nothing. She burrowed under the comforter. She finally allowed sleep to overtake her while keeping her mind as closed as possible.

The sound of running water woke her. Blinking, she looked at her watch—6:00 a.m. She stood up and stretched. Her mind drifted back to the middle of the night encounter. It was hard to recall the details. *Had it been a dream?*

Leaving the door open to the bedroom, she headed into the study. Picking up the phone, she ordered breakfast, including Nyles in her order. She debated going and waking him, but she knew he needed his rest. Their flight was wheels up in three hours. He would probably be getting up on his own quite shortly.

As if summoned by her thoughts, she heard a soft rapping on the study door. Stretching out her senses, she felt Nyles's familiar presence on the other side of the door. Walking over, she opened it with a smile. "Good morning," she said, opening the door wide to grant him entry.

His expression was relieved, and his face broke into a smile at her words. "Good morning, yourself. Your alarm went off about half an hour ago. I figured you would be up here as well," he said.

"I'm so sorry I completely forgot to tell you to unset it last night."

"It's fine. Gave me a chance to get a shower and be here for breakfast."

"I just ordered it. Father is in the shower. When he gets done, since you're here, I'm going to slip down to my room take a shower. I'll grab my bag and be back to eat." She tried not to notice how his dark hair shone when wet. So black, it was almost blue, reminding her of a raven's wing. He wore a burgundy sweater that nicely defined his well-cut upper body.

The air between them was thick with unspoken emotions. She moved toward him. Her head tipped up, and he bent down. A kiss was eminent.

"Kyra?" her father called from the other room.

His voice broke the tension. She felt the blush rising to her cheeks as she rushed into her father's bedroom to answer his summons. She was relieved that he didn't ask why she was blushing.

"Yes, Father. Sorry. Nyles was woken by my alarm. I ordered breakfast for all of us." Her words tumbled out.

"Oh, good. I just wanted to let you know to go ahead and order food. I'm going to need my coffee."

"On its way with a good breakfast. Road meals are not nearly as good as what comes from Gus. I'm going to nip round to my room, grab a shower, and my bag. I should get back just as food arrives."

"Excellent plan, my dearest daughter. What would you suggest I wear? I haven't been in the field in ages."

She had never seen him in casual clothing. The closest he had ever come was khakis and a polo shirt.

"Do you own a pair of jeans, hiking boots, and some sweaters?"

He laughed. "Believe it or not, I do."

"Then, that is what I would suggest. Probably a coat and hat as well. Nights can get nippy. I'll be back in twenty minutes." She left the room without waiting for a reply.

* * * *

The Architect entered the study. "Good morning, Nyles. Ready for our adventure?"

Nyles did a double take.

The Architect wore jeans, hiking boots, a gray turtleneck, and a navy blue cable knit sweater. He laughed. "I know it's a bit out of character for me, but it's what Kyra suggested." He packed his pipe with tobacco.

"I think it's going to be refreshing for you to come out into the field with us," Nyles replied.

"Since it is just you and me, I would like to speak to you about something," he lowered his voice.

Nyles moved in closer.

"I'm going to have to speak with the indigenous Fae of the area. From the maps I've consulted, they are a warrior Fae, and a particularly brutal tribe at that. I have to find out what contact they had with the Imps that lived in that house. Perhaps, they can shed some light on who our mysterious third party is.

"I am concerned about Kyra. I do not wish them to know she is there, but I know they are going to sense her. Given her previous encounter with them, they will be expecting her. I would hope they have enough respect for Scíath that they would not try anything; however, I can never be certain of anything.

"When I speak with them, I want you to take her somewhere else and occupy her. I expect she would want to accompany me, to protect me. So, the when will have to be our secret. I'll take her wrath once the meeting is over with."

"Take Tinka with you? She will be much less enraged if you don't go completely alone," Nyles pointed out.

The Architect nodded his agreement. "I hope to come away from this with a lot of answers," he said thoughtfully.

"I agree. We still have to get the paperwork from the prison. I know Leland has much to do on the sample we found. Then, there are the identities of the bodies," Nyles replied.

"I think we are all going to be very busy, but I do not want to delegate outside us, and I want this to remain as hush-hush as possible," the Architect said, more to himself then to Nyles.

A soft knock halted the conversation. Nyles went to the door. He was clearly surprised to see Anna standing on the other side of the door.

"Please, come in," the Architect said, hiding his surprise at her appearance with a wide smile.

"I'm so sorry to bother you. I know you are leaving for the house very shortly, but I was hoping to speak to the three of you," Anna replied, looking around.

The Architect took in her appearance. She was dressed in her classic black suit. Her hair, her makeup—nothing was out of the ordinary. Her look was worried, though, and her mocha complexion was faded. Bruise-like shadows under her eyes spoke to sleepless nights. Her brow was furrowed, the lines deep.

"Kyra will be here in a moment. Please, have a seat. Can I get you a cup of tea?" The Architect kept his eyes on her, but his expression stayed impassive.

"No, I'm fine. I appreciate you seeing me. You have some busy days ahead of you." She sat on the edge of the chair. Her hands fidgeted in her lap, and she threw nervous looks at the door.

The Architect wondered briefly how she had convinced Nikkos to let her out of Medical to come here.

* * * *

The door swung open, and Kyra strode in, looking ready for action. Her eyebrow rose in surprise as she saw Anna. She looked her over.

"Perfect timing, as always," the Architect said.

"Anna just arrived, saying that she wanted a chance to speak to us before we took off," Nyles explained.

Kyra sat across from Anna. She could feel the fear rolling off her in waves. Something had her very upset.

"Nikkos has allowed me to keep working on the project, to keep me from going stir crazy. I have identified a number of the bodies that we found in the house. There are the bodies of four Fae, which we have no way to further identify. Since you will be seeing the local Fae, I thought perhaps you could ask them if any of their members went missing around that time," Anna said.

Kyra's eyes narrowed.

"However, that is not the reason I am here. The last body to be identified caused Simon to bring up all kinds of red flags, so I thought I would bring it right to you," Anna continued.

Her listeners leaned in, intent on the words to follow. Anna took a deep breath. "It came up as Trina Mawkawee," she said, watching their expressions.

Kyra's mouth fell open. The Architect gave a tight frown. Nyles sounded a strangled cry.

The Architect was the first to recover, "You're sure?"

"Nikkos did DNA and dental records. All of those were recorded when she signed up to be a diplomat," Anna replied.

The Architect pulled himself to full composure. "You did the right thing. Go back to Medical, and make sure it goes no further than you, Nikkos, and Leland. I will handle informing Tinka."

As Nyles gently escorted Anna out, breakfast arrived. Kyra no longer had an appetite. Once the server left, they automatically filled their plates. Appetite or not, Kyra and the others had to eat before heading out to the field. A thick silence filled the room.

Eventually, Kyra spoke up, "This places serious complications on this field mission."

"Very much so. First off, we have to decide whether to tell Tinka before or after about finding her sister's body. Tinka became so interested in spirits after her sister disappeared, shortly before the war began. It is possible that if she knows ahead of time, she will be focused only on finding and talking to her sister. On the other hand, if her sister's spirit is lingering, I do not want her to go in blind," the Architect said.

"Not to mention the grief. I know deep inside she was hoping to find Trina alive," Nyles added.

Silence descended again before Kyra spoke up, "I have known Tinka almost my entire life. She is strong, smart, and dedicated to Scíath. While I am sure it will be very hard for her, I believe she has the right to know, to have some closure. Who knows? If the spirit of her sister is still around, it may be very useful to us. I think if we tell her on the way there, it will give her a chance to get over the shock. She will be better able to deal with her sister's spirit if it does make an appearance than if she was surprised by it."

The Architect smiled slightly. "Very sensible, my dear. I will tell her. I'm the one who sent her sister on the mission that seems to have led to her death," he said, his tone grave.

Nyles glanced at the clock. "We'd best go. We have to take those horrible tubes to the runway."

The Architect agreed. "I'm not a fan of them either, my boy. While practical, they are my least favorite form of travel."

Due to the early hour, the halls were sparsely populated. Kyra kept her eyes out for Tinka. They approached the tubes without running into her.

A short while later, they climbed out of the cramped tubes. Tinka had arrived ahead of them and was chatting idly with the pilot. She waved to them, her grin wide. They returned her greeting with forced smiles.

"It's only ten to nine! Did everyone sleep in or something? I've been here for an hour," she said in a mock lecture.

They boarded the plane, taking up their usual spots. Tinka settled in beside the Architect. She took out a black bag and pulled some items out, placing them gently on the table. "I have brought along a number of cleansing items. Hopefully, once this is over, and we know what we need to, we can set the spirits free and let them rest."

Kyra recognized some of the items but most were a complete mystery to her. Some might refer to her Fae powers as magic, but Kyra viewed magic to be something performed by Witches and Wizards. It was not something she was overly comfortable with. Anything that could be used to steal someone's will, or force them to do things, was something she wanted to stay far away from.

Tinka placed the items back in the bag. Her excitement was palpable. The Architect drew in a deep breath.

Tinka looked around at them. "You are all acting so nervous. Like long-tailed cats in a room full of rocking chairs. What is going on?" she asked.

"We have something important to tell you, and it's not pleasant," Kyra said. She looked to the Architect to finish explaining.

The Architect laid his hand over Tinka's. "Anna came to see us very early this morning to let us know that one of the bodies identified in Medical from the house raised a number of red flags. After they did a thorough identification, they discovered it was your sister Trina."

The smiled dropped from her face, leaving her expression completely blank. That was shattered as tears flowed down her cheeks. The Architect held her while she cried. Several minutes later, she sat up, taking the proffered tissue from Kyra.

"I apologize for my outburst of emotion," she said, her voice still full of tears.

"Don't be. It's quite a blow. All of us here care deeply for you," Nyles said.

"I want you to know that I won't allow this to derail our mission. After we get this wrapped up, I'm going to request a leave to take her body back to my tribe's land to be buried," she said, regaining her normal tone.

"Perfectly understandable. I would also like to hold a memorial for her in the chapel, if you will agree," the Architect added.

"I would really like that. She had a lot of friends within Scíath, and they also deserve the chance to mourn for her," Tinka agreed.

Silence settled over the cabin. Surprisingly, it was Tinka who broke the silence. "So, what is our game plan?" she asked Kyra.

Kyra was pleased. She had been right about Tinka not letting the personal trauma affect the mission. "There are a number of things that we need to accomplish. I have set the return time for three days; however, since the plane will be landing in the field beside the house, we will be using the plane as our home base and can change our departure time at will. We'll start with a full tour. There are a number of things in the house itself I want to show you both.

"Following that, we will do a limited sweep of the grounds. I can show you where we encountered the animal. That should take up most of an entire day. I would prefer we were back in the plane by nightfall. The next day, we will devote to the spirits and collecting any further evidence you may think will be helpful. The next day or days are going to depend largely on what we discover on day two," Kyra explained.

Nyles and the Architect exchanged a knowing glance and a nod that Kyra felt left out of.

"If no one objects, we have about three hours until we land, and last night's meeting threw off my sleep schedule. I'm going to lean my head back and catch a nap. This is going to be a long couple of days, I think," the Architect said with a yawn.

"Fine with me. I'm going to go over the information we do have to make sure I didn't miss anything. Also, finalize the list of things I want to look for specifically," Kyra said.

"I'd like to use the viewing crystal I brought and look for any unusual vibes as we pass through the surrounding area. Nyles, will you assist me?" Tinka asked. He nodded, and the two of them moved toward the rear of the plane.

For the next several hours, they all kept themselves busy with their tasks. The announcement from the pilot brought them all back together as they buckled in for wheels down.

Kyra's watch said it was just after one. They would have time to cover the house and perhaps the outbuilding, today. The plane landing was turbulent. Kyra let out a breath she didn't know she was holding when they finally came to a stop.

"Right, take your packs from the overhead. Each has a name on it. They are light packs, since we are using the plane as our home base, and we will not need to take everything with us. Nyles, will you also grab the evidence box, please?" Kyra said.

They exited the plane. Kyra was surprised to find the temperature had dropped considerably since her last visit. The quartet made their way through the field, all senses on high alert.

As they reached the gate, the Architect held up his hand to halt them. "We are being watched," he said, his voice low.

Kyra closed her eyes, stretching her senses out. At first, she felt nothing. She was about to ask him for a clarification when a violent, red blur passed through her field of vision.

"I see a signature, a Fae aura," she whispered back, drawing her weapon.

"It's just watching us. We have no need for weapons just yet," the Architect responded.

Kyra wanted to believe him, but it was nearly impossible for her to feel comfortable around pure blood Fae. After glancing at the bandage on her arm again, she holstered her weapon grudgingly.

Fae, especially warrior Fae, were adept hunters and could move without being seen. They moved forward again, and every crackle or sound from the woods drew anxious stares. Kyra knew she could take at least two Fae; however, they always went out in packs. Anger rose inside her. She was glad she wasn't full-blooded Fae. The ability to kill for no reason was a trait she did not ever wish to have.

Slowly, they made their way to the house. Kyra held up her hand to call a stop as they approached the front door. She scanned the ground, looking for any signs of traffic. It looked undisturbed. She slipped her key into the lock they had left behind. Everything seemed undisturbed. They moved into the front hall.

Tinka let out a soft sigh. "This is elegance. I can just imagine the grand parties that went on here," she said, studying the soaring ceilings and marbled tile.

Kyra paused and actually looked at the house as a home instead of a mission. It was truly beautiful. She could see women in fancy dresses, men holding drinks and chatting as soft music played.

She shook her head and cleared it of the vision. This was not the time for such flights of fancy. "We will start with the kitchen and the Imp nests in the basement." She walked to the kitchen door, not waiting to see if they followed. She inspected the cabinets under the sink. The image of the little girl haunted her. She made herself move forward toward the dank chamber below.

After flipping on the light, she held her breath as the flickering, naked bulb decided if it was going to stay on. At last, its harsh light once again illuminated the mess before her. She stood on the bottom step, leaving room for Tinka and the Architect to view what was below without having to step into it. She heard Nyles's hooves clacking on the tile floor above her and was once again reminded of the things about him that kept them apart.

"I simply cannot fathom living in such squalor with a huge, amazing house overhead." Tinka's nose wrinkled from the toe-curling smell.

"They are the one race that is truly as disgusting outside as they are inside," the Architect said as he walked away. The other two followed silently. They gathered in the kitchen. Kyra could not keep her eyes off the cabinets.

"As you will notice from the stench and rotted food here, something else has been eating out of here. There is no way this is thirty years old." She gestured to the rotting piles of meat. Given the time we spent cleaning the servants' quarters, we did not get to clean this out.

"I am not interested in guessing what kind of meat that is," Tinka said while backing toward the door.

"We'll clean it out before we attempt to go after the spirits tomorrow," Nyles added.

"I would appreciate it," Tinka said.

The group left the kitchen. For the rest of the afternoon, they went over the entire house, room by room. Both Tinka and the Architect took notes and photographs. When Kyra looked out the window as they finished up the second floor, it was twilight.

"We should head back to the plane." Kyra noticed Tinka's fixed stare on the door to the third floor. The chill of the restless dead danced down her spine.

"I can feel them. They are all still trapped here, and we must set them free," Tinka whispered, a tear sliding down her cheek.

The Architect slid his arm around her. "We will. No matter if they help us or not. We will not leave the souls in torment." He gently turned her away from the door.

Kyra and Nyles moved quickly to place themselves behind them. Silently, they made their way back to the plane. Kyra was surprised that she felt or saw no other presences in the woods. Both she and Nyles had their weapons drawn as they watched the shadows jump.

Once they were back inside the plane, Kyra flopped on to one of the beds. The pilot had taken the time to turn the passenger compartment into sleeping chambers, and she was thankful.

"After dinner, we will go over what we observed today and add it to the deductions made by your team," the Architect said as he struggled with the packaging of a microwave meal.

Kyra went to help and wound up making everyone's dinner. The conversation was sporadic and forced. Everyone's mind seemed occupied. After dinner, the Architect moved to open the side hatch, lighting his pipe. Kyra thought to warn him against it but then realized if there was anything hostile out there, he would know it.

Everyone settled into a seat. Kyra pulled out her notebook, ready to take notes.

"I'm going to go first," Tinka said. "Aside from my general dislike of Imps and the restless spirits, I concur that there had to be some third race here. The lab room and the lack of traps, but these are things you realized long before you brought me here. Here is what I think—the spirits are what want us here. They sense that we are good. Your first visit here must have stirred them up, reenergized them.

"I think we will be able to learn a lot from them if we can keep them from overwhelming us. Until we have them completely cleared out, this place will be unusable. There are enough spirits here that if riled up, or focused by an entity that could control them, they could easily open a rift between our world and theirs."

Kyra had never even given that kind of thought to the spirits. They were a variable, sure; however, she never thought of them as a threat. She noted a similar look on the face of Nyles. This mystery did not need yet another facet, but that is exactly what Tinka had brought. Scribbling a note into the notebook, Kyra felt even more weight add itself to her shoulders.

With a deepening frown, the Architect tapped his pipe out and pulled the door closed. "I agree with you, Tinka. I do believe this was a secondary happening. It was not something that was planned, but it was caused by the careless taking of life here. Even after we get this cleaned out, I'm not even sure we will be able to use it. There is a great deal of bad blood here." He settled back onto his bunk.

"It would be a shame not to use it. It's truly a magnificent place," Nyles commented.

"Agreed. However, we will have a lot to go through to make sure it's safe, and I don't mean just structurally. After we clear it, and Lev's team makes sure it's sound, I would suggest we bring some of the Witches out and have them make sure everything is quiet," Tinka added as she stifled a yawn.

Kyra sighed softly and added another note to her pad. She brought her attention to the Architect for his observations.

The Architect drew in a deep breath. "I must say I'm impressed to see that ninety percent of the things I noticed were already in your reports. You did an excellent job investigating. That being said, the things I am most concerned with are the hybrid animals and the accomplices to the Imps. I trust those on our team to take care of the spirits. In all honesty, they have never been my strong suit."

He caressed his pipe, looking as if he'd like to have another bowl. "We need to find out how many of these beasts exist, where they are living, and are they reproducing. In theory, if we could tranq one and bring it back to the compound, that would be ideal. Sadly, the clues about the other race are not as tangible. I saw nothing that gave me any more ideas than I had before. If we can get a description from the spirits, that may be our break there." He clamped the empty pipe between his teeth.

"I don't know what kind of tranquilizers will work on the beasts. I can call Leland and see if he can give us some kind of idea from the genetic makeup. Do we have a containment unit to get it back to the compound?" Tinka asked.

Kyra shook her head. "Not knowing its physical capabilities, we should have a maximum security crate. I can call Galerius and see if he can coordinate with Lev to get it out here as soon as possible." She picked up her phone and dialed.

Tinka picked her phone as well and dialed Leland. Both of them moved to opposite sides of the plane to avoid interfering with the other's conversation.

* * * *

"Well, I guess we just get to sit here and look pretty," the Architect said to Nyles with a grin.

"Not one of my strong suits," Nyles replied with a similar grin. He could not take his eyes off Kyra. She was pacing. Her eyes looked so serious. One little lock of hair had worked its way loose and hung over her eyes. She flicked it out of her face impatiently, but he loved it. She was so amazingly beautiful to him.

* * * *

Tinka closed her phone and headed back to the group. "Leland says he can give us a base tranquilizer and a recommended dosage but can in no way guarantee it's going to work."

"Galerius said he would send out the crate. He can't guarantee that it will work on this creature, as we have never trapped one before," Kyra said.

The Architect smiled. "So, we have what we need but have no way of knowing if it is actually going to work."

"Pretty much," Kyra said.

"Well, that's promising," Nyles said with a laugh.

The rest of them shared his chuckle.

"Right, let's get to bed. We will head out about 7:00 a.m., and start with the spirits, as they may be able to give us some useful information about the Fae, the beast, and our third race. This will most likely take us most of the day, and we can't go after beasts until we have the tranquilizers and cage, anyway." Kyra placed her gun under her pillow.

Tinka went to her black bag and affixed several dream catchers around the plane. She smiled when she caught them watching her. "Can't hurt," she said with a smile and a shrug.

"Every little bit helps," the Architect said with his eyelids drooping.

Kyra's sleep was uneasy. While no specific visions assaulted her, she woke several times, because it felt as if she was being torn apart by hands. Their very grips burned her, and their strength made her feel as if she should be ripped asunder. She lay in her bunk, waiting for the memory to fade.

* * * *

Several time, Nyles had to fight with himself to keep from rushing to save Kyra from her nightmares. He envisioned himself gently waking her—her expression grateful to him for saving her from the images that tormented her. Pulling her into his arms, comforting her in the near dark. As tempting as it was, he knew he must not. In the light, things were easily definable. He was a Centaur and she was…well, she was beautifully human. In the dark, as the shadows played over their faces, it could be easy to ignore, to allow the passion to overcome him and to kiss her as he had longed to do so many times. His heart was heavy as he finally settled into sleep.

* * * *

Kyra woke confused, as she didn't immediately recognize her surroundings. Her hand was on her weapon before her eyes were fully open. Blinking, she remembered where she was.

Nyles sat watching her as he sipped a cup of steaming coffee. The Architect was going through some papers, and Tinka appeared to be meditating over some powdered doughnuts.

"I can't believe I'm the last one up," she said. Her watch read 6:15 a.m.

"I would have woken you about fifteen minutes ago, but you looked so peaceful," the Architect replied.

Kyra took her bag to the tiny bathroom to change. On the way, she snagged Nyles's cup of coffee from his hands.

"Hey!"

She sipped it and smiled. "Hazelnut cream, just the way I like it. Thanks."

For a moment, Nyles sat there dumbfounded, his mouth hanging open. The Architect chuckled and shook his head. Nyles tried to put on an angry expression, but it lasted mere seconds before he too was grinning.

She disappeared into the bathroom.

The numbers on Kyra's watch turned to 7:00 a.m. After leaving instructions with the pilot to inform them when their delivery arrived, they ventured out into the field.

On top of her gear Tinka carried her large, black bag of tricks. Her face was set into a hard expression. Kyra could feel the nervous vibes rolling off her.

The Architect looked thoughtful but far less perturbed.

Nyles felt closed off to her. Reaching out with her senses, Kyra attempted to read him. It was like running into a cold, steel wall. A response from him that was very new, it troubled her, but there were other things that would require her time and attention, today.

Kyra approached the house on high alert. She was certain everything around them would now be aware of their presence.

"I'm going to go clean out the kitchen. That way, we can start in there," Nyles said.

"I'll grab a garbage bag and help you." Kyra followed Nyles into the kitchen, leaving the other two in the entryway.

* * * *

Tinka watched them go before speaking. "Not that this is the time or the place, but he is so completely in love with her."

"It breaks my heart. They would be so wonderful together, and I know he would take care of her."

She nodded in agreement before changing the subject. "I'm not sure we should try to speak to the spirits in the room they died. Perhaps on the landing just below. That way, I might be able to control the flow of energy and spirits that come to speak to me."

"I will trust your judgment on this and be here to aid you," he replied.

"I am going to need about an hour to completely set up all my equipment. I'll ask for Kyra's help—that will free you and Nyles, if you want to go check the grounds." She left unsaid that he and Nyles needed to meet the Fae without Kyra.

"You, my dear, are a blessing."

* * * *

"I thought I was your favorite blessing," Kyra said playfully as she exited the kitchen with a bulging bag in her hands.

He laughed. "You're a blessing and a half."

"Kyra, I need to set up my tools, and I need some agile fingers to help me," Tinka said.

"Well, since I am anything but agile, we can take this opportunity to scout for the beast." Nyles went to the front door, taking Kyra's full bag and adding it to his own.

The Architect nodded. Before Kyra had a chance to object, they were out the door.

"Turn on your radios!" she yelled after them, slightly perturbed that they had made their own agenda. They both knew what they were doing, though. If she had more time to think about it, she probably would have suggested the same thing.

* * * *

The two men moved quickly away from the house, cutting off any chance Kyra had to object to their mission. Once they were completely clear, the

Architect closed his eyes. Nyles suspected the Architect was hunting for the beings they wanted to rendezvous with.

The Architect started out walking due south from the house. Nyles noted it was the very same direction Kyra had been wandering off in when she had been distracted. The Architect moved with purpose, pulling away from Nyles as the forest floor grew more cluttered, and Nyles had to become more aware of his footing.

Just as Nyles was about to call out to him and ask him to wait up, the Architect stopped dead in his tracks.

"I am here. We are friends, and I want to talk," he said aloud. Nyles scanned the forest, but he could detect no one present other than them. He moved up closer to the Architect and waited.

"Architect, you may speak," a melodious voice floated down to them from an overhead branch.

Nyles looked up and stared into wild, violet eyes. A stunning Fae sat perched on the branch. Unlike Kyra, her skin matched her eyes. Her long, white mane fell down to her waist in perfect waves. Most astonishing were her wings. They resembled a moth's—large and pearly white, but they were shaped like those of a swallow-tail butterfly. Streaking through the satiny white in a random pattern were swirls of the same unique purple of her skin. Her body was toned and taut. A simple, woven garment covered most of her. She clutched in her hand a wicked looking spear.

"I thank you, and I appreciate you coming to see me." He stepped back to position himself against a tree to better look up at her.

"We respect your position within the supernatural world, even if you shelter the abomination," she replied.

Nyles's fists clenched. This wild creature had no right to judge Kyra. He felt the Architect's hand on his arm.

"I am not here to discuss her. I'm here because of the beasts that roam this forest. We know they are hybrids of your guard beasts. I need to know how that happened," he said, keeping his voice level.

Nyles and the Architect both knew that while he could only see one, there were at least two more nearby.

The Fae let out a high-pitched sound that could have easily been a laugh or a shriek of anger. Nyles had never spoken to a Fae before. Other than what he knew from his books, he was completely unprepared if some kind of confrontation broke out.

"It would be easy for us to take her from you, now. Finish what was started so long ago. Though, we wish no war with you. Yes, the beasts came from us. One was captured by an Imp patrol when they were originally securing the house. We assumed they killed it, however, when we witnessed humanoids coming from the house and heard the growls, we began to wonder. Then, shortly before this site was abandoned, we caught sight of the hybrid beast. We have not engaged it, as it has not been aggressive toward us," she explained, never resting in her battle-ready stance.

"How many have you seen?" The Architect kept his manner at ease.

"They are breeding. There are at least twelve of them at varying stages of age," she replied.

The Architect sucked in a quick breath, but he kept his expression the same. "Can you tell me about the humanoids?"

The creature shrugged.

"They were humans. About ten to fifteen of them came and went right before the end. Many of them smoked, as they would congregate on the porch in the twilight. I could smell their filthy ash from our place," she said.

"We are going to try to take a beast back with us for study," he replied.

"Why are you here? What are you plans with the human dwelling?" she asked.

Nyles noted her enhanced grip on the spear. It was obvious she was anxious over the coming answer.

"We plan to use it for a place for traveling diplomats. If and when the house is cleared and ready to go, I will meet with you to set up boundaries, so we don't encroach on your homes. We want this to be mutually beneficial to everyone involved," the Architect replied.

Again, she made the noise. Nyles was still unsure of what it meant, but he definitely didn't care for it.

"There is nothing beneficial for us in having outsiders trekking through our woods," she replied.

"We will do our best to be as unobtrusive to you as we can be," he said, not giving in to her baiting.

She nodded. "Do what you can for the spirits here. They make the air uneasy, and also keep your abomination close. I can't say the rest of my tribe is as forgiving as I." With a rush of gossamer wings, she was gone.

Nyles heard two more sets of wings take flight from neighboring tree tops, although he could not catch a glimpse of the Fae themselves.

The Architect walked calmly away and pulled Nyles alongside him.

Once they were closer to the house, the Architect sighed softly. "They never change, the Fae. So much could be done if they would just not be so stubborn." There was a hint of annoyance in his voice.

"I dunno, but wiping that smirk from her face came to mind when she chose to sling threats," Nyles replied, folding his arms over his chest.

"I understand. Let's go back before Kyra decides to come looking for us," the Architect said, worry lines creasing his forehead.

The two made their way back to the house, neither speaking. As they approached the house, the front door was opening. Their timing was perfect.

* * * *

Kyra observed them. She knew something had gone on; however, neither one of them was being forthcoming, nor did she want to press.

"You ready?" she asked.

"We are here. Let's get this show started," the Architect replied, making his way toward the kitchen.

The room smelled of smoldering sage—gone was all the traces of rotten food and debris. On the center of the island, a small cauldron sat bubbling. The room was lit softly by alternating white and blue pillar candles. Tinka sat in front of the sink. Her eyes were closed, and she was chanting softly. Kyra motioned for them to stand on either side of her and raised a finger to her lips to signal silence.

"Please, focus your energy on giving this room a calm and serene presence. I will attempt to make contact with the little girl, now," Tinka said, her voice low and soft.

Everyone did as they were told. Kyra closed her eyes, reaching out with her senses. She drank in the golden vibes that were shining out from Tinka and did her best to make her own match them. She knew it was just her imagination, but the room felt warmer. The tension ebbed away, unable to combat the four strong spirits.

Tinka hummed softly. It had no discernible tune to it, but it was soothing. Kyra's eyelids drooped. At the sound of a familiar, young voice, she snapped her eyes open wide.

"You came," she said.

Kyra was surprised to see the girl again, this time with no dream or vision to convey her. She stood in front of the kitchen cabinets, with the same simple nightgown and bed-rumpled hair. Her expression was stoic.

"Yes, dear. We are here to help you," Tinka said softly.

"I want to be with my family," she replied.

"I know you do, dear, and as soon as we can, we will unite you with them. I just need to ask you some questions, if you don't mind," Tinka said.

The girl took in the others in the room. Her eyes lingered on the Architect the longest, but then, she nodded.

Tinka continued, "I need you to tell me everything you can remember about what happened to you."

The girl frowned in concentration. Kyra recalled reading somewhere that spirits had a hard time keeping memories intact, so she wondered how this girl was going to do.

She closed her eyes, and Kyra watched as her transparency changed from opaque to a hazy film. Kyra hoped the concentrated effort would not cause her to lose her ability to remain visible.

The girl said, "We had a party the night before, a big one. Lots of music and ladies in beautiful dresses, lots of men and their stinky cigars. The music was so beautiful. I hid on the landing and watched the party. Mama thought I was asleep, but I just wanted to watch." Her eyes glazed over.

"It was the next morning. The last of the stay-over guests had left, and Papa was nursing a headache that Mama said was because of his damn gin. My big brother was playing quietly in the foyer when I heard him shout. I was in here, filling up another pitcher for Papa. Following his shout, it was like a thunder storm—shrieks and screams, breaking glass, splintering wood. I heard Papa shout, 'Dear God', and then, his gun went off. I was scared, so I hid under the sink," she said, her voice shaking.

A tear rolled down Tinka's cheek, but she encouraged the child to go on.

"They were beasts—huge, smelly, and scary. They found me. I cried for my mother, but she never came. I was afraid. I thought they were going to eat me, and then, the men came in—humans, like me. I thought they were here to save me, but then—"

As the girl looked up at them, a deep gash appeared across her throat, as if her memory of her death brought about a manifestation of it. The image shuddered and wavered, and then all at once, it was gone.

Tinka's chin fell to her chest. Kyra closed her eyes, wishing she could have done something to help this child. This happened before she was even born. This poor child's spirit had been rattling around this place for decades.

"She was fairly lucid, still. Perhaps, the lack of spiritual activity in the area will keep the rest of them that way. If she saw these men, perhaps the others did as well, and they may be able to help." Tinka stood. Kyra could see the pain in her eyes. "I'm going to suggest we go up to the landing, now." Tinka picked up her misting pot. She headed out, not waiting for a reply.

The others followed silently, making their way to the landing. Tinka stood inside a large, chalk circle.

"Please, enter the circle at the open gap, Kyra. I'm going to ask the two of you to wait outside. You will be our backup, in case things go wrong in here," Tinka explained.

Everyone followed her instructions. Kyra felt ill-equipped for this assignment, but she trusted Tinka to know what she was doing.

Tinka closed the circle and took a deep breath. "Let us begin."

The air from the attic was cold and reeked of death.

Tina continued, "Spirits, I am here to help you. I need to speak to you, but I can only do so one at a time. If you can hear and understand me, please come to me slowly, and I promise you will all be free."

Kyra moved nervously behind Tinka. The vision of being overwhelmed by a mass of faceless spirits was terrifying. She sat as still and as straight as possible. She was here to help. Once again, the slow humming began, but instead of the soft voice answering her, a horrible shriek filled the air. Its vitriol sound caused Kyra to cover her ears to try to block out the sound. The air around them swirled and filled with smoke, she could smell rotting bodies, hear death cries as they had sounded when they were originally made. Every fiber of her being told her to run. She had to shut down her Fae senses to avoid them being overloaded. The onslaught continued only a minute, but it felt like ages being lost in the dense fog.

As quickly as it had begun, it was over. The air cleared, the silence was more deafening than the sound with the swiftness it clamped over them. Tinka spoke again, her voice visibly shaken, "If there are any spirits here that can speak to us, I invite you to do so, now."

They all waited, with no result. Kyra was about to suggest they give up when a voice spoke clearly.

"Tinka?" it asked.

Kyra searched for an apparition, but none was visible.

"Yes, Trina. I'm here," the voice replied. Kyra could not see Tinka but knew Tinka was crying.

"The little girl was right. She said you were coming. I've been waiting so long, holding on, and just hoping you would somehow find me here," Tinka's sister, Trina replied.

Kyra noticed a very faint waver in light at the base of the stairs, almost like heat rising off the pavement in the summer.

"I'm so sorry it took me so long to find you. I never gave up hope," Tinka replied.

"Listen, it's hard for me to speak. Now that the spirits are roaming the house, the sooner you clear it out, the better," Trina replied.

"The men who came here, they helped the Imps in the war. They were men of science. I never got close enough to find out their race; however, their eyes were black." The heat wavered less, now.

"I am losing my hold. The veil is wearing thin, perform the rite and set us free," Trina's voice grew faint.

"No! You can't leave, yet. Please. I love you," Tinka cried out.

"I love you too, Little Sis. Please, let me rest," Trina replied, her voice barely audible.

Tinka sobbed softly. She exited the circle, and the Architect pulled her into a strong embrace. Kyra stood slowly, making her way out. She stood beside Nyles. Displays of strong emotion always made her uncomfortable, and Tinka was distraught.

Kyra was disappointed with how little information they had actually gotten from the spirits, but she would never voice that. Black eyes, while a clue was not as limiting as one would think. It wasn't much to go on, but they might be able to enter it into Simon with the other criteria and get a narrowed down list. After a long moment, Tinka released the Architect and stood up straight, wiping her eyes.

"I do not have the power to completely cleanse the house. I can set up a portal to the other world, and the ones that are lucid enough will go through on their own. The more scattered ones will need the help of a Witch to make it to the other side." Tinka gathered up her supplies. "I'm going to set up in the front hall. It's central, and I should be able to draw them all to me."

Kyra knew it was better to just let her go forward. The time for grief would come after they had finished.

Kyra's radio sparked to life at her side, causing all of them to jump.

"Miss Kyra, the cage and tranquilizer darts have arrived," the voice said.

"Thank you, Mister Veloute. We will be back shortly to retrieve them. Seems like our supplies are ahead of schedule," Kyra said to the rest of them.

"Excellent. Nyles, if you and Kyra want to head back and bring it here, I will assist Tinka in setting up the portal," the Architect suggested.

Kyra frowned. She was not keen on the idea of splitting up, but the Architect would be much more help to Tinka than she and Nyles would be. Nyles would be the only one who could transport the cage. Logistically, it made sense to split up, but she could not shake the sense of dread she felt at letting them out of her sight. She nodded. "Keep the radio close by. If anything at all happens, you are to hit the button immediately," she said, stressing the word anything.

"Will do." Tinka knelt down at the base of the stairs to begin preparations.

Kyra and Nyles headed out into the forest. The sun was high above them, indicating that it was just past noon.

"Galerius and Leland really outdid themselves in getting this to us so quickly," Nyles commented.

"I have to agree, although more on Leland than Galerius. We have the cages in storage, but Leland had to engineer a tranquilizer," she said.

"Just goes to show that the people in the positions are the right ones for the jobs," Nyles replied.

"I'm inclined to think that perhaps some form of magical transport was used," Kyra added.

They broke into the clearing. The cage sat just off to the side of the plane. It was a massive, forbidding structure made of iron bars and Kevlar padding. It stood easily eight feet tall and six feet wide. The beast would fit, and hopefully, it would be asleep during its confinement. The cage's wheeled base made hauling it much easier. Upon seeing them, the pilot exited the plane. He carried a silver case which Kyra assumed contained the tranquilizers.

After a short demonstration on the tranq gun, and attaching a rope to the cage, so Nyles could pull it along, they were on their way. Kyra could tell by Nyles's expression and the bulge of his muscles that even though he would never say it, pulling the cage was straining him.

The going was slow. The wheels caught in ruts and on tree roots. After what felt like an eternity, they saw the house looming before them. The front door stood open. Kyra's senses went on high alert. Something was decidedly wrong. A scream from inside the house set them both running for the door.

Nothing could have prepared them for the sight before them. On the floor, an intricate circle was drawn and a pillar of luminescence rose from it. Several steps up the staircase, the beast stood on its hind legs. Its mouth opened to reveal its many rows of sharp teeth. Five steps above it stood the Architect, who was doing his best to shield Tinka from the rampaging creature. Kyra raised the gun, aiming for the back of the creature's neck. Before she could fire, a thick mist of swirling spirits rushed toward the portal, blocking her view.

The beast looked back at the newcomers and released another menacing growl. It returned its focus to the Architect just as Kyra burst through the fog of spirits to again have a clean shot. A blast of deep blue, pulsing energy shot from the beast's eyes.

"Father!" Kyra cried out in a panic. It was too late. The blast hit him squarely in the chest.

Time crawled as the blast struck him. A grimace of pain and torment crossed his face. In that final moment, as his body crumpled to the ground, Kyra saw the light in his eyes dim. Only the empty shell of her great mentor was left behind. Just above him, a shimmer of light seemed to be floating.

"Close the portal," Tinka screamed.

Kyra heard the words but found herself unable to move. Beside her, Nyles crashed into the portal, using his hooves to smear and erase the runes used to cast the spell. A shriek of anguish filed the air as the spirits were scattered and denied their rest.

The beast turned its focus on Kyra. Her eyes welled with tears, but she was able to aim the tranq gun at where its heart should be. She fired three times in succession. The darts struck the beast. Nothing happened. Kyra feared the end was near for all of them. The beast charged. Reaching the landing, it collapsed with a floor-shaking thud.

Kyra raced over to pull her father's limp form into her arms. He was breathing, and his body showed no visible wounds. His eyes opened. The once warm, bright eyes were glazed and fixed. She looked up at Tinka, whose own eyes were overflowing with tears.

"What happened?" Kyra asked quietly, cradling her father in her arms.

"We had just opened the portal. We were calling the spirits to cross over when the beast burst through the door. I believe it said something telepathically to him, because he spoke back out loud. He told it we were here to help the spirits, that we meant it no harm. It charged at us, and we backed up to the stairs. Then, you arrived." Tinka let loose another shaky sob before continuing, "We have to get him back to Scíath. Great minds there can help him. I believe the beast's blast has separated his psyche from his body." Tinka gently placed a hand on Kyra's arm.

Kyra nodded.

She looked over to see Nyles loading the beast into the cage. "We should take him with us. It may help us to find out what he did," Nyles said.

Kyra had to keep it together, but all she wanted to do was break down and cry. She stood up. Carrying her father's limp body tenderly in her arms, she headed back for the plane.

She laid him on his bunk and secured him with the seat belts. She refused to leave him. Nyles and Tinka struggled to get the beast aboard and into the cargo hold. Night was falling as they all buckled in for takeoff. Her father looked so peaceful, almost as if he was sleeping.

Kyra glanced over at the cabinet that contained all the medical equipment. All her preparedness did nothing to help the most important person in the world to her.

Tinka sat down beside her. "I know you don't want to hear what I have to say right now, and you will probably think me heartless for even bringing this up, but the Architect is incapacitated, and we have to think of the leadership of Scíath. As you know, he chose a successor, and it was ratified by the council. That person is going to have to step in until he recovers." She watched Kyra's expression keenly.

Kyra sighed, taking her eyes off her father's form to look at Tinka. "Right when we get back, you and Di can get all that in place. I'm going to make sure Leland doesn't stop until he helps Father."

"I understand completely your desire to be at your father's side at all times, but that can't be." Tinka raised her hand to hold off Kyra's coming reply. "The new leader of Scíath is you."

Kyra's mouth dropped open. "You can't be serious."

"Your father believed you to be the best choice to carry on his leadership role," Tinka replied.

Kyra's mind spun violently. *Why would he do this?* She had no idea how to run Scíath. He had made a point of saying he was going to stay on to train the new person until they were comfortable in the position. He hadn't intended for her to be simply tossed into the position. She stared at his serene face. She knew she had to take the position, to honor him.

Looking through the window, she watched as the stars guided her back to her home, rushing toward destiny with a heavy heart and a turbulent mind.

Epilogue

Time flew since they had returned home. In only a day, so very much had gone on. Sitting in the silence and semidarkness of the Architect's room, Kyra breathed deeply and reflected.

The beast was quarantined in Security while it was examined. It never regained consciousness before dying. There was no way of knowing if it had been from the tranq or a side effect of the use of its power.

Leland was running an entire battery of tests to make sure the Architect's body had not been affected. Those skilled in telepathy and magic had already confirmed that his mind had been forcibly ripped from his body and thrown onto the astral plane. Others were attempting to track it.

Seamlessly, she had been sworn in to the position of leader of Scíath. Kyra remembered very little of the actual ceremony.

Sitting beside her on the floor was a stack of files she needed to go through. Regardless of personal tragedy, life went on. Not to mention what needed to be done out at the house. One file contained a list of species that fit the parameters they had compiled on the humanoid accomplices. Then, there was report from the Witches with recommendations on the handling of spirits. A report from Maria about the structures, the body list, and missing person matches they had made.

There were rumblings in the ranks about her appointment, but she had expected that. The conspiracy theorists were probably having a field day. Ever suspicious of people's intentions, she had twenty-four-hour security posted outside the door. She was taking no chance of anyone trying to harm the Architect while he was incapacitated.

He lay so still under the covers, wires of various sizes and colors led from him to the machines that surrounded him. She imagined he would be proud of her. She had taken on the mantle of leadership with a strong front. Yet, it was only the beginning. Within a week, she would be expected to attend the Halloween ball, and then, the holiday season. Father had so loved the holidays, she knew she had to uphold the traditions and make sure everyone enjoyed them.

A tear escaped her eye, and she wiped it away angrily. Now was not the time to feel. Now was the time for action. Mentally, she ticked off a list of things that needed her immediate attention. It was just so overwhelming. She stood shaking off those thoughts and moved to her father's beside.

Slipping her hand into his, she squeezed it gently.

"Don't worry. Soon, you will be back with me, and we will continue your dream together," she whispered.

She bent down to kiss his forehead, just enjoying the quiet moment together.

A soft knock invaded her peace, and she glared at the closed door. "What?" she asked, unable to keep the annoyance from her voice.

"Miss Kyra, I'm so sorry to disturb you, but a body has been discovered in the flower gardens. It has been determined she was murdered." The messenger kept his eyes down.

Kyra's mouth went dry. "A murder? Within the walls of Scíath? It can't be. Who was it?" she asked, moving toward the door.

"She appears to be a clerk from Gilly Relations." He continued, edging backward as she approached.

Kyra took a deep breath. She looked at her father's still form. Turning toward the door, she began barking orders at the messenger.

Pausing, she glanced back once more at the closed door flanked by two grim-faced security guards.

Her era of leadership had begun.

About the Author:

Born in the late seventies, author J.A. Castelli, was raised on the collected works of Horror master, Stephen King, whose influences can be found throughout her first self-published work, *Eden*. When not being spoken to by the magical denizens of Sciath, Castelli can be found taking care of her family, or losing herself in the work of many writing greats.

Visit her online at:
https://www.facebook.com/pages/JA-Castelli-Author/283726373427
https://twitter.com/JACastelli

Also from Eternal Press:

Where Shadows Lie: Bay City
by JE Cammon

eBook ISBN: 9781615723041
Print ISBN: 9781615723058

Paranormal Urban Fantasy
Novel of 55,186 words

Book 1 in the Where Shadows Lie series.

In the underbelly of the eastern US seaport of Bay City, supernatural and non-supernatural creatures alike strive to understand the meaning of life, to belong, or simply exist. David is one of them. He is far, far away from his clan. Before Nick, his only friend used to be a vampire named Jarvis. However, Nick's only gift seems to be more of a curse: he brings change wherever he goes. When the three unlikely companions finally find the answers to their questions, they also find more mysteries needing to be solved. Eventually, they will all wish not to have been present on the evening when everything changed forever. Were the answers they received worth trading everything to darkness? After all, shadows lie. What's a supernatural creature to do where the shadows' lies carry the promise of home?

Also from Eternal Press:

Humans and Demons and Elves
by Donaya Haymond

eBook ISBN: 9781615724352
Print ISBN: 9781615724369

Young Adult, Urban Fantasy
Novella of 41,387 words

The Elves of North America use dimension-bending magic to conceal their woodland villages from humans, though it fails to protect them from the beautiful-but-deadly Eudemons. Edofine is less prejudiced than many, even befriending an Archaedemon, whose people are known for switching sides in the ancient conflict. But when young Edofine's clan is destroyed, he has only one person to turn to: his cousin Kryvek, who was adopted by humans who established the Official Magics-Humans Institute (OMHI).

Will Edofine be able to adjust to human society? Can the OMHI help him despite facing its own crisis? Could he possibly be falling in love with Kryvek's friend Lira, a half-Elf half-Eudemon working for the OMHI? His life has fallen to pieces, and the reconstruction is full of surprises.

Eternal Press

Official Website:
http://www.eternalpress.biz

Blog:
http://www.eternalpress.biz/blog/

Reader Chat Group:
http://groups.yahoo.com/group/EternalPressReaders

Twitter:
http://twitter.com/EternalPress

Facebook:
http://www.facebook.com/profile.php?id=1364272754

Google +:
https://plus.google.com/u/0/115524941844122973800

Good Reads:
http://www.goodreads.com/profile/EternalPress

Shelfari:
http://www.shelfari.com/eternalpress

Library Thing:
http://www.librarything.com/catalog/EternalPress

We invite you to drop in, visit with our authors, and stay in touch for the latest news, releases, and more!

CPSIA information can be obtained at www.ICGtesting.com
Printed in the USA
BVOW07s1323290114

343192BV00001B/34/P